IDENTITY CRISIS

The Team pilot was lying on her back, her arms crossed at the junction of sheet and hospital gown and her face like a long winter.

"So, Auglaize DeWellesthar," Dancer began. "What brings you all the way out to my territory?"

At the sound of Dancer's voice, the impostor's head jerked around, her pupils dilated, and her jaw dropped. She looked as if she had just seen a ghost—which, in effect, she had. "My God, am I hallucinating? Who are you?" Even the voice was Dancer's, almost.

"Precisely what I wanted to ask you. I do know, however, who you are *not*."

"I don't believe this. Is that really you?"

"Now, there's a particularly inane question. If I am I, where does that leave you?" Something hovered on the edge of Dancer's memory; she *knew* this person. Or had known her . . .

DANCER
OF THE
SIXTH

Michelle Shirey Crean

A Del Rey Book
BALLANTINE BOOKS • NEW YORK

This one's for me.

A Del Rey Book
Published by Ballantine Books

Copyright © 1993 by Michelle E. Crean

Library of Congress Catalog Card Number: 92-97053

ISBN 0-345-37912-8

Manufactured in the United States of America

First Edition: March 1993

Acknowledgments

Many thanks to my technical advisors:

Patrick H. Crean, Systems Engineer, Zenith Data Systems, who—coincidentally—built my first word processor, then left me alone to learn how to use it;

Lt. Col. Robert L. Shaw, USAFR, author of *Fighter Combat*, who doesn't read fiction and therefore won't know that I didn't take all of his suggestions;

and Joseph A. Ventolo, Jr., Museum Curator (Aero), United States Air Force Museum, and his wife Martha, proprietor, Ventolo's Bed & Breakfast.

Prologue:
The Lioth Massacre

The shouts sounded like murmurs to her numbed ears, murmurs far away and having nothing to do with her. Even when she opened her eyes and saw the black bootheels only inches from her face, and the black cape-hem brushing them.

"I've never seen anything like this before in my life."

"Pray that you never do again," a steady male voice answered. "But you will. Where's Ford?"

"He . . . uh, wasn't feeling too well. Gad, there's blood everywhere! How do you ever get used to this?"

"You don't. Careful with those bodies!" he snapped. "You're not stacking firewood over there! These people may be dead, but they're still deserving of our respect."

"Look at that one . . . they didn't even touch the face."

The bootheels receded slightly, and she blinked.

"My God, it's still alive. This one's still alive."

"You sure? Careful, damn it! Pass the word for a medic." A face swam before her; the words, soft and caressing, seemed directed at her, though they didn't make much sense. "Are you in there somewhere? Look at me." The tone sharpened. "I said, be careful! Gently, now. Let's see what we've got."

The sound of retching, overlaid by the voice whom she had identified as the leader. "Unbelievable. If that mind is still intact . . . no, let me."

Motion, a blur of color, predominantly red. Her mind shied away from it and her eyes closed.

"Don't leave me now, child." Were the words whispered in her ear, or only in her brain? No matter. The voice spelled safety, and she struggled toward it.

"Easy, child. Easy. Is there a cocoon on the way? Call again. Now! In the meantime, get me a blanket. Oh, for . . . All right,

1

use this." A swirl as something black settled over her, and she flashed once again on bootheels and cape-hem.

"Sir, the blood . . ."

"Be sensible, man! The cloak can be replaced. The life cannot. But mark this: if the mind survives, this one is *mine*."

1: O'Brian's Stake

Chapter 1

"Traffic control. *Traffic* control! Two of the hottest pilots of the Sixth Service stuck in a lumbering ground vehicle, chasing down speeders and handing out parking tickets, for the love of . . . !"

The lament was cut short by a snort from her partner—Seven had heard it all at least a dozen times in the few hours that they had been on duty. "For the last time, Dancer, it isn't my fault you're not out in the cloudy gray."

Dancer allowed herself the luxury of a monosyllabic exclamation of distaste. "No, it's Michael's. That was *my* high-level recce mission he gave to Cler."

"Clermont needs the hours. You don't."

Dancer settled back with a grunt. Actually, ground patrol wasn't all that bad. Their compact little all-terrain vehicle could outrun any other ground-bound on the planet, and carried, besides Seven and herself, a small arsenal. It also had the distinct advantage of never having to stop at any of the numerous small stations along the highways to refuel.

For that matter, it wasn't a bad planet to be stuck on. O'Brian's Stake, the not-very-romantic name given to coordinates 27–15–32–81 on the Galactic Grid, had come a long way in the century since Mahoning O'Brian first led an adventurous band of three thousand hardy souls to homestead the planet. They had come, as had all colonists probably back to the first splinter group of cave dwellers, to escape what they considered intolerable conditions on their home world and set up a society governed by their own rules. "Intolerable conditions" in the case of the O'Brians meant what they considered excessive spending of their tax dollars on the military. Planetary defense systems were a waste of money, since the Confederacy would protect them—after all, wasn't that why there was a Confederacy?—but even the Confederacy spent altogether too much on "defense," since no one dared to attack it. The fact that military strength and military spending were *why* no one dared challenge the Confederacy meant nothing in peacetime.

O'Brian's Stake now boasted a thriving, self-sufficient economy, diverse but unmatchable scenery, an abundant variety of growing things, unusually pure air, and a concentrated population of close to six million. These folks were, for the most part, tractable enough, although the recently ended war hadn't changed attitudes passed down from their ancestors—after all, O'Brian's Stake hadn't even been involved in that war. They didn't mind having a Confederacy force quartered on them, though, as long as someone else was footing the bill. In fact, these outsiders proved a convenient supplement to their own meager police forces. So, the O'Brians went about their daily business with no idea of who their peacekeeping force really was, or how strategic their little ball of rock was in the grand scheme of things. Nor did they care.

Part of Dancer's job was to keep it that way. Not too difficult, up till now, but something was in the air. She could feel it—more to the point, Michael could feel it, and he wasn't the Commander just because nobody else wanted the responsibility. For one thing, there was that weapons cache they'd been watching on the far side of the planet. Why would a society that eschewed all things military and had strict limitations on the importation and manufacture of weapons secretly stockpile such things? Either someone was engineering a challenge to the government, or somewhere there abided a collector obsessed with things that went boom, bang, hiss, and whine-warble.

The far side was one huge, sparsely inhabited continent with numerous lakes, virgin forest, and blessed silence. More than once since their preliminary explorations Dancer had fantasized about a cozy cabin on one of those small lakes with no company but the indigenous wildlife. Not easily accessible, it was a wonderful place for a getaway—or a rendezvous. Obviously, she wasn't the only one to think so.

Though she had frequently argued for an outpost on the far side, they simply didn't have the manpower. Nor were they allowed, by the terms of the peace, even the most rudimentary of weather satellites. Hence the frequent, top-secret, high-level "eye-in-the-sky" flights from their well-camouflaged under- and above-ground launch sites just outside the city limits.

Which brought her back full circle to the fact that no matter how beautiful the scenery or how superior the ground vehicle, she would rather be flying. Especially when Seven was driving.

Her partner glanced skyward at her sigh, no doubt invoking the Auryx gods to forestall another round of complaints.

"Dancer, my friend, admit it—you're jealous that Clermont is flying with Michael."

"Am I?" She pondered the novel thought for the brief space between mile markers. "Maybe. I've been at the Commander's back for so long that I don't trust anyone else there, I guess. Even in peacetime . . . Will you look at that?" she added, pointing to a massive collection of vehicles clogging the road ahead.

"Not another accident," Seven groaned.

As he accelerated toward the snarl of cars, Dancer visualized the plethora of paperwork attendant upon reporting twenty-vehicle pileups on the freeway and uttered a few words appropriate to the situation.

"That's one of the things I like about you, Dancer." Seven grinned. "You know how to curse constructively."

"It's all that good Fourth Service training," she replied absently, trying to figure out what the problem was. There didn't seem to be any broken glass or bent metal.

Seven glanced skyward again, hit the brakes, and almost skidded them into a guardrail.

"Will you keep your eyes on the road!" Dancer exploded, just as a red blur streaked in front of them so low that they could count the pilot's teeth as he flashed them a smile and a wave. Thank God the craft wasn't armed! Dancer thought. Sheepishly, she put away the weapon that had leapt reflexively into her hand.

"Beautiful," Seven said, craning his neck to watch the other twelve aircraft roar by overhead.

"Too bloody low. Park this thing before you kill us," Dancer ordered; he obligingly placed them at a vantage point on the fringe of the crowd as she radioed back a strongly worded reminder that such flying over and around the main highway was strictly prohibited, no exceptions. The exercise cooled her temper enough for her to admit, "Not bad."

"Not bad," Seven echoed. "Only you would find fault with the famous Fourth Service Interplanetary Precision Aerial Demonstration Team."

"Strictly sour grapes, my friend," she replied, a critical instructor's eye on the formation now passing to their right. "As far back as I can remember, I've dreamed about flying with the Team."

"You, too, huh?" was Seven's comment. "Somehow I never figured you for such a peaceful pursuit."

"You forget, I used to be Fourth Service—and the Team is why

I joined up.'' His quirked eyebrow was the closest he'd come to asking, but she never had been reticent about her past. "I was ten when my parents sent my application to the Fourth Service Academy, and twelve when I was accepted. Six years of academic slavery to earn my commission, eighteen grueling months of flight training—then, just as I started piling up the hours, just when the dream was finally within reach—whomp! The Karranganthians decided to annihilate the population of Danton. Within twenty-four Standard hours, the Team was disbanded and flying combat sorties with us mere mortals. So much for my one goal in life.''

"The Big K messed up a lot of people's plans with that move," her companion observed mildly.

Not for the first time, Dancer experienced a fleeting curiosity as to what and who Seven had been in that shadowy Real World to which they in the Sixth Service had been declared dead. His given name wasn't Seven, any more than hers was Dancer, or Michael's, Michael. When dealing with an enemy who habitually delighted in making war on women and small children, it was wise not to be too free with true identities. Though, unlike her, most of her Auryx compatriots no longer had families to protect.

"They didn't waste any time reconstituting the Team after the cease-fire was signed," Seven continued, as if unaware of the speculative scrutiny. "Though how we lucked into getting our little backwater on their schedule is beyond me.''

"Michael," they replied simultaneously. The Commander could arrange anything, and he undoubtedly had ulterior motives.

Reorganizing the Team had been a sound move, both politically and militarily. On the surface, the cream of the Fourth Service fighting machine gave a good show and the reassurance that the war was, indeed, really over. At the same time, they served as a friendly reminder of Confederacy military presence and skill, were excellent public relations, gave yet another generation of kids something to dream about besides fighting and killing—and could easily get into places and see things that otherwise might go unnoticed.

Dancer's Sixth Service mentality again. With a shake of the head, she returned her attention to the sky. "Fair formation," she commented, not missing a beat in the conversation. "Number Five's a bit wide, though.''

"You're right, as always. Good thing this is only an orientation flight—he's going to get his empennage chewed.''

"They're all going to get something chewed for practicing in restricted airspace . . . Give me the glasses, Seven. Number Five still doesn't look quite right. The starboard wing . . . look out, she's coming down!''

Seven already had the brake off and the ATV moving as the trim red-and-white aircraft plummeted nose downward. It looked like a "mort"—a fatal crash—for sure. Then, just at the last moment, the pilot adroitly recovered control and, as gently as a leaf, set the plane down in a small grassy area.

Dancer flung herself out of the still-moving ATV to hit the ground running. Even so, the pilot had the canopy open, helmet off, and was scrambling out of his . . . *her* harness as her rescuer approached. Dancer had the impression of carrot-colored curls, green eyes wide with fear, and a survival knife flashing open in front of her face before she reacted automatically with a right to the jaw.

As the pilot fell back, unconscious, across the seat, Dancer felt, rather than saw, the threat from behind. Seven yelled a warning at about the same time the massive hand closed over her shoulder and jerked her away from the cockpit. Next thing she knew, she was flat on her back in the grass looking up at what, from her vantage point, was the biggest man she had ever seen. Surprise, evident in his eyes as he looked down into hers, made him hesitate just long enough for her companion to subdue him with a simple nerve block.

"Thank you, Seven," Dancer breathed, cursing herself for her carelessness. The Team Gypsies seldom flew with the backseat occupied, but she should have stopped to think: preshow practice hops were always VIP/Public Relations flights. All thirteen backseats were undoubtedly strapped onto various sorts of media persons trying not to be sick. However, this man wore a Fourth Service standard-issue flying coverall and boots, and a nasty expression that was not prompted by a queasy stomach.

"My pleasure, Red. You okay?''

Hauling herself to her feet, she dusted off the seat of her pants, then winced as her hand ground grit into bare thigh and an eight-inch gash in her leg. Damn! Dancer thought she'd successfully sidestepped that knife. Obviously not. "Yeah,'' was her terse reply. "It's just a scratch; serves me right for not moving faster. My uniform, on the other hand, is totaled. That's going to cost her!''

Seven nodded. "You're okay. I'll get our friend here into restraints, then come back for the other one.''

"Pilot's small. I can handle her.''

"You sure?'' he asked, ignoring a protest from his captive and forestalling further violence from him with a casual but well-placed swat with the heel of one hand.

"No sweat.'' Though the pilot was the same size as Dancer, it was no great matter to drag her up by the front of her tailored red show jumpsuit and toss her over a shoulder for the short distance back to the ATV. What bothered Dancer more was that the kid was still out cold, even after the necessary five-minute wait for backup to keep curious onlookers from walking away with souvenir pieces of the Gypsy.

"I didn't hit her that hard." Dancer must have said it ten times on the swift ride back to their headquarters complex.

Seven was silent the whole time, though his frequent glances between the face resting on his partner's shoulder and her own were eloquent. Their other passenger, bound hand and foot and strapped in the backseat, made one or two attempts to communicate, then gave it up. If what he spoke was a language, neither Dancer nor Seven had ever heard the like.

They were met, as requested, by both medical and security teams. The big guy put up such a fuss when they started to take the pilot away that Dancer gave permission for him to accompany her down to the Medical Section. Under heavy guard, of course. She herself went along for the walk, and because—well, she really *hadn't* hit the girl that hard! Meanwhile, the report came back that a crash team was swarming over the downed aircraft, and it looked peculiar. Mighty peculiar.

So, what else was new? First, there was that incredible emergency landing. Immediately thereafter, the pilot pulled a knife on her would-be rescuers. Granted, it must have been a shock for her when she saw Dancer's face, but that was no excuse for her to try to rearrange it. Then, there was the giant in the backseat, evidently a bodyguard of some sort, who didn't seem to speak any known language. Last but not least, there was the girl herself, still showing no sign of waking up. It would have been peculiar if there *were* a simple explanation. Basically, Dancer thought, it was just one of those days.

The puzzled meds called in the psychs, then, with nothing better to do, started harassing Dancer about the mess on her leg. By this time, it had bled enough to stick the khaki to the skin in a sodden scarlet stripe all the way down to her shoe top. Even she had to admit that it looked disgusting. "Come on, Dancer, off with the pants and let us take care of that for you."

"It's just a scratch," she insisted, pulling what was left of the fabric aside with a grimy hand. "I don't have time for this nonsense. Michael's due back any minute, and he'll want a report. If you'll excuse me, I'm off to find myself a uniform that isn't air-conditioned."

"Will you at least take the time to clean up that 'scratch' and put some of this on it?" Hawk-eyed Preble had already ascertained that the wound wasn't deep enough to require artificial aid in healing. "You'll wind up with a nasty infection if you aren't careful."

"Yes. All right. Thanks." Dancer took the proffered tube from the med, then stopped a moment to lay a hand against the pilot's cheek. "Who in the worlds are you?" she couldn't help whispering. The gesture, if not the words, seemed to reassure the pilot's companion; his hand closed over Dancer's with a gentleness that surprised her. Even more surprising was the thrill his touch sent down her spine. She jerked away with a smile. "We'll talk later," she told them both, and exited before the hovering Preble could change his mind about bandaging her leg.

The Team commander was in his office aboard the Warlord Starlifter, "mother ship" and transport for the Interplanetary Precision Aerial Demonstration Team, when he received word that one of his planes was down on the planet's surface.

"Who?" was his first reaction, though he had a feeling he already knew.

"Number Five, sir," the voice on the other end of the communications link informed him. "DeWellesthar."

DeWellesthar and Callicoon, the Team commander's memory supplied. Callicoon, that flarking bastard traitor! If this "incident" was an accident, he, the commander, was a Dantonian dance instructor.

With a string of oaths, the commander grabbed the first thing on his desk that came to hand and sent the gold nameplate bearing the inscription COL. H. DAVEN crashing against the opposite bulkhead. It was intelligent of Summit not to deliver this news in person; it could just as easily have been him lying on the red carpeting on the far side of the room.

Daven didn't need to ask, but he did anyhow: "Survivors?"

"Both of them got out. Minimal damage to the Gypsy."

"I want them in my office immediately."

There was an uncomfortable pause before the reply: "I'm afraid they're out of our hands, sir. Confederacy enforcers got to them before we could. They're under 'medical observation.' "

Well, of course. What else could go wrong today? Aside from his entire operation being jeopardized just because one of his men was weakling/fool enough to fall in love with the enemy.

As for that damned redhead—there was something familiar about her, something . . . he couldn't put his finger on it. Just a feeling he'd had ever since he'd first laid eyes on her. That one was trouble.

Well. She wouldn't tell those thrice-damned Confederacy stooges anything; he'd seen to that. Still, she was in a hospital, and medicos loved nothing more than to poke and prod and analyze. And those analyses would show . . . nothing, he'd been assured. The drugs were supposed to be untraceable. They had better be! As for DeWellesthar—she and that crewchief/lover of hers would be back in his hands in a matter of hours. Then he would make them both pay.

"Sir? What do you want me to do?"

"Get them back, Summit," Daven said reasonably. "If you value your life."

"Yes, sir," the other replied hastily.

Daven sighed. He was getting too old for this nonsense. Too old. And he missed Kalelle. Of all his wives, she was the only one he had allowed into his heart. Even after all these years, and many children, the thought of her still had the power to excite.

But Kalelle was weeks away, at the end of the mission, the end of the tour. After he had finished planting the seeds of the new Karranganthian Alliance.

For now, he'd have to once again ease his . . . loneliness . . . with what was at hand. There were several among his command who had proved both eager and adept. Still, his thoughts kept returning to the redhead.

Chapter 2

The ruined uniform bothered Dancer a lot more than the damaged thigh. Skin would heal; its attendant pain would remind her, at least for a while, to be more careful. The destroyed trousers and the blood-, sweat-, grass-, and mud-stained shirt, however, were another story.

Most people didn't recognize the Sixth Service's identical cut and style but individual choice of color and combination as a valid uniform—Dancer had had problems with that herself, at first. Fresh from the strictly regimented Confederacy flying service—generally known as "Fourth"—she had been amazed that each member of this strange, secret Sixth Service picked a favorite shade which was then recorded as his exclusively for the rest of his life—and sometimes beyond. In a way, that had been helpful, since most Auryx were black-haired, blue-eyed, compact in build, and, according to an old Sixth Service joke, all looked alike. "Don't worry about telling us apart," she had been told early on. "We're all color-coded."

For Dancer, the decision had been trivial: she had spent better than half her existence in Fourth Service red, and the color was already part of her identity. In the painful adjusting process, she'd needed all the help she could get.

There were several uniform combinations, all in cuts and fabrics geared toward maximum comfort while still maintaining a little bit of style. The high-collared tunic and trousers were the most popular, though vests, buff-colored shirts, and jackets could be added for a more formal look. Summer editions included short sleeves and pants, and, for the women, optional skirts. Adhering to the attitudes of her old Service, Dancer had disdained the last as a valid uniform item. She always felt awkward and half-dressed in a skirt.

There was also what was euphemistically referred to as a "ceremonial uniform" of severe black, much like Michael's everyday wear. Service members didn't talk much about this outfit, with its stand-up collar, long, tightly cuffed sleeves, knee-length boots over straight-legged pants, and black gloves. A black cape could be fastened at the throat with an enameled black clasp. The effect was stark, almost frightening, and this combination was kept out of sight as much as possible. Even glimpsed on a hanger, even after all these years, the costume filled Dancer with a sense of foreboding and triggered a flash of the nightmare of bootheels, capes, and blood that sent chills down her spine.

No official headgear of any kind was included—and no insignia, because there were no ranks in the Sixth Service and no individual units. Surprisingly to her, though, jewelry of all types was encouraged. This meant that she hadn't had to part with her precious Fourth Service Academy ring.

All in all, she'd come to appreciate the individuality this Service encouraged while still enforcing its own brand of discipline. Unfortunately, Sixth's current assignment required its members to be instantly recognizable as a police unit; therefore, those having any contact with the public were required to wear a utilitarian Confederacy-standard khaki outfit that they all detested.

Not only were the things aesthetically limited, but, due to space, time, and budget constraints, only two per person were issued. Consequently, Dancer's other set was always in the laundry. Which, in turn, meant that she would have to go all the way down to Wardrobe for a spare. On top of that, since she was taller than the Auryx women, either she'd have to return to duty showing two extra inches of booted leg and bare forearm, or one of her slenderer male counterparts would have to donate to the cause until Sixth's overworked part-time seamstresses could tailor her another suit of her own. All things considered, it would have made sense to keep an extra set of everything in her size, but that just wasn't the way things worked. By the time she reached the barracks floor, Dancer wasn't in the best of humor. This place didn't make it any better.

The living quarters had undoubtedly been mapped out by a crazed maze builder. Space was at a premium here as everywhere else in the complex, so, to give the illusion of much-coveted privacy, the floor was divided up, seemingly at random, into areas—to make it appear more "homey." Each of these areas consisted of a group of cubicles end-to-end and back-to-back, with narrow corridors here and there for access, on or near a common lounge, which had furniture, artificial plants, bad lighting, and half-a-dozen computer terminals, and a communal bathroom thrown in anywhere it would fit. All alike; all sprinkled around with no apparent rhyme or reason. What this building must have been used for before it had been turned over to Sixth defied even her active imagination. Warehousing, maybe, or movable offices for myriad government workers who never saw the light of day. She shouldn't complain about traffic control; at least it got her out into the fresh air.

Each cubicle was large enough for a bunk, a chest for clothes, and a few personal items. Very few. The rule had been "only what you could carry in the baggage compartment of a fighter," but the advent of peace and the Sixth Service's involuntary involvement in bureaucracy allocated its members an extra transport for equipment and—given the ingenuity of the troops—a little added space for the nonessentials. Dancer's treasures included a number of copies of old-type photos of archaic aircraft to decorate her walls and a custom-crafted dulcimer which habitually sat on top of the chest. Stringed instruments were popular with the Auryx because, unlike the wind instruments, they could be sung along with. Music was one of their main forms of relaxation. It didn't necessarily take a lot of energy.

Not that any of them had much recreational time. Theirs was a typical bureaucracy, understaffed and overworked. For instance, Dancer's present job dealt chiefly with intelligence gathering, enforcement of the laws of the Confederacy, and liaison both with the O'Brians, as the "natives" called themselves, and with the constantly rotating contingents of regular service troops with whom was shared the responsibility of keeping the peace. In what spare time she could scrounge from the endless paper-shuffling, she flew reconnaissance patrols. And, every once in a while, she got a chance to return to her quarters. When she could find them.

Her cubicle was in Section 4–A4, and more than once when she had been particularly tired she had missed it. Today, after three tries, she finally marched through a bead curtain that should have been a folding wooden parquet door, kicked the fur-covered bunk that should have boasted a hand-worked quilt, and tumbled out a sleepy technician who should have been her.

"What the hell's going on, Marion?" Dancer demanded. "When I left here this morning, this was *my* room."

The tech in question blinked up at her, then shook his head to clear it. "Dancer? Haven't you heard? Word came down that you've been confirmed as Michael's second-in-command. He figured you'd be more comfortable upstairs with him, so we did some rearranging."

"Look at this face, Marion. Do you see anything to indicate that I am amused?"

"I'm not joking. Your stuff was moved upstairs with the Commander, by his order. Go see for yourself."

"I fully intend to. But if this is a put-on . . ."

He grimaced. "We all know your sense of humor, Red. I tell you, you got a promotion. Congrats. Now, let me get back to sleep."

"Right." She spun around on her heel and strode out.

Promotion, huh? In practice, Dancer had been Michael's second since . . . Lord, when hadn't she been? Almost from the day of her first check ride with Sixth, when they'd been jumped by half-a-dozen Karranganthian fighters. She had immediately dispatched two of them, then clipped a third from Michael's tail while he dealt with their leader. After that, they had calmly double-teamed the other two, who elected to run away—and had proceeded to blow them to kingdom come. Their adversaries' obvious lack of skill and/or experience fueled Dancer's suspicions that the Commander had deliberately flown them into a hornets' nest to test her nerve, but he had never admitted it. Either way, he was impressed enough to keep her at his side whenever possible—in a whole lot of places she would rather not have gone. They were gifted with a unique rapport, Dancer and Michael, and she occasionally wondered if he had the same high level of unspoken communication with the others that he shared with her.

But a promotion in a Service that recognized only two ranks, Commander and commanded? If that indeed were so, what did it mean? She didn't like to consider the implications of Mike's paving the way for a successor.

"Commander, there's been a incident," were the words that greeted Michael as he stepped off the shuttle in the courtyard of Confederacy headquarters.

The terse wording of the report told him that an aircraft was down with no fatalities, and that the aircraft in question was not one of theirs. Ergo, it either belonged to the Fourth Service contingent on the other side of town—in which case, it was Fourth's headache—or it was a civil matter. He dismissed the whole thing with a negligent, "Get Dancer on it."

"Dancer is . . . involved."

Trust that red-haired pain in the backside to be smack in the middle of any trouble that came along, Michael thought with an inward smile. His punishment for rescheduling Clermont for this morning's flight? As if flying with Cler wasn't punishment enough . . . No, that was unfair. Cler was a good pilot; Michael was just so used to having Dancer glued to his wing, anticipating his every move, that having to play instructor to anyone else was a real chore. These days, he had enough chores. "Perhaps you'd better give me the details of this 'incident,' " he suggested to the slight, black-haired woman who was trying to match his stride. "Where is Dancer, by the way?"

Fayette followed him into his downstairs "office" and took a seat while the Commander poured himself a cup of coffee and situated himself behind his desk. "Down in Med Section, far as I know."

"She hurt?" he asked abruptly.

"She says it looks worse than it is."

Michael tilted his head, his eyes vague as if he were listening to something far away, then, satisfied, nodded. "Start at the beginning, Faye. What's this all about?"

"Excuse me, Michael," his assistant interrupted. "Commander

of the Fourth Service Interplanetary Precision Aerial Demonstration Team—now, there's a mouthful! Anyway, he wants to talk to you about getting his plane and personnel back.''

"The . . . oh, yes.'' Suddenly, the situation became quite clear. "Handle it, Will.''

"I tried. He insists upon talking to you.''

Surprise, surprise. "Put him on hold, then. Let me find out what's going on here. Faye, in twenty-five words or less, if you please.''

Tersely, Fayette reported that no serious damage had been done to either plane or occupants, and that the latter were getting a routine going-over by Preble even as they spoke. Michael's reaction was, "More paperwork. Just what I need to round out a perfect day. Jeremiah, I'll take that call now. Audio only.''

When dealing with an unknown, the Commander habitually preferred audio-only communication. Though most citizens of the Confederacy wouldn't know an Auryx if one bit them, Michael's ingrained sense of security—Sixth Service paranoia, Dancer jokingly called it—urged caution. There were still those who could pick one of his people out of a crowd of fifty thousand, generally with evil intent.

Besides, Michael didn't need to see the face on the other end of the comm line. It would be a well-coached underling instead of whoever was really in charge, and the command computer had been painstakingly programmed to analyze nuance as well as content of verbal communications. Michael would be able to reinforce his own impressions that way. Quite aside from the psychological effect on that well-coached underling of not being able to see *him*.

As suspected, the sum total of the conversation consisted of the Team representative reiterating his request that the aircraft and personnel involved in the morning's unfortunate incident be turned over to the Fourth Service for return to the Warlord immediately, and Michael's reiterating standard investigatory procedure as spelled out by Confederacy law. All pro forma; the Fourth Service had made its token protest, and he had answered it. Now his people could get on with their accident reports and have the Team's property returned to them in about two hours.

Just one more annoyance in a morning rife with annoyances.

Speaking of which, there was a small matter he needed to discuss with Dancer before she tried to return to her quarters. "Jeremiah, is Dancer still in Med Section?''

"No, sir, she's on her way up—''

"Michael, about that incident," a fresh voice cut in on the intercom. "We have a problem."

"Why doesn't that surprise me?" He sighed.

"Sir, Dancer . . ." the computer known as Jeremiah pursued.

"Later, Jeremiah. I have a feeling she already knows."

Chapter 3

Michael occupied an entire top-floor "penthouse" suite by himself, begrudged him by no one. His people knew how little time he spent there, and what percentage of that he spent hunched over his worktable. Dancer had been a frequent visitor, of course, but she still had a feeling of awe as the door swung open at her voice.

So, his lock had been expecting her, at any rate. Nice place, comfortable-looking but not lived in. No dust, live plants so well-groomed as to look artificial, shaded blue shag carpeting immaculate. A beautiful deep-cushioned easy chair that bore no sign of ever having been sat in, a glass-topped coffee table that had never seen the bottom of a mug, a sleeper sofa with the protective covers still over the cushions. Michael's cherished carved oak rocker that looked lonesome to support the curve of his back.

Ah, but a private bath—with a tub *and* a shower—and a kitchenette! Now, that looked used, though the dishes beside the sink were clean. Michael liked to cook. Another way they complemented each other, because Dancer liked to eat.

She wandered back to the computer console, unwilling to open the bedroom door. There was still that uneasy feeling of trespassing, and she quite frankly wasn't sure how she would react if her belongings turned out to be sharing space with his. Enlightening as the influences of both her Services had been, she didn't like the thought that the Commander might have had ulterior motives for moving her up here. *If* he had moved her up here.

"Second door on the right, Dancer."

"Reading my mind again, Commander?" Dancer asked the empty air as she obeyed his voice via the receiver implanted behind her ear. Good grief, a real bed, with her embroidered quilt folded over the foot of it. Her airplanes tastefully arranged on the pale pink walls. Her hairbrushes on the mirrored vanity table; her dulcimer propped next to her books on a shelf over the bed. In fact, the only object in view that wasn't hers other than the furniture was the carved wooden model of a Gypsy fighter adorning the top of the dresser. As Dancer's forefinger traced the inlaid Fourth Service insignia on its wings, her mind recognized the tail number. Her former bird, of course. Michael was the only one who knew. This was his handiwork, fashioned by nervous hands while the mind was occupied with the problems of several worlds.

Silently thanking him, she crossed the room to investigate another surprise: a window! This was the only floor in the entire building with windows. She couldn't help twitching back burgundy drapes and white lace curtains to look down at the folks strolling through the tree-lined courtyard.

"Later, Dancer," the receiver hummed. "I need you downstairs."

Her master's voice. The spell broken, she grabbed a hangerful of clean red Sixth Service uniform out of a closet that looked empty holding only her few things and headed for the bathroom. At least his summons had saved her the trouble of getting another khaki from Wardrobe.

"Michael?" she queried, sliding into her accustomed chair in the small conference room a short time later.

"He's on his way," violet-clad Gallia told her. "Since you returned, we have taken three communiques from the Team hierarchy demanding their pilot and aircraft back. Michael's handling the latest one now. By the way, they did not appreciate your reprimand."

Dancer refrained from vocalizing just how much she cared, saying only, "Okay, what have you got?"

"First of all, the meds report that your pilot has been using some pretty weird drugs."

"Like what?"

Gallia shrugged. "No idea. They're doing every analysis known to computer now. Ditto with the aircraft. As usual, you were right; there was a winglock loose."

The Service's new second-in-command acknowledged the offhand compliment with a grunt. Something very strange indeed was going on here. The type of carelessness evidenced by that loose winglock was inconceivable in a Team technician; even more inconceivable was that it should go undetected through numerous rigorous inspections. The pilot had been extremely lucky that the entire wing hadn't ripped off.

Maybe she had been luckier than she knew—had somebody been trying to kill her? In one of the murder mysteries popular with the school-age set on this planet, one of the backups might conceivably resort to such a thing, but in real life that was hardly likely. A well-orchestrated publicity stunt, then? With no advance promotion, the Team had to rely on the local media coverage of today's flight to get the audiences out for tomorrow's demonstrations. If such were the case, they would probably have planned some small drama on the ground, too, that Dancer and Seven's timely arrival on the scene had ruined. Yes, it could have been a publicity stunt—but for the drugs in the pilot's bloodstream.

The drugs. Perhaps that would explain her trying to knife Dancer; who knows what kind of a monster the kid had seen her as? But recreational drugs were something no self-respecting member of the flying profession would indulge in, nor again would they go undetected. The only conclusion that came to mind was that someone had deliberately fed the girl chemicals for some reason or other, which supported the attempted murder theory, which still sounded ludicrous.

And the girl. The girl . . .

A soft step behind her told Dancer that someone else had entered the room; Gallia's respectful greeting confirmed that it was Michael. Dancer had known, of course, as soon as he had set foot in the corridor. Nine times out of ten, she knew when Michael was near. The tenth was usually when she was doing something she shouldn't have been.

"Don't stand on my account, Dancer," was his mildly ironic statement as he stationed himself behind her chair and folded his arms.

"Gallia tells me that the Team is rather vehement about getting their pilot back," she returned.

"Indeed. I explained to their commander that our medical facilities are far superior to theirs, but the information did not seem to reassure him. He claims not to understand why she should need medical attention, and as much as accused me of kidnapping the child. My reminders that we are supposedly both on the same side resulted in threats. I have gained us a few hours, though, before they try to storm our defenses. Still no change in her condition?"

"None," Gallia answered.

"I didn't hit her that hard," Dancer mumbled in response to the unspoken accusation.

Michael said only, "The child has a name?"

With a flourish, Gallia tapped the keys that called the computer files of the Team onto the screen. "Auglaize DeWellesthar."

"DeWell-LES-thar," Dancer corrected automatically as the picture flashed before them.

"She looks just like you, Dancer!" was Gallia's reaction. "The hair's different, of course, and the eyes aren't brown like yours . . ."

So, after pulling her out of her aircraft and holding her in her arms all the way back here, Dancer wasn't going to have noticed that? Still, her hand strayed to her own waist-length braid as her eyes remained riveted on the image before her. Young, very young, was Dancer's first thought. Too young to have accumulated the requisite hours for consideration for the Team, barely out of training, in fact. Wordlessly, she examined the carrot-colored curls, regulation length identical for male and female in the Fourth Service; the wide, innocent-looking green eyes, the freckles across the bridge of the upturned nose. She could almost feel the stiff, heavily embroidered red collar of the brand-new dress uniform chafing her neck as she posed for the official records photo. . . .

The name was Dancer's name; the face was Dancer's face, but for the altered eye color. And, except for some judiciously doctored numbers, and one or two conspicuous omissions, so was the Service record. She knew it; Michael knew it—the light tap, tap, tap of his forefinger on the opposite sleeve betrayed his agitation—and they were the only ones.

"Any ID on the guy in the backseat?" she found herself asking in an interrogatory tone that belied her wandering attention.

Gallia, clearly disappointed that her revelation had produced so little apparent sensation, banged a couple more keys. "Not much. He's her crewchief, supposedly. Name's unpronounceable, and he remains unresponsive to all our efforts to communicate with him."

"Yes, DeWellesthar's commander did mention something about her having had problems with her craft and the crewchief going along this flight to see if he could detect anything," Michael interjected.

"Makes perfect sense, on the surface."

"The more we learn, the less we know," the Commander murmured with his usual flair for understatement. "Has anyone thought to question what the Team is doing in our sector to begin with? In the best of times, these small population centers were not included in their itinerary.''

"You didn't arrange it?''

"I knew nothing of it until their mother ship encountered one of our deep-space patrols and announced itself en route. Coincidental that they're just in time for our local Fourth Service open house and fly-in, isn't it? Especially when O'Brian's Fourth Service Commander also knew nothing about the Team's arrival in advance.''

"Well, then.'' Dancer pushed herself up to a standing position with both hands on the arms of her chair. "We'd better get to work.'' Her reasons were purely personal. Who was this woman, and why was she impersonating Dancer? Or rather, who Dancer had been . . .

Michael gave her the ghost of a smile and walked her down to the Med Section.

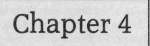

Chapter 4

They were definitely in a world of hurt if even Dancer had ceased questioning odd occurrences on the theory that the Commander had probably ordered them, Michael thought wryly. Perhaps others had known him longer, but she knew him best. And she should have known he wouldn't have arranged for this damnable airshow without telling her.

Then he sighed. *When* would he have told her? When had they been in the same room long enough for him to have told her? He hadn't even found the time to tell her the Team was on its way when he'd been informed of it himself. Fact was, it hadn't seemed very important.

Hadn't seemed very important, he castigated himself. The very-much-in-demand FSIPADT suddenly changes its itinerary to include O'Brian's Stake—largely considered the backside of nowhere—and he hadn't considered it very important?

Come on. Why would the Fourth Service send the Team here without first notifying him, as nominal commander of the Confederacy support troops, and Tom Trumbull, his counterpart with O'Brian's Fourth Service contingent? Answer: they wouldn't. Not unless they were checking up on the performance and vigilance of one or the other forces—in which case, both had failed the test! And if that had been the case, Michael would have been informed via his Sixth Service sources.

The only other answer was, someone else had come to the conclusion that the backside of nowhere was really an arrow pointed at the heart of the Confederacy.

And who might that someone else be? The Karranganthians, of course. They weren't cowed; they weren't subdued. Capitulating when they did had been in their best interests.

It was a classic example of the Confederacy's winning the war but losing the peace. Confederacy sanctions should have been structured to allow for its forces to press their military advantages and ensure future peace by forcing unconditional surrender, the dismantling of the Karranganthian war machine, and the restructuring of the Karranganthian government. Instead, when crushing defeat was imminent, the Karranganthians had merely pulled back inside their prewar interstellar borders—as the Confederacy had been demanding since the unprovoked "annexation" of a small but economically significant planet called Danton. By its own laws, the Confederacy had been unable to pursue. So, the Karranganthians, nominally under the guise of defeat, were now being given the opportunity to rearm, retrench, and reassess their strategy.

Meanwhile, what territory had they lost? Nothing but what they had taken by conquest, and they'd already raped those worlds. The Confederacy called for reparations, but reparations to whom? The populations of those conquered colonies had, for the most part, been wiped out.

Punishment for even that had been deferred. Some of the soldiers doing the deeds had been apprehended, but who had given them their orders? By Confederacy law, a War Crimes trial could not take place on speculation. No witnesses, no proof—no trial. And the Karranganthian hierarchy definitely did not want any proof to surface; all intelligence indicated ignorance of these deeds by the general Karranganthian-governed populace. Michael had no doubt that there would be a great deal of trouble at home should unequivocal evidence of these atrocities be discovered.

Granted, the Auryx solution of annihilating the entire Karranganthian civilization was as contrary to Confederacy law—and as morally repugnant—as the Karranganthian policy of "annexation" by conquest. Still, the Sixth Service, with its limited but highly trained and motivated resources, should now be employed in tracking down the Karranganthian torturers and murderers, bringing them into the full light of publicity, and ensuring that they lived to stand trial. So far, the pitiful few actually apprehended by the Confederacy had practically been handed to Karranganthian assassins, so ineptly were they guarded.

Instead, after the Confederacy had used his people for all the operations the military commands of the other five services didn't want to know about—not to mention rescues that the other five combined couldn't have pulled off successfully—Sixth's reward had been banishment to O'Brian's, with the admonishment to be neither seen nor heard. It seemed that the peacetime Confederacy didn't want reminders of its own less-than-lawful wartime forays walking around where they could be questioned.

Bitter? Michael? Not much.

There were those who would say that such strong feelings were coloring the Commander's judgment, that he was seeing Karranganthians around every corner. Perhaps they would be right. After all, how would *anyone* get away with taking over a Warlord Starlifter and a group as prominent as the Team with no one the wiser? Even given the satisfactory accomplishment of that impossibility, what would be the purpose?

No, the answer had to lie elsewhere. Only in his mind was this minor nuisance a threat to the universe.

But how came this "minor nuisance" to take the form and identity of his second-in-command?

"She's awake and talking, but not saying anything we want to hear," was Preble's report as Michael and Dancer entered his domain. "The young lady may be the image of our Dancer, but she certainly doesn't have Dancer's sweet disposition."

The Commander smiled his thoughts; Dancer spoke them. "That's the first time I have ever been accused of being 'sweet.' "

"Exactly," was Preble's pointed reply. "However, this one is arrogant, condescending, spiteful, and thoroughly unpleasant. Furthermore—"

"Furthermore," Michael interrupted, "she's probably frightened out of her wits. Any progress at identifying the chemicals in her blood?"

"So far, we've isolated two hallucinogens, a possible depressant, one of the more obscure stimulants, and two additional compounds that, at this point, are totally beyond us. It comes as no surprise that she has no recollection of ingesting them, nor that she doesn't remember her arrival here. She does remember you, though, Dancer. Keeps demanding to see 'the bitch who decked her.' ''

Dancer wanted to see her, too: she had a few demands of her own to make. With a wry smile for Michael, she nudged the room door open with her knee. ''Mustn't keep the lady waiting any longer.''

The Commander nodded and relaxed into an observer's stance. This was his second's show, and he trusted her implicitly to handle it. Still, it couldn't be easy on her, after all of these years, to suddenly be confronted with her name, face, and service records in use by somebody else. He had a very uncomfortable feeling about the whole affair, but couldn't yet pinpoint it. Something to do with Dancer, something to do with loss. Try as he might, he couldn't keep the two concepts from sliding together, side by side, in his mind.

The Fourth Service Interplanetary Precision Aerial Demonstration Team pilot was lying on her back, her arms crossed at the junction of sheet and blue-flowered hospital gown and her face like a long winter. Her crewchief/bodyguard sat erect in a chair beside her, his wary eyes darting back and forth at the slightest movement. Of course. Good. It would be prudent to study his reactions, too. Or lack thereof—other than the alertness of those eyes, his face was totally impassive as Dancer walked through the door.

''So, Auglaize DeWellesthar,'' was her opening gambit, ''what brings you all the way out to my territory?''

At the sound of Dancer's voice, the impostor's head jerked around, her pupils dilated, beads of sweat broke out on her forehead, and her jaw dropped. In short, she looked like she had just seen a ghost. Which, in effect, she had.

''My God, am I hallucinating? Who are you?'' The voice was Dancer's, almost. Almost. A shade higher, perhaps, or maybe it was just the different intonation.

''Precisely what I wanted to ask you. I do know, however, who you are *not*.''

''I don't believe this is happening. Is that really you?''

''Now, there's a particularly inane question. Then again, if I am I, where does that leave you?'' Something hovered on the edge of Dancer's memory; she *knew* this person. Or had known her. Some quality in her voice, in the back of her eyes, in the way she held herself, told Dancer that here was no stranger for some unfathomable reason dressed up to resemble Auglaize DeWellesthar. This girl *was* a DeWellesthar.

A DeWellesthar. Which one had the grit to try to step into Auglaize's shoes? Antonia was the likeliest candidate, but Antonia was just a child. Antonia was . . . a little mental arithmetic added the intervening thirteen years to the kid she'd once known.

Dancer's impassive face hid the shock of recognition, and the unreasoning anger accompanying it. Antonia? How? Damn her, why?

"It can't be," the girl said, shaking her head. "It can't be. You're . . . dead!"

"Aren't I just. We're all dead here, child," Dancer informed her in a voice that chilled even herself. "Every one of us. In fact, in some quarters, we are facetiously known as the Service of the Dead."

If possible, the girl's face turned two shades paler. "You can't mean . . . "

Michael's voice whispered into her ear receiver, "Easy, Dancer."

She ignored it. "That you are dead, too? What an interesting concept of the afterlife. I don't know, are you?"

"You are rapidly frightening her into that state," Michael admonished. "Ease off."

"Sir," she responded, with a mock bow toward the door. The bodyguard rose menacingly, and so did Dancer's right eyebrow. "Call off your dog, child. The last time he was at my throat, he took me by surprise. This time, I'll kill him."

Her cool, almost indifferent tone must have made an impression; the girl's hands sketched a motion like fluttering birds, and the man relaxed back into his chair, his eyes locking defiantly with Dancer's. So. She wrinkled her nose into what she knew was an engaging grin, and tapped her chest. "Dancer."

A hesitant smile was his response, followed by a string of consonants that could have been syllables or the sound of a buzz saw ripping through the trunk of a petrified tree. The voice was soft and rich, though, and the delivery graceful.

Dancer's breath caught in her throat. God damn. The man sent chills up her spine and a flush down her face at the same time. She hadn't reacted to anyone physically in that way since . . . Deliberately, she shifted her attention back to the girl. "Translation, please."

"I have no idea. I call him Troy; he reminds me of someone I used to know. Handsome, isn't he?"

Handsome, he was. Despite his massive build, the man's features were finely molded; light hair, clean-shaven face, mild gray-green eyes. Dancer found herself inexplicably drawn to him, at the same time wondering what the devil was happening to her. She'd thought herself long since immune to that kind of sensual magnetism.

Well. Perhaps, in some indefinable way, he did resemble Morgan Troy. She should have resented the girl's calculatedly casual use of the surname, but she was still too busy resenting the other's usurpation of Auglaize DeWellesthar's identity to care about her taking Troy's name in vain, too. "You communicate by sign language?" she asked impassively.

"Mostly. Technical diagrams are the same in any language, and since all Fourth Service personnel are required to know Standard Sign, no problem."

"Interesting. Where does he come from, to be so indispensable to the Service that they overlook a small thing like his not understanding the regulation language?"

"He knows enough to get by. Where he comes from . . . " She shrugged dismissively. "I don't think I ever asked."

"I see." Dancer sneaked another quick glance at the man; he met it with a blank-eyed smile. Either the Fourth Service had changed tremendously since she had left it, or there was a lot more to this one than met the eye. She was inclined to believe the latter. "And you," she continued, turning her attention back to the girl. "You never did answer my question. Are you yet among the living?"

"I'm not afraid of you any more, so you can stop bullying me."

"My dear . . . " a marked pause before the name, ". . . Auglaize. Was I bullying you? Forgive me. But I would like to know how you came here. I would also like to know who sabotaged your aircraft. Any ideas?"

"My dear Auglaize,"—the tone mocked Dancer's own—"I have no idea where I am, or how I got here. All I remember is, you hit me."

"Straight?"

"Straight, Glaize." Tears came to the other's eyes at the use of Dancer's childhood nickname, tears Dancer somehow knew to be genuine. "Why did you let us think you were dead all these years? Why did you let us mourn you all these years?"

"Little Antonia . . . " Dancer's voice softened. "We all do what is necessary."

"Necessary? Allowing your family and friends to grieve for you—after twelve years, they still grieve for you! That is *necessary*?

A lot of people loved you, Glaize, and you don't give a damn about them, do you?''

"The farm is doing well, especially since Alan decided to return home," Dancer recited calmly. "Of course, Father was overjoyed, and Mother is up to her matchmaking tricks again. Our Alexander refused to resign his Fifth Service commission at war's end and is still shuttling supplies back and forth across space, much to everyone's dismay. Next time you see him, ask him if he remembers the Auryx wife of the Ramses ambassador, the woman who turned out to be such an unexpectedly accurate marksman. Tell him that ebony hair he was so enamored of was in reality a strong dye hand-painted strand by strand over DeWellesthar red. Ahannah married Thaddaeus Moon, and they have, let me see, it's three children now, isn't it? Shall I remind you of their names? And Ash. Uncle Ash is still suffering the effects of his captivity during the war. Now, tell me again that I don't give a damn for my family!''

Dancer had kept up with the details of her former life whenever possible, though that information was not necessarily current—obviously, since she hadn't known what this chit was up to. She'd still thought of Antonia as the child she had said good-bye to so long ago. And it had been one of the hardest decisions of her career not to reveal herself to the captain of that Fifth Service freighter Michael and she had arranged passage on, who also just happened to be her older brother and childhood best friend Alex. In fact, when it came down to the wire, the only factor ensuring her silence was the knowledge that she would have been signing Alex's death warrant as well as Michael's and her own had she confessed her true identity. Perhaps one day she would tell Antonia that. Not now—she didn't deserve to know that now. "Enough of the games. Why have you taken my name?''

The girl shrugged and eyed her coolly. "You weren't using it. Besides, I knew something of you, and we do resemble one another.''

"We are enough alike to be twins," Dancer interjected. "Is the likeness natural, or surgically enhanced?''

"Ironic that you mentioned Cousin Alex earlier, because it was your dear brother who first gave me the idea that I could be you. He came home from the wars quite a hero, as I am sure you already know. I was at his homecoming. When he saw me, he rushed past everyone else and grabbed me with a hug that took my breath away. 'Auglaize,' he said. 'Thank God, you're alive! Why didn't anyone tell me?' Well, I thought, if I could fool Alex, maybe, just maybe,

I could make one or two of my own dreams come true. I had my nose altered, and my chin, and the eyebrows—just a little bit.

"It was your training and flight records that got me onto the Team, or have you figured that out for yourself? Well, why not?" she blazed at Dancer's glare. "I fly as well as you, if not better. After all, I *am* on the Team, not stuck in a peacekeeping force on some backwater world not even worth the effort of setting up a real base. What do you fly here, anyway, Auglaize? Puddle-jumping patrol craft!"

Dancer allowed herself a tiny smile. Antonia would never know about the smooth, sleek Dart interceptors poised and waiting on their catapults ten feet below the surface of the courtyard just outside those walls, nor of the multipurpose Weasel fighters tucked away on that hidden airfield a stone's throw from the city limits. "I am known as Dancer now, Tonia," she quietly corrected. "As for our 'puddle-jumpers,' they are faster than they look, and the vertical takeoff and landing capabilities get us in and out of places that can't be reached by ground vehicles. You, of all people, should know the wisdom of utilizing whatever is most suitable for the environment. After all the emphasis the Team places on study of the atmospheric conditions of its show planets?"

Antonia colored under the thinly veiled sarcasm. "Forgive my continued curiosity, but how in the name of All did you happen to choose 'Dancer' as your . . . pseudonym?"

"Really, child, I am surprised at you. You blithely assume my identity and background without even knowing that 'Dancer' was the nickname given me by my fellow cadets at flight training? I was called 'The Dancer,' " and she chuckled at the memory, "because I couldn't seem to master the art of formation flying."

"I trust you eventually did."

"I daresay. If I hadn't, where would you be?"

"I may have used your records to get onto the Team in the first place, but I stayed on it by myself!"

"I don't doubt it. You always were very . . . competitive. Tell me, where exactly did you learn to fly?"

"You remember Myles Ashland?"

Of course Dancer remembered the man who had given her her first airplane ride, in a fabric-and-wood craft that he had built himself. Indeed, how could she ever forget the exhilaration of the wind in her face, roaring past her ears, and trying to tear her hair out by the roots? "Yes."

"And his son Mydge, who was Fourth Service?"

"Myles junior. Of course. He was a year or so ahead of me at the Academy."

"He received a disability discharge, bought up a couple of surplus Gypsies on the black market, and taught some of us kids to fly them in his spare time."

Dancer cocked an eyebrow at what the girl had omitted saying. Certainly, she had been just a child. And certainly if her parents had known what she was up to, they would have locked her in her room to make sure she had a chance to grow up. On Triterra—Third Earth Colony, their shared home planet—society was based on a rural economy, highly family oriented. It was unusual for a man to join the military except in time of war, and unheard of for a woman to do so at any time. Certainly not the Fourth, where women looked, dressed, acted, and talked like men, and "voluntary" sterilization was required for a career pilot of either sex. Dancer and Antonia both had eaten, slept, and breathed flying since the day they were born, and the military was the only way either had been able to do the kind of high-performance aerobatic flying each had dreamed about. Dancer had been lucky: her parents, especially her father—the one who had put aside his own dreams to stay behind and mind the farm—backed their nonconformist daughter completely. While Mom consistently encouraged her in the face of seemingly insurmountable odds and societal pressures, Dad and Uncle Ash had moved heaven and earth to get her into the Fourth Service Academy.

Antonia, however, lacked this parental backing. As a result, she had taken her advanced training in illegally obtained, war-weary Gypsy fighters to which Dancer wouldn't have entrusted her own pilots, from a famous former fighter jock whom the Service had been grateful to have the disability excuse to retire because he pushed his men, equipment, and himself past their limits. Dancer's respect for the girl was grudging, but it was genuine. As was her pride. "And the records? Did you doctor them yourself, or did you have help?"

"I know a little bit about computers; Mydge showed me how to get into the Fourth Service records. He thought it was a great joke—and a personal coup for him if I pulled it off. Of course, the confusion caused by the war helped. A lot of data conveniently . . . got lost."

"Very good. I'm impressed. I would still like to wring your neck, but I am impressed."

"For the love of . . . look, Auglaize . . . "

"I told you before, Auglaize DeWellesthar is dead," she said abruptly. "Perished rather horribly along with seventeen squadron-mates in a Karranganthian torture cell. Like a phoenix rising from their ashes, Dancer emerged whole and strong. Very strong."

Dancer flexed her fingers, leaving Antonia to infer what she might from the revelation. It was true, all right; her screams had mingled with those of her dying comrades, and somehow, she had survived. But the Sixth Service medical wizards were as adept at eradicating scars from the mind as they were from the body. At least, as far as she had allowed them to.

"I'm sorry; I didn't know."

"You damned well *should* have known! Antonia, I lived that record you're capitalizing on. When you were still playing with your dolls, I was flying planetary defense. While you were giving tea parties for your schoolmates, I was killing other intelligent be-ings who were hell-bent on killing me. At the time when your major concern was whether or not you would be asked to a Saturday-night dance, I was watching my people being tortured to death. Knowing that my turn would come soon. Do you have any conception of what that was like?"

"Oh, come on, Glaize. Don't try to snow me with all that anti-Karranganthian propaganda."

"Propaganda!" Dancer exploded. "You've seen Ash, and you still call it 'propaganda'?"

"Surely the reports were exaggerated."

"I assure you, little girl, from firsthand experience, that what you've heard is only a very small part of what the Karranganthians actually did."

"Well, of course they didn't coddle POWs; one would hardly expect them to. But tell me why a civilized people would massacre whole planets, kill innocent women and children?"

Dancer just shook her head, trying to rein in her temper. This wasn't the first time since the cease-fire that she had heard that same line of reasoning, but coming from someone wearing her face and a Fourth Service uniform, it was too much. "Unfortunate that you couldn't assume my education along with my identity. All right, see if you can follow this.

"The basis of all war, as any first-term cadet knows, Antonia, is acquisitiveness. Greed. Somebody has something that somebody else wants. Wealth, resources, land, power, it's all the same. When you try to take something somebody else has, he's going to fight you for it. You have two choices: either enslave him—bend his will to yours by force—or kill him. The latter solution crushes resistance permanently. If there are others who will take up his fight—kill them, too. Unless, of course, you need workers to mine the wealth, manufacture the goods, or exploit the resources. In which case, you use threats, torture, and terror to keep the conquered people in line. You with me so far?''

"Yes, Professor. I'm not stupid.''

"Good, because here's where it starts to get tough. Terror is also a military weapon, though a two-edged one. The certainty of torture upon capture will either make the opposition turn tail and run, or fight to the death. I've seen both.

"Toughest of all to comprehend is the human factor, the innate cruelty that war gives excuse to. The Karranganthians have precedent, as far back as human history reaches. A barbarian named Genghis Khan, who terrorized an entire continent. A supposedly civilized man named Hitler who used genocide to rally his people just twenty years before the first space shots. Have you ever read Caesar? Even the idealized Roman Republic wasn't above burning a city down around its inhabitants as an example to quell further resistance.

"Add all this to the assurance that you are the superior race, that life is cheap—and you have an oversimplification of the official policy of the Karranganthian state.''

Antonia shook her head. "They're saying now that—''

"I know what they're saying now. *That*, child, is the propaganda.''

"Obviously, after all these years of fighting them, you can't be objective.''

Raising her eyes to the ceiling in exasperation, Dancer let the matter drop. "As you will, Antonia.''

"Anyway, the war is over now, Glaize. Can't you come home?''

"Wouldn't it get just the tiniest bit confusing with the two of us?''

"They don't know where I am or what I'm doing. All they know is, I'm in Fourth.''

"And all those in Fourth who knew me are dead.''

"Not all, but I haven't been challenged yet. You were missing for so long, you see, that of course when you came back, you were changed. For that matter, they're changed.''

"Surprise, surprise. One of the effects of war, I'm told. Just for the record, where had I been while I was 'missing so long'?''

"Even easier. You had been seriously injured, took years to rehabilitate, then did alternate service somewhere very vague. Not a story anyone could really check up on.''

Inwardly, Dancer shuddered at how close Antonia's rationalization came to the truth. Except for the part about returning to Fourth, it was pretty much what *had* happened. Michael made no comment, though she imagined she heard the sigh of fabric against paint as he shifted his weight just outside the door.

"Well," she said. "You are good, Antonia. You must be. Just remember that I am better. Because I am ruthless. And I can break you—"

"Easy, child," Michael's voice caressed her ear.

She nodded once, sharply. "But I won't. I will, however, tell you why I can't come home. I am Auryx now; there are few who remember that I was born otherwise. And our war isn't over. We have been fighting the Karranganthians for generations, and we will be fighting them until the last one is dead. Each of us has personal reasons for wanting to bring that day around as quickly as possible."

"So, what happens to me? I'm not a prisoner of war, since the Confederacy"—with emphasis on the words—"recognizes no war, and I'm not ill, so you can't use that excuse to keep me here. I want to go back to the Team."

"You will. When we say so. First, though, you'll have to tell us what you're doing here."

Michael unobtrusively nudged the door open a crack with his foot. Dancer's anger was almost palpable; though she had it in check, it was clouding her judgment. Therefore, it was time to terminate the interview. He hesitated a moment to observe, though, smiling slightly as his eyes rested on the two redheads.

It was a little eerie, he had to admit. Side by side, the pair weren't mirror images—more like a single image displaced in time. The younger DeWellesthar was near the age Dancer had been when she had come to Sixth, with the same fear-roughened edges and the same mischievous grin. The same chip-on-her-shoulder attitude, though for a different reason. Looking at the girl, Michael could plainly see what Dancer had been before the war had hardened her. Young, eager, and ignorant. Did she have the feeling she was talking to herself, back across the years?

Michael eased himself through the doorway, allowing the portal to close noiselessly behind him, for a better vantage point. The third member of the party, the crewchief, also watched the other two, as if he were trying to figure out Dancer's role in the affair even as she was trying to figure out his. For the younger girl, his regard held proprietorial amusement. Toward Dancer, it was blatantly sexual. Puzzling to Michael—perhaps troubling was a better word—was that consciously or not, Dancer was responding. Over the years, he had seen a lot of men look at his second in that way. This was the first time he had ever seen her look back.

Dancer was asking again about the crash, about the Team's appearance in the skies over O'Brian's Stake.

"I don't know . . ." Tonia began, then her eyes slid past Dancer and widened as they rested on him. "Who are you? *Who are you?*" The words took on a hysterical edge as the girl flattened herself back against her pillow. "Keep him away from me, Glaize!"

Startled, Dancer followed the girl's horrified stare to where Michael lounged in the doorway. "Mike? He's not going to hurt you. He might as well come on in; he's been listening anyway."

"No! Get him out of here, Glaize!" she pleaded.

Michael met Dancer's stunned gaze with an almost imperceptible negative gesture—Antonia was literally terrified of him, and he hadn't the vaguest idea why. Her bodyguard still sat where he had been ordered to, clearly torn between his instinct to defend her and obedience to her directive not to.

"Tonia," Dancer said reasonably, "Michael is our leader. He is also my friend. He won't hurt you."

"If he is your leader, Auglaize, then why is he wearing the uniform of the Death Squad?"

Again, Dancer looked to him. How would even a genuine Fourth Service pilot know anything about the Death Squads, known inside the Sixth Service as Black Teams for the uniforms they wore?

"Tonia, listen to me. You trusted me once; you can trust me still. That's only Michael. He prefers to wear black, just as I prefer to wear red. He thinks it brings out his masculine charms. I tend to agree, don't you? Look at him, Tonia," Dancer continued in a soothing tone. "Look at Michael's eyes. Have you ever seen anyone with such beautiful blue eyes?"

She involuntarily looked, then locked. Good. A little mild hypnosis wasn't out of place here. Later, Tonia would trust him to probe her mind more deeply, though his first impression was that he wouldn't learn much from the exercise.

With a nervous giggle, the girl broke eye contact, and said, a trifle too hastily, "He is very good-looking, though I prefer my men somewhat bigger." This, with a glance at her bodyguard, who had meanwhile relaxed. "Michael. Michael what?"

"Just Michael," he replied easily. "I am the only one. Dancer, a word with you, if you please."

To Tonia's obvious relief, Dancer followed him out of the room.

As the door closed behind them, she leaned up against the corridor wall with something like a shrug. "What do you think, Mike?"

"I was going to ask you the same question."

"I have never seen a woman react that way to you before. Usually, they fall all over you. She was scared silly."

"Your prologue didn't help, of course, but still. She was also quite vigorously resisting me, probably unconsciously. That and her selective amnesia seem to suggest that someone has been tampering with her mind. But why? Again, more questions than answers." With a weary sigh, he shifted the focus of his concern. "How are you, Dancer? Does it bother you, looking at your face on someone else's body?"

"Damn it, Michael, she knows nothing of how Auglaize De-Wellesthar lived and died. Just put on my identity like it was a comfortable jacket tossed over a chair, taking advantage of the warmth that someone else had already paid dearly for."

"You obviously knew our young lady before. Cousins, I believe she said?"

"We were . . . acquainted."

"I see. We'll discuss it at a more appropriate time. Right now, you had better talk to her, get to know everything you can about her. Tomorrow, you are going to take your jacket—and your identity—back."

"That ought to be interesting," Dancer muttered.

Michael rewarded her with one of his rare, beautiful smiles. "Indeed."

Chapter 5

"Jeremiah?" Dancer called as she entered Michael's—their—quarters.

"Yes, Dancer," was the immediate reply. "I was told to expect you. The Commander informs me that we'll be working together from now on.''

"Does he, indeed." Dancer unfastened the top two buttons of her shirt, rolled up her sleeves, and made herself comfortable in the straight-backed chair in front of the terminal. "Do you mind if we talk later? Right now, I have some concentrating to do.''

She must have been having a rough day—there she was, concerned about hurting a computer's feelings. As if it had any. With a snort, she reached over and flicked his voice off. It was hard not to think of Michael's Jeremiah as a person.

The Command computer was certainly going to take some getting used to again—the voice-recognition and vocalization capabilities were seldom used downstairs. With so many people trying to work in so small a space, it would have sounded like the Tower of Babel, and no one would have gotten anything done. Trained eyes could scan a screenful of data faster than the machine could read it to them, and pick out pertinent facts almost as quickly, and users quite frankly preferred the relative privacy of the keyboard. But for the Commander, who habitually juggled a dozen projects at once, having a machine that could talk back was a must.

Dancer had a feeling she'd learn to appreciate the feature again, too, but for now, she'd rather do things her own way. She started to tap out RECORDS, FSIPADT, DEWELLESTHAR, AUGLAIZE but on impulse hit cancel and typed instead RECORDS, AUGLAIZE DEWELLESTHAR, 6TH, CON—confidential. The machine asked for a clearance code, and she unashamedly fed it Michael's. Instantly, her latest Service photo flashed up on the screen, then flashed off again as a lowercase "override" appeared in the top left-hand corner.

"Keep your mind on the business at hand, Dancer," was Michael's gentle admonition.

Punching the intercom button for his personal receiver, she shrugged it off with, "Can't blame a girl for trying."

There was amusement in his voice. "Don't try again, Red."

"Understood." She wasn't sure what she had hoped or expected to find, but there was obviously something in her records that the Commander didn't want her to see. No, she chided herself, it was more likely that meeting Tonia again, and looking into the mirror of her face, had made Dancer unusually edgy. How else to explain the fact that in all the years she'd been in Sixth, this was the first time she'd ever tried breaking into Michael's computer records on herself?

With a sigh, she turned the voice recognition back on and asked for the most recent show tape of the Team. Within seconds, the first of the red-and-white Gypsy fighters flashed across the screen and her stomach muscles gave an involuntary squeeze. All vague worries and unformed doubts fled before the realization that she was soon to be piloting one of these beauties again. How many hours had she put in, in this, her first love, before coming over to Sixth? Not enough. Never enough.

Dancer's fingers reflexively reached for nonexistent controls; her body automatically responded to every maneuver. For a full five minutes, she *was* a Gypsy fighter, feeling the air rushing past, reveling in the euphoria of the disciplined freedom the aircraft knew. Tomorrow afternoon at this time, her lifelong dream, dormant these many years but still very much alive, would be coming true. The *real* Auglaize DeWellesthar would by Gypsy Five; *she* would be weaving and spiraling and rolling in perfect synchronization with the rest of the Team! The supreme irony.

No, the supreme irony would be if she wasn't ready.

"Back 'er up, Jeremiah." She sighed. "I'm going to want to take notes."

The child Auglaize, the Academy cadet, the young Fourth Service pilot, had known the Team's routine by rote—but that had been a long time ago. Even if she hadn't forgotten anything in the intervening years, the format surely had been changed. Logically, then, Dancer's first move was to reacquaint herself with the basic maneuvers; Jeremiah listed them in order, and made her memorize the list before allowing her to review the tape again.

The aerobatics alone would pose no problems; these were nothing any fighter pilot worth her salt wouldn't have mastered long ago. After all, aerobatics had originated as a means of waging aerial combat, or so she'd been told. The difficulties lay in the tight formations and the synchronous execution of those maneuvers. Timing was everything. An error of a few milliseconds could result in disaster.

Therefore, the next time through the show tape, Dancer choreographed Number Five, counted out the precise timing, noted, reviewed.

From there, she went on to request a full cockpit layout for the Gypsy, its specifications, its updated performance graphs. Not that Dancer hadn't joyously pushed the aircraft to the limits of both their capabilities on numerous occasions—but again, that had been a long, long time ago. Sixth's Darts and Weasels might have been built for roughly the same purpose, but they had a whole different feel. What she really needed, lacking an actual Gypsy, was a good simulator.

The nearest simulator was two star systems away, but they did have an actual Gypsy. Didn't they?

"Afraid not, Dancer," Jeremiah informed her. "The Commander sent it back already. A good-faith gesture, I believe he called it."

"I do wish he had waited on that. All right, then, Jeremiah—can you give me a visual of the entire show from the perspective of one of the participants?"

"Of course. Number Five, I presume?"

Dancer had also forgotten the computer's knack of anticipating her. Michael's programming, no doubt. "Yes, Number Five," she said with a smile. "Also, I want full-size hard copy of the cockpit layout."

"I can give you simulation control using my keyboard."

"What I need to do, Jeremiah, is make sure I know where everything is."

"Of course."

She stood up and stretched the knots out of her neck as she read the specs on the Team's Gypsies. There had been a few modifications, but for all the years the old girl had been in service, she had remained essentially the same craft as the original production run. Can't improve upon perfection, Dancer thought affectionately.

The Gypsy was small, sleek, fast, highly maneuverable, and deadly. Easily transported, too, with swept wings designed for easy removal and reassembly. Perfect for the Team to shuttle from their modified Warlord Starlifter, visible overhead in low orbit, to the host airfield. And as beautiful in flight as the Triterran hawk she was named for.

"Ready when you are, Dancer," Jeremiah stated.

After spreading the freshly printed sheets into a reasonable facsimile of a cockpit, Dancer gave Jeremiah the go-ahead. The first few minutes were awkward, but soon she was flying her paper airplane as if all those intervening years had never been. Her mind projected her past her immediate surroundings: the instruments in front of her were real, the switches under her gloved fingers actual switches, the scenery on the screen before her the true panorama of sky and ground. She felt herself alternately pushed against the seat as G forces multiplied her body weight several times, then abruptly floating against the restraints as those forces were reversed. Though Jeremiah was just going through his self-programmed routine, allowing for no variations on her part, in her mind Dancer was flying.

How long this continued, she had no idea. So complete was her concentration that time had meaning only in the context of the aerial maneuvers she was executing; after a while, even that wasn't conscious.

Damn, but those people were persistent about getting their pilot back! Strained courtesy masking his impatience, Michael ended the latest conversation with the Team commander's representative. *If nothing were wrong with her, why was she being held in their medical facility?* Observation, to make sure there were no hidden problems. *Surely the Fourth Service flight surgeon aboard the Warlord was skilled enough to care for one of their own.* We are constrained, by law, to conduct an investigation, surely you understand that. *But what of* our *investigation? Surely* you *understand that! And what of the crewchief?* Michael couldn't quite pass along the information that the crewchief was, at the moment, one of their major subjects of investigation; or that the man fought anyone who tried to separate him from the girl. And back and forth, and back and forth, through the same groove they'd traveled at least three times before.

This was usually Dancer's job! Her knowledge of the Fourth Service, coupled with her inventive mind, would have had these people eating out of her hand long ago. Ooh, Commander, are you admitting you're losing your touch? he could almost hear her say in answer to his thoughts.

Michael smiled to himself. Where was that redheaded bane of his existence, anyway?

A quick check with Jeremiah told the Commander that Dancer was still occupied learning the new Team routine, that she had been for a long while, and that, in Jeremiah's opinion, it was high time both of them took a break. Michael quirked an eyebrow at the machine's insubordination—did Dancer realize, he wondered, how many of *her* character traits he had programmed into the Command computer?

A good meal would definitely be in order, though. And—it was nice to have someone to go home to. She'd have a thing or two to say about her move "upstairs," he had no doubt. He looked forward to hearing them.

The Commander's half smile as he rose prompted a few startled looks which blossomed into full-fledged grins behind his back when he announced, "I'll be in my quarters if anyone should need me—and I trust no one will." It was obvious what everyone was thinking. Let them think.

Dancer didn't turn as the door to his quarters opened and shut, not that Michael expected her to. He knew that intense, single-minded concentration she could slip into; it had once saved her life, and he had since trained her to use it at will. Standing silently behind her, he watched the unconscious play of expression across the rapt face reflected in the monitor screen—no more than a tiny tug at one corner of the mouth, or the infinitesimal drawing together of the eyebrows—as she flew. She was beautiful in the combination of sun and artificial light in this corner of the room, her brown eyes almost black and the fire of her hair sparking out defiantly from its confining braid.

He'd always loved her hair, as short as Antonia's when they'd first met; how many times, in those days, had she talked about having it cropped off, back to Fourth Service regulation length? Roughly the same number of times she had been admonished that the Sixth Service had no such ridiculous regulations. Indeed, he'd known Sixth had her for sure when she stopped threatening a trip to the barber. Now, though she would vehemently deny even the suggestion, she was justifiably vain about the rich, luxuriously waving cascade that, when loose, tumbled to her tailbone. Had she realized yet that as a Team pilot she'd have to sacrifice it?

The full impact of the thought struck him. Child, it looks like you finally are returning to the Fourth Service. That feeling of foreboding assailed him again; only this time, he assured himself there was nothing to fear. The assignment was only temporary. She'd be back in Sixth day after tomorrow. . . .

Look at her, though. She *was* Team Five in her mind, and as happy as he had ever seen her.

The Commander marveled at this ability to ignore everything outside her own mind, even intense physical pain. Marveled at it, and secretly feared that someday he might not be able to penetrate the wall she built and bring her back to the "real world." The psychs still averred that given the right set of conditions, it could happen.

My, but we're morbid today, he could almost hear her say. Giving himself a rough mental shake, he returned his attention to his excuse for escaping to his quarters this early in the day: a hot meal and some good company.

His hands automatically settled on Dancer's shoulders, kneading, massaging tension points, the back of her neck, her upper arms. Gradually, she responded as he had conditioned her to. Taut muscles relaxed, a true smile bowed her mouth, and her head eased back to rest against his midsection. Hands dropped limply to her lap, then rose again to cover his in a gesture at once intimate and innocent. The relaxation was his conditioning. The gentle pressure of her fingers around his was a refinement all her own, and it never failed to send a thrill throughout his body.

"No need to ask how you're doing," was his quiet comment. "Will you join me for dinner?"

"Mmmm, is it that late already?" Her stomach grumbled that indeed it was. "Yes, I'd like to. Thank you, Jeremiah. I'm going to need some personnel information later, and I have to talk to Tonia again."

"I think you'll find her much more cooperative," Michael said as he disentangled his fingers from Dancer's.

"Oh, really?" was the dry retort.

"She and I . . . had a discussion this afternoon. I explained to her a few facts of life; at least she agrees that you have good reason to be angry with her." That the "few facts of life" included a brief but graphic description of what the Karranganthians had left of the Lioth installation, Dancer didn't need to know. No sense having her angry with *him*, too. "As for you, Red. . . . "

"Here it comes."

"Kindly remember that she's drugged, dazed, and in shock at seeing you alive. In dealing with her, anger is counterproductive. Hmm?" At her reluctant nod, he continued lightly, "If you start to lose your temper again, think of this: she may have traded on your reputation to get what she wanted, but she will be the instrument to get you what *you've* always wanted, a chance to fly with the Team."

"The Commander," Dancer replied with a smile, "is always right."

"The Commander is always right," she repeated under her breath as she stood, stretched, and followed him out to the kitchen. For a while, she'd actually forgotten his high-handedly moving her into his quarters without her knowledge or consent, as if she was some piece on a flarking game board. The Commander is always right. . . .

"Michael. Now that I've taken over your bedroom, exactly where are you going to sleep?"

"Thirty-seven seconds," was his amused reply. "I wondered how long it would take you to broach the subject. Look here." With that, he swept back the deep blue draperies on the wall beside the kitchen to reveal, not the large window that Dancer had expected, but a neat bunk set into the wall. "I had it put in soon after we arrived," he explained, pointing out the drawers underneath, the wardrobe at the foot deep enough to hold his uniforms on hangers, the communications buttons set into the narrow shelf between the mattress and drawers in the wall where his hand would automatically fall when he was lying down.

"Not bad," was her admiring appraisal.

"I'm glad you approve. This is close enough to the heart of things"—with a nod at Jeremiah—"that I don't feel guilty about grabbing a few hours' sleep now and then."

"The mighty Michael actually does sleep?" she asked in mock surprise. "Will wonders never cease?" As he turned with a snort to the kitchen, Dancer parked herself on the firm but comfortable mattress, her legs crossed in front of her and her back against the wardrobe.

Compact, attractive, and efficient, she thought. Add the word *brilliant*, and you'd have a fairly accurate description of the Commander. His hands had polished the rich wooden drawer fronts and doors, she knew. The woven blanket upon which she sat was black, as were the satiny sheets and pillow cover, the contrast of textures resulting in an effect that was far from somber.

With something akin to delight, Dancer spied the corner of the Auryx harp peeking out of its niche on the floor next to the wall. Mmmm. What would it be like, lying in Michael's arms here in this cozy little cave . . . ?

"Make yourself at home."

The Commander's voice jolted her back, and she grinned up at him. How long had he been standing there with that loaded tray, watching her?

"I think she likes it," he added with a wink. "No, sit still; just because we have a dining table doesn't mean we have to use it."

There was the tiniest bit of censure in his tone, but his smile as he handed her a mug of steaming vegetable soup and a grilled-something sandwich countered it. No need to ask what was in the sandwich; Michael was a superb cook, and had fed her often enough over the years to know what she liked.

He set a glass of cold milk on the shelf beside her—she had never gotten used to the swamp ooze the Auryx called coffee—then wedged the pillow behind his back on the other end of the bed, the tray, still containing his lunch, between them.

"There's something else you wanted to ask me, I think," he prompted.

Knowing that his motives weren't sexual mollified her somewhat. Still . . . "Why did you move me up here? And why did you have me promoted?'' An unpleasant thought struck her. "You're not thinking of leaving the Service, are you?''

"You know the only way out for me is death.''

All members of Sixth were aware of that, but Dancer still shivered at his putting the knowledge into words. Her imagination balked at even considering a world without Michael. "The thought had crossed my mind.''

"Have no fear on that account, child. I am not yet so tired of living as to contemplate taking my own life. Even on my worst days—and I must admit this may well rank right up there—I am not so heartless as to wish this job on anyone, even a certain red-haired pain in the backside. Whose 'promotion,' I might add, is nothing more than recognition of the portion of my burden she has assumed over the years.''

A surprising relief washed over her. "Thank you—I think.''

"Don't thank me, child; it was not my idea. Or at least, not entirely. As for the other—why I had you moved up here with me— I so seldom see you any more. Quite frankly, I missed you, missed sitting and talking like this. I thought perhaps if we shared accommodations, we would at least pass each other coming and going. Besides, it seemed a shame to let that whole big bedroom go to waste. Although I'm sure you know the conclusion everyone else has come to concerning your move.''

"Right,'' she said wryly, holding up her soup mug in a toast. "Most of them are convinced we've been sleeping together for years, and it's about time we were open about it.''

"It has served my purpose for them to believe that. Ironic, isn't it?''

"Ironic.'' That described her mixed feelings about his motives, too. Why was it she was so glad it was her companionship he wanted and not her body, when in truth Michael was the only man she had really desired since she had come to Sixth? "A girl likes to be asked, though,'' she mused aloud.

"What, you mean you don't care for the idea of being ordered to be my mistress?'' he teased. "All right, then; if I ever decide to take that foolish step, I'll be sure to ask you first. Feel better now?''

She wrinkled her nose at him, and laughed. "You know, Mike, I've missed you, too.''

"Just out of curiosity, though,'' he began, and then stopped.

Dancer let her eyes meet his and saw, beneath the humorous sparkle, the serious intent. If he were to take that foolish step and put his ego on the line, what would her answer be? Easy. First,

she'd make him sweat for about thirty seconds. Then—"I'd say yes,
of course."

Chapter 6

In his office aboard the Warlord Starlifter, the Team commander
waited impatiently for his operations officer to report. "Well?" he
snarled when the man appeared in the doorway. At least he'd come
in person this time; must be some progress with those planet-bound
bureaucrats below.

"Well, we got the airplane back."

"Wonderful," Colonel Daven said sarcastically. "The airplane
couldn't tell *them* any more than it can tell us. I want that trouble-
making redhead and that damned traitor crewchief of hers!"

"I don't think you're going to get them tonight. At least," the
man hastened to add as his commander's eyes blazed, "not the way
we've been going about it. I think it's time to try Plan B."

"And what might that be?"

"Simple. We call the local news media. . . . "

Antonia was wide awake and in much better humor than she had
been when last Dancer had spoken with her. She was joking with
one of the techs as Dancer came in; Dancer didn't miss the way he
looked at Antonia on his way out. Tonia's bodyguard was watching
it all with an expression of contemptuous amusement. At Dancer's
nod of greeting, he leaned back in his chair and folded his arms,
his face once again blank, but she hadn't imagined that emerald
sparkle in his eyes at her approach, any more than she had imagined
the warmth suffusing her body in reaction to it.

Talk to Antonia, Michael had directed. Observe. Converse. Con-
fine your questions to what you need to know about her day-to-day
life. Let the others do the interrogating; you have enough to worry
about learning to be Fourth Service Interplanetary Precision Aerial

Demonstration Team Pilot Number Five. The Commander was right, of course. She would be briefed about anything else she needed to know. At least, discussing it over dinner had helped rid Dancer of the worst of her antipathy for the girl.

"Your boss was in to see me earlier," Tonia commented as Dancer pulled up a stool beside her bed. "I was dozing, and when I woke up, he was just standing there, looking at me." She shivered. "Those eyes—like he could see right through me."

"Michael can be very intense at times. Also somewhat intimidating, if you don't know him. He'll grow on you."

"I will admit he's not bad looking. In fact, if he'd crack a smile, he'd be a knockout. His accent is cute, too."

"Accent? Michael?"

"Sure. He can't seem to say 'z'. Kept calling me 'Auglaise.' "

"Glaise." It seemed to Dancer that someone had deliberately mispronounced her name that way once, but she couldn't seem to remember. An Auryx, she was sure, but not Michael—except in the line of duty, he never called her anything but Dancer, or "Child," or sometimes a teasing "Red." "The Auryx use the z phoneme very rarely in their language," she finally said. "I suppose that some of them have difficulty mastering it." If this was Michael's one flaw, Dancer found it rather endearing, though it seemed strange she had never noticed it herself. "Maybe next time you see him, you should ask him to say 'a zillion zealous zebras' three times fast."

"You're kidding, of course. Even when he's being nice, the man gives me the screaming weirds."

Dancer stifled a chuckle. "You haven't known many Auryx, have you?"

"Of course not; aren't they almost extinct? I never even saw one until I woke up in this place, and now I'm surrounded by black-haired, blue-eyed short people. How do you tell them apart? They all look alike."

This time, Dancer laughed outright at the inadvertent repetition of the standing Sixth Service joke. "If you recall, they used to say the same thing about that red-haired, green-eyed DeWellesthar clan. You get used to it. Me—I'm uneasy when I'm not surrounded by Auryx."

"Are they all like him?"

"Michael? No, he's one of a kind, thank God."

"You two are pretty close, huh?" she pursued.

"Not in the way you mean."

"Come on, Auglaize; you're roommates, don't try to tell me you're not sleeping together."

"News travels fast around here, doesn't it?" Dancer cut in. "No, Antonia, we are not, we haven't in the past, and we probably never will. Not that I wouldn't like to," she added with a grin. "Unfortunately, Michael does not share my desire." In fact, he'd long ago confided to her that he was incapable of physical love, but she never had believed it—not when she knew firsthand the extent of the knowledge and skill of the Auryx medical wizards. She had no doubt that Michael did have a problem. But she also had no doubt it was of his own making.

"The way he looks at you? That's hard to believe."

Dancer swallowed the coarse pun that was on the tip of her tongue—after all, Michael was probably listening, and if this conversation continued, she would shortly receive a curt reminder to get her mind back on business. "To tell you the truth, Tonia, we don't have much time for that sort of thing around here. Believe me, when I finally do fall into bed, the only thing I'm interested in getting is a little sleep."

Tonia choked back a laugh. "Will the real Auglaize De-Wellesthar please step forward? To use your own analogy, when I was still sleeping with a teddy bear, your prowess was legendary."

"Oh?" Michael's voice, dry, amused, not unexpected.

Dancer cleared her throat and started to giggle. "The rumors"—emphasis on the noun—"were greatly exaggerated. I was always highly selective about with whom I slept."

"I believe the issue was quality, not quantity. At any rate, your brothers and their cronies thought it was shit-hot, and your sisters were scandalized."

"They were scandalized by my very existence," Dancer said wryly. "I'm sure my death came as a great relief to them. A dead hero is so much more comfortable than a live embarrassment. And where did *you* hear about all this, anyway?"

"Mydge Ashland."

"Good old Mydge. Well, he ought to know."

"He said when you brought Troy home with you that last time, everybody figured it meant you were finally going to settle down."

There it was, at the mere mention of his name—that sharp pang of loss that Dancer hadn't let the psychs program away. It was clear and sharp as it had been the day she had woken up to her new life—sharper; she'd been in shock then. But Dancer wanted to remember Morgan Troy and what he had been to her. "Career officers in the Fourth Service do not 'settle down,' as you very well know. Besides, it probably wouldn't have worked out, anyhow. A commander shouldn't have that kind of relationship with a subordinate. It's like walking a tightrope under the best of circumstances. When it comes to the possibility that you are ordering your people to their deaths . . .'' Dancer shook her head. How many times had she heard Michael say those same words? And how many times had she disagreed with them? She could almost feel his amusement at her repeating them now.

Again, Tonia chose not to comment directly. ''You and Troy sure gave a great imitation of two people in love. I, of course, idolized you both. Did you know that I got in all kinds of trouble for cutting up my red dress to make a flightsuit for my teddy bear?''

''No great loss; red never was your color anyway.''

Antonia just looked at Dancer for a moment, and the latter shrugged to show she hadn't intended the double meaning that had emerged. ''It is yours, though,'' Tonia finally replied. ''You always looked so good in your uniform. I was—still am—envious.''

''My hair is just that little bit darker than yours. It's funny about the teddy bear, though; I did the same thing with a rag doll and the bottoms of the living-room drapes. They hung down behind the couch; I didn't think anyone would notice. Somebody noticed. I never found out for sure, but I think it was 'Lisha. She was going through that goody-goody stage.''

''Really?'' she giggled. ''I never heard about that.''

''There's a lot you never heard about. Troy and I figured you could get into enough trouble without our giving you ideas. There were those who thought you spent altogether too much time with us as it was.''

''I couldn't believe you two put up with me hanging around practically your entire leave.''

''As I recall, there was nothing unusual about my dragging you all over the place with me whenever I was home.''

''Yeah, but you'd never brought a boyfriend with you before.''

''I must admit, there was one time we sent you off on a wild-goose chase so that we could have a little time alone together.''

''So that you two could go out into the woods and jump each other, you mean. I know. I followed you.''

''Of such stuff are legends made,'' Dancer murmured.

''It certainly furthered my education. That and that drinking party you took me to.''

''I remember that. You got totally wiped out on carbonated fruit juice. Troy had to carry you home.''

"*You* weren't drinking carbonated fruit juice. It's a wonder he didn't have to carry you home, too."

"Don't think we both didn't hear about it in the morning, either." Dancer's face relaxed into the first warm, genuine smile she'd given the girl. "Damn, but it was worth it!"

"We did have a good time, didn't we? I was devastated when you had to leave. I lived for your letters. Then, they stopped."

Dancer's fingers flexed again, an unconscious gesture that generally manifested itself when she was uneasy about something. "What did they tell you?"

"Oh, it was all very solemn; the whole neighborhood turned out at the sight of the local Fourth Service recruiter and a chaplain decked out in full-dress uniforms that looked about a size too small—I giggled, because I remembered you bitching that full-dress uniforms were *always* at least a size too small and it ought to be against the law to be forced to wear them home on leave just to impress the old home town. These two kept running their fingers around the insides of their collars, just like you and Troy did. Except they were a lot more nervous.

"Your mother knew why. She said, 'Which one?' There were, I think, four of you in Fourth at that time: Uncle Ash, you, Alan, and Amadeus. 'Auglaize, ma'am.' 'Dead?' 'Missing in action. Presumed dead.' "

Dancer nodded; she could picture it. She had pictured it, many times over the years. Mom, very collected, serving them refreshments on the front porch while the neighbors stood around talking quietly in small groups. All the right words. Careful omission of the fact that she had been captured; you never tell the next of kin that their loved one died in agony. God knew Dancer had weasel-worded enough letters of that type herself to have the spiel down pat.

"For a while, we hoped you would turn up somewhere safe and sound, you know how you do when someone's listed MIA. Then— oh, it was a long time later—we were notified that your body had been found. Nothing more. Not how, or where, or anything else. Unless you count the citation and medals that the same delegation came back to present a few months later.

"The family had hardly begun to come to terms with that before Uncle Ash was reported missing, and we finally got word he was in a prisoner-of-war camp."

"Yes, I know." Dancer would have let the subject drop, but Antonia's inquiring glance told her she wasn't getting out of it so easily. She sighed in capitulation. "Who do you think sent that message? Or, for that matter, eventually got him and the others out of that reeking hellhole?'' Her eyes clouded at the recollection. The Karrangeenan, allies and offshoots of the Karranganthians, were not so hell-bent on indiscriminate genocide as their parent race. Still, their POW camps were no vacation spas. It had been one of her earlier missions with Michael, back when she still had to look in a mirror to make sure that the black uniform was adjusted properly. A mission she would have long remembered even had she not stumbled across her favorite uncle, emaciated, broken, barely alive, amid the squalor. Sharp eyes had focused on her face, though, as she tenderly lifted his once-imposing body into her already-bloodstained arms.

''Strong lass you are,'' he had whispered through cracked and swollen lips. ''You remind me of a niece I once loved very much.''

''What happened to her?'' Dancer had asked conversationally, her heart a block of ice in her chest.

''Dead. Butchered by the Karranganthians in one of their charnel houses. You take care, girl,'' he'd added later as she strapped him into a pallet on the medical transport.

''Never fear, Uncle Ash, I have no intention of dying again.''

''Auglaize?'' he'd queried, eyes narrowed and seeking to hold hers.

''Dancer,'' she had replied to one who had helped give her the nickname. ''My name is Dancer.''

Tonia's matter-of-fact reply brought her back to the present. ''You know, he always maintained you were still alive. We thought it was just . . .''

''His mind? No. I was careless with Ash.'' At the time, he had been so ill that she hadn't thought it mattered. Besides, Colonel Ashtabula DeWellesthar, of Fourth Service Intelligence Section, knew the risks even better than she.

''You two always were especially close. He'll be glad to know that he was right.''

''He must never know. No one must ever know.'' Dancer shook herself, tried to recapture a light tone. ''So I really did die a hero, huh?''

Tonia looked at her oddly, but let it pass. ''You always were my hero. I was trying to think—what was it Troy called you? 'Lead'?''

''Among other things. You were the Ant.''

She nodded. '' 'Hey, Troy, what say we walk down to the creek and go wading?' 'Roger, Lead. Let's take the Ant along; make it a picnic.' 'Sure thing, Buddy. What's a picnic without an Ant?' Funny the things you remember.''

Dancer Flight from Dancer Leader. You know the game plan; we're going in hot. Good luck.

Roger, Dancer Leader, gotcha covered. Let's blow 'em away . . .

Yes, it was . . . funny what one remembered. "You were very fond of him, weren't you, Tonia?"

"He was my first love," Antonia answered wistfully.

"And my last." Dancer's tone unconsciously echoed hers.

"What happened to him, Glaize?"

"Who, Morgan?" She gave herself another mental shake. "He died."

"How?" she persisted.

Dancer met the girl's eyes coolly; she'd thought she had gotten over the guilt for Troy's death long ago. "You don't want to know."

"Were you with him?"

"Yes."

Antonia started to pursue the matter further, but thought better of it. Instead, she asked, "There really hasn't been anyone else for you since?"

"No." Dancer didn't bother to add that it wasn't from misplaced loyalty to the deceased; rather that first the opportunity, then the urge, had been lacking. Perhaps the psychs had programmed that out of her, too, though she doubted it. She preferred to think that she had finally outgrown the obsessive need to constantly prove herself.

"You have changed, Auglaize." For a moment, Antonia's eyes bored into Dancer's skull as if she would see into her thoughts; the look that Dancer gave her in return assured her that she would not like those thoughts if she could read them. "At least you still drink."

"When the situation warrants it."

"Curse?"

"Fluently"—Dancer laughed—"in twenty-seven languages."

"Thank God," Tonia returned. "I thought you were going to shatter all my illusions! All this time, I've been trying to live up to your reputation."

"You have my sympathy. So, tell me all about Auglaize De-Wellesthar. How am I doing these days?"

Antonia chuckled. "Great. With a little time, luck, and practice, you might even make Lead again. Your . . . *my* current goal is the solo slot. After that, who knows? My personal life isn't doing too badly, either." This, with a patronizingly affectionate glance at the man still sitting patiently at her side.

"Yes, I wanted to ask you about that." Dancer had been watching him throughout the conversation, and not once had he shown the slightest interest when Troy's name was mentioned. This seemed odd. If indeed that's what Antonia had been calling him, he would have been expected to display a little natural curiosity as to what the two women were saying about him. Perhaps he had no more intelligence than the pet dog Tonia treated him as, but even a dog will look up at the sound of its name.

"Delightful, isn't he? No intellectual, but I assure you he lives up to every other expectation."

He met Dancer's gaze disinterestedly, yet she had the impression he was appraising her even as she was appraising him. She sensed amusement; it was ridiculous that his approval should matter, and yet it did. Only partially because he would be returning to the Starlifter with Auglaize, and Dancer didn't delude herself for an instant that he would ever believe she was Tonia. Which could present a problem, because as of this moment, Dancer didn't trust the man as far as she could spit with her mouth closed.

Tonia had been watching this byplay with amusement. "I think he likes you, Glaize."

"How can you tell? Where'd you pick him up, anyhow?"

"Actually, he picked me up. I found myself in the middle of a brawl one starry night, and he hauled me out before I could get hurt. On top of that, Troy here is the best Gypsy crewchief in the Service." A slight smile from the subject of this praise; but then, she had been looking at him while she spoke. "He could build a fighter in a day from a couple of crates of parts."

"I would assume quite a bit of Fourth Service experience, then." Or intensive schooling elsewhere. "How long has he been with the Team?"

"Since it was reconstituted after the war, I think. Before that, he was with some maintenance group or another; I forget just which one."

"What's the name on his records?"

"Funny, I never bothered to find out. Or if I have, I've forgotten."

"You say that he speaks and understands very little Standard. Don't you find it odd that a Fourth Service maintenance crewchief has difficulty communicating with his troops?"

"Just because he doesn't speak doesn't mean that he can't communicate, Auglaize," Tonia said defensively. "And just because *you* can't understand him doesn't mean that the rest of us can't."

"It's Standard Sign that you use, then." Dancer tried a simple nonsense statement about the weather on him, and he chuckled and signed back that he liked her ring. Fourth Service Academy, she told him, and it had been with her for years.

"We wondered what happened to that," Tonia interjected.

"Don't get any ideas; it stays on my hand. Does he write?"

"What do you mean—oh, can he write? I suppose so; I've never given the matter much thought."

"You haven't known each other very long, then."

"Long enough. And very well."

"I have no doubt. Does he fly with you often?"

"Occasionally. He enjoys it, and I like having him around."

"That's why he was with you today."

Tonia looked at her oddly. "I suppose so. Why?"

"Just curious. Someone suggested that you might have been having problems with your plane, and he was along for a diagnostic check."

"Sounds plausible. Funny, I don't remember."

"You don't seem to be able to remember much of anything," Dancer commented. "Are you on any kind of medication?"

"You know better than to ask that. If I were, I would have been grounded. Some things don't change."

"But if no one knew about it . . ."

"For God's sake, Auglaize!" she blazed. "Give me credit for *some* sense!"

"Then do you have any idea who fed you what, and why?"

"No. This is beginning to sound like an interrogation."

"Sorry, kid." Dancer pulled back slightly. "You know me. When I have questions, I look for answers, and about this situation, I have a lot of questions."

"Yeah, your boss explained to me that my accident might not have been so accidental, and that you're in charge of the investigation. Okay. Interrogate away."

"What do you remember about the crash?"

"Looking down and seeing you, and thinking I had gone crazy."

"The same thought crossed my mind when I saw you," Dancer admitted. "I'll tell you, though, Seven and I were sure you were goners, the way that bird of yours came screaming down. Your recovery was just about the best I've ever seen. You're a hell of a pilot, Antonia; in that, you're certainly living up to my reputation. Something wrong?"

She shook her head, but her eyebrows remained knit. "I just don't remember any of it."

"Nothing? Well. I expect you will, in time. Shock, probably; it happens. There is one thing I'm really curious about, though. As you so accurately remarked before, O'Brian's Stake isn't exactly on the main trade routes. How did we happen to luck into a slot on your schedule?''

"Don't ask me. When this season's schedule first came down, it was the usual route—then someone upstairs decided to change it. Most of the places on there nobody had ever even heard of.''

Interesting. "When were these changes made?''

"Oh, let's see.'' She shrugged. "I don't remember for sure. Happened shortly after we changed commanders, I guess.''

"Oh?'' Dancer sat up a little straighter; the motion startled the bodyguard and he shot her an uneasy glance. She had to work to keep her questions nonchalant—the records she had been studying, supposedly incorporating the latest updates, didn't mention anything about a change of command. "What happened to Colonel Montgomery?''

"I don't really know. He was a good guy; left before we could have a going-away party for him. It's Colonel Daven now. Funny, I'm not even sure what he looks like. We've only seen him once or twice. He doesn't fly with us. Just moved Terry Woods up into Colonel Montgomery's solo slot, and sat back to shuffle papers.''

"Sounds like he must be busy, what with the new schedule and all. When did you say he took command? After the season started?''

Antonia looked at Dancer through narrowed eyes, then gave a sigh of frustration. "I don't remember. I don't remember. I know what I had for supper last night, I can tell you all the latest Team gossip, but I can't remember the simplest things. You people tell me that I have traces of at least six different chemical compounds in my bloodstream, but I have no idea how they got there. You say that what was to my knowledge a perfectly good airplane just fell out of the sky and through some incredibly adept maneuver I recovered control and managed to land the thing—all I can say is, I'd've liked to have seen it, because I sure don't remember doing it.''

"Could he have?''

"Who, Troy? No way. Unlike the original, this one doesn't fly. Oh, he can keep a plane in the air; he's even managed a landing or two. But nothing of the caliber you're describing. So, it had to be me; I just don't remember. Am I losing my mind?''

"I don't think so.''

"Then what the hell's going on here?''

Dancer glanced uncomfortably at Troy. "That's what I'm trying to find out. Listen, could you get rid of him for a while? There are several forms of entertainment available in the solarium down the hall. An escort is waiting just outside the door.''

''Why . . . ?'' the girl started to ask. ''Okay, sure.'' A few gestures, a slight argument, and it was done. The man left them alone with a grumble and a dark look back over his shoulder at Dancer. ''Now, what was that all about?''

''Did Michael tell you that my investigation will take me back to the Warlord in your place for a few days?''

''Now, wait a minute!'' Tonia protested. ''What makes you think that you could find out anything I couldn't? You don't even know your way around!''

''So, Antonia, tell me again exactly how you regained control of your Gypsy this morning.''

''Your point,'' the girl snorted disgustedly.

''Also, I've got the training and experience.''

''For snooping around, maybe, but can you fly a Gypsy in close-formation synchronous maneuvers? Although—we could figure out some way to let you handle the detective work and smuggle me in to do the flying.''

''Uh-uh. I go''—Dancer jerked a thumb ceilingward—''up there, and you stay here where we can keep an eye on you.''

''What if I refuse to tell you anything more?''

''Then, Antonia, you might just get me killed.''

''God, Auglaize! Are you kidding? Okay, okay, I'll go along with whatever you and that blue-eyed boss of yours have up your sleeves. But . . . my reputation is on the line here, you know? And have you ever seen what's left when two Gypsies try to occupy the same airspace at the same time?''

''Yes, I have. But it's not gonna happen tomorrow. At least,'' Dancer added calculatedly, ''not if I go in completely prepared. And *that*, kid, is up to you.''

''Okay,'' Tonia said decisively. ''Where do I start?''

With a minimum of prompting, Antonia launched into a recitation of who her friends were, what parts of the Starlifter Dancer should be familiar with—and more to the point, what portions had recently become restricted for reasons never revealed or just 'not remembered.' In fact, the gaps in Tonia's memory were particularly noteworthy, since they dated mostly from the time of the change of command.

Not that Dancer had the opportunity just then to consider them, because about her daily routine Tonia had total recall, and she wouldn't allow Dancer to get a word in edgewise. She gave Dancer a few unnecessary tips on close-formation flying. She recounted her usual schedule, including how long she brushed her teeth, and what her favorite breakfast drink was. Dancer didn't intend to be with the Team long enough to use half of what Tonia told her, but she filed everything away anyhow. You never knew what might be important. Tonia's overbearing ego was a bit hard to stomach at times, until Dancer reminded herself that the kid was young, scared, and pulling off a bluff that Dancer might have attempted herself, given the same circumstances.

Antonia wanted—perhaps needed—to talk about herself, and Dancer wasn't averse to a little conversation. There would be time enough later for her brain to analyze all the information being poured into it. Admittedly, she was enjoying indulging in the unaccustomed "girl talk" as well. It amazed her how easily she had fallen back into the speech patterns of casual chatter, though she repeatedly lapsed into Auryx idiom instead of Antonia's Fourth Service colloquialisms. Tonia remarked on the precise diction at one point, and Dancer took pains to correct herself.

Altogether too soon, though it had been hours, the voice in Dancer's ear receiver informed her that they were ready for her down in Wardrobe to cut her hair, tint her eyes, and fit her for a Team jumpsuit. Almost guiltily, she rose. "If you'll excuse me, Antonia," she said a lot more abruptly than she intended, "I have things to do, and it's getting late."

Antonia matched Dancer's suddenly crisp tone. "Sorry to take up so much of your valuable time. I have enjoyed it, however; I hope we can get together again sometime."

"I do, too, Ant," Dancer reassured her, "but don't count on it. Perhaps I shall see you again before you leave our sector. Perhaps not."

"There's no way we can keep in touch, is there?"

"No." Though she knew she could arrange something if she wanted to, and part of her wanted to. But Dancer had been in the Sixth Service too long—and Auglaize DeWellesthar had been dead for too long. "Nor, when this is finished, will you remember ever seeing me. I do regret that. It has been an interesting acquaintance—it's not often that one gets to talk to oneself. I'll leave you a little piece of advice, though: my reputation was hard enough for me to live up to. I wouldn't wish it on anyone else."

Dancer was out the door before Antonia had a chance to reply.

Chapter 7

It would have been simpler for all concerned if Dancer could merely have stepped into Tonia's jumpsuit; were it normal Fourth Service issue, she would have been able to. For that matter, if it had been normal Fourth Service issue, she could have changed the nametag and patches and worn her own—she still had two of them. But the Team had opted for a classy, minutely tailored coverall that didn't allow for the fact that there was a little more of Dancer than Tonia in some places and a little less in others. This meant tedious measurements, fittings, and refittings, ad infinitum. It had to be perfect, even if perfection drove her insane.

Meanwhile, there was the question of communication. She normally used a tiny transmitter built into her Fourth Service Academy ring, but Tonia wore no jewelry, not even an identity disk. When one of the techs suggested a voice-activated throat implant, Dancer took his head off level with the shoulders. It was bad enough having the receiver permanently embedded behind her ear so that she was on call constantly, without having every sound she uttered subject to monitoring, too. A person was entitled to some privacy! She finally told them to annoy Tonia with the problem. Let her add something constructive. If it weren't for her, Dancer wouldn't be in this mess to begin with. Her precarious goodwill toward the kid had worn off with the first pin that had tucked flesh instead of fabric.

By the time Dancer made it into the barber's chair, word had spread that she was in a decidedly testy mood. Though that was a condition with which none were unfamiliar, they all trod lightly just the same.

She watched silently in the mirror in front of her as Clarke unplaited her habitual braid and smoothed the wavy red-brown-gold mass over her shoulders. The one thing about herself that she had always considered attractive, the rare times she had contemplated her appearance. People were always complimenting her on her hair. . . . With an abrupt kick, she spun the chair so that the mirror was at her back and signaled Clarke to begin.

Snip. Dancer shuddered. *Snip*.

"I remember the last time I had my hair cut," she said to distract herself from watching each long lock snake to the floor. "It was just before I flew my last combat patrol with Fourth. A very long time ago."

Snip. "The barber was a little more talkative, though."

Snip. She winced. This was ridiculous. It was not somebody's funeral here; it was just hair. It would grow back. In another ten years or so.

Snip. It's about time I got this mane cropped back to regulation, chimed a voice in the back of her mind that she recognized as memory.

We in the Sixth Service have no such ridiculous regulations, child. We like our women to look like women, and you are shaping up to be a very beautiful one.

Snip. A touch on the cheek, a hand holding a mirror. Brown eyes, *her* eyes, extra large and liquid in a setting somewhat thinner and much whiter than usual. Framed by a living, shimmering halo of deep-red fire that moved when she moved, and thus must be part of herself. The first time since her childhood that she had seen herself with hair longer than the base of her jawline, hair that she had never thought of as being the much-admired DeWellesthar red. A man's voice, telling her once again that she was beautiful. A man's voice, warm, familiar, beloved . . . but to which she couldn't put a name.

Snip.

"In the name of the Seventeen Imbeciles of the Council, can't you just take it all off at once?"

Hesitation, then an even pull, a sharp jerk, and her head snapped forward, feeling about five pounds lighter.

"Is that what you had in mind?"

Dancer turned in time to see Michael, a coil of red still wrapped around one fist, resheathing his boot knife. "Yes, thank you."

The Commander nodded for Clarke to continue, with the admonition, "Leave it a little long over her ears, and don't shave the back of her neck too closely. By Fourth Service regulations, DeWellesthar is looking a bit shaggy. It wouldn't do for us to return her freshly barbered."

He stood back to watch for a moment, then, with a satisfied nod, left.

As for Dancer: she surveyed the wreckage in the mirror, unprepared for the shock of what she saw. The face staring back at her wasn't hers; it belonged to someone she had known a very long time ago and yet had been talking to just this evening. Closing her eyes, she slumped back in the chair to let Clarke finish, wishing fervently that Tonia had never been born.

The persistence of that Fourth Service commander would have been comical if Michael hadn't had so many other things on his mind.

Well, of course, it was harassment pure and simple, this siccing on them of the media hounds. Lights, cameras, and so-called reporters besieged the place, clamoring about laws and rights and the people's privilege to know. Know what? The girl was in bed, asleep, as they all ought to be and Michael wished fervently *he* could be.

Dancer should be handling this. She'd dealt equitably with the newspeople before; her occasionally abrasive style and ready sense of humor were well suited for defusing such situations. It didn't hurt that she was also very pleasant to look at.

Michael allowed himself a short, barely audible chuckle. Dancer *would* handle this. A flip of a switch connected him with the "front office," the only section of the building the public was ever allowed to see. Brown-haired Perry was on duty; the Commander didn't have to see her face to picture the surprise there when he said simply, "Tell them they'll have their interview."

His next call was to Dancer. "So, child, are you ready for your first performance as Auglaize DeWellesthar?"

"Depends on what you want."

"Network Twelve News is banging at the door demanding an interview. Think you can handle being awakened at this ungodly hour to talk to them?"

A sigh that he wasn't meant to hear, then, "Sure. Why the hell not?"

When the lone cameraman and two reporters—Network 12 and a representative of the print media—were ushered through a long, confusing maze of corridors to finally end up in what certainly looked like a standard infirmary room, one tousled, irate FSIPADT pilot was there to greet them.

"Look, people," she said, squinting and holding a hand up against the camera lights, "make this short, okay? It's been a tough day, I've got a show to do tomorrow, and I need my sleep."

"We have reports that you are being held here against your will," was the first question.

"I don't believe you guys." Team Five laughed and gestured around her. "Does this look like I'm being held against my will? Honestly. The bed is soft, the food is good, and the doctor says I need observing. Normally, I don't go along with doctors, but, as I said, the bed is soft, the food is good—and the doctor is cute."

"Lieutenant DeWellesthar, can you tell us exactly what happened this afternoon? Was there a mechanical problem with your aircraft, or was it pilot error?"

"Come on, guys. You know I can't talk about that until after the investigation. I'll tell you one thing, though, off the record," she added arrogantly. "It wasn't pilot error. *This* pilot doesn't make errors."

Michael smiled at her from his concealed vantage point. Nice touch. He was almost sorry when Preble stepped in on behalf of his "patient." The doctor made a standard statement on her condition, then the Network 12 reporter, a blond woman who, Michael recognized, usually got her facts straight, recorded a plug for the airshow the next afternoon. After that, the group was politely shown the door.

"Good going, Dancer," he congratulated her dryly. "That ought to bring them out in droves tomorrow."

"Thanks, boss," she returned. "Unfortunately, it's not going to satisfy our persistent friends upstairs."

"It's going to have to. I'm not taking any more calls from them!"

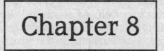

Chapter 8

Tired as she was, there were still things Dancer had to do before she could rest—facts to double-check, faces to be sure she could match with names—details, details, details, and not enough time, even in a planet-day three hours longer than Standard. Why, then, did her weary legs take her back down to Med Section and the red-haired problem child asleep there?

Why, indeed? she asked herself as she stood looking down at the girl in the semidarkness. Asleep, with the bulldog set of her jaw relaxed and the lingering fear in the back of her eyes hidden from view, she looked again the lonely child whom Dancer had befriended so many years ago. Back in that other life, where Morgan Troy and she had acted out dogfights from *Rhombyan* for a little girl's bedtime stories. With a gentle hand, Dancer tucked the sheet up around this not-so-little girl's shoulders.

I must be tired, she told herself. At the best of times, overt sentimentality was not one of her strong suits.

A slight rustle off to her left reminded Dancer that someone else was in the room. Turning to the other bed, she silently regarded the still form of the sleeping bodyguard, his bare arms relaxed on the sheet, his semiexposed yellow-furred chest rising and falling with his breathing. He certainly was easy on the eyes, despite the unsettling effect he had on the pit of her stomach. Suddenly, she wanted to see the rest of the body outlined under the blankets. Nobody really knew all that much about him, she reasoned; the techs had been unable to get him to cooperate for even the most rudimentary of examinations, and when coercion had been tried, the result had been bruises and smashed equipment. The med team had exercised the better part of valor and turned their attention elsewhere.

So much for token rationalization. The bottom line was, good old Dancer just wanted to look at a well-made male body. Or maybe—maybe there *was* the slightest resemblance to her former lover.

The breathing continued slow and steady as she took the three strides to his bedside, slow and steady as she eased back the covers and chuckled softly to herself. As anticipated, the man was totally nude and exquisitely constructed. No wonder Antonia's half smile, Dancer thought wryly, sidestepping so that what light there was fell full on him. Beautiful. Then, even as she admired the living sculpture before her, her professional side took over.

Without thinking, she leaned closer, looking for telltale signs of race, such as extra ribs, off-side navel or navels, peculiar patterns of hair or lack of same—any of the easily concealed nonstandard genetic traits. Then she paged down through mental lists to see if his size contained any clues to his origin, and couldn't think of one race that routinely produced classical gods. Her considered opinion was that he was human, and a very superior physical specimen at that. Not unlike Morgan Troy . . .

Her eyes were once again drawn to the body hair, catching and reflecting back light like small jewels. Troy, though somewhat shorter and not of this bulk, still had been of much the same build; his hair, a golden-bronze flame in the dappled sunlight of a forest glade on Dancer's home planet . . . without thinking, she reached out to touch a memory. Instantly her wrist was snatched into a viselike grip, while emerald eyes bored into her face in the semi-dark. Then recognition softened his gaze and her hand was released as abruptly as it had been grabbed.

Recognition. With her hair cut and colored, clad in a robe, there was no way for him to have known that she wasn't Tonia, yet Dancer was sure he did. She was just as sure that he had been asleep when she came in, that he hadn't seen or heard Antonia in the bed behind her. Dancer stood still, waiting for him to make the next move. He, in turn, waited for her. Both sensed that neither was a danger to the other at this point, and both were curious about how the other would react.

Finally, he sighed, and made a gesture that she took to be an inquiry whether she liked what she had been so obviously staring at. Dancer's reply was a nod. The corners of his eyes crinkled, and a laugh slipped easily from between his parted lips. He had marvelous, strong, even white teeth, she noted. He had also eased himself into a sitting position and in the process very unobtrusively obscured most of his body from her view with the blanket. She laughed, too, at that, drawn to him for his unexpected modesty, his smile, the personality that was emerging from the former studied passivity. When he patted the edge of the bed next to him, Dancer sat without hesitation.

A sadness tinged his smile as he touched a finger to her neck in what she correctly interpreted as sympathy for her shorn locks. "It was so beautiful long," he signed. "And you have done something to your eyes."

Perhaps he didn't know for sure that she was not Tonia. If it was just a suspicion on his part, she wasn't about to confirm it. "I haven't had long hair since I was a kid, and you know it."

He shook his head, smiling, and his lips shaped the word "Dancer." "You are like," he continued in signs, "yet unlike. The child"—his intent, not her interpretation—"has not yet your strength."

"You were awake when I came in."

He shook his head, reinforced it with a strong negative gesture. "I know her well, and I have been watching you closely."

"I figured you'd be able to tell eventually, but I certainly didn't think you'd see through me so fast."

"I knew there were two of you. Your secret is safe with me."

"Is it? How do I know that?"

"I love her," was his simple reply. "It was I who . . ." A faint crease in his forehead, and he dropped his hands.

"You who what? Tell me what happened this morning."

He made a diving motion with his right palm and shrugged his shoulders.

"Uh-uh. That won't wash with me, friend. You know a lot more than you're telling. What's going on up there?"

The forehead crease deepened; he looked almost frightened as he once again shrugged and shook his head. The thought struck Dancer that he had staged the crash, that he had brought Antonia here for a reason, and that he wouldn't—or, more likely, couldn't—tell her what that reason was. After all the trouble he had gone to to get Antonia away from whatever it was, it didn't make sense for him to just sit tamely by and watch her be sent back. There were ways to lock a mind so that it could remember but not communicate; Michael was an expert at such things. Unfortunately, seldom could even the Commander bypass a lock that someone else had the key to.

Dancer's eyes narrowed, hardened as they sought the man's. She saw fear there, but not of her. For her? Of all the questions she could have asked him at this point, the one she did took him most by surprise. "What is your name?" she asked aloud.

He answered aloud, a meaningless jumble of sounds that might have approximated what she had seen spelled out on the computer screen hours before.

"I don't understand."

His eyebrows drew together, and his hand slid up her arm. Dancer reflexively jerked back out of his reach; his hands clenched in frustration, then rose in the sign for "Trust me."

"Uh-uh. You understand every word we say, don't you?"

A hesitation, then an affirmative.

"Stupid! Stupid to assume that just because someone can't talk, he automatically doesn't understand, either. God, I can't believe I did!"

"Shh! You suspected," his hands told her. "I had to be careful. I have had much practice."

"Who—no," she modified, "what are you?"

"Trust me."

"Trust you? How can I trust you when you conceal who and what you are, when you feign ignorance of Standard, then sit there and take in every word everyone says? And because they think you don't understand, everyone talks very freely, don't they?''

"A mixed blessing. They think I am an idiot and call me names. Even that one.'' With a nod toward Tonia's bed. "I am not what you think, Dancer. I have my reasons.''

"I suggest you enlighten me.''

His left hand was held out to her, palm up, before it reached for her arm. Again, she sidestepped, and again, the frustrated imperative. "Trust me!''

Every rational part of Dancer cried out not to, and every instinct she possessed whispered that she could.

Dancer always went with her instincts. She let him draw her back down beside him, didn't protest when he laid her hand on his chest and slid his up her arm and behind her neck, relaxed into him as he guided her head to his shoulder, turned slightly so that he could more easily find her mouth with his. Instinct suspended reason for a moment as she let him hold her close, pushing into the background the observation that he was very nervous, much more nervous than the simple act of physical trespass warranted. Pushing into the background momentarily her awareness of who she was as she parted her lips for his exploring tongue . . .

. . . which wasn't . . . quite . . . all there. Enough to eat somewhat normally, but no control for the intricate patterns required to produce comprehensible speech.

Everything tumbled into place with a resounding crash. "Paulding Callicoon!'' she exclaimed into his still-open mouth. The letters and sounds of his name suddenly made perfectly obvious sense. "Paulding Callicoon,'' she repeated as she drew back far enough to look into his face.

"You understand now,'' he gestured sadly. "I was certain you would.''

"My God, who did this to you? No, you don't have to answer. I know.'' She had seen the bizarre mutilation only once before, and that, on a corpse. It was a punishment reserved for some forms of treason. By the Karranganthians. It was not generally known; the Fourth Service doctors had probably passed Callicoon off as a victim of torture. Which, of course, he was. "Yes, I understand. Your Fourth Service peers are an unforgiving lot; they would do much more than call you names if they knew.''

"And you, Auglaize? Are you unforgiving? You could, I think, kill me without a second thought. Your war isn't finished until the Karranganthian race is extinct, I believe you said.''

"Oddly enough, my friend, now I *do* trust you.''

"I am afraid," he replied simply.

"Not of me."

"No. But I am afraid . . ."

She was framing a reply when Tonia's voice startled them both. "If you want him for the night, Auglaize, he's yours. I'm finished with him. It might be interesting to find out how we compare."

"Sorry I have to turn down your generous offer," Dancer said sweetly, her eyes still on his—Calli's—face. "It sounds like fun, but I really don't have time for that now."

Calli's hand lightly brushed her hair again. Out of Antonia's line of vision, his fingers asked Dancer if she would reconsider. With a regretful smile and shake of the head, she rose. The look she gave Antonia on the way out was one of sheer loathing.

"By the way, Ant," she tossed back over her shoulder, "did you know you're being monitored? The camera is right over your bed."

Aboard the Warlord, the Team commander was pleased with his subordinate's plan to utilize the media, even if the effort had not resulted in the return of his personnel. In fact, that damned redhead was proving to be useful, after all.

Most of the Confederacy puppets encountered by the camera team had been average, ordinary types, indistinguishable from the cattle they "protected." The black-haired, blue-eyed doctor who had hovered in the background, however, who had given the oh-so-short summary of his patient's condition, was another story. The power he exuded didn't come merely from an overinflated opinion of his importance as a healer.

Colonel Daven knew an Auryx when he saw one. And where there was one Auryx—there was usually a whole nest of them.

He smiled his satisfaction as he planned more carefully the Team's itinerary for its stay on O'Brian's Stake.

Chapter 9

Dancer knew she needed nothing more than bed and sleep, yet when she got back to Michael's quarters, something drew her again to the computer console. Calli, she thought. She trusted him, yet there was still that nagging doubt. Something didn't quite click. She had Jeremiah flip through the crewchief's records once again, but there were no clues in the cut-and-dried figures on the screen. Even the fact that the records were incomplete meant nothing. In his case, Dancer would have been suspicious if they hadn't been. She smiled again at his method of passing information—she had always been told that you could learn a lot about a man by the way he kissed. Wonder what Antonia had made of it? Probably didn't have the wit to realize there was anything wrong.

Dear Antonia. Half thinking, Dancer had Jeremiah blow up the Team publicity photo until just her face was visible. Antonia. On impulse, Dancer accessed her own Fourth Service personnel file and found the corresponding photo of herself. "Split screen, Jeremiah. I want to take a look at these two side by side."

It was true, she thought critically, Antonia and she were enough alike to be twins. But Tonia—or Auglaize, as she was now known and Dancer supposed she would have to start thinking of her—had an infinitesimal something that Dancer herself lacked, or had lost prematurely with her own youth. No wonder all the men on the station were distracted around Tonia; even Dancer, her harshest critic, found the girl's irrepressible sparkle, her carefree smile, engaging.

For the second time that day, a pang of jealousy shot through Dancer. Wait a minute: she, jealous? She had thought that emotion long dead.

What did Tonia think of her? she wondered. That she was an enigma to the girl went without saying; Tonia was still having trouble accepting the fact that Auglaize was alive. Did Tonia also feel as if she were talking into a mirror? Was it as strange to her to be calling Dancer by what was now Tonia's name as it was to Dancer to think of Tonia by what once was hers? Did Tonia compare what Dancer had become with the so-much-younger version that she had known?

Dancer flexed her fingers—funny, she couldn't even remember which ones were plastic anymore—and wondered for the first time just how much rebuilding they had had to do on her face, and the memories stored behind it.

"Dancer?" Michael's breath tickled her ear, and she slowly became aware of his hand resting lightly on her shoulder. "That's enough for tonight, child. You need rest. It has been a long, difficult day for you, and tomorrow will be another such."

"Did I ever look like that?" she queried, gesturing vaguely at the two images on the screen. It was a rhetorical question; Michael and she hadn't met until long after that wide-eyed innocence had succumbed to the harsh realities of a Confederacy at war.

Nevertheless, the Commander took his time answering, seriously considering his reply. "From what I know of you, I think perhaps you were always more serious. Very strong-willed, and much more confident."

"I don't know any more. What I was. Not so very different from what I am today, I thought. Now, I wonder. I look at her, and I wonder."

"Dancer . . ."

She shrugged off his hand. "It's eerie, you know? I look at her, and I start thinking about things that haven't crossed my mind in years. I think I miss Auglaize DeWellesthar. Whoever she was."

"Child, she was—she is—you."

"I don't know, Michael. I have this feeling . . . like there's something important about her that I don't remember. What if she . . . I . . . did something so horrible that the psychs had to program it out of my mind? What if she were responsible for the others' deaths? What if she somehow betrayed them, and that's how she survived?" It was out, it was spoken, and the mere thought chilled her to the bone.

"Hush, child. You did nothing of the sort." His tone was soothingly matter-of-fact. "Flight Leader DeWellesthar conducted herself with the utmost courage and honor. She was a woman I would have been proud to know. As are you."

Dancer shook her head. "There was something, Michael. I'm sure of it."

"All right, then, what *do* you remember about that time?"

"Of Lioth and the deaths of my people, altogether too much. Vague recollections of months of recuperation and"—she smiled suddenly—"being under Madison's tyrannical rule for most of my retraining. And Serious, of course. I still miss my dog."

"Sounds like that about covers it."

"No," she stated with certainty. "There was something . . ." Or someone. A heavy feeling of dread at the thought. Another death? Instinctively, she shied away from mentioning it to the Commander. Why? She'd always been able to talk to him about anything. "Damn it, Michael! I can't even remember what it is I can't remember!"

"Trust me, Dancer, there are no shameful secrets in your past." Michael drew her to her feet, concern evident in his very touch. "But are you certain that you want to go through with this masquerade? There are other ways of getting the information we need."

"Not as quickly or efficiently. Of course I want to go through with it. I'm all right."

"I think you will be, but I would prefer not to take any unnecessary chances. You are too valuable."

"To the Service."

"To the Service," he agreed lightly, "and to its Commander."

Dancer raised a hand to her butchered, tinted curls, and half turned so that the light accentuated her green-dyed irises. "It's too late to turn back now." As another thought struck her, her slightly ironic tone changed to one of unaccustomed eagerness. "There's one thing I *do* remember: I've always wanted to fly with the Team. No way am I going to pass up this opportunity. I can do it, Michael!" she added in emphatic defiance of his continuing silence.

"I have no doubt whatsoever of that," he replied evenly. "Sleep now. I want you at your best."

Dancer nodded, resisting the absurd urge to ask him to tuck her in.

It could have been the unfamiliar bed, or all the names, faces, and aerial maneuvers chasing themselves through her brain—or even the unaccustomed silence and privacy which had earlier seemed so attractive—that now kept sleep at bay. Perhaps she was too used to having to block out some kind of noise, low-voiced conversations, the normal day-to-day living sounds of so many people packed so closely together. Here, there was nothing to distract her from the throbbing in her head that was the cumulative effect of exhaustion, eyestrain, and the loss of the accustomed weight of all that hair.

Then, from the living room, the soft, sensual, relaxing strains of Michael's harp filtered through the walls and under the door. As the music entered Dancer's brain, the tension drained from her body, and she started to drift off—until the thought struck her that Michael's restless fingers seldom found the time for music unless he was disturbed and needed to think. She was afraid she knew what he was thinking about now.

Her hand clenched reflexively as her mind flashed on black. Wearily, she catalogued the fleeting but all-too-familiar vision: black bootheels, black cape, that damned disembodied voice. With a stifled curse, she flung herself out of bed and jerked the curtain back so that she could see outside.

Mountains looming black against a velvet sky. The navigation lights of a distant patrol craft a sudden streak of red, like blood. Blood. The smell of it in bright, sticky pools at her feet. Her own blood, mingled with that of so many others. Red on black. "This one's still alive. My God, this one's still alive."

She shook her head to clear it, and steadied herself on the windowsill. Images from other half-forgotten nightmares reflected in the glass in front of her face, and her face—wasn't. Panic, swift and fleeting, then Dancer was again in control.

Breathing deeply, she gazed down at the sleeping city. Now, she could see a kind of serene beauty in the sparkling lights and the shadows of the mountains in the distance. They slept securely down there because of the Sixth Service; for Dancer's part, she wondered at their blind trust. Had she ever been so trusting, so secure?

Suddenly, it struck her that the nightmares, the flashes, the voices, were memories clamoring to be released from the hidden storehouses deep within her. Her sense of humor reasserted itself with the thought that the timing on this could have been better; the coward in her said that what was buried was buried for a reason, and better left so.

And she knew what she had to do.

Hoisting herself up onto the wide windowsill, Dancer slowly and painstakingly tried to remember. It was difficult at first; the psychs had done their jobs well, and it was nearly impossible to break through their conditioning. But Michael was also right about her strength of will.

Who had Auglaize DeWellesthar really been? Dancer wanted to know, needed so badly to know, that at last she breached the wall, and the whole thing came rushing back to her like a Dart fighter spiraling down, out of control. . . .

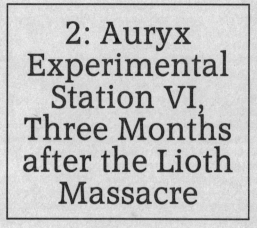

2: Auryx Experimental Station VI, Three Months after the Lioth Massacre

Chapter 10

There was no pain inside the cloud in which she drifted, no sights, no smells, no sensation whatsoever except for an extremely pleasurable feeling of floating, now in free air, now in a comfortable womblike warmth. After a long time, there was added a faraway sound, a pulsating golden tone inside her head, at one with the beauty and peace of that place. She could have happily existed there forever.

Gradually, however, she became aware that that faraway sound wasn't inside her head, and it wasn't so far away, either. No . . . it was a voice, a masculine voice, droning on and on close by her ear. Though it intruded upon her consciousness, that wasn't unpleasant, either.

Eventually the drone resolved itself into words, and the words slowly became comprehensible. He was reading something—something familiar—*Rhombyan's Manual of Fighter Tactics*? Yes, that was it, and he must have been at it for quite a while, because he was reading from the last section, the one headed "Classic Combat Engagements." The section began with records from the ancient times, when flying machines were little more than wooden kites, but the voice was reiterating details of an engagement that had taken place a mere generation ago.

She tried to move, and it was then that she realized she couldn't feel her body. A stray lock of hair tickled her cheek, of that she was aware, and she knew there was a light on the other side of her closed eyelids. But below her chin—nothing. She had an absurd vision of her disembodied head being carried about on a gold-tasseled pillow before the panic set in. Complete paralysis, then? No, reason asserted. If that were the case, there certainly wouldn't be a man at her bedside doggedly plowing his way through *Rhombyan*. Even a cadet cramming for the interminable exams would

71

have the sensitivity not to do so aloud in front of a pilot with no hope of ever flying again.

So, who was that with the magnificent, if somewhat hoarse, voice?

She forced her eyes open a slit, just enough to focus on the expanse of startlingly bright dark blue that they were level with. It was a sleeve, connected to a tunic of the same color, completely without insignia or identifiers of any sort. Her head, surprisingly enough, moved of its own accord to complete the picture, taking in the beige-jacketed manual resting on a blue-trousered lap, held open by tanned, strong-looking fingers. The face bent over the book, by contrast, was gray and drawn, the lines of fatigue etched beside red-rimmed eyes accented by dusky velvet stubble shadowing the jawline. Auglaize wondered how long he had been sitting there, and why, and wanted to reach out to him.

The movement of her head finally caught his attention. She found herself being assessed by a pair of penetrating eyes the same startling blue as his clothes. "Well, hello there," he finally said.

She tried to answer, but none of her facial muscles seemed to work.

"Do you understand what I am saying?" he asked in a normal, conversational tone.

She inclined her head slightly in assent.

"Excellent. Oh, that problem you are experiencing is caused by the medication," he continued, almost as if he could read her mind. "You'll be able to articulate when it wears off. I am Makellen Darke. Who are you?"

Confederacy Fourth Service Flight Leader Auglaize De-Wellesthar, service number 8305437W. Dancer to her friends. But what came out was, "Glaise."

A sudden smile transfigured his face. "You're all right. You really are all right. For a while there, I thought we had lost you."

Lost her? How? And why did this Mac-whatever care so much?

"In due time," he assured her. "In due time. Now, though, you sleep, child. I'll be here with you."

And he was there whenever she opened her eyes, reading aloud, sitting silently, occasionally singing quiet songs the words of which she did not understand. Always immaculately groomed, but still looking perpetually tired. Only once did she catch him dozing.

"Are you here all the time?" Auglaize asked as soon as she could string words together coherently.

"Just about."

"When do you sleep?"

"Very seldom," he answered ruefully.

"Am I that desperately in need of a nursemaid?"

"Yes, though we prefer to call ourselves Guardians. Everyone who comes here is assigned one; it was my turn for the duty."

She wanted to ask him to define "the duty"—she suspected it had something to do with the hours and hours of Rhombyan, but she couldn't imagine what. That question brought up so many others so fast that all she could say was, "Why?"

"Because we want you to live, child. Because you will be an asset to our Service."

"What Service? Why do you keep calling me 'child'?"

"Because," he answered with obvious reluctance, "when we found you, there was no identification, and we . . . it was impossible to immediately determine your sex. Now, it's just habit." Then, as if conscious he had said too much, his voice became firm. "Enough questions for now, ch . . . Auglaise. Sleep, if you can. Heal. I want to get back to my flight."

"It's 'Auglaize,' " she corrected.

He winked. "I know. But do you remember what you said when I first asked you your name? 'Glaise.' I rather like the sound of that."

"To tell you the truth, so do I." Auglaize returned his slightly ironic grin and closed her eyes obediently.

However, there was too much now to think about to surrender once again to the creeping oblivion. This man beside her, for instance. Instinct told her that he was much more than he was letting on. But instinct also told her that she could trust him. Still . . .

Auglaize stole a cautious glance at him: he was sitting in an attitude of utter exhaustion, head bent, eyes covered, slender fingers unconsciously massaging the bridge of his nose. "It's not yet the time," he murmured in reply to some voice only he could hear. "She is not ready. I will not chance losing her now."

"Woman trouble, my friend?" she couldn't help asking, though she was fairly certain that the "she" in question was one talking head formerly known as Auglaize DeWellesthar.

His head jerked back, but he recovered nicely. "Always. The words are synonymous."

"Well, I do have the reputation of being a good listener. I somehow managed to become privy to the romantic entanglements of my entire flight. Ah, the responsibilities of command."

The look in his eyes made her uneasy, but his words were light-hearted enough. "Indeed. How about you? Any 'romantic entanglements'?"

"A few. At the moment, my wingman and I are pretty close. Why do you keep looking at me like that?"

"Jealousy, perhaps."

She doubted it. Again, he had his head tipped to one side as if listening, and again, she startled him. "Tell me about her."

"Who? Oh. No. It is not yet the time." Emphatically. Over her head, as if to unseen listeners.

"Yes, it is," Auglaize stated just as emphatically. "What is this place, and how did I get here? What are you? Why do you look at me so strangely whenever I mention Dancer Flight? Where are my people? Am I a prisoner of some sort?" Her voice had taken on an imperious edge; after all, she was—had been?—a flight leader, a not inconsiderable achievement for one of her years.

Makellen regarded her silently for so long that she was convinced he wasn't going to answer. His gaze went no lower than her chin, though, making her once again uncomfortably aware of her complete lack of feeling from there on down. All that was visible to her was a tanklike contrivance, with some sort of blue liquid that occasionally sloshed into her line of sight. The blue of Makellen Darke's eyes. She couldn't help but wonder what both concealed.

He had been following her look, following her thoughts, and waging an inner battle. Now, a sigh, a shrug, and a shake of his head signaled that the battle was done. "What is the last thing you remember?"

She frowned at the effort of concentration. Since her awakening here, Makellen had subtly steered her away from remembering. Now, her mind flat out refused.

The blue eyes holding hers darkened to the color of the sky at midnight. You could become lost in those eyes, Auglaize thought before his quietly commanding voice snapped her wandering attention back. "The last thing you remember, DeWellesthar."

"We were returning home from combat patrol," she heard herself responding in her calm, unemotional, debriefing-room tone. "Dancer Flight. Twelve of us—three four-ships, my command and my friends. It was very quiet in our sector, too quiet. A couple of minor skirmishes, just enough to deplete our ammunition, but neither side drew any real blood. Not like them at all. Needless to say, it made us all edgy. I knew something was up, but there was nothing I could put my finger on, you know? So, we stayed on patrol until we were low enough on fuel that we had to head for home.

"We were still quite a way out when we first saw the flashes, then the radio message came for us to divert to Soloman. Refuel, rearm, and return; the base was under attack.

" 'Dancer Lead to Tower, no can do. Repeat, cannot comply. We're coming in now.' 'Dancer Flight from Lead, you heard the situation. This is for the ballgame. Good luck.'

"The engagement was brief. We had only one squadron in the air, and half of them were, like us, returning from patrol with bingo fuel—enough to get us back to base with a small safety margin. Certainly not enough to fight with. We took hordes of Karranganthians with us, but they had the numbers to lose. We didn't. It was all over in a matter of minutes. No time for help to get to us, though we did manage to buy enough time for some of our people to escape. I was forced down and among the eighteen captured. Eighteen left alive out of three hundred.

"Believe me, we tried our best not to survive. We fought in every way we knew, both for our Service and for ourselves. I, myself, didn't use my escape capsule; I soft-landed my Gypsy, used the last of my internal power to maneuver myself into a defensible position, and expended the rest of my ammunition. Including handgun, flare launcher, and emergency tool kit.

"I figured that when it came down to the wire I'd simply insert the point of my survival knife about an inch below my breastbone with a sharp upward thrust, as the textbooks say. But damn, if at the last moment my hand didn't slip and let that knife open up a Karranganthian belly instead. The others all had similar stories. And we knew when they didn't just blow us to atoms what they had planned for us. We'd seen the intelligence briefings on the fate of Karranganthian prisoners of war.

"I'm sure you know that the Karranganthians aren't interested in any information they may or may not gain along the way; they simply torture for entertainment, for an evening's diversion over supper. It can go on for hours, and their . . . pleasures . . . don't always end in death. Sometimes they'll go at someone until he no longer responds, then toy with another until the first is sufficiently recovered to afford further amusement. That's how it was with Troy—my wingman. My . . . lover. He held out for three days."

"Auglaise—"

"No, Makellen. No, please, pass on my report. Someone should know exactly what happened. My people deserve that much." Was that her, so calmly reciting the deaths of her friends? "The first of us was the luckiest; he didn't have to watch the torments of the rest. And anticipate his own. We hit upon a form of resistance, though; it helped some. It started with Keri. He was tough, but he finally broke. 'Dancer, for the love of God, help me!' I'll never forget his . . . scream. Well, of course they would call on me; I was their leader. I yelled back the first thing that came into my mind, the Four F's—'Food and friendship, fu . . . fornicating and flying.' The others picked it up, made it into a chant. Over and over, until there was nothing else in our minds. Even after they silenced our voices, it was still burned into our brains. It eased Keri's death, if only by a little. It gave us the illusion that we were fighting back.

"After that, all any of us had to do was call 'Dancer Flight' and the rest of us responded. We chanted, we recited checklists, we sang drinking songs. We had the bastards going, too—they actually went so far as to promise freedom to any who would betray our leader. Me. None did, though the temptation . . . well. But then, of course, we knew they would not honor their promises.

"Mine was a gutsy bunch. Monty—she giggled through multiple rapes and laughed in their faces as they destroyed hers. But she was broken in the end. Troy—his resistance was taunts. 'How many Karranganthians does it take to change a light bulb? None; they're too stupid to have electricity.' Troy was electrocuted by degrees. Three days. He died by my hands; I strangled him with my manacle chains."

"That's enough, Auglaise."

She shook her head. "No. I thought so, too, thought I had reached the end of my endurance with that act, but the horror went on, and so did I. One by one, I watched them die. Seven . . . ten . . . then it was my turn. I was so vain of my hands. And the pain . . . I didn't know a body could hurt so much and still function. Funny, I feel nothing now. I wonder if the nothing isn't worse than the unrelenting, excruciating torments, piled one upon the other until—Dear God." Auglaize stopped dead as a new thought struck her. "Dear God, I am still a prisoner. You didn't kill me; this is just some new torture!"

"No, Auglaise; you're safe now. I promise you, you are safe now!"

"Bullshit; I know the game. I don't know what you could possibly want of me, but you won't get anything more."

"Dancer, look at me!" The voice was becoming sharp, but that made it easier to ignore. It was his gentleness she had fallen for; now that he was reverting to type, she could fight him. After all, some of the Karranganthians had had blue eyes, too. Davenger. How could she ever forget Davenger, the blue-eyed Karranganthian?

Once again she was back in the cell, the one with the crimson-stained white walls, the stench of blood and death so strong it seemed to clog her nostrils. Flight Leader DeWellesthar shook her head violently, raging aloud with what she thought had been only in her mind. "No. I will not give you the satisfaction. I will not scream. I will not . . . !" The hiss of her own sharp intake of breath as remembered agony clawed at her body. "God help me. Dancer Flight . . . Dancer Flight! There are so few left. Give them the strength to continue resisting. Give *me* the strength to continue resisting!" Over and over, Auglaize pleaded with a deity who, despite recent events, she still believed must exist. There were no atheists in battle . . .

A stinging slap first on one cheek, then on the other, and that voice demanding, *demanding* that she look at him. Instead, she clenched her jaws together, squeezed her eyes shut and turned them inward on herself, determined to resist with her last ounce of strength. She had done it once; she could do it again. And again, if need be.

Auglaize could still feel the repeated blows to her face, but she could endure. She would endure, until her body died, cheating them of their amusement.

From a great distance she heard that voice, nearly frantic now: "Come on, Auglaise, look at me. Look at me! Auglaise De-Wellesthar, you will open your eyes!" As if he could will her to do so merely by ordering it.

Then another voice: "You're losing her, Darke!"

The first one, frustrated, angry, employing all the colorful oaths of the five Services as he indicated his awareness of the fact. "If you had let me do this my way . . . don't slip away from me, Dancer. You're mine. Do you hear me? You are *mine*!"

Her facial muscles relaxed into a smile as her lips formed the words, "No way, Davenger. You lose."

"Damn it, Darke, do something!"

Auglaize was drifting away when a scream split her skull. "Dancer Flight!"

Hang on. Hang on; it will end soon.

"Dancer, help me!"

"Dancer, look at me."

No. It was too late. She'd done her part. Let someone else. . . .

"Dancer!"

"Child, please. . . ."

Someone had called her 'child' once, someone with a voice like velvet and eyes that were deeper than space. But the screams, the screams . . .

Then Auglaize was struggling as something held her down, something clamped under her chin and pulling her hair, something bruising her lips and trying to force its way into her mouth . . . What? What was this?

The pressure eased for a second as a voice whispered, "Come on, Glaise. Come on."

Glaise. Strange way to say her name. Glaise. It sounded like a smile. The pressure returned, though more gently this time. Very gently. Almost like . . . a kiss? Warm breath on her cheek, and . . . Experimentally she moved her head, instantly feeling, rather than hearing, the words "Come on, child, we've come too far together for you to leave me now."

Gentleness from a Karranganthian? Impossible. Then, what—? In spite of herself, she relaxed under his caressing hands and mouth, then very gradually began to respond. When Auglaize had finally come out of herself enough to realize what was happening, she had already begun to lose herself in Makellen Darke.

His lips formed the words "Thank God!" on hers, and she expected him to pull away—his job was done, after all. Auglaize was still alive, for whatever reason.

He did pull back, but only far enough to survey her face with wide eyes that were all pupil. Then, with a shudder, he kissed the tip of her nose, her forehead, her cheek. This was no Karranganthian. Without thinking, she turned her head and recaptured his mouth with hers.

A passionate man, Makellen Darke. She intensely wanted to feel his arms around her, his body pressed against hers . . . she intensely wanted to *feel*.

Suddenly, deep down inside where her abdomen should have been, there was a spark. Just a small spark, but it gave her such a jolt she gasped.

Makellen jerked away with a shaky apology, and she wished with all her heart she could have pulled him back.

"Thank you," was all she managed to get out. The smile that lit up his face was like the sunrise.

"When you are out of this thing . . . Damn!" That last, with the heel of his hand pressing the skin behind his right ear. It suddenly dawned on Auglaize that there must be a communications device of some sort implanted there, an insight confirmed as he continued, "They're buzzing at me like a swarm of angry hornets. It seems that they do not approve of my brand of therapy. Would they perhaps prefer to see you dead?" He drew a deep, calming breath, and his voice quieted. "Do you think you can sleep now, Glaise? It would be best. We can talk more later."

"What about you—can you sleep now?"

A half smile and an affectionate, "Only when you do."

With his hand twined in her slightly-longer-than-regulation curls and the words of what might have been a lullaby floating around her head, she drifted off.

Chapter 11

How long Auglaize lay in that deep, drugged, dreamless slumber, she had no idea. However, when she was again allowed to awaken Makellen was beside her, his eyes clear, his face rosy-cheeked and unlined.

"You're certainly looking better," was her comment.

"Good morning," he returned with an ironic twist of a smile. "And so are you."

"I wouldn't know."

"Are you always this cheerful when you wake up?"

"Only when I don't know where I am, can't feel my body, and have a strange man practically in bed with me." Then, astonishingly, she found herself blushing a deep scarlet.

"Auglaise, what is it? Are you all right?"

She waved him off with an unconscious toss of the head and a half smile. "I was just thinking that . . . I have the oddest feeling you saved my life before. Your methods are certainly unorthodox."

Comprehension slowly replaced the concern in his face. "Is it all right, then?"

"That you kissed me? It was delightful. I wish you'd do it again."

"That I love you," he said steadily.

It was hard for her to hear her own choked reply over the pounding of the blood in her ears. "Whatever there is left of me to love."

"Auglaise, it is very important. They'll replace me if you will it."

"Don't leave me, Makellen!" was her panic-stricken, knee-jerk reply.

"Hush, child, you won't be alone. There are others here; you will never be alone."

"You saved my life. You saved my sanity." You gave me something else, something that I'm not even sure of yet, she added silently, but I want to find out. "As you said, I am yours."

Relief shattered the composed mask that had obscured his face. "Indeed. You are. I shall hold you to that."

"I want you to hold me. Such as I am."

He purposely ignored the question inherent in her tone, grinning nervously. "It isn't unusual for patients to fall in love with their caregivers, but it's not supposed to happen the other way around. I'm afraid that my superiors aren't too happy about it."

"I don't understand how it could have happened at all. We practically just met."

"Let's just say I've known you longer than you've known me."

Calculatingly, the flight leader watched him for a moment, noting that he wouldn't meet her eyes, then nodded abruptly. "Mak, I have some questions that need answering."

He hesitated. "I had hoped we could defer this for a while longer. They . . . we were concerned about your reaction."

"For crying out loud, Mak, I know the worst! I *lived* the worst! Did any of the others survive?"

The reply was as brisk as the question, his face a bland mask once more. "I'm sorry. No. The others were all dead. We are still not sure why you weren't."

"Neither am I—I certainly wanted to be badly enough."

"Not as badly as you thought, or you would have been."

"Conceded. Our base?"

"Those who made it to the underground command post held out until reinforcements arrived. Two from your barracks: a Myles Clinton and Hardin Wyandot."

"Wyandot." The flight leader smiled grimly. "She was on sick call that morning. Minor sinus problem. Furious because I upheld the orders grounding her. So, I inadvertently saved one of them, did I? And Clint. He was working his command-post rotation. Who else?"

Makellen gave her that now-familiar, searching look, then nodded slowly. "As you will, Auglaise. We have the casualty lists. What do you wish to know?"

"For starters, how am I referred to on those lists?"

"Missing, presumed dead. Your body has not been recovered."

Auglaize looked down at the giant pickle jar encasing her, and snorted. "*There's* an understatement. You were with the reinforcements?"

"I was. The fighting had scarcely ended before word reached us of your group's capture; a sufficient number of us were detailed to form a rescue party. We came for you as soon as we could track you down, but it was too late. They slit the throats of the last three prisoners as we fought our way through the door."

"At least they died easily."

His eyes flashed. "But I assure you, their murderers did not! I watched each of your people die, too, Auglaise. I watched your torture."

"They recorded the event, of course. Well. Better to be the subject of future intelligence briefings than an evening's home video entertainment."

"The recordings went into a file accessible only to our Commander," he said shortly. "How much more do you want to know?"

"All. I would see the tapes myself, were it allowed."

He nodded. "I expected no less. Though I thank the gods it is not allowed. I wish that I had not been required to watch it." His jaw set, and Auglaize recognized the flash of helpless anger in his eyes. It was a feeling she knew well.

"So," she said to rid her mind of certain images, "how did I hold up?"

He snapped his attention back to her. "Well. Almost . . . too well. You didn't make a sound. Throughout the whole ordeal, you didn't make a sound. I don't know how you endured it; I couldn't have. The look in your eyes . . ." A shiver, and a shake of the head. "It finally even got to them. They slid a knife between your ribs and threw you into the pile of bodies. It was almost like you went so deeply into your own mind that nothing touched you."

"It touched me, all right," Auglaise assured him grimly. "I remember some of it. I remember . . . him."

"Yes. Yes, but when we found you there, I looked into your eyes and *you looked back at me!* And you trusted me."

His tone challenged her to deny it. She couldn't. "Yes."

"When you arrived here, the first reaction of our med wizards was shock that a body so badly damaged could still live. They were determined that it would survive, though your mind—your sanity— we were not certain could be saved. You remained withdrawn, unresponsive, unreachable; I refused to consider that that spark of intellect I had seen had been extinguished. I knew that if I persisted, I could reach you. So I talked to you constantly, sang, read your

Service record aloud so many times I can recite it from memory, racked my brains to come up with something that would be familiar to you.''

"Rhombyan."

"Indeed. *Rhombyan*," he confirmed. "Next, I would have tried the *Gypsy Pilot's Manual*. After that, something else. Whatever it took. All the while not knowing what I would find if . . . when I did break through. You understand what I'm saying?''

"I understand.''

"You also understand why you must not remember too much too quickly. The next time you slip back inside yourself, I might not be able to bring you out again. Eventually, though, you will know what is necessary for you to know, and it will cause you no pain.''

"You people place a peculiar emphasis on numbness.''

His eyes became veiled. "Child, in my Service, that is often necessary for survival.''

It was almost a relief to take that opening and change the subject. "You keep alluding to your Service. Just what Service is that, Makellen?''

"The Sixth.''

"Wait a minute, there are only five Services.''

Makellen's smile was smug. "So we would have outsiders believe.''

"What do I have that your secret Sixth Service would go to such pains for?'' Auglaize couldn't help asking. "Why didn't you just let me die?''

"Don't you realize that you are the only person in recorded history ever to survive a Karranganthian torture cell? Through sheer strength of will?''

"So, you only want me for my mind, huh?''

Her attempt at levity was met with an appreciative chuckle. "They want your mind. I want your body.''

"Sure you do.'' Which brought them back to the question that was uppermost in her thoughts. "But do I have a body?''

"Of course. Would I fall in love with just a mouth? I assure you, when you leave here, you will be as good as new. Better.''

"How?''

"Ah, child, this is a place of wonders; our medical and psychiatric wizards routinely rebuild shattered bodies and minds that others give up as hopeless. In peacetime, this complex was a secret Auryx research facility which few even now realize exists. We are extremely selective about whom we choose to transport here.

"Look, Glaise." He drummed his fingernails on a surface just out of her line of sight; the sound generated was a solid clack. "You are encased in what we call a Van Wert apparatus, or Van Wert's Womb; your body is floating in a solution containing a deep anesthetic, various nutrients, antibiotics, and the like . . . in effect, the damaged portions of your body are being regrown."

"That's impossible!"

"Nothing is impossible. The fact that you are talking to me now is proof of that."

Auglaize shook her head. "This whole thing is just a horrible dream. Any minute now, the alarm will go off and I'll wake up in my own bed, with a roommate who snores, and a fight over who gets the last clean flightsuit."

"This is a new reality for you. You'll adjust. We'll help you. I'll help you."

"If I get out of this thing, what will I be?"

"*When* you get out," he quietly corrected, "you'll be what you always were. Same height, same weight, same proportions, if that's what you wish, since your body is reconstructing itself from its own gene patterns. I'll warn you, though, that the process is not always one-hundred percent effective. Grafts, and in some cases, prostheses, may be in order. But in the end, I promise you, you won't be able to tell them from original equipment. If you should decide you want something changed—that can be arranged, too."

"How long?"

"As long as it takes, child. What measure of time would you have me use? Then, of course, there will be physical therapy to reeducate muscles, and the psych wizards will have their work to do."

"How long will you be with me?"

"As long as you want me. For whatever form eternity takes."

How poetic. How frightening. This talk of love made Auglaize uncomfortable. She had once known very well what the word meant, but there was nothing like it in her existence now. "When this is all over, will I remember Morgan Troy?"

"Morgan. . . ? Oh, your friend."

"My lover," she quietly, ruthlessly, corrected.

"You will remember what you wish to remember."

"I want to remember Troy. I want to remember what it felt like lying in his arms, arguing theoretical tactics, walking hand in hand together on a winter's evening. He and I were as one once, Makellen, and now I feel nothing."

He met her eyes evenly, reading, she hoped, deeper things yet unsaid. "Nothing?"

"Gratitude. Curiosity. Apprehension. Nothing more."

"I see. The rest will come if you wish it."

"Mak, I don't even know you."

"Hush, child, I understand." Then he calmly and rationally tried to dry the tears squeezing past the corners of her eyes with his lips.

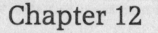

Chapter 12

There followed another on-again, off-again period distinguished by short intervals of awareness alternating with dreamlike nonexistence, punctuated occasionally by a recurring nightmare that Auglaize couldn't remember long enough to relate to Makellen. It had something to do with the Karranganthian, that much she knew as she clawed her way to consciousness in dry-throated terror. That security in the form of Makellen Darke awaited her when her eyes opened, she also knew. Somehow he could sense the turmoil within her, though he told her that she made no outward sound or sign. He could sense it, and he was always there.

Oddly enough, the same presence that reassured her also made her uneasy. Despite Makellen's gentleness and seemingly honest affection, the fact remained he was the only person she had been allowed to see here. On top of that, there was very obviously somebody looking over his shoulder every minute. Perhaps she had hit upon her true condition in that moment of irrationality which they still didn't discuss. Perhaps she was, in reality, still a prisoner of the Karranganthians. Perhaps they both were, he being used to ensnare her, though what possible motive there would be in that, she couldn't fathom.

A flash of Makellen's smile would banish all such thoughts for a time, but inevitably they would return.

Reassurance finally came in an offhand way: Makellen staggered into her line of sight carrying a large, obviously heavy box which he deposited with a thud in his accustomed chair.

"Your personal effects," he explained without preamble.

Her personal effects. It was as simple as that. The Karranganthians looted, pillaged, and burned, but they had never yet been known to box up neatly what they didn't want and parcel-post it home to the victim's next of kin. Her relief was almost tangible. Mak was *not* the enemy.

"There was some damage to your barracks," he was saying, oblivious for once to her true feelings, "but most of this is intact. We've been sitting on it for as long as we could. The families have been getting insistent, though, yours among them. They know that it takes just so long to inventory and process. You understand."

So, her return from the dead, and all her programmed pattern of sleeping and waking, equated to the time it took to salvage the shambles of an established base, sift through the rags and scraps representing hundreds of lives, ascertain ownership, and package for shipping. The attendant paperwork alone would occupy months, and they would be understandably shorthanded. Great gods above, how long had she been here?

"I understand." Suddenly, she laughed aloud. Time was immaterial. What mattered was, Makellen was not the enemy, she truly was safe, and this was all for real, this . . . thing . . . that was repairing her body. She would walk, she would fly—her spirits were already soaring—she believed that now. And the way her pulse jumped whenever Makellen Darke touched her—that was all right, too. She might even love.

Mak was looking at her oddly, picking up on her euphoria but totally misinterpreting it. "Perhaps I'd better tell you first, you can't keep everything. We travel light and fast, and the sum total of all our worldly possessions must fit into the baggage pod of a fighter."

"Besides which, being dead, I don't need any of it, right?" she said flippantly, feeling gloriously alive.

Makellen's reply was a raised eyebrow and a smile of amused tolerance. "Exactly. However, if a few of your possessions were found to be missing, no one would think very much of it, under the circumstances. What we have to do now is sort out those few things."

"You said the families were getting anxious. Why did you wait so long?"

"Why do you think? They were concerned as to how you would react."

"Ah, yes, my fragile mental state."

"More so than you think, child," Mak murmured. "However," he continued in a cheerful tone, "prevailing theory was that you might feel more secure with some of your own belongings."

Auglaize chuckled. "And just whose theory was that, might I ask?" As if she didn't know.

"Who knows you better than anyone else alive?"

Makellen Darke, of course. But she'd be damned if she'd tell him how right he was.

"They" were also correct, to a point: with surprisingly mixed emotions, Auglaize watched Makellen shake out the spare flightsuit and dress uniform which had been used as packing material and unload the boxes. Memories—some good, some bad—unexpectedly came crowding back too thickly to disentangle. She didn't even try. That was for the future, when she had hands to wipe away the tears.

Almost all of her worldly possessions would be shipped back. The antique aircraft prints, some dating back hundreds of years to the crate-and-wire days, could easily be computer-stored and re-copied at any later date. New clothes and uniforms would be provided when she needed them—though she couldn't yet part with her old Fourth Service flying gear—and she knew that every one of her treasures would be missed by a loving family. A few she kept, though: a silver bracelet that had been her last gift from Troy, an odd-shaped rock—an ordinary pebble, really—that she had in her cadet days picked out of a freshly plowed field back on the family farm.

The books were the most difficult. Old friends, two baker's dozens of them, which Mak piled one by one before her eyes on a table he had pulled up for the purpose. Auglaize had always loved books—loved the feel of them, the smell, that wonderful tactile satisfaction of holding them in her hands and physically turning pages. They could, Makellen assured her, be entered into the computer's library, but it wouldn't be the same.

"As a matter of fact," he said, "I'll scan them in myself. Or perhaps I could read to you and record? And you can pick a favorite or two to keep. Or three; I can always find room for one." She caught the way he unconsciously ran his hand up and down a simulated leather binding and smiled inwardly.

How long had it been, she wondered, since he'd sorted through all his worldly goods for the few that would, along with his uniforms, fit into a travel pod? Not so long that he didn't remember the pain of it. It wasn't just objects being relinquished here; it was an entire life.

Then, she laughed again as her dog-eared, faded red, Fourth Service Academy–issued volume of *Rhombyan* appeared. "That's a keeper."

Mak flashed her a startled glance, then grinned. "When you were back on your feet again, I had thought to give you mine. If you would allow me to do so. This—your family would treasure, because you did."

"Thank you. For the gift, and for the thought."

"Nonsense," he said mischievously. "If I give you *Rhombyan*, then I can replace it with something here that I haven't already memorized."

Finally the boxes were empty, or seemingly so. When Makellen turned the second one upside down and shook it, something that had been caught in a corner clattered to the floor.

"My class ring!" Auglaize exclaimed while he was still down on his hands and knees trying to figure out where it had rolled. "I never had that off my finger from the day I got it, except when I was flying." The item that would be missed the most by her family, for that very reason.

Mak said something, but his voice was muted by the apparatus he was crawling under so that all she heard was, ". . . easily lost."

"I know. I know. It goes back," she told him as he emerged triumphant, the familiar circle with its burgundy star ruby set in yellow gold clenched in his fist. "I don't even want to see it." But if she had had hands, she would have snatched it from him. Its engraving slightly worn where her fingers had rubbed, the ring was a symbol of everything she had loved and would see no more. She turned her head away, ashamed to have Mak see tears in her eyes over such a trivial thing.

"What I said was, small items such as this are easily lost," he repeated matter-of-factly. "Not to mention how extremely valuable monetarily Service Academy rings are, due to the quality of the precious metals and stones. A fortune for anyone who came across it and knew that the owner was dead and wouldn't miss it."

"So? There's my ring. No one stole it."

With a mysterious smile and a flick of Mak's wrist, the item in question disappeared from sight. "Someone just did. No one will ever know who, child, and I'm not telling. Are you?"

Auglaize flashed him a smile of pure gratitude as she finally caught on.

"Out of all of this, that's the one thing that means the most to you, isn't it, Glaise?" Makellen asked.

"Yep."

"May I ask you why?"

"Well—let's just say it signifies something I wanted badly enough to give up just about everything else for. Where I come from, nice girls did not join the military. My daddy once said to me, 'Glaize, as I see it, you've got two choices: you can either be a run-of-the-mill *nice girl* or you can be one hell of a pilot.' I took the easy way out."

Makellen's only comment was a raised eyebrow. "There's a lot more to you than meets the eye, my dear."

Auglaize gestured at the tank obscuring her body and laughed. "I should hope so!"

Chapter 13

Then something went wrong. Auglaize awoke suddenly in the half light, alone. Trapped. Trapped in a chamber of horrors where white walls spun dizzyingly above her and a strange, flickering blue glow danced all around. Nothing—anywhere!—for her wildly searching eyes to grab onto to allay her vertigo; no sound except her own harsh breathing to reassure her straining ears. Through the swirling void she plummeted, like a sparrow in a cyclone, squeezing her eyes shut and praying that if it was death she was spiraling down to meet, it would claim her soon. The Karranganthians . . . no. The Karranganthians . . . !

"Mak!" She cried aloud the name that meant safety. "Makellen!" Feebly, she struggled against the liquid bonds that held her in thrall, able to feel arms flailing, legs kicking, body twisting and squirming.

Panic engulfed her as she fought against a liquid thicker than water—blood?—and, her head free of it, she took a deep breath and screamed. The sound was so satisfying that she repeated it again and again, only dimly hearing the voice from above trying to get her attention over the echoes bouncing back at her from the walls.

"Flight Leader! It's all right. Calm down—you're not alone. It's all right!" The tone of the unfamiliar voice was calculated to be soothing, but it abruptly turned sharp. "Damn it, fetch Darke! He's *where*? Oh, for . . . get a tranquilizer into her. Then use a stronger one! Move!"

The last command was preceded by a string of expletives that Auglaize didn't have to speak the language to understand.

Hey, guys, did you realize you left the intercom on up there? The thought made her giggle; then the giggles dissolved into sobs.

A hand feathered her hair, hesitantly but caressingly, and that unfamiliar voice murmured right beside her. "Flight Leader, I am Davis Ashur. They call me Van Wert. Kellen is on his way. Do you hear me?"

How could she help but hear him? She nodded slightly.

"Kellen is on his way," the voice repeated softly. "He's flying this afternoon. We thought he would have plenty of time . . . Child, are you in pain?"

Auglaize cocked her head, as if listening, then gestured in the negative. At his touch, the whirling vortex she'd been caught up in settled back into just a hospital room once more, and she ventured to open her eyes.

"All right, then. You must lie still. Do you hear me? Calm down; lie still. If you don't, you're going to hurt yourself."

Just then, the door burst open with a violence that sent it crashing into the wall, followed by an out-of-breath "I'm here, Glaise," and a familiar palm cupping itself around her cheek.

She snuggled into it. "The Karranganthian . . . had you. He was killing you, and I couldn't stop him . . ."

"Hush, child; Mak's here now, and it's all right. No one can hurt either of us. You're safe." His voice was low and musical and tickled her ear.

"The Karranganthian . . ." A leering face with glittering eyes and a predatory smile, etched on the inside of her eyelids, made her shudder. "The Karranganthian—"

"Is dead. Understand? The Karranganthian is dead."

She nodded, sniffling, as his palm flattened to push the damp curls off her forehead. "I'm . . . sorry. I don't know what happened. I woke up alone and . . . panicked."

"It's all right, Glaise. Your reaction is not atypical. I should have been here. It's just that no one expected you to awaken for hours yet. Ah, child, I will not leave you again.''

"Kellen? He called you Kellen?'' she asked.

"Who, child?''

"Dave . . . Ashur, I think he said his name was.''

Makellen's voice held surprise. "Van Wert told you his true name? Child, we . . . you should be flattered. Kellen, I was called in my childhood. Van Wert and I have known each other for a very long time.''

"I like him. Is he one of 'Them'?'' she asked, stalling to get her composure back.

"Davis? He's on our side.''

At last she turned to him, able to smile, and the smile became wistful. Makellen was still in his flying clothes—he had taken the time only to shed helmet, life-support equipment, and one glove. The other, soggy now, still sheathed the hand touching her face. His tan flightsuit was unfastened about halfway down his chest, revealing a light knit shirt of the electric blue that she'd come to identify with him. His sweat-matted, longish black hair had been sketchily combed with his fingers, and he was self-consciously smoothing it down now, a tentative smile playing across his flushed face, where the lines of the helmet pads were still visible.

He smelled of damp fabric, exertion, and warm man, with just a hint of the indescribable but unique combination of rubber, metal, and electronic components; in short, the comfortable, familiar, debriefing room smell. To Auglaize's sense of smell, grown accustomed to the sterile nothing that usually surrounded her, it was a reassurance that her old world really did still exist. She wrinkled her nose in pleasure, and the tears started again.

"Glaise? What is it, child?''

"I am . . . I *was* . . . a pilot.''

"And will be again,'' he stated, relief evident in his voice. "Though obviously 'They' were correct in instructing me not to remind you of it.''

"Oh, really?'' she sniffed, wiping her face on that still-convenient glove.

Hooking a booted foot around the leg of his accustomed chair, Makellen pulled it close enough to collapse into, and grinned innocently. "Really.''

Her eyes narrowed, Auglaize watched him sit back, stretch, and take a couple of deep breaths. It was the first time she had ever seen him looking less than perfectly uniformed and immaculately groomed—barring their initial meeting—and she decided she definitely liked his disheveled appearance. "You look damned sexy when you're half out of uniform. And I don't give a fairy frigate what 'They' say, I want to hear all about it. What do you fly here?"

Mak leaned forward, eyes sparkling sapphire, and gave her a brief but thoroughly enjoyable kiss before launching into a spirited recitation of his day's accomplishments.

As Auglaize watched him, the thought crossed her mind that if Makellen had nothing in the world but a maneuverable aircraft and Auglaize DeWellesthar, he'd be the happiest man alive. That was when she realized the feeling was mutual.

Some time later, the sense of detachment from a body she shouldn't have been able to feel told Auglaize that whatever chemicals had been introduced into her system were finally taking effect. Mentally, she was fully alert and knew that she would be for some time yet; she also knew that Kellen—she savored the aftertaste of the nickname in her mind—would feel it his duty to keep her company all that time. So she injected a drowsy note into her voice and allowed her eyelids to drift shut. Her unseen monitors would know that she was shamming, but perhaps they'd understand. Makellen could change his clothes and get some rest, and she'd have a little time alone with her thoughts.

It worked; after sitting quietly by her side for about five minutes, Kellen dropped his accustomed kiss on the bridge of her nose and stood. The breath of his sigh was barely audible; strangely enough, it was the same as the sound of the door opening.

Evidently this Dave Van Wert person, whom she assumed to be her doctor, was waiting in the hall; surprisingly, she found herself able to overhear the ensuing conversation.

"What happened?" was Mak's low-voiced but sharp query. "Another nightmare?"

"I don't know. Maybe. More like a claustrophobic panic attack, I think. What worries me is the way she was thrashing around."

"She shouldn't have been able to do that."

"No shit. Nor should she have been awake. We have a definite problem here. Our girl apparently has built up a resistance to standard drugs—painkillers, tranquilizers, sedatives. Dosages have been increased to the danger levels, yet they continue to lose their effectiveness. Very odd."

"Life-threatening?" Makellen's voice held a note she hadn't heard before, a crispness, an urgency—an air of command?

"Not in the conventional sense, no. However, we must keep her immobile to heal properly. I'm much more concerned about her mental well-being.''

"I saw no signs of withdrawal."

"There were a couple of moments when she might have started to slip . . ." Van Wert's voice was thoughtful.

"But she didn't."

"Not this time. However, as you well know, we have no idea what might trigger memories that will send her so deeply into her own mind that even you cannot get her back."

"So. I'll stay with her."

"You can't be there every minute, Kell. No. I'll take another look at her Service records. The answer is in there somewhere, and I intend to find it. Until I do . . ."

"I'll stay with her," Makellen reiterated.

"That's something else," Van Wert said quietly. "My people hadn't time to notify you, and I know for a fact your flight plan didn't have you back on the ground for another hour. How did you get here so quickly?"

"I aborted the flight," was the grim reply. "I felt . . . I knew she needed me."

"Yes, but *how* did you know?"

"Dancer is one of us, Van Wert," Makellen said intensely. "I just knew."

One of us? One of who? One of what? My God, he really *did* read minds, were the thoughts chasing themselves around in Auglaize's brain. Then, inconsequentially, He called me Dancer. He's never done that before.

And, evidently her "mind-reader" learned she was awake—probably informed by her monitors upstairs—because he and the doctor continued their most interesting conversation in a language she'd never heard before.

No, that was wrong. It was the language of Makellen's songs, and of his whispered endearments when he thought she was asleep.

Yes, indeed, she had a lot to think about.

Chapter 14

Auglaize thought she was seeing double—the only reassurance that her eyes weren't playing tricks on her was that the two men before her were dressed differently. Makellen she recognized by the vivid blue of his shirt. The other wore blue also, but a lighter, less obtrusive hue.

The lines around his eyes deepened as the man allowed himself a chuckle at her perplexed stare. In that instant, she could see a distinct difference. This one's face was slightly rounder than Kellen's, the lips not as full, the black hair shorter and more carefully tended, the blue eyes not so startlingly blue.

"Are you brothers?" she finally asked.

Kellen just laughed; it was the other who answered. "Brothers of the mind," he said pleasantly. "Our race is the product of a genetic engineering experiment; we all look alike to outsiders. You'll soon learn to tell us apart, though—we're color-coded."

She'd heard the voice before. "You're Van Wert."

"Right the first time, Flight Leader."

"So, we finally meet face to face. I've been meaning to ask you, is this your real estate I'm occupying?"

He shook his head. "I wish I could take credit for it. However, when the previous owner of the name died, I inherited both it and her duties."

"Numbered among which is raising people from the dead?"

"Here comes the lecture on Confederacy statutes concerning laboratory creation of sentient life, yes? Set your mind at ease, Flight Leader. We believe that the creation of life belongs to a higher power. However, the enhancement and preservation are our responsibility. Confederacy law was written to keep less scrupulous races from using technology such as ours for growing slave labor and replacement-parts donors. As Kellen told you, this is a highly secret installation; what the Confederacy doesn't know won't make them uncomfortable.''

"Since I wouldn't be alive if you felt otherwise, I have to agree with you. So. To what do I owe the honor of your acquaintance? I was beginning to think that Makellen was the only other person in the world.''

"He likes to think so. Listen, Flight Leader, we have a problem, you and I.''

"Something about my developing a resistance to your drugs?''

"Exactly. We're doing a records search now, but if you know anything that might help us out here, it would be to your advantage to tell us.''

"Well, I always had a real high tolerance for alcohol,'' she answered. "That's about the only painkiller I've had much experience with. Sorry.''

"You've no need to apologize. There are other means of easing discomfort, just not so convenient in your case.''

"I'm not afraid of hurting,'' Auglaize assured him. "It would be a nice change of pace at this point.''

"That is immaterial. We have to keep you immobile to assure proper healing. Sleep, at this point, is the best thing for you.''

"But I do not *want* to sleep nine-tenths of my life away,'' she stated in frustration, appealing to Makellen, who shrugged. "My body may be pickled, but my mind still needs exercise.''

"My patients have always preferred being in limbo,'' Van Wert replied. "They find themselves unable to cope with the boredom of confinement otherwise.''

"I'd rather be bored than inert!''

"That may be the key,'' Kellen interjected. "She's strong-willed, our Auglaise.''

"You may be right.'' Van Wert regarded her speculatively, clinically, for just a moment before relenting. "You win, Flight Leader. I'll talk to the psychs and see what we can arrange. No, Darke.'' Van Wert cut off Makellen's protest before he could even voice it. "That's the way it must be. If she is alert and alone, she will begin to think. We have no idea what may trigger memories with which she cannot cope.

"We've all grown rather fond of you here, Flight Leader. It would be unthinkable to chance losing you now. Tell you what, I'll leave the two of you alone to talk it over. I've some detective work to do.'' With that and a shake of the head, he hustled out.

"Nice meeting you, too,'' Auglaize called after him with a smile. "He's cute,'' she added with a sidelong glance at Makellen.

"Of course he is. We all look alike, remember?"

"No, you don't."

"Well, don't get any ideas. Van Wert's married. Besides, I've already lost one girl to a friend; I don't intend to lose another."

"Hmm. I wondered why you never brought any of your buddies home for dinner," she teased.

"Well, now you know." Kellen leaned over to press his lips across the bridge of her nose in his usual greeting.

"Mak, c'n I ask you a question?"

"What is it, child?" He grinned.

"It's silly, but I've been wondering. Why do you always kiss me there? Why not on the cheek, or—revolutionary thought—the mouth?"

"Oh, that. It's just a custom of the Auryx. To tell you the truth, I do it without even thinking. I will amend, if you prefer."

"Actually, I like it. But what are . . ." she paused momentarily, wrapping her tongue around the unfamiliar syllables, "aw-ricks?"

Kellen laughed outright. "*I* are Auryx. Van Wert are Auryx. All of us here, with the possible exception of one charming redhead, are Auryx."

"Is that a race, religion, or sexual preference?" she snapped back in exasperation.

"Race, love. My Service oath forbids me to divulge the name or location of my planet of origin."

"Oh. Auryx!" She pronounced it *Orks*.

"Auryx," he corrected gently. "I take it you've heard of us."

"Not much. Rumor and innuendo, mostly. Something about the Auryx stealing peoples' minds and turning men into puppets."

"Oh, God, is it that bad?" He laughed. "Listen, Glaise, we do *not* turn men into puppets. Women, maybe . . ."

"That's 'sex slaves,' " came a familiar voice from above—Van Wert, letting them know he was back on duty. "You don't actually believe that nonsense, do you, Flight Leader?"

"Of course I don't! On the other hand, you two are the only representatives of your race I've ever met."

"We are fairly representative of our race, at that," Kellen said. "Brilliant, sexy, devastatingly handsome—"

"Modest," Auglaize added. "Give me your best, Service-approved, five-minute lecture on Auryx culture."

"You're serious, aren't you? Don't look at me like that; it's been my experience that outsiders, even those who are our allies, are much less concerned with learning about what we are than with making us what they wish us to be."

"But I'm not an outsider, remember? I'm a new recruit. Besides, I never considered my curiosity about other lifestyles particularly unusual."

"It's not your curiosity I find unusual. It's your attitude. You lack the arrogance that yours is the best and only way to live."

Open-mindedness, her superiors had called it. That, along with her facility for languages, had led to early temporary assignments as liaison officer between the Fourth Service and various planetary-defense air forces. She had tackled this challenge with a cheerful enthusiasm that had netted her commendations—and, more importantly, a logbook full of flying hours in all sorts of exotic aircraft not normally available to her Service. Thinking back on it, she realized she had also made a lot of friends. It was all in her records, the ones he purported to know by heart.

"Service records present deeds, not attitudes," he replied to her unspoken thoughts. Then, with a what-the-heck shrug, he settled into his chair beside her. "My best, Service-approved, five-minute lecture on Auryx culture. All right. Let's see, we are, as Van Wert mentioned, the product of a genetic engineering experiment generations back, which gives us all roughly the same physical characteristics. The purpose of the exercise, however, was to exploit, by careful breeding, certain innate mental capabilities—empathy, telepathy, that sort of thing. The experiments," he added hesitantly, with a defensive glance upward, "were to some degree successful."

"Oh?"

"The effect has been diluted, for the most part, over subsequent generations after the experiments were . . . discontinued. The race remains nearly pure in every other sense, though. Not so much through our prejudice against outsiders—though I do admit that one exists. But ours was an isolated planet; few outsiders came in, and the bulk of our people had no desire to leave. The war has changed that, of course. Those of us who remain are scattered for survival, but we are still left to ourselves by our allies."

"Tell me about your family, Kellen."

"My family. Well, my father's name was Cael—Makellen is a sort of diminutive, I guess you'd say. He was a pilot. He also taught at what you would call a university. A brilliant, gentle man who could dance tons of airplane around the sky like a leaf on a breeze. You would have liked him."

"What did he teach?"

"Science of the Mind," Mak said with a smile. "My mother, Ariel, was an artist. She worked miracles in glass—she could sculpt crystal as easily as some artists work in clay. She was also a musician—as are all Auryx, in one way or another. The true Auryx harp has a glass frame, producing a tone of unrivaled clarity. Ariel Darke's were among the best. I don't know if any yet exist."

Auglaize chose to ignore the implications of his last statement. "Siblings?"

"One each."

"Older or younger?"

"It matters not, child. You are a rarity among us: you are dead, but your family is still alive. Most of us are sole survivors."

"Lord, Kellen, I didn't know."

"It's not something I often discuss. I was an adolescent when the Karranganthians destroyed my home. One way and another, I and several of my friends escaped with the intention of mounting some sort of resistance. We were young; what did we know? It was a game. The rescue party found us wandering through the carnage, trying to pick up the pieces. My father's plane never made it off the ground, and I, mercifully, have no recollection of what happened to the rest of them. My friends and I were raised and trained Sixth Service. That's how it is with Sixth; you're either born to it, or a recruited survivor. No outside ties to distract. Most of us don't even know each other's real names. I was surprised that Van Wert told you his."

"Makellen Darke—is that your real name?"

"Yes. Most here know me simply as 'Darke.' "

Auglaize filed the information away for future reference. For now, though, there was something else bothering her. She did some mental arithmetic and shook her head. Lioth, the base she had supposedly died defending, had been her second combat assignment, her third out of the Academy, since they hadn't yet been at war when she graduated. That would mean that Makellen was still only in his teens. "How old are you?" she asked bluntly.

He laughed. "We are roughly contemporaries, Auglaise. I may have a year or two on you; I never stopped to figure it out. It didn't seem important."

"What I meant was, the Karranganthian invasion of Danton may have seemed like it happened in another lifetime, but in years Standard, it was only . . ."

He stopped her with a gesture. "Auglaise, it's not something I am allowed to discuss. I've said too much already."

"Tell her," came a quiet voice from the doorway. Van Wert hesitated momentarily, then crossed the room to stand behind Kellen's chair. "The monitoring system is turned off; tell her. If she is to be one of us, she has a right to know."

"It's not a pretty story," Makellen said. "We Auryx are by nature a race of poets and philosophers, Glaise—musicians and lovers of all life. Bred to peace and the pursuits of the mind, to us war and violence were as alien as the concept of universal brotherhood is to the Karranganthians.

"Until our children were wrenched from their mothers' arms and tortured before their eyes, our women raped and murdered— and our men left untouched except by the horrors they had been forced to witness, helpless to prevent. What better way to humble a proud race than kill off its hope of a future, condemn it to slow extinction? You know how the Karranganthians work. But they did not reckon with the capacity of a disciplined mind for ingenious methods of retaliation."

"The Sixth Service."

"Not the Sixth, child. The only. We have been dueling with the Karranganthians since long before the Alliance. We will be fighting them until one or both of our races is just a memory, even though a treaty be signed in this war. A duel to the death is our only chance for survival."

"Why?" she asked. "Why are the Karranganthians and the Auryx so hell-bent on mutual extermination?"

"I told you that our race was the product of a genetic experiment. It was a Karranganthian experiment."

Her involuntary gasp was the only indication of her reaction to the revelation. "Funny, you don't look Karranganthian," she managed to get out in a more or less normal tone.

"We're not supposed to. We were bred small and dark to make us instantly recognizable—so we could be kept in our place."

"Obviously, that part of the experiment was a failure."

"You could say that. When they started treating our people like livestock, pairing and breeding and exterminating offspring that didn't exhibit the proper characteristics, their own scientists rebelled. There were enough of us by that time, and the planet was far enough from reinforcement, that the rebellion was successful. The Auryx fled as far from the Karranganthian sphere of influence as possible, evolved their own language and culture, and sought to live peaceful, productive lives."

"Ah, yes," Auglaize said. "The Karranganthians never were ones to allow their mistakes to live to reproach them."

"No. Even after the Auryx became recognized members of the Confederacy, we were not safe. The Confederacy for years found some reason not to get involved, and our people continued to die. The Karranganthians became bolder, and the Danton raid was planned. I honestly do not believe they expected the Confederacy to react with force this time—not after so many 'incidents' passed by with mere verbal protests and ineffective sanctions levied by council.''

"Danton was a mixed colony of economic importance," she interjected ironically.

"Perhaps so. But as far as the Karranganthians are concerned, we are still recalcitrant children and they are the disciplining parents.''

"So, this war, into which have been drawn all the human worlds in the Confederacy, is merely a family squabble. I'm sure the inhabitants of the other planets devastated by the Karranganthians would be glad to hear that.''

"But, you see, even after we have pushed the Karranganthians back where they belong and Confederacy troops all pack up and go home, it still won't be over for *us*.'' Mak raked his fingers through his hair and turned away, breathing deeply to calm himself. "Look, Auglaise, our fight is not your fight. You still have hopes of peace and a home to go to. If that is what you decide to do, I won't try to stop you.''

"You mean, I have a choice?''

"Of course you have a choice," he answered abstractedly. "To the 'real world,' you are merely missing. If you stay with us, we will 'find' your body and ship it home for burial in a sealed coffin. Full Service honors, of course. Or, as soon as you are well enough, you can miraculously reappear among your own people, if you prefer. Though if you do go back, you will remember nothing of what has happened to you here.''

"Nothing, Makellen? Not even you?''

Mak shook his head. "Not even enough to regret the necessity. We will provide you with an adequate cover story, of course.''

"What if I do join you, and come across someone I know—knew? How do I explain?''

"If you like, we can restructure your face so that your best friend wouldn't recognize you. It's not an option we prefer, but when sufficient security risk is involved, it has been done.''

"It's not an option *I* prefer, either," Auglaize stated emphatically.

"Good. Then you simply convince this 'someone you knew' that he is mistaken and you aren't who he thinks you are. It's a little parlor trick that will appeal to you. You are strong-minded enough that it would be trivial for you to impose your will on someone to that small extent.''

"Then, how do I know if the choice is really mine, or if you people are just more strong-minded?''

"You're learning. That's where trust comes in. You have to believe that we see the path of the rest of your life as too important for any coercion. We didn't have to tell you that there was a choice to begin with, did we? But the decision does not have to be made now. There'll be time enough to discuss it again after you get back on your feet, get to know us better.''

Get to know *you* better, her mind supplied. Once again, he had given her a lot to think about.

Chapter 15

All measurement was arbitrary. Seasons varied in length from world to world, as did ratios of daylight to darkness and the cycles of natural satellites. Most of the worlds settled from Earth or Earth colonies stuck with traditional terminology, though an hour might be longer or shorter than sixty minutes, or the minutes themselves lengthened or shortened as needed to keep the requisite number. Thus, three Earth days meant a week to the residents of New Appalachicola and the average span of one period of darkness for the Dorians. Which made for a great deal of confusion.

When the original five nations of the Confederacy had banded together for mutual trade, communication, arbitration, and protection, the first order of business had been establishment of Coordinated Universal Measurement and Time Standards. Originally, the Mother Planet was, for obvious reasons, selected as Standard, and all other member worlds had to convert to it when dealing with each other. This worked out until nonhuman species were invited to join the Confederacy and took umbrage at the lack of consideration for *their* Mother Planets. Thus, the New Coordinated Universal Standards of Time and Measurement came into being. The Coordinated Universal Communications Standards had evolved into the New Coordinated Universal Communications Standards in the same manner. Most people cut through the bureaucratese and called both measurements and language Standard; few anymore even knew the official titles. Except at the five Service Academies, where "Seven Standard" became "Seven Days New Coordinated Universal Standard Time, sir!"

There had been one grading period at the Fourth Service Academy when the combined final exam for all courses consisted of the single problem: "Your next duty assignment is on Lyle Field, Fallowans. You will be accompanying a factory-fresh Gypsy. In what uniform combination will you report to your new commanding officer?" It sounded fairly simple, but unless one was a very good guesser, to answer correctly one had to know what type of transport would be necessary, in order to compute length of journey Standard, which could be converted to arrival date, Lyle Field time, telling what seasonal uniforms would be required—the specific combination to be determined by protocol which should already be memorized. Certain conversion charts, a pencil, and several sheets of paper were all that were provided for computations.

Now, with nothing better to do, Auglaize reworked this and several variations of the problem in her head. As much as it galled her to admit it, Van Wert had been right about her succumbing to boredom.

Well, it was really no wonder. With no physical activity to tire her out, she didn't need much sleep. On the other hand, both Van Wert and Kellen did, as well as having other duties besides baby-sitting her, so she tried to make as few demands on them as possible.

Then, of course, there were the three men Van Wert introduced to her as "psych wizards," who arrived twice a day to enliven her existence with their emotional bloodletting. Warren, Vinton, and Sandusky—Dusky, she immediately dubbed him—all appeared to have been stamped out of the same mold as the other two Auryx men. Where were all the Auryx women? she wondered. Luckily for quick identification, each man actually did wear a different color.

Life was not dull with these three around. The first thing they had done was to push her into the state that everyone supposedly feared so much, her total withdrawal into her own mind, from which it had taken Kellen several feverish minutes to recover her. After that, they worked on teaching her to recognize the warning signs accompanying the onset of this withdrawal so that eventually she could combat it. In the process she would have to remember every agonizing moment of her ordeal at the hands of the Karranganthians, to actually relive the experience not once but many times, while the trio minutely examined her emotions, her thoughts, her every reaction. In the end, she was assured, she would be able to remember what she wanted to remember, and it would hold no more horrors for her.

Meanwhile, these sessions boiled down to sheer hell. Perversely, she looked forward to them simply because they presented a challenge—not only to conquer her own reaction to traumatic memories, but to build up a resistance to the psychs' probing. Warren proved to her, time and time again, that if he could just get her to look into the deep purple velvet of his eyes, he could reach into her mind and extract the information he wanted as easily as drawing a snail from its shell. She would find herself paralyzed, unable to struggle free until he released her. That kind of intrusion on the privacy of her thoughts, she resolved, was going to stop.

As for Makellen—having moved a cot back into her room, he had appointed himself in charge of her physical and mental wellbeing. Upon awakening every morning, he'd pad out barefoot in his bathrobe to attend to his own needs, then return fed, groomed, and properly uniformed to attend to hers. From her first awareness—even before, she was told—it had been Makellen, almost exclusively, who had taken care of her, who had washed her face, cleaned her teeth, kept her hair shining and snarl-free. This last was his favorite chore; he loved running his fingers through the thick, ever-lengthening copper-brown-gold strands, or brushing them until the electricity in the air pulled them out into a reddish haze around her face, tickling her nose and making her giggle. She, in turn, liked to tease him about having it cut back to Fourth Service regulations, somewhat shorter than his. It was nice to be told she was beautiful, even though she didn't believe it herself.

His challenge came in inventing imaginative means to keep her sanity intact and boredom at bay. At first, he spent hours reading aloud to her, even contriving a way to hold a book so that she could read aloud to him. Enjoyable recreation, but limited. She could only do it when he was there, and, while he would have remained at her side every waking moment had she willed it, she figured that would be the quickest way to drive them both crazy.

His solution: a wafer-thin computer monitor mounted on the Van Wert at a comfortable distance from her face so that she could read on her own. A sensor followed her eye movements to automatically turn pages, and a voice-activated microphone relayed her preferences to the recreation computer. There was also a hookup with their communications control so that she could talk to Kellen any time she felt the need, and vice versa.

The next trick Makellen pulled out of his electric-blue sleeve was her "window." With the enhanced computerized holographic imaging technology usually reserved for flight and combat simulators, he created several breathtaking living landscapes for her, complete with sunlit warmth, the sounds of birds and insects, and appropriately scented breezes. Somehow, he had found the time to program in different seasons, different times of day, places he thought she would like to see, all framed in a homey red-curtained window reminiscent of the one in her bedroom back home.

Music was his best innovation. He had a beautiful singing voice and wasn't shy about entertaining her with it and the upright, lap-held, wooden-framed instrument that was the Auryx harp. With Van Wert's reminder that recordings were available of everything touching Auglaize's constantly monitored world, she was provided with two tiny but powerful speakers mounted on either side of her pillow. Not only could she play back Kellen's singing any time she wanted, but her unseen—and hitherto unheard—watchers in Van Wert's monitoring room could share and discuss their favorite compositions with her. The result was a computerized music-appreciation course that would have been the envy of the universities of several worlds.

Given her quick mind and natural curiosity, it was inevitable that she would develop an interest in separating the jumble of phonemes of Mak's songs into understandable language. Thus, enthusiastic lessons in Auryx grammar and culture were added to her daily routine. And that was how she discovered that the "lullaby" Kellen so often sang to her was, in reality, one of the tenderest love ballads ever written in any language—and quite impossible to translate.

Auglaize held the knowledge close to her heart, along with the warm pleasure that it gave her. The hours between his visits stretched considerably longer than the too-brief intervals when he was at her side.

To her, Kellen's laugh was the sunshine; it filled the room with tiny bubbles that tickled the ears and pushed even the most recalcitrant facial muscles into a smile. She loved to watch him talk, watch light and shadows play over his mobile face, catch the flash of pearl white but endearingly less than even teeth between finely drawn lips that could shape a kiss as expertly as they could turn a phrase. And his eyes, his eyes were the peculiar blue/indigo of the night sky after the colors of sunset had faded and the first stars had come out, with a sparkle that he was never quite able to suppress.

His hands were perfect, his shape was perfect, and he moved with an unconscious grace that made her breath catch in her throat and her pulse rate double.

In short, he was quite the handsomest man she had ever seen—and with her usual sense of humor, Auglaize recognized in herself all the nauseating symptoms of a woman in love.

Odd, then, that her last memory of Makellen Darke should center around her ordering him from her sight in a rage.

Chapter 16

It was a wonder they didn't fight more often. Two strong-willed people in close contact, both chafing at confinement, both frustrated with circumstances that allowed a physical attraction so intense that sometimes the merest touch was sheer torture for them both, but prevented them from any real intimacy. Makellen, at least, could get out into the air for a while, take long walks—even find himself a woman if need be. Auglaize, on the other hand, physically active all her life, was flat on her back without even thumbs to twiddle, and envied him his freedom. Never again would she take for granted the joys of motion, the physical engineering of joints and muscles!

Of course, Van Wert slowly began letting her feel her body—only for short intervals, but she was allowed awareness of belly and knees and elbows and fingers and toes. There was occasionally pain and always a vague discomfort, but that didn't matter. Eventually, near the end of her sojourn in the Womb, she would be given some simple exercises to start rebuilding muscle tone.

She and Kellen savored every triumph together, even dared to talk about the day that she would be free of her life-restoring prison.

They would talk—and then he would walk away to attend to his other duties.

The fly in the ointment as far as Kellen was concerned seemed to be Morgan Troy. Auglaize seldom spoke of her former love, partly because she saw no need to and partly because the mere mention of the name was enough to set Makellen's teeth on edge.

And she quite honestly couldn't understand why. Insecurity was the last thing she would ever have expected of Makellen Darke; he was so confident, so sure of himself. As for her relationship with Troy—he had gone his way, she had gone hers, and they had always gravitated back to each other, to compare notes and laugh together over their less successful romantic sorties. Buddies. Very *affectionate* buddies. Oh, very well, she had been in love with the man, but it hadn't been the kind of love upon which to build a lasting relationship. She saw that now. Now that Kellen had come into her life.

Trying to convince *him* of that, though, was a losing battle. In fact, most of her attempts ended in a vicious display of temper on both their parts—for all his sweetness and light, Makellen possessed a disposition at least as hotheaded as her own, tempered with considerably less self-control. Van Wert's intervention was occasionally necessary.

So the stage was set for that last battle, when the combined pressures of confinement, boredom, claustrophobia, frustration, and jealousy all came together in an explosive brew. It started innocently enough, with Mak stating, "You know, you never did tell me how you and Troy happened to meet."

Her reply was a cautious attempt to change the subject.

"Really, Glaise, I'd like to know. You keep telling me how much we would have liked each other. I took the liberty of taking a peek at his Service records, and I was impressed."

"You *would* have liked each other; you and Troy are a lot more alike than I care to contemplate. Listen, Mak, do you think you could sneak me in just a tiny little piece of chocolate?"

"No," came an amused voice from above. Van Wert, as usual. It was good to know that he was up there.

"That answers your question," Kellen interjected. "Now, why don't you answer mine?"

"Because we'll end up yelling at each other."

"I just asked how the two of you met. Seems like a fairly innocuous question."

"*He* was a persistent son of a bitch, too. All right. I got into some trouble my first year at the Academy, and he helped me out of it. We decided we liked each other.''

"What kind of trouble?''

"Do the words, 'I'd rather not discuss it' mean anything to you?'' Oh, damn. That was a particularly stupid thing to say. Now he'd never let it rest. If she didn't answer his question, he'd keep after her until she either told him in self-defense or ordered him from the room. Which would make him even more persistent. Auglaize never even considered making up a plausible lie. How could she lie to someone who made a practice of looking into her soul?

"All right, Makellen.'' She sighed, defeated. "There was an upperclassman in our cadet squadron who liked to coerce first- and second-term cadets into bed. I was one of his . . . conquests. Hey,'' she added as Kellen's eyes narrowed, "he threatened to have me thrown out of the Academy, and I knew he could have done it. I hated him, but I hated myself even more. Not an episode in my life that I am particularly proud of.''

"Obviously, Troy found out somehow.''

"Yeah. The guy actually had the balls to brag about it, and Troy came to me for confirmation. I figured he wanted some for himself, so I went for his throat. If I had been a little stronger or a little more experienced, I might have made the mistake of my life. As it was, he wore a necklace of my fingerprints for a while.'' A thought struck her, and she laughed harshly. "Ironic, is it not, that in the end I strangled him?''

"Ah, child.'' Kellen sighed. "So, what happened?''

"Cadets pretty much watch out for their own. When word got around of what had happened to me, we rounded up proof that I hadn't been the first or only wog Scioto had forced himself on. A dozen others came forward. A Cadet Board was convened, we all testified, and poor Sci met with a terrible accident which necessitated extensive reconstructive surgery and artificial hormones for the rest of his life. It also resulted in his quiet expulsion from the Academy.''

"You got away with it?''

"Sure. The administration didn't want to know the details. If we'd brought formal charges, Sci still would have been expelled, probably would have brought down a stiff sentence in a military prison, and definitely would have created all kinds of scandal. It wouldn't have done our own careers any good, either. As it was, things settled down real fast. Of course, I still got physically ill every time Sci's name came up, and went into hysterics if anyone touched me, but the others assured me it was par for the course, and I'd get over it in time."

"Not exactly the kind of help I would have prescribed."

"Troy's sentiments exactly. By the ripe old age of seventeen, he had developed a fairly refined appreciation of the basic sensual pleasures, and was not at all happy at the possibility of emotional scars preventing anyone from developing the same appreciation. Therefore, he took matters into his own hands, and signed me out for the weekend."

She knew she had said too much even before Mak's eyebrows came crashing together at the oblique confirmation that Troy's therapy had entailed much more than polite conversation over tea. "So the bastard exploited the situation," he muttered darkly.

"He didn't do anything I didn't consent to, my friend. At that, it still took the better part of that weekend for him to get me to trust him enough."

Makellen's answer was a glare.

"Look, Mak, I was no prize package at thirteen, certainly not what Troy was attracted to, and I knew it. He did care about me, though, and years later he still agonized over whether he had done the right thing. Particularly since soon after our only weekend together, he left on an Academy exchange program. But, he said, a person always remembers the first time, and when I thought of mine, he wanted me to remember a lover, not a rapist. No, his exact words were, 'I want you to remember *me*.' I didn't see him again for years, but I certainly did remember him. And he remembered me."

"How touching."

Auglaize was beginning to lose it. She knew she should have said something soothing to Mak's ego, but she was just about fed up. "I thought so. We had some good times together over the years, Troy and I. When I got to my last duty station, there he was to greet me. Dancer Flight by rights should have been his, but he recommended me because I was better suited for the job—then was content to be my wingman when I was promoted over him. A very special man, Morgan Troy."

"I'm sure. What chance for a mere mortal against such a paragon?" Mak said bitterly.

"What is your problem, Darke? You brought the subject up!"

He rose, his face shadowed, his voice husky. "For the last time, I assure you."

"Makellen, what do you want from me?"

"You don't know by now? No. Just drop it, Glaise."

"Kellen, for God's sake!"

"I said, drop it, DeWellesthar!" he thundered, the overstretched thread of his temper snapping.

Auglaize cursed herself for not being able to reach out to him, and him for being such a stiff-necked, unreasonable child of a gypsy cur.

Makellen stared at her coldly for a full minute before turning abruptly. "I need some air."

"Oh, that's just great, Darke. Go on then, get your ass out of here," she yelled after him, "and don't bother coming back!"

"Could you stand some unsolicited advice from a not-so-disinterested observer, Flight Leader?"

The soft voice in her ear made her jump; she hadn't heard Van Wert come in. The scent of Mak's anger was still on the air, and she shivered. "God, why do we do that to each other?"

"You don't really need an answer, do you? The man is so much in love with you he can't think straight."

"This is not a situation I know how to handle, Davis."

"So I've noticed. Consider this, child: perhaps he uses Troy as a convenient shield against his own fears."

"What could Kellen possibly be afraid of?"

"I already told you, the man is in love. Sometimes a person can be so afraid of losing someone he loves that he will take any excuse to push her away before she can leave him."

"That doesn't make a whole lot of sense."

"My dear Flight Leader, *love* does not make a whole lot of sense."

"You've got that right! It was so much simpler with Troy. Although that may have been because we could jump each other whenever we felt like it." She made a face, and Van Wert chuckled. "You know what's frightening to me?"

"What's that?"

"When I try to imagine a future for myself without Kellen, I can't. It hurts too much. I've never felt that way about anybody before."

His mouth curved in a slight smile of amusement, but his expression remained serious. "For Kellen's sake, I'm relieved. I must warn you, though, They are very displeased about the situation."

" 'They'? Once and for all, Van Wert, who the hell are 'They'?"

"The ruling Council who directs those who direct our Service."

Auglaize whistled softly. "Mak must be pretty high up on the chain of command to elicit such personal interest."

"He has a very promising career."

"Obviously, I don't fit into their plans for him. I take it that your Service discourages the pairing off of its members."

"No. Many of us are—or have been—married. I myself am lucky enough to have a beautiful wife of many years, who also happens to be under Kellen's command. Of course, she flies only rarely now."

"I had wondered . . . I mean, I haven't met any Auryx women. Even—up there." She pointed with her chin in the general direction of the monitoring booth. "I was beginning to wonder if there were any."

"Not many, child. There are in fact so few that they have assumed the role of breeders, encouraged to bear children to as many different men as they desire to enlarge the gene pool—then those children are hidden away in places of safety so that they can mature and breed and fight and begin the cycle all over again."

"It's because I'm not Auryx, then," Auglaize pursued.

"No, child. It isn't you at all. It's Darke. They have plans for him that require his single-minded devotion to the Service. He must have women, of course, if that's what he wants, but not one who may possibly divide his loyalties."

"Divide his loyalties?"

"If it came to a choice between you and the Service . . ."

"Son of a bitch," she breathed in understanding. "Does Makellen know about this?"

Van Wert met her eyes for a fraction of a second, then looked away. "What They want for Kellen and what Kellen wants for himself are . . . diametrically opposed at this point."

"What do I do, Davis?"

"Let him determine his own future. However, you could help by telling him how you feel about him, before . . ."

"Before it's too late?"

"There's always that possibility, too. Sometimes, the dying is easier when a man knows he'll be mourned. Before he makes the wrong choice, is what I was going to say. I know it's not easy for you, but tell him. Because out there"—he jerked his head toward the wall—"people are killing each other. Makellen's duty routinely takes him into the thick of it, as will yours when you're able."

Auglaize smiled her thanks, and he uncharacteristically bent forward to kiss the tip of her nose. "You're a good friend, Dave."

"I hope so, Flight Leader. For all our sakes, I hope so."

It was a sheepish Makellen who appeared a long while later. "Forgive me," he said simply. "I'm an ass."

"Succinctly put. Even so, I think it's time we settled this thing once and for all."

He nodded, resigned. Fearful. "You're right; we have to settle it. Say what you have to say."

"Mak, in my Service, touching of any kind except that strictly required in the performance of our duties is prohibited, not just during working hours but any time we are in uniform. Even out of uniform, public display of affection is strongly discouraged. While verbal declarations aren't forbidden, they are frowned upon. From the moment I took my cadet oath, I had this drilled into me. It's the way I am."

"In our Service, we are encouraged to express ourselves freely. It's the way *I* am. So where does that leave us?" he asked coolly.

"No matter. I have been alone most of my life. When you are gone, I shall be alone again. I expect I'll survive."

"Excuse me, just when did I say anything about leaving? I'm not letting you push me out of your life that easily, Darke. In fact, you're going to be stuck with me for the rest of it, if I have any say in the matter."

Mak tipped his head back and squeezed his eyes shut, his tightly meshed lashes wet. "Don't stay with me out of pity, Auglaise, or gratitude, or friendship, or because I excite you physically. You would be doing neither of us any favors."

"Kell, I love you." The words were choked, barely audible, but she got them out. "There was an empty place inside of me that I wasn't even aware of until you moved in to fill it up."

The blue eyes opened slowly, damp-bright but clear, to level that peculiar, soul-searching stare on her. Then, his face sun-rayed into a smile; his head tipped back again, and his shoulders shook with laughter.

"Lord knows I may not always be physically faithful to you," she continued almost nervously. "I couldn't promise Troy that, and I won't promise you. He taught me too well."

"I don't care if there are others, as long as I'm the first!"

"So you say now. Well, that much, at least, I will promise you. When I am free of this thing, you will be the first. Now, for God's sake, will you quit being so jealous of poor Troy? He's dead, and I for one don't believe in ghosts."

The sunshine smile was back. "You are a part of my soul," he said in a whisper, just before his mouth touched hers.

Oh, God, she wanted him! In a matter of weeks, she'd be able to feel his arms around her; after that, another handspan of days before they could truly be together. That was the farthest ahead she would let herself think. Down the road waited the world, the war, and any number of events that could wrench them apart.

As if he had read her thoughts, he jerked away suddenly, eyes wide, face frozen. "Oh, ye lords of creation, not now! Not just when—" He was on his feet before the door banged open, and out in the hall before whoever awaited him had even made himself known.

Makellen was back as quickly, more upset than Auglaize had ever seen him. "Glaise, my love, something has happened. I have to go. It may be a while before I can come back to you, but I will come back. I promise you," he told her breathlessly.

Fear sat like a dead weight on her chest at the suddenness of it all. "What is it, Mak?"

"I don't have time to explain, and oh, my Auglaise, I couldn't even if I did. It is . . . my duty; leave it at that. You understand?" Seeing the vein jumping in her neck, he tried to reassure her, his words jumbling together in his haste. "Ah, no, love, you have nothing to fear; this area is secure. I swear to you, you'll never fall into their hands alive again."

"Cheering thought." She strove to be lighthearted as she conveyed her real fear. "See that you don't, either, Makellen. You mean too much to me alive. Go on, get out of here, before they drag you. Do whatever it is you have to do, and keep yourself safe." Above all, keep yourself safe! "Maybe I'll be out of this contraption when you get back."

"I want to walk with you in the garden, Auglaise, and lie with you under the stars. I want to hear you say you'll never need anyone else as long as I am there—"

"Darke!" a voice interrupted urgently from the hallway.

"Coming!" He dropped a quick kiss on her forehead and dashed toward the door. A second later, he was back, the kiss on her mouth deep enough to bring tears to her eyes.

"Darke, now! You've barely time to change as it is."

"I will come back to you, Glaise. I swear it!"

"I love you, Makellen," she called to his back.

"Wait for me!"

The door swung shut.

"I'll never need anyone else as long as you are there," Auglaize whispered into the frightening silence he had left behind.

Chapter 17

The days dragged interminably without Makellen, but if there was one thing Auglaize had learned from this whole ordeal, it was patience. She waited unquestionably for his return. After all, he had promised, had he not?

He had promised to be at her side for what Van Wert facetiously referred to as "systems checks," when she swallowed tracers so that digestive functions could be tested. Submitted meekly to more tracers being injected into her neck to outline patterns of blood flow. Allowed technicians to attach sensors to her head so that they could stimulate and track nerve impulses. It was Davis who figuratively held her hand throughout this necessary torment.

Makellen had promised to be there on the momentous day that she was taken out of the tube, frustratingly weak in spite of the exercises and with skin so sensitive that the very air currents caused pain. His face would be the first thing she would touch. He would bring her her first real meal, and feed her himself, if need be. A med, one of the few Auryx women left alive by the Karranganthians, had that honor. Auglaize never asked.

Some crooked fingers had to be repaired and one or two other defects remedied. She went to sleep with the certainty that Mak would be beside her when she woke up. But a turquoise-eyed cadet was sitting in Kellen's chair when Auglaize opened her eyes.

Surely Mak would be back in time for her long-awaited first excursion outside. But it was another patient, a stiff, cool, almost angry man with wired jaws and a heavily bandaged face who showed her Mak's cherished gardens and pointed out, in Standard sign, constellations in a night sky she had never before seen.

"Where is he, Davis?" she finally asked Van Wert.

His answer was a shake of the head and a forefinger against his lips before he changed the subject.

Right after Van Wert left her, Auglaize heard angry voices in the hall. When they stopped, the door opened and he stood there with thunder in his face but tears in his voice. "Flight Leader," he finally said, the appellation as always taking on the tone of an endearment. "Flight Leader, you no longer need me, and I have other patients. You understand."

She understood nothing save that for some reason her staunchest ally was being taken from her. "Visit me occasionally?"

"If I can, child. When you are able, come to me. But don't ever ask . . ." The cryptic warning was left unfinished. Auglaize knew, though, that he meant not to ask about Makellen, that her one query had somehow resulted in her removal from Van Wert's care.

What was going on? Where was Kellen that his mere mention caused such repercussions? When in the name of heaven would he come back to her?

Later than night, patience exhausted, she cried out for him in her sleep, continued to scream his name until someone rushed in to sedate her. The next day, her team of psychs arrived at the crack of dawn to discuss this dream man she had conjured up. No matter how real he had seemed, they informed her, he had never existed.

That was when she knew that Makellen Darke was dead.

It took all three psychs to sedate her again.

Interim: Quarters of the Commander, O'Brian's Stake

Michael pushed himself away from the computer console with a sigh. Another dead end in his records search for information on the elusive Paulding Callicoon. Since Dancer had first reported the Karranganthian's identity, Michael had nearly exhausted all of the considerable resources at his disposal, and had found nothing concerning the man postdating his reported defection.

Of course, the records of how and where the Confederacy had exploited Callicoon's talents would be sealed and highly classified, but there wasn't much that was kept from the eyes of the Sixth Service Commander. If legal inquiries produced no results, he'd have to resort to illegal ones. But if the information existed at all, Michael *would* have it.

Thus, with a keystroke and two whispered commands, he had set into motion yet another search. All that was left to do was wait.

Sleep was his first impulse, a couple hours' respite for his exhausted body. On the heels of that thought came a second: Dancer. What would it hurt for him to lie down beside her for that couple of hours? She need never know, just as she'd never known in the past . . .

The past! Suddenly what had been nagging at the back of his mind for hours burst to the forefront. Yes, Dancer had been troubled, but it wasn't her ambivalence about Antonia DeWellesthar that disturbed her slumber, nor excitement over her childhood dream of flying with the Team about to come true on the morrow. Not even pleasant fantasies concerning a "drop dead handsome" Karranganthian defector.

No, it was the past troubling his red-haired second-in-command. Specifically, her early days with Sixth, those days full of pain and uncertainty, loss and love and loss again, alienation, homesickness—Michael had been so sure he was going to lose her back to her own Service. Turbulent days for him, too.

He moved silently toward the bedroom, stopping in the doorway, from which he could see her sitting motionless on the windowsill. The battle raging inside her certainly wasn't visible on her face, though her wide-open eyes were glassy with unshed tears as they stared out over a landscape she didn't see. The tumult in her mind, though, he could almost reach out and touch.

Then, as he watched, her lips soundlessly shaped a word, just one, but enough to make the Commander's stomach lurch. ''Makellen . . .''

So. She remembered Darke. It had taken her a dozen years, but she had remembered. Well, good for her! Though of what possible benefit the knowledge would be to her now, he couldn't fathom.

She stirred, almost back with him from that faraway place of remembrances. Almost back, but still struggling.

It's all right, child, he wordlessly reassured her. I'm here, and it's all right.

Dancer relaxed, eased her mind toward him, but he stopped her. Not yet. There was more that she should know. Again, what possible use it would be to her in her dealings with false Auglaizes and Karranganthian spies—defectors—he wasn't sure. Perhaps it was only to ease his own conscience that he began, one by one, to remove the rest of the memory blocks he had been forced to implant between Dancer and her past.

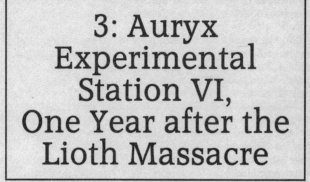

3: Auryx Experimental Station VI, One Year after the Lioth Massacre

Chapter 18

The next time Auglaize opened her eyes, it was to an apparition standing at the foot of her bed. She blinked hard to make sure she really was awake. The man was Auryx, but as different from Makellen Darke as . . . well, dark from light. He was attired in unrelieved black, from the soles of his handmade, calf-hugging boots to the high-necked tunic under a nonstandard quilted flying jacket. His hair, black and glossy as a raven's wing, fell into soft waves despite the short regulation-style haircut, and his eyes . . . his eyes were of a deep-sea blue that seemingly took light in, but didn't let it out again. Slight he was, and only a couple of inches taller than Auglaize, but with such an aura of power that she knew: this man was a Commander—or the devil incarnate.

Stripping off his supple leather gloves to reveal characteristic Auryx slender-fingered, graceful hands, he glided over to her side.

"So, Dancer, you're finally awake. We had begun to despair." The resonant voice was barely audible, yet Auglaize heard each syllable as distinctly as if he had shouted in her ear. "You are working for me now. How soon before you can be at your duties?"

That was her introduction to Michael.

She saw the Commander often after that, too often. Blessed with more than her share of nerve, she hadn't yet let anyone intimidate her, not even a Karranganthian "executioner." But she was afraid of Michael. She would almost have preferred the standard torture; one knew what to expect—it was going to hurt. Michael's brand of torment was more subtle, however: he preyed on the mind. Auglaize never knew when she was going to turn around and find him watching. His coldness, the speculation in his eyes every time he looked at her, the biting sarcasm in his voice, his deliberate efforts to cause her pain, both physical and emotional, all conspired to

119

reduce her to the status of a child begging for parental approval and meeting only contempt.

In self-defense, Auglaize learned to return sarcasm for sarcasm—after all, the penalty for insubordination could scarcely be any worse than what she was already enduring from him—all the while strengthening her determination to excel, though every muscle in her body had to be retrained. While Makellen had urged her to take one day at a time, under Michael's too-watchful eye she was working steadfastly toward the day when she would not only be on her feet again, but would have some semblance of her old flying skills back. To prove herself to him, though she didn't look at it in quite those terms. Everything along the way was incidental.

The physical-therapy troops didn't approve of what they called her "shortcuts," but Auglaize got her way, deriving no small satisfaction from the fact that as hard as the Commander tried to push her, she was always at least one jump ahead of him. The payment was bruises and aching muscles, but the pain was worth it—if only for the one time she surprised a grudging approval in his usually expressionless eyes.

Every night, just before she drifted off into an exhausted slumber, she indulged herself in elaborate fantasies of blowing her fearless leader out of the sky. Not that she really wished him ill, in spite of his callous treatment of her. No, she only wanted to see him humbled, human, not so everlastingly damnably cocksure of himself. She wanted to see him smile at her as she had in her dreams, the ones over which she had no control. The ones her cheeks flamed at the thought of.

Neither fantasy did she discuss in those daily sessions with the psychs. Her imaginary life was none of their business, and her resistance even to Warren's will-stealing eyes had built to the point that they could no longer force her to disclose information she preferred to keep to herself. Her increasingly frequent attacks of claustrophobia they attributed to stress and dismissed with a few breathing exercises. The "real problem" upon which they concentrated—and which she resisted more constructively—was convincing her that the man she had "fancied herself in love with" had never existed.

Why was it so important that Makellen Darke be eradicated from her mind? Auglaize asked herself time and time again. Was that the way the Auryx routinely dealt with the deaths of loved ones, or were "They" just getting revenge upon her for diverting his affections? Occasionally—just occasionally—she wondered if she had unwittingly been the cause of his death.

She would never know. Even Van Wert, who was also Makellen's longtime friend and brother-of-the-mind Davis Ashur, refused to speak of him.

So now, outwardly, at least, Auglaize was beginning to accept the fiction. She knew Makellen had existed, had died mysteriously on that last mission when he had been called away so abruptly; even Warren's hypnotic stare would never convince her otherwise. By herself, she mastered the grief, the loneliness, the irrational feeling of betrayal that he had not kept his promise to return—and the mind-searing fear that it was somehow all her fault. Mastered, but did not forget. Every once in a while, when it seemed too much for her to bear alone, she would consider succumbing to the psychs' efforts to erase him from her mind.

Only briefly, though, and with a rush of guilt at the thought. Van Wert's prophetic words would always haunt her: Sometimes the dying is easier when a man knows there's someone to mourn him.

The trust was hers. She accepted it.

Chapter 19

Then, the day arrived that Auglaize had been looking forward to for half her life, it seemed—her first shot at the complex's basic flight simulator. Her flying clothes and equipment were her own, salvaged from the boxes of personal effects simply because she couldn't bear to part with them. There was confidence woven into the cloth; even so, her palms were sweaty as she drew on her gloves, then awkwardly bundled her now-shoulder-length hair under her helmet.

The shape of the seat felt good the entire length of her body; the restraints, as the techs buckled her in, were like the welcoming embrace of an old friend. The faintly metallic smell of the breathing apparatus, the slightly distorted voices through the helmet receiver; the dials, knobs, switches of the controls; the simulated hum and vibration of the engine—all were so achingly familiar that she feared she was going to break down and cry. Flying was the only thing Auglaize had ever wanted to do with her life, and now, at last, she could let herself believe that she would soon be living again.

Then the computers came on line.

Fifteen minutes of it was all she could take, and it was the longest fifteen minutes of her life. "Interesting technique, Dancer," the sim instructor stated as she unstrapped.

"Cram it, Wayne," she replied wearily. All she wanted to do was crawl back to her room and lick her wounds, and—maybe later, when she had the energy—kick out a wall. But when she emerged from her computerized tormentor, shaking and defeated, her Auryx tormentor was there waiting. Michael. That was all she needed.

"Congratulations, Dancer, on the worst primary sim flight I have ever been privileged to witness."

Charming, charming man. She tried to brush him off with a cool "Thanks," but what came out was a sob.

His reaction was scalding. "Damn it, DeWellesthar, I can't . . . oh, come on!" Suddenly, his arm was around her shoulders and he was steering her down the long corridor toward the living quarters. Stunned and still battling for self-control, she didn't protest, even when instead of turning right into the section that contained her room, he went straight on into a part of the complex that she had never seen before. The door closed behind them, locking them together, alone, in what she instantly recognized as his combination office/sleeping accommodations.

"If I had known it would be so easy to persuade a woman to accompany me to my quarters, I would have tried it long ago," he quipped.

Michael, joking? Sarcastic, she had seen him, altogether too often, but joking? Auglaize stole a sidelong glance at her companion and received another shock as he flashed her a dazzling smile.

"I think it's about time you and I got to know each other a little better. No, not that way," he added hastily as her head turned to where his bunk should have been. "Not that I am disinterested. I simply do not have the time."

If his casual statement was calculated to put her at ease, it had the desired effect. Auglaize may have feared for her life, but at least she didn't have to worry about her virtue. At the thought, she even managed a tiny answering smile.

Michael nodded approval as he indicated a deep-cushioned armchair. "Sit." He lowered himself into a wooden rocker opposite, and folded his hands in his lap. "Comfortable? Excellent. Let's talk about today. What happened?"

Here it comes, she thought, meeting his eyes defiantly. "I fracked up."

"Specifically?"

"Specifically, Fourth Service's finest did not manage to perform even one routine maneuver correctly. I crashed three times on take-off. On takeoff, for God's sake!"

"I must admit that takes a certain degree of talent."

"Finally, we agree on something!" Dancer held up her hands, palms out and fingers spread, and flexed each joint one after the other. "I was a natural, Michael. One of the best. Now I can't even do a decent takeoff in a damned primary sim!" There followed a string of expletives that ended with her sobbing out her frustration, her despair, and her fear against the silky black fabric covering his shoulder. She forgot whose arms were around her, or she just plain didn't care.

Astonishingly, Michael said not one word, made no sound of either sympathy or condemnation. He only held her close, rocked her slowly, and let her cry. Gradually, with his unhurried breathing and the slow and steady beating of his heart, a comforting warmth crept in, an unspoken understanding. Auglaize had started reassembling the scattered remnants of her self-control when he reached over to palm the damp hair back from her face with a gesture she'd never thought to feel again.

"Makellen," she gasped painfully, and the sobs started again.

"No, child," Michael stated with a gentleness of which she had not imagined him capable. "Never Makellen again. Weep for him, then forget."

When she tried to shake her head, his hand pressed it to his shoulder, his thumb almost absentmindedly stroking her cheek. Then she realized that he knew of her deception of the psychs, and was giving her an out.

Why? Why had the tyrant suddenly assumed the role of protector? Was it some new form of amusement at her expense? This time, when Auglaize pulled back, he let her. For at least an eternity, she tried to read his impassive face for some clue to his behavior.

He continued to regard her steadily, a tiny sparkle working its way up from the velvet depths of his eyes. When she sat up, he had stopped rocking, ceasing the slow, rhythmical tensing and relaxing of muscles in legs that by now must be numb from midthigh down from her weight. His arms stayed around her, but loosely, allowing her to go, stay, or make a complete fool of herself again, as she chose.

Go, she wouldn't; she liked it too well where she was, well enough to make it worth the risk. It wasn't the first time she had been so acutely aware of Michael as a man—and a damned attractive one at that—but it was the first time she hadn't fought it. It would be so natural to simply lean forward and taste that beautifully defined mouth now tantalizingly relaxed in a half smile.

What would he do, she wondered, if she actually presumed to kiss him? Would he freeze in indignation at her effrontery? Or would he melt into her arms as she so longed to melt into his?

"Why don't you try it and find out?" he suggested softly.

Involuntarily, her eyes searched the room again.

"The bedroom is behind me, to your right."

Blushing, Auglaize informed him that his perception was more than a little unnerving.

That elusive sparkle burst to the surface as the corners of his eyes crinkled into a full-blown smile. "Your train of thought isn't all that difficult to follow. For instance, at this moment, you're recalling all the stories you've heard about Auryx clairvoyance." At her reluctant nod, he continued, "I'll tell you our secret, Dancer: most so-called mind-reading is merely observation. Intuition, you would call it, though it's even simpler than that. We 'mysterious Auryx' are just trained from birth to observe. You do it yourself. Body language. Tone of voice. Scent. Eye contact, or lack thereof." His eyes locked briefly with hers before he shifted his gaze. "A little bit of hypnotism, though we seldom exert the kind of control over others for which we are so feared. It's a talent in which few of us are instructed."

Dancer had no doubt whatsoever that Michael was one of the few.

"The 'trick' isn't anything you can't learn," he continued, ignoring the aside he surely saw in her face. "And in the process of learning how to read others, you also learn how to make yourself unreadable."

Could it be . . . was he obliquely trying to tell her that it hadn't been merely wishful thinking those rare times she thought she detected compassion, almost even affection, behind those hooded eyes? It was quite possible that the man wasn't an inhuman monster after all. A novel concept.

This time, he replied to her unspoken thoughts. "You're learning already. Rule Number One: Always trust your instincts. You knew well enough to do that when you were flying."

"When I *was* flying is right," she snorted.

"It's not like you to give up this easily."

"Easily? Give me a break, Commander! You were there! You saw me!"

"I saw you attempting something for which you were not yet ready."

"Not ready? It's all I've been working towards since I got out of that . . . thing!"

"I say again, you were not ready. Everyone knew that but you."

"Wait a minute." Comprehension made her voice sharp. "You set this whole thing up, didn't you?"

"No. I allowed it to happen. There's a difference."

"Let's not split hairs, Michael. You imply that you could have stopped me from making a total ass of myself, yet you didn't do it. I hope you had a damned good laugh."

"Child." The word came out on a long, exasperated exhalation. "We must all be allowed to make our own mistakes. I was there to make sure you learned from yours."

"Oh, I learned, all right, you black-haired son of a bitch. If I still had my wings, I'd throw them in your face!"

"So, you *do* intend to give up because of one failure." His voice was even.

"Failure? A mild term for that debacle!"

The corners of his lips twitched. "Momentous failure, then. Tell me, Dancer, were you named for your flight, or was your flight named for you?"

"This is a hell of a time for twenty questions."

"Just answer."

"Dancer has been my nickname since pilot training," she replied shortly. The good old days, when air-to-air combat was just a game and your friends didn't die before your eyes.

"Why 'Dancer'? Why not 'Red'? or 'Ace'? Or any one of the hundreds of other nicknames of which your culture seems so fond?"

"What's that got to do with . . . all right, all right!" she acquiesced as the blue of his eyes got two shades darker. Michael didn't need hypnotism; he had intimidation going for him. "I had a little problem with formation flying."

"A little problem. Now who's understating? Wasn't there something about a near midair collision? Not to mention your initial average of three landings for every takeoff?"

"You are a sadistic bastard, you know that, Commander?"

"So I have been informed—though I believe the full epithet went something like, 'sick, sadistic bastard of a perverted storm trooper,' with a 'face of granite and the mind of a gonad' or some such . . .''

"What I said was, you had more balls than brains, and a person'd need a microscope to find *those*," Auglaize muttered darkly.

"Replete with specific references to supposed deviant sexual acts with various of my family members, as well as several types of animals and a rare plant or two," the Commander finished, unperturbed. "All astonishingly delivered in one breath, I'm told. I was highly impressed."

"I live for your approval," was the acid rejoinder. "What'd you do, bug my room?"

"Invade your privacy with listening devices? Indeed not! Van Wert thought your opinion of me might appeal to my twisted sense of humor. He was correct."

So, Michael knew all about those clandestine visits to Van Wert, and Davis had been the one to tell him. Auglaize didn't know whether to laugh or to cry, so she laughed. "Damn him!"

"That's better. Tears frighten me."

She couldn't conceive of his being frightened of anything, any more than she could comprehend the sudden about-face in his treatment of her. "Forgive my deplorable lack of self-control. It just seems like everything's coming apart, you know? My folks used to tell me that in every generation of DeWellesthars, there was one born pilot, and that was me."

"Excellent; you are making my point for me; you're just too busy feeling sorry for yourself to see it. Child, you were born with an instinct for flying. It was all you ever wanted, and your entire life up until you actually began training was in preparation, correct?"

"I guess you could look at it that way."

"Yet still, with all this innate talent and preparation, you had some difficulties. So. Now, you are a baby again, Dancer, newly emerged from Van Wert's Womb. You had to relearn balance to walk, coordination of muscles to feed yourself, dress yourself. Your mind knew how to do all these things, but it had to retrain your body. Flying takes another kind of balance and coordination, to which your body must be retrained. You must shelve the self-pity and start working constructively toward that goal. Yes?"

"Yes," she reluctantly agreed. She still would have liked to kick out that wall, though. She figured she'd earned the right.

"We have done things your way and failed. Now, we do them my way." He reached up again to push a stray lock of hair back behind her ears, and she ducked away.

"It's also time I had this mane cut back to regs."

"We have no such regulations. I think . . . Yes, I think you will start wearing braids. Two. That will serve."

"Now, wait a minute—"

"Don't interrupt. You speak passably fluent Auryx."

"As well you know. Speak it, and read it fairly well."

"Good. Then you shall learn to write it, too. In longhand, legibly, if you please. We have rather an unusual character set which I would like you to master."

"Terrific. What does all this have to do with flying?" He ignored the question, continuing brusquely, "Do you sew?"

"Good Lord, no! Nor do I have any desire to learn."

"I have in mind someone to teach you. You'll like her, I think. She is also a skilled musician and can instruct you on any instrument; that I know would appeal to you. A keyboard would serve the purpose best. Yes. And the Auryx harp, if you're so inclined. I myself could . . . no. Best leave it to Madison."

"Excuse me, but don't I have anything to say about this?"

"No. If you are to remain with our Service, the first thing you must learn is unquestioning obedience of my orders. If you decide to leave us—the discipline will not have been wasted. Yes," he continued as if to himself. "Merylys will have some ideas. She is a pursuit pilot."

That Merylys was the afore-mentioned Madison, Auglaize understood. She also understood that if Michael knew both her names, they must be very close friends indeed. How close? It was difficult to picture him as a lover, and if this Madison was as rigid and uncompromising as Michael seemed, it would be an interesting mating. Still, he did have a certain warmth, a genuine compassion. Auglaize found herself the tiniest bit envious of the unknown Merylys, and that was total nonsense. "Well, at least we'll have something to talk about," she finally said.

"I expected more of a fight from you. Very well. I'll tell Madison to come for you first thing in the morning. Then you and I will meet at the primary simulator tomorrow evening."

"Oh, no, we won't." She wasn't ready for that kind of humiliation again so soon.

Michael evidently had other ideas. "You'll be there if I have to track you down and drag you. Understood?" This sounded more like the Michael she knew and loathed. Dancer turned her head away; he grabbed her chin and jerked it back around. "Understood?"

"Sir," she spat from between clenched teeth.

"Good. You will find me demanding, but not entirely insensitive." His voice—and his grip—softened. "Trust me, Dancer. I know something of what you're going through."

She looked him in the eye for a minute, then shook her head. "I can't quite figure you out, Commander. You scare the hell out of me, and if anyone even suggested that someday I'd be sitting on your lap crying my heart out on your shoulder, I'd have told him that he was out of his rabbit-assed mind. But for all that, I trust you. I don't particularly like you, but I do trust you. Don't ask me why."

"Your instincts again. I may be a sadistic bastard, but you know by now that I am a man of my word. Hmm? Perhaps we can work on the liking. Oh, there's one other thing: no more sneaking over to the Medical Section to chat with Van Wert. If you want to talk to him, go talk to him. What you do on your own time is no concern of mine."

That earth-shattering smile again, throwing her even more off-balance. "Why, Michael?"

His slow, thoughtful drawl let her know that he understood. "The Service needs you, Dancer. That alone would justify my expending my energies to the utmost on your behalf. It also happens that no matter how you may feel about me, I like you. Besides, every man should have a hobby.

"Enough," he added firmly, rocking forward, rising, and setting her on her feet all in one smooth, fluid motion. "I'm hungry. We'll talk further over dinner; I want you to tell me all about Flight Leader DeWellesthar. First, however"—he winked—"I'm going to get out of this wet shirt."

Chapter 20

It was one Standard week before Michael could keep that appointment at the simulator, one Standard week of new challenges—and new frustrations.

Much as Auglaize hated to admit it, she liked Madison on sight. If this was indeed Michael's woman, he had excellent taste; she would have been considered attractive by any standard. Petite as were all Auryx females, Madison had the same core of steel as her Commander, but hers was cloaked behind wry humor and a devilishly mischievous spirit. Her ebony hair tumbled in shimmering waves to the waistband of her emerald-green-and-gold uniform, and Auglaize's first words to her were, "What do you do with all that when you're flying?" The answering laugh boded well for their association.

However, Madison was not without her personality flaws, chief of which was her constant assertion that the Commander was always right; by extension, since she was working under the Commander's orders, *she* was always right. Auglaize had a tendency to argue that point. Whereupon, Madison's stock reply was that they either played the game by her rules, or she'd take her toys and go home. The threat as to where that left Dancer remained unspoken.

That was another thing: it wasn't difficult for Auglaize to get used to being addressed as "Dancer"; after all, it had been her nickname for a lot of years. It was, however, hard for her to get used to the idea that this was the only name she would be recognized by as long as she was with the Sixth Service. Which, in Madison's opinion, wouldn't be long.

Being back in uniform again, even the strange Sixth Service combinations in any color of her choice—provided it wasn't already registered to someone else—felt really good. That she was allowed Fourth Service red was even better, and the icing on the cake was that she didn't have to part with her precious Academy ring. Personal comfort seemed to be the watchword here, and individuality was stressed; still, there was an underlying sense of comfortable discipline. Used as she had been to strict Fourth Service regimentation in everything from dress to diet during duty hours, the ease with which she seemed to be adapting surprised her. The Commander would approve.

On the other hand, Dancer took to sewing like a pig to parasailing. Her first few attempts at braiding her hair were classic exercises in ineptitude, and coaxing anything that sounded remotely like music from the electronic keyboard was totally beyond her. That rollercoaster week had given her back some measure of self-confidence, though; at least she was mediocre or bad at everything. Okay, so the Commander had been right: just because she could walk and chew gum at the same time did not mean that she was combatready. Any more than that admission meant that she was ready to face Michael again.

Therefore, Dancer was calculatedly late for their meeting—she took the long way around. Instead of using the connecting corridors or tunnels between sections, she fled outside for the fresh air that she would never again get enough of, and thus had to jog around several buildings and across the courtyard. She reveled in the exertion. There was a storm on the way; the clean, bracing north wind swirling around her promised rain and smelled so good that she laughed out loud. Dancer was still laughing as she flung open the door, sprinted down the last hallway, and skidded to a halt outside the portal marked with the Auryx characters for "Standard Primary Aircraft Simulator Apparatus": six Standard letters, two chicken scratches, and a snail trail. Then she figured it politic to pause, slow her breathing, and curb her spirits before gazing once again upon the dour countenance of the Commander.

As anticipated, Michael was waiting. Totally unanticipated was his winsome smile of greeting. "You've been outside, I see."

"Yes, sir." Auglaize self-consciously pushed back a wisp of fine hair that would not stay where it belonged. Funny how she didn't think about having it cut off anymore. "I like being outdoors, but I don't have much time to myself here, and . . ." At the last minute, she thought better of saying that the Auryx seemed to be paranoid about not being encircled by four walls.

His smile took on a trace of irony as he finished her thought. "Yes, our people are somewhat uncomfortable out in the open. As you are uncomfortable being shut in. You have your reasons, we have ours. They are not so dissimilar. I'm like you, though; every once in a while I have to break away and breathe unfiltered air. Perhaps after we are finished here, we can take a walk together. Or a run, if you prefer.''

"I'd like that, sir.''

"Michael, if you please. We're not much for military formalities here.''

"I'd noticed.'' The words slipped out before she could stop them.

Michael raised an eyebrow but shook his head. "Always feel free to speak your mind to me, Dancer. Though it may seem like it, I can't look into your head and read your thoughts. Come. We are going to work over here today.'' Leading her past the maze of various computerized cockpits and through an archway on the far side of the building, he halted in a small room with what appeared to be two ordinary desk chairs amidst a cluster of boxes on a slightly raised platform. "You know what this is?''

Upon closer inspection, the boxes proved to be mountings for interchangeable instrument panels that could be snapped into place later to represent other functions of the multipurpose CRT displays of the more advanced aircraft. It would be a while before she would have need of the various weapons-delivery and attack modes. "A basic trainer. Where I should have started out to begin with?''

"Exactly. We retrain your muscles first, so that what should be automatic is, then we add the distractions one by one. Computers are wonderful tools, but they can only do what we tell them to do.''

"*Are* you always right?'' Auglaize asked wryly as she took her seat.

A fractional pause. "No, child. Not always. But close enough. Now, then, we shall begin at the beginning. I'll name an item; you show me where it is and describe its function. Ready?''

Flexing her fingers, she took a deep breath and nodded. Michael's pace was slow and easy at first, imparting the impression that the simple cockpit drills were primarily to put her at ease. The pace gradually quickened, though, until he was snapping orders and her verbal responses took on the crisp manner of an Academy underclassman: "Sir! The thrust reverser switch is located next to the pinky position on the throttle control and is used to supplement the braking action of the aircraft upon landing, sir!'' Dancer's muscular responses were clumsy, but even she noticed an improvement with repetition.

Finally he rose, stretched, and moved around behind her, so close that her head rested against his midsection; so close that she could feel his belly muscles expand and contract with his breathing. Hers quickened, and her blood coursed hot through her veins.

Her hands, though, remained steady as Michael flicked a braid back across her shoulder so that his fingers could shutter themselves over her eyes.

"Excellent," he murmured. Unsure as to whether he was referring to her reaction, her mastering of same, or the fact that she was finding everything with a minimum of fumbling, she waited. "Now we do it blindfolded."

The mood was shattered, and they got back to work.

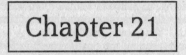

Chapter 21

Michael was coming through the woods behind her. There wasn't so much as the sound of a twig snapping to give him away, but somehow Dancer knew he was there. Come to drag her back to the compound, no doubt. It would have been foolish of her to think her refuge here would go undetected forever, but she could have wished for the privacy of a few more solitary hours.

Out here, Auglaize could be herself, by herself—isolated from the rigid, autocratic Auryx who ruled her waking moments and did their best to restructure her thinking in their own image. Not even the smallest decision affecting her life was hers; the children in the compound nursery had more freedom than she was allowed. Madison, her friend and jailer, was increasingly sympathetic as she noted Dancer's struggles to adjust, and tried to vary the routine— but she had her orders, and Dancer had her schedule. The atmosphere of the Fourth Service, which Dancer had before considered uncompromising, was looking more and more permissive by comparison. Its strictures were limited to duty hours; its constraints mostly physical. A member's thoughts—and her memories—were her own.

That was the major bone of contention between the two women: Madison's forbidding Auglaize ever to talk about her past. Auglaize understood the Auryx definition of security. What Madison didn't seem able to understand was that her charge's former life was all she had to define herself by, that and her time in the Van Wert—which she certainly wasn't going to discuss, as tied up with Kellen Darke as any recollections of that period were. She hadn't been Dancer of the Sixth long enough yet to know who she was, while she'd had a lifetime of experience being Auglaize DeWellesthar—an identity complete with friends and family, all of whom she missed with an acuteness directly proportional to the number of times a day she was admonished to forget them.

It certainly wasn't Mad's intention to be cruel. Indeed, she saw her attitude as a kindness. The rare glimpses of her past that their growing friendship allowed were very painful for Madison. Dancer vaguely recalled Kellen's veiled references to the preferability of a mental numbness that, she was beginning to understand, was a cultural trait.

Not surprisingly, Auglaize had gained a reputation for reticence among the dozen or so Auryx adults with whom she was allowed contact. With the installation's children, however, it was another matter. To them, she was a master storyteller.

It started with a long-distance gift from an absent parent, an archaic weapon—a crossbow—that the recipient didn't know how to hold, let alone use. Auglaize found herself clumsily demonstrating what she, as a child herself, had been proficient with. Uncle Ash had come upon a beautifully crafted crossbow somewhere in his travels and sent it home to her brothers and her, along with a legend about an ancient hero by the name of William Tell. At the request of an appreciative audience, Dancer recounted this historical background, too.

Somehow that lazy afternoon, on a planet who-knew-how-far from medieval Earth, the legendary Swiss freedom fighter was transmuted into a legendary Auryx freedom fighter, and the Austrian invaders became the Karranganthian hordes from whom some of these innocents had only narrowly escaped themselves. The tale of a father's imperiling his son by refusing to submit to tyranny, then subsequently rescuing him through skill, appealed to them.

After that, the kids insisted that favorite characters, including a strong heroine with a prowess to match the hero's, be inserted into every tale, and that the tales themselves be tailored to the eternal Auryx-Karranganthian enmity. Drawing upon her own experiences and those of her former colleagues to supplement the wide repertoire of stories recalled from history and literature, Auglaize willingly obliged.

Thus was born Auglaize DeWester, who, the girls decided,

should have exotic red hair and deep brown eyes. The space to be occupied by Flight Leader DeWester's best friend and constant companion was filled by none other than the Auryx Willemtell.

These storytelling sessions, surprisingly enough, gained official sanction as "language lessons." Couldn't the adults in the compound guess that Auglaize DeWester was, except for the simplification of the name, the former dashing persona of their own reserved Dancer? To Dancer, this served to emphasize exactly how isolated she really was, isolated and imprisoned by well-meaning people whose dislike of the outside—and outsiders—bordered on the agoraphobic.

Inevitably, somewhere along the line, the walls between which she was forced to spend most of her time started closing in on her. There were no two ways about it; she had to get out. Somewhere, there *must* exist a place Auglaize could escape to, once in a while, to make the rest bearable.

One afternoon, breathing deeply to keep from screaming and trying to climb the windowless expanse of paneling hedging her in, she desperately cast about for an escape. Suddenly, Makellen Darke gave it to her. Almost too vividly for mere memory, she heard his dreamy, sensual voice describing the river on the other side of the stone boundary fence. Without a thought for the consequences, Auglaize pitched her sewing into a corner, graphically told Madison what she could do with it, with the psychs, herself, and the whole bloody place, and fled.

The refuge was there, all right, just as Makellen had promised: a beautiful world of sunlight and shade and the silence of growing things. She waded in the river, bare feet slipping on rocks under the cold water; she stretched out on the cushion of moss beneath an ancient tree, the smell of fresh grass in her nostrils and shafts of white light through the leaves creating strange dancing shadows across her face. Fingers locked together behind her head, Auglaize reveled in her solitude.

Whenever the pressures built up back in the compound, her mind drifted into the forbidden land. Though she tried not to go there too often, when the limits of tolerance were reached her feet reacted automatically. Freedom was sweet. She had become addicted.

And now it was about to end. A low growl from the hound stretched out at her side alerted Dancer that they were no longer alone.

As for Michael—he came on unerringly, as if he knew exactly where to look. Maybe he did. If asked, Serious's master would have had to tell him. The dog's tail thumped as Auglaize retrieved her electronic notebook and stylus from the grass by his paw. Perhaps if she appeared to be hard at work, the Commander would leave her alone.

She hadn't seen much of him during the weeks past—only a smile of greeting across a room, a word of encouragement or praise, a quick tug on a braid in passing. The opportunity for private conversation would have been a delight under other circumstances, but now she resented—and feared—his intrusion.

Serious's tail thwacked the ground with the abandon of a pagan mating drum as Michael broke out of the underbrush and strode over to where Auglaize sat.

Pretending absorption in the translation of a tricky line of poetry that she had earlier tossed aside in disgust, she turned back into the sun the first time his shadow fell across her computer screen and ignored it the second. Hard as it was not to look up under his glower, Auglaize managed. She even managed to slow her heartbeat and steady her writing hand as it, with no direction from her brain, proceeded to mark out appropriate Auryx characters in careful but strong strokes.

Finally, on a long exhalation of breath, the shadow over her relaxed, and hands dropped from hips. Full light flooded the screen as Michael eased himself down onto the grass and gave the dog a quick but affectionate chin rub. Serious dozed again, and Dancer was becoming truly engrossed in her lesson when light fingers teased the pins out of her carefully anchored coronet so that the two braids, which had been crossed and pinned at her crown, plopped down over her shoulders.

Playing games now, are we? she thought as the hairpins were tucked into the pocket of the jacket she had been wearing earlier. Then those relentless fingers unraveled the painstakingly neat plaits, one after the other, combing through the hair until it fell in soft waves around her face. Dancer automatically tossed her head to get it out of her eyes, and it was gathered up into a bundle and thrown over one shoulder as a light touch across the back of her neck sent shivers down her spine.

Dammit, Troy, you know that drives me crazy! flashed through her mind as she jerked out of reach.

"You're going to have to acknowledge me sooner or later, you know."

Michael's voice, so close his breath feathered the fine hairs just behind her ears. She managed a shaky laugh. "Tickles."

"Sorry." He didn't sound it. He sounded absurdly pleased with himself. He looked absurdly pleased with himself, too, with that disarming smile of his. Here he was, reaching out to play with her hair again, and she was too much of a fool to get out of his way. The Auryx, it seemed, were fascinated with red hair.

"You and the kids," she couldn't help giggling.

Michael unwound a long lock from around his hand and let it drop. "Forgive me," he stated stiffly. "When I am with you I sometimes forget myself."

From his tone, that could have been either a compliment or an insult. Dancer let it pass. "How did you find me?"

"I recalled your mentioning that when you needed to get away from everything, you used to seek refuge in a certain clump of trees down by the river that flowed behind your family's farm. Upstream from the pastures," he added with a smile. "I naturally came here first."

"I don't remember telling you anything of the sort."

The smile this time wasn't quite so playful. "You didn't. I know everything there is to know about you, Flight Leader De-Wellesthar."

"Surely not everything," she countered.

He suddenly raised his hand to signal silence, paused momentarily to listen, then spoke in the general direction of his left sleeve. "She is with me," was his patient assertion. Again he listened, repeating with less patience, "I said, she is with me!"

"Someone else with the temerity to talk back to the Commander, hmm?" Auglaize couldn't resist saying. "Just off hand, I'd guess it's Madison, demanding that you haul me back in irons."

"Something like that. She tells me this is the third time in two weeks you've conveniently forgotten to show up for lessons."

"So, she sent you out after me? I'd have thought you had better things to do with your time."

"Madison merely reported you missing after she learned of your most recent altercation with the psychs. She was concerned. I came because . . . ." He hesitated, then continued at her prompting look, "because I guessed where you would be."

"You came because you thought I might need a shoulder to cry on."

His almost imperceptible lifting of one eyebrow indicated that she was right on target. "It's occasionally available for that purpose. I also thought you might need to talk. Or rather, to listen. You must concede that the psychs have helped you."

Auglaize stiffened at the suggestion, then remembered all the times she had awakened with screams stifled in her throat. Or worse, the waking dreams, beside which all nightmares paled in comparison, through which she had struggled as the full horrors of what she had survived surfaced in her memory. Dancer could face them all without flinching now. Almost. That much, the psychs had given her—perhaps her sanity, through their aid in forgetting things best left unremembered. She acknowledged that debt with a shrug and an inclination of her head.

The divergence in thinking came, however, in the determination of what memories she should be allowed to keep. The cessation of Makellen's life, she had long ago accepted. It was the negation of it that she could not condone. And her total rejection of his existence was what the psychs still insisted upon. Her lips set in a harsh line; her head lifted. "But perhaps their job is finished."

"Perhaps not," he countered mildly. He sighed, then spoke haltingly, as if considering each word before he uttered it. "Child, it is immaterial whether or not Makellen Darke ever actually existed outside of your own mind. Pertinent now is the fact that as far as you are concerned, he exists no longer. With that, you must deal."

Dancer felt his eyes searching her face as he waited for a rebuttal, or at least the question she knew wouldn't be answered if she asked. The psychs had succeeded in planting the doubts. Had her tortured mind melded a sea of similar faces into one and then woven some elaborate fantasy around it? No. Mak had been a man, as warm and as real as the one beside her now, and They would never, ever, take that away from her. "Fine," she acquiesced bitterly. "Tell that to the psychs."

Eyes on a point far away, he nodded slowly. "You are beyond their ken, Dancer. Your mind works very differently from ours in many respects. Because we have grown to consider you one of us, we are less tolerant of these perceived disparities. Sometimes we all forget that different is not necessarily bad."

Auglaize's only reply was to run her hand over the dog's sleek brown fur in long, relaxing strokes. His leg jerked as she found his kick reflex. "Some things are the same everywhere," she said without thinking. "Dogs are dogs, and thank God for small favors."

Michael sat silently watching the tension drain from her neck and shoulders as she transferred the bulk of her attention to the animal. "The perimeter guards usually aren't so friendly," he finally observed in an amused tone.

Dancer smiled at his stratagem to keep her from dropping too deeply into her own thoughts and, not for the first time, silently speculated on whether or not he had once been one of those so-called psychological wizards the Auryx set such store by. "So Serious informed me on our first meeting," she admitted, in answer to his comment. "I vaulted the boundary fence, and he was waiting on the other side for me. We discussed the matter at length before his handler showed up." When a discreet glance at Michael assured her that no reprimand was in store for the kennel master, she continued, "After that, Shelby ordered me to take Serious with me whenever I went out wandering. He doesn't know I know he keeps track of me through the tracer in Serious's collar." She ruffled the golden neck fur with a chuckle.

"He certainly likes you."

The statement could have applied to either Shelby or the dog; so could the answer. "It's mutual. I used to have dogs, back ho—" Auglaize snapped her teeth together on the rest of the sentence as repeated admonitions against discussing her former life were belatedly recalled. Resignedly, she awaited the Commander's censure.

But again Michael surprised her. "Back home on your family's farm? Don't look so startled, child; you can say anything you like to me. I know all about you, remember?"

"Yes, I'm sure you get all kinds of reports," she stated dryly. "Madison constantly threatens me with your wrath."

"For all the good that does," he replied in the same tone. "Actually, Madison's reports are unfailingly complimentary. In a lot of ways, she admires you. On the other hand, she's thoroughly convinced that you do not know the meaning of the word 'discipline.'"

"Semantic disagreement. She's not too familiar with the word 'compromise.' If the Commander didn't cover it specifically in his orders, forget it. Don't get me wrong, I really like Mad, and we usually get along very well. But when we don't . . ." Dancer made a double-handed gesture sketching an explosion on the air. "Sometimes I think we're too much alike."

He nodded. "In a lot of ways, you are alike, but I'm surprised you recognize it. And Highland? What is your assessment of him?"

After only three sessions together, Michael had informed her that he could no longer scavenge the time to see to her retraining himself, so he had assigned her to someone named Highland for intensive instruction. In rational moments, Dancer acknowledged that the change was to her benefit, that this Highland would get her back into the cockpit much faster than if she had to rely on being squeezed into the Commander's erratic schedule. But disappointment was not rational. Auglaize had come to look forward to those stolen hours under Michael's tutelage, and the brisk walk to his quarters for dinner and conversation afterward. She suspected he felt the same way, that that in part was what prompted his decision to end it.

"Highland is a good man. He's taught me a trick or two about handling a fighter, and I didn't think anyone could do that. Especially in a simulator. Though I'd appreciate it if you kept that between the two of us—his ego is inflated enough."

"Highland was an engineer and chief test pilot at another of our research facilities as well as part of that facility's air defense; he has probably forgotten more about flying than most of us will ever learn, as the saying goes. He came to us in pieces after an escape capsule misfired. He is, like you, a Van Wert, so he understands your particular difficulties. Unlike you, he is not eager to fly again. He quite simply cannot climb back into an actual cockpit; even the simulator is a strain. I hope someday to have him back on full active status. Until then, his job is transferring his expertise to others. I don't need to remind you that I'm telling you this in the strictest confidence."

"Of course." Dancer replied automatically. She was too aware of the emphasis these people placed on keeping their private lives private not to realize the enormity of the confidence Michael had entrusted her with. "But what can I do for him?"

"I thought perhaps you might challenge one another. Unlike Madison, Highland has no complaints about your lack of enthusiasm. Staying one jump ahead of you isn't always easy. I have difficulty doing so myself, occasionally."

"That I will definitely take as a compliment."

"Do you find him attractive?" he asked idly, returning her smile.

"You knew I would when you selected him for me." No doubt Michael would infer the double meaning that was intended. "And, before you ask, I also enjoy his company. Just not as much as he'd like me to."

"You could do worse."

"I know. Blaise has told me that himself at least a dozen times. However. He's a good friend, and that's all there is." The use of Highland's given name was enough to get the point across. No need to go into the details of romantic expectations gone sour for both Highland and herself, of the one attempt at a more-than-casual kiss which had been very pleasant, true, but had generated no spark. There once had been a time when that wouldn't have mattered. No longer.

"I see. While we are on the subject, you know, of course, that there is talk about us."

"Us. You mean, you and me, as in . . . Skek!" Dancer murmured a gentle Auryx imprecation that would have blistered a heat shield. Was that why he had kept his distance all this time? "I assure you, Commander, I have said or done nothing to warrant it."

"The idea never even entered your head, did it?" he commented wryly.

"I wouldn't say that, exactly," she conceded. "I might have nurtured a fantasy or two. Which makes me no different from most of the women on station, and some of the men." Then, she blushed, remembering discussions openly and frankly voiced in what she had come to call the "Ladies' Sewing Circle," the group of women in various stages of pregnancy whom Madison and she frequently joined during the time set aside for stitchery practice. It was incongruous enough to watch them working on delicately detailed baby clothes while the topic of conversation revolved around combat flying, but even harder to get used to was the other favorite: speculation on the Commander's sexual habits.

"I think I would like to hear your fantasies," Michael said softly.

"Not mine," Auglaize stammered. "Theirs. The other women."

"Ah. Well. Being grounded gets wearing after a while, as I think you know; there are worse ways to cope with that frustration than rechanneling it. Besides, I'm a safe enough topic of conversation. If any of them knew for sure, they'd keep it to themselves."

"Uh huh. Mad won't let me disclose any of the secrets of my former life, which means I don't have any war stories—and I never was very good at speculative gossip. Signifying, in their minds, an acute lack of experience in the former, and an overabundance of it elsewhere?"

"Another of our cultural differences," was his amused agreement. "Just out of curiosity, what does Madison say on the subject?"

Dancer met his eyes levelly. "Not much. She does theorize that you encourage your female combat pilots to contribute to the repopulation effort so that you can ground them and keep them safe."

"So, now you know my terrible secret," Michael replied with mock horror. "I like women. While we're on the subject, Red, I would venture to guess that a good number of the men have nurtured a fantasy or two about you, too."

"The Commander among them?"

"The Commander is a man. May I see that?" He pointed to her notebook, and Dancer handed it to him. With only a slight qualm, she watched as he flipped the switch on the side from Write to Read and fingered the command that would take him back to the beginning of the file.

"Does it bother you, the rumor?" she couldn't help asking as he paged through some of her early attempts to master the Auryx characters.

"Not at all. Let them think what they like; it takes the pressure off me," was his offhanded reply. "Your Auryx is exceptional."

"Madison permits me to speak or read nothing else when she's around. On the other hand, I have been instructed to speak only Standard with the children. It gets confusing sometimes."

"That would explain the interesting blend of the two that you use in conversation with me."

"Sir?"

"You tend to lapse into Auryx when you're trying to express yourself emotionally, or to describe something in precise terms."

"You people seem to have a word for every aspect of everything. I'll have to start listening to myself more closely."

"Do. Here, it doesn't matter, but there are places in the known universe where one Auryx word would be worth your life.

"Do you enjoy working with the children?" He asked it abstractedly as he continued to scan screens full of progressively neater handwriting, but Dancer knew he was listening.

"As additional duties go, it's among the better ones I've had," she said noncommittally. The sixty or seventy kids here were mostly those of Service members, with a fair sprinkling of orphans, Auryx and non-Auryx, brought in from some unspecified "elsewhere." Due to the nature of the Service and the concerted efforts of the Karranganthians and their allies to obliterate the Auryx race, family life had been sacrificed to the necessities of survival. Children were kept in the most protected part of the compound, seeing their parents only when the adults stole the time to visit or pulled additional duty in the nursery. As a result, the kids had everyone—and no one. At the inevitable contrast with her own boisterous, loving family, an unacknowledged homesickness stirred yet again.

"Ironically, I keep having to remind them that I'm *not* Auryx. Especially when I try to correct their pronunciation—they don't believe that Standard is my first language. For that matter, they don't believe that Standard is *anyone's* first language. They're all picking up Fourth Service idiom very quickly, though."

"From the sampling that I've heard, I hope not! About the first time Eire calls me 'gonad brain' you and I are going to have a long talk."

"Give me credit for some sense! Besides, I never actually called you 'gonad brain.' At least, not in so many words. I may start, though, since you seem so enamored of the phrase.''

"Hush, child, I was only teasing. I've listened in on a few of the adventures of Flight Leader DeWester and her faithful Auryx companion, Willemtell. Though I think perhaps the prototype for the latter was a tall redhead by the name of Morgan Troy, yes?''

"Yeah, but I don't think he'd mind the race change. He was a sucker for kids.''

"A weakness I share, I fear.''

His casual statement brought to mind remembered glimpses of the Commander in the nursery, changing diapers, playing ''horsie,'' drying tears, initiating games that more pressing duties never allowed him to finish. ''Mike . . .''

"What is it, Red?'' he prompted.

"It's none of my business. I was just wondering if any of them were yours.''

"Figuratively speaking, they all are. Biologically, no. I regret it occasionally, but my contact with women has been limited.''

"That's a shame. I'd like to think that there was a little piece of you growing up in a sheltered garden somewhere.''

He smiled at her imagery as he tapped the Screen-saver/Hold key with his forefinger. ''Would you bear my child, Dancer?''

Chapter 22

"Why, Dancer; you're blushing!'' His tone was light, but his manner wasn't—not completely.

"Is that a proposal or a proposition?'' she sputtered.

Michael shrugged. ''Merely a hypothetical question. It seemed rather a logical follow-on to our previous discussions of sexual fantasies and nurseries.''

"Uh-huh. But figuratively speaking, Commander, I *am* your child.'' The left corner of Michael's lip quirked in appreciation of the way she had turned his words around, but the steady gaze of those eyes, a deceptively lazy gray-blue in this light, made it an effort for Dancer to sustain the humorous note. "Biologically, I had that system disabled at the medical mill with most of the rest of my class the day after I graduated from the Academy. I have never regretted it."

"You forget that your extremities were not the only damaged portions regrown during your time in the Van Wert," was his mischievous rejoinder.

"Yeah, that can be remedied, too, can't it. I'm not the maternal type. Besides, any of your Auryx women would fall all over themselves for the opportunity to, uh"—she gestured vaguely—"help you enlarge the gene pool."

"But wouldn't you like to know that it was a small piece of both of us in that sheltered garden of yours? I'm sure the universe could handle another red-headed Auryx."

His tone was joking, his smile whimsical, but there was an earnestness behind the twinkle in his eyes that made Dancer the tiniest bit nervous. Leaning away from him, she picked up a flat stone and shied it out over the water, watching it skip once, twice, three times before it disappeared beneath the surface. "Michael," she answered finally, eyes still on the spot from which the concentric circles rippled the calm water, "I would do anything you asked me to."

"Not anything, I think, child."

She turned quickly back to him at the deadly serious inflection in his voice. "I trust you not to ask what I cannot give."

"Don't," was his quietly vehement rejoinder. "The choice is not always mine.

"This is very good," he added in his normal cool tone, indicating the poem she had been struggling with earlier and thus adroitly changing the subject again. "Although here, you might want to use *verihan*, 'home of the heart,' instead of just *han*, which is merely a dwelling. Take out the repetitive, and it keeps the rhythm of the line better, too. This is not something Madison has assigned."

As if thirty-eight seconds ago they'd been idly chatting about the weather. But that was how conversations with Michael went. Someday, maybe, Dancer would learn to anticipate his abrupt shifts, even to forestall them, but for now she could only shake her head and try to follow him.

"Uh, no, most of what's there I've done on my own. I had an instructor at the Academy who asserted that the best way to truly learn a language was to translate poetry. To try to keep the rhythm of the words, as you say, as well as the meaning. So, I've been doing some practicing on my own. My lack of discipline, you know.''

He gave her a mock frown at the allusion to his earlier disclosure of Madison's criticism. "So noted. Is this original?''

"The poem? No. It's an old song. 'My home, it lies over misty seas/But I'll never see it again,' '' Auglaize quoted in the dialect of her people, then closed her eyes and put the words to the tune that was running through her head frequently these days.

> "My home, it lies over misty seas
> But I'll never see it again.
> My love, my life waits there for me,
> She'll wait for eternity, then.

> "She'll wait, for I am bound to die
> Here, under the sky of green,
> Where the waves break high and the wind sings low,
> And no woman has yet ever been.

> "My home, it lies o'er the Milky Way,
> But I'll never go there again.
> My love, my life, ah! she waits for me—
> We'll meet in eternity, then.''

Michael joined in about halfway through, translating back into Standard from her Auryx. His slightly husky voice and echoic harmony gave the simple but haunting tune an eeriness that hung in the air after they finished and made Auglaize shiver.

She cleared her throat. "Legend has it the poem was found in the log of an early exploratory team that vanished without a trace. Personally, I think it was more likely the product of a maudlin night in a bar somewhere. No matter. My group could identify with the sentiment. 'She'll wait, for I am bound to die/Here . . .' We knew that two out of three of us wouldn't survive to see our next duty station, let alone home.''

"You want to go back, don't you?'' he probed gently.

His question startled her, but not as much as her instinctive reply: "Yes, damn it! I miss my family; is that so unbelievable?'' This last was directed at herself; she was suddenly discovering a part of herself she had never known existed. "The little things, you know? Like helping Dad mend a fence. Refereeing one of Alicia and Alan's epochal battles. Walking with my dogs through the little cemetery up on the hill where I'll have a headstone, but my body will never lie. All the things I took for granted, because I would always have the next leave to look forward to. Your Sixth Service doesn't have home leave, does it?''

''We don't have a home.''

''Yeah. Well, neither do I, any more. I could handle that if I just had *something*, you know?'' His slight frown showed that he didn't know; Dancer wasn't sure she did, either. ''It's not real easy to explain.''

''Try, child.'' At her continued reticence, he prodded gently, ''Just tell me what you're feeling.''

''What I'm feeling,'' Dancer repeated. ''Look, Michael, my former life no longer exists for me, but I'm not a part of yours, either. It's like, except for my time with the kids, I'm watching you all through a glass door with no handle on my side. They accept me for what I am; the rest of you consider me an alien to be kept apart. Like an animal in a cage—seeing only those select few of your people and those areas of the compound necessary to my 'training,' forbidden even to talk about where I come from unless it's with the psychs—so that I don't contaminate them with that alienness. Is that a word? I'm sure there's a good one in Auryx. Madison would know.'' She fiddled with her writing stylus for a minute, then jammed it point downward into the ground. The sensitive electronics squeaked in protest, but neither paid any attention.

''Good God, Michael, I understand your people's paranoia for security, truly I do, but I don't even know who I am anymore! My mind, like my speech, has become such a hybrid of Standard and Auryx that the only times I'm completely comfortable are when I'm with the children or . . .''

''Or with me?''

Dancer shrugged, too embarrassed to meet his eyes.

Closing his fingers around hers, he nodded once or twice, but said nothing for a very long time. When he finally did speak, his voice was scarcely audible over the sound of the water lapping at the rocks by their feet. ''I will send you back, if that's what you truly want.''

Dancer's grip on his hand tightened as her eyes squeezed shut. What *did* she truly want? ''I never even seriously considered the possibility before. I had been told it existed, of course, but I just naturally assumed . . . Mike, what would happen to me if I did go back? Would I be returned to active service?''

''I think not.'' Michael's shoulders straightened; he was the

Commander again, but his fingers did not try to disentangle themselves from their basket weave with hers. "You would be worth much more as a media hero. A great deal of publicity, then recruiting, perhaps, or training. An Academy professorship would be a very real possibility. A few, high up in your Service, would know the truth of what happened to you. For the rest, there would be a believable story to explain the gaps in your memory, but no one would entirely trust your stability. I doubt that you would ever again be allowed in a combat zone."

"That's about what I figured. Funny, when I first came here, I couldn't stand the thought of being a noncombatant. Now, I almost think I would be content to go home, settle down, teach. I never dreamed I would be good at that, but I find I am. I would miss flying, of course, but I could check out for my civil ticket and do some exhibitions on weekends, maybe give lessons," Auglaize thought out loud, spinning a civilian fantasy she'd never even contemplated before. Trying it on for size. Intellectually, she saw the exercise for what it was—just an exercise—but emotionally, it was very appealing.

"I've done my share, Michael. I've done enough. I'm sick of this whole damned mess." Dancer widened her eyes against the unexpected blur of tears, but didn't protest as Michael turned her head toward him. He could read her voice; what did it matter what he saw in her face?

"I don't want to lose you, Dancer, but I have said that I will send you back. Tomorrow, if you like. Today, if you like."

"And deprive you of your one and only hobby?" The humor fell flat; the Commander's eyes were unreadable as the water spilled down Auglaize's cheeks. If she did return to her own people, how she would miss this gentle, perceptive cipher who was, in spite of himself, fast becoming her closest friend. Even if she weren't allowed to remember him, she would still feel the loss, of that she was certain. And yet . . . Dancer jerked away violently. The whole discussion was academic. She couldn't go back.

"I can't go back," she whispered.

"Why not, child?"

She shook her head again and tried to get herself in hand. Another minute, and she would be able to joke her way out of this whole maudlin exhibition. But Michael refused to give her that minute.

"Talk to me, child," he persisted. "Why can't you go back?"

"I've never told anyone before. Michael, I—" Dancer took a deep breath and shrugged off his hands. "I have seen the aftermath of a Karranganthian raid on a civilian population. The wanton destruction, the indiscriminate slaughter. Those who resisted killed as examples. Those who didn't resist taken as slaves, and murdered at leisure. Marchand was supposedly a rear area. As is my home.''

"I was also on Marchand.'' His simple words spoke volumes; Dancer nodded shortly.

"Then you know. After that, they sent us home on leave—we were all in varying degrees of shock. My father was the only one I told, and then he showed me the shelter he had built beneath the barn. It didn't take much imagination for either of us to see the farm in flames, my sisters scattered like chickens trying to escape the slaughter. With any luck, there would be enough warning for them all to make it to the shelter. With a lot more luck, they'd be able to stay hidden. If not—my father had provisions for that, too. Death would be quick. He meant to reassure me. I let him think he had.''

"I begin to see,'' Michael interjected.

"Do you? Do you see that the only thing truly reassuring to me is the belief that as long as I continue fighting, my family will be safe? That every man I kill is one who will not threaten their lives? That every piece of equipment I destroy, every inch I help push back the front, as long as I am out there, somewhere, somehow doing something . . . my family will be safe? That's why I can never go home.'' She forced a laugh. "Just a silly superstition.''

Michael squeezed her shoulders. "My little Dancer, here is something *I* have never told to anyone. I saw my home destroyed and my family killed. I was the only survivor, because I was late in returning from an errand. Because I stopped to look at the clouds, to play adolescent love games with a girl. At first, I was overcome with guilt. Why should I have lived when my parents, siblings, most of my friends were dead? For a time, I even sought death myself. Then, revenge. Now—an end to it all. So, you see, child, I do understand. We all do what we must, and our reasons are essentially the same in the final analysis.''

"It's so hard, Michael. If I could just let them know that I'm still out here . . .''

"It would be no kindness.''

"Maybe not. The thing is, though, no matter what happens deep down inside, Dancer will always be Auglaize DeWellesthar.''

"As I will always be . . . who I was. I understand,'' he repeated.

"You, Van Wert, one or two others.''

"Child, have you ever considered that perhaps I often feel the outsider myself?''

Dancer blinked. "You?"

"I. Luckily, I seldom have the leisure to reflect upon it. On the rare occasions that I do, my reaction is much the same as yours. I would give everything I have to be able to go back to the security of home and the love of family."

"*Verihan*," she supplied.

"*Verihan*. Would that I could return with you to yours."

Dancer looked at him in surprise. "But everybody here adores you! The way they talk, you could walk across the river without getting your feet wet."

He didn't quite smile. "Deities are notoriously lonely, Red. At any rate," he added in a different tone as he hauled himself erect, "I'll leave you to your solitude. Don't stay out too long; Madison will worry. She's already afraid I intend to dismiss you."

"Isn't that what she's wanted all along?"

"Child, we have grown very fond of you. Perhaps we're hard on you simply because we *don't* want to lose you. Remember the losses all of us—you included—have already sustained, and try to understand. In her own way, Madison is protecting your family, too. What she doesn't know, she can't be compelled to disclose. Think on it. We'll talk again."

"Wait a sec, Mike; let me get my shoes on, and I'll walk back with you."

"Back to the cage?"

Dancer shrugged. "I like your company. Look, Commander, don't worry about me. I'll cope. I've always managed before, and I'll manage now. You just caught me on a bad day."

"You don't run out here on the good ones, do you." He extended a hand to help her to her feet, then stooped for her notebook and jacket, his face clearing suddenly as he came to a decision. "Are you up for a bit of a walk, Dancer? There's something I want to show you."

Chapter 23

With a groan, Dancer grasped the hand Michael held back for her and let him pull her the rest of the way up a small rise. The Commander's ''bit of a walk'' had turned out to be a full-fledged hike. He wasn't even breathing hard, but she was all in. So was Serious, who, with a groaning sigh, flopped down on the grass by their feet. Dancer gave him a sympathetic ''Good dog,'' and contemplated joining him.

Then, she heard it, a humming roar behind her that could have been made by only one thing. She turned her head just in time to see a Gypsy fighter approaching low and fast. ''Oh, Michael.''

''Look here.'' His wrist rested casually on her shoulder, the thumb stroking her cheek to get her attention as the forefinger pointed to the panorama below.

Dancer's eyes followed that finger, and she gasped. There, spread out as far as she could see, was a vast flight line—buildings that were unmistakably hangars, a maze of runways and taxiways, a fleet of support vehicles and, making her heart beat so fast she thought it was going to leap out of her chest, every type of aircraft known and a few she'd never seen before. The Gypsy passing overhead on a VFR approach drowned out her exclamation of pure, unadulterated joy, but what she felt was mirrored in Michael's face, so it didn't matter whether or not he had heard.

Fatigue forgotten, Dancer watched as the rest of the flight of Gypsies roared in—watched and whooped and yelled with delight until her throat hurt, oblivious to the fact that she had tucked in closer under Michael's arm, wrapping one of her own tightly around his slender waist for balance.

''This is the most incredible thing I've ever seen!'' Automatically, she started mentally sorting and classifying the hundreds of aircraft on view. Besides the three stalwarts of the Fourth Service fleet—the Gypsy, the Gonif, and the flying-wing Gryphon—there were Fifth Service shuttles, which meant, in all likelihood, an interplanetary transport or two in orbit above them; a batch of Third Service Corsairs, numerous varieties of transports, gunships, a ferry from a Starlifter . . . These people had a Warlord Starlifter? She gave a low whistle, and shook her head. "Unbelievable. Gypsies. Lord, I never thought I'd be this close to one of them again. Trainers, interceptors—what's that little beauty over there?"

Michael shaded his eyes with his free hand and smiled affectionately. "That, my dear, is a Weasel. Very fast, very versatile—fighter, ground attack, recce. Doesn't look like much, but it can fly up its own exhaust."

At the pride in his voice, Dancer grinned. "We used to say that somewhat more crudely about our Gypsies. Your bird?"

"My bird," he agreed. "Though you would probably prefer a Dart—next row over. Transatmospheric interceptor. Very, very fast, but limited range. And temperamental in the extreme. You don't even sit in a Dart until you prove that you can fly anything else not just in your sleep, but comatose."

"Can you?" Dancer already knew the answer.

"I, and a handful of others. I prefer my Weasel, though. I cannot afford the single-minded concentration that the Dart demands. Which is why I think it may suit you."

"Single-minded, demanding, and temperamental, am I?"

"Occasionally."

"Hmmm. That group there, extreme right. They look like Karranganthian T-Twelves."

"You have good eyes. They are."

"Tango Twelves? Where in the name of Third Earth did you get Tango Twelves? The pilots either kamikaze or blow themselves up rather than land a damaged aircraft, and the things are booby-trapped on the ground so they can't be stolen. And you have half a dozen sitting there!"

"Give or take a few. There are the same number of 'Fourteens sitting in the hangar over there," he added with facetious nonchalance, "where they are also constructed, to manufacturer's specifications. We keep them around for dissimilar air combat training, among other things."

"Sure you do," was her prompt response. "Gad. No wonder Highland is so well versed in aircraft characteristics."

"You name it, we've got it."

"Is it always this active?"

"Generally. We do most of our training here."

"You'd never even guess, back there." She inclined her head in the general direction of the medical complex. "I'm not supposed to know about any of this, am I?"

"No, and anyone else bringing you here would be in deep trouble. But they tell me the Commander can get away with murder. Look up, quick!"

Dancer snapped her head back just in time to see something small and sleek spiraling rapidly groundward. Her breath caught in her throat, so sure was she that it was going to impact, but Michael stood beside her like a rock. A scant second before the craft scattered itself all over the pavement, the pilot pulled out and executed a victory roll as he screamed past their vantage point.

"How many do you lose from exhibitions like that?" she asked tartly. "If one of my pilots ever pulled that kind of stunt, I'd have him grounded until his feet took root."

"We haven't lost one yet. That, child, was a Dart, and its pilot was one of our trainees. If he had crashed, we would have had to wash him out of the program."

"If he had crashed, you would have had to wash him off the runway," she corrected. Still, her eyes followed the dust speck against the clouds that was the Dart, and she couldn't deny that she wanted it.

"Feeling a little better now than you were an hour ago?"

Dancer answered his question with a question. "Have you ever been in love, Michael?"

"Once or twice." He grinned in understanding. Then, "Damn!"

His joking tone had changed so abruptly that Dancer jumped. "What?"

He sighed. "Seven is coming for me; I am needed."

"How did they know where you are? Oh, yes—Serious." The dog still sprawled in the shade, watching them with tolerant amusement.

"You're close." He pushed back his left cuff, revealing what she at first took to be a simple pilot's wrist chronometer. "My dog collar. A communications link with the Command computer. Jeremiah always knows where I am."

"That's how you spoke with Madison."

"Yes, all communications go through the computers, which sort them out and transmit them on the frequency of the individual implant receiver."

Serious leapt to his feet barking a split second before a two-wheeled motorized vehicle topped the rise a short distance away. Auglaize realized she and Michael were standing like interrupted lovers and, embarrassed, pulled away on the pretext of quieting the dog. One of the hardest things for her to get used to was the Auryx's easy familiarity, the—as she considered it—indiscreet and indiscriminate touching that was so natural for them. However, she tended to forget her distaste for the practice whenever the Commander was within grabbing distance. "This ought to be good for some choice gossip," she muttered under her breath as the newcomer parked his bike and strode over to them.

Michael merely performed the introductions. "Dancer, this is Seven. He's a friend. Seven, take Dancer back to the compound and see that she gets something to eat, will you?"

Seven's uniform was a vivid blue, almost but not quite the shade Makellen had favored, lending a faint bluish sheen to his night-black hair. He was tall for an Auryx, broad-shouldered and proportionately hefty—roughly of Troy's dimensions—making his trimly built Commander look fragile in comparison. That his genes were not pure Auryx was obvious by his physical characteristics; that his heart and mind were, was equally obvious by the way he held himself. His mild protest—"I was detailed to take you down to Operations, you know"—was uttered in a voice good-naturedly deep.

"I prefer to walk. Go ahead."

Seven nodded, and turned on Dancer eyes that were the rich dark brown of the soil in her father's cornfields. Auryx eyes, yet very like her own. "So," he said. "At last, we meet face to face. I've heard a lot about you."

"You have the advantage of me." Dancer laughed. "Your voice is familiar, though. Where do I know you from?"

"I'm flattered you remember. I was one of your monitors when you were in the Van Wert."

"Uh-oh. Then you do know a lot about me. I'm sure I can find some way to exploit that."

Michael cleared his throat. Auglaize expected some joking comment about her fickleness, but when she turned back to him, he had retreated into his image as Commander. He held out the jacket and notebook that she had dropped, unnoticed, when the first Gypsy had come into view. "You will want these."

As if the intimate conversations, the confidence shared during the course of the afternoon, had never taken place. "Thank you again, Commander. What about Serious?"

"I'll keep an eye on him. If you get . . . homesick again," he added in a murmur for her ears only as he helped her into the jacket, "you know where my quarters are. If I'm not there, I can always be found. Come to me; we'll talk."

"As you will, sir," she returned neutrally, conscious of Seven's curious scrutiny.

"Ready?" the brown-eyed Auryx asked, turning toward his conveyance. "Just sit behind me, and hang on tight."

Michael stood aloof, seemingly amused by the whole game. Dancer let her eyes smile into his, then laid her face against Seven's broad back as he started the machine and once again admonished her to "hang on." The next time she looked back, Michael was disappearing into the trees, a shadowy black figure with his hand on the head of the dog padding contentedly at his side. She watched until she could see only the tip of Serious's tail waving back and forth like a flag. Then they rounded a bend in the road.

When Seven finally left Dancer at her door that evening—after a protracted dinner in the third-wing cafeteria and additional lingering over coffee and conversation—she discovered that she had a new roommate. Serious, ignoring his own bed in the corner, was sprawled full length across hers, and greeted her with a joyous rearrangement of half the room with his tail. A handwritten note from Michael amidst the rubble conferred guardianship of the animal upon her for as long as she could properly care for him. The Commander, Dancer realized, would indeed be keeping his eye on her from now on. She found the thought curiously reassuring.

The next afternoon, over the strong objections of the flight medicine people, Highland, and Madison, Michael hauled Dancer into the rear seat of a tandem Weasel and took her up for her first orientation flight.

"I think you'll live to regret this day's work, my love," was Madison's sotto voce comment to the Commander immediately following that flight.

Michael looked across to where a jubilant Auglaize stood with a less-than-jubilant Highland, supposedly out of earshot, and replied, "On the contrary, dear one, 'this day's work' might just have saved them both."

The next day, Auglaize was out of the simulators and into actual flight retraining.

All talk of going home was forgotten—and within a month, Highland was in the cockpit of his own Weasel, flying air-to-air against her. The Commander was always right.

* * *

Almost overnight, it seemed, Dancer had been accepted as an Auryx by her growing circle of friends. She even came to think of herself as "that red-haired Auryx"—when she had time to think of herself at all, what with her new Service's exhausting work schedule.

She was forever briefing, debriefing, studying, in the air, or in the hangars, with Serious at her side when he could be, waiting patiently for her back at Ops when he couldn't. Whenever possible, they walked to and from the aerodrome, her four-pawed buddy and she; it wasn't nearly so far if they stuck to the road, and she and the dog enjoyed the time alone. Besides, though she refused to let on to anyone, riding in the underground shuttles was modified torture for her. The closed-in spaces and tons of rock and dirt pressing down on her head triggered a panic that still took all of her self-control to squelch.

In addition to flight-line duties, Dancer still budgeted several hours a week with the children. The sewing lessons also remained a requirement, though she discovered to her chagrin that, as her skill increased, she actually enjoyed working the intricate Auryx embroidery Madison had sweated over drilling into her.

As for Madison, a subtle shift toward equality took place in her attitude toward her pupil. The tentative friendship firmed as she allowed herself, at last, to get to know Dancer. In private, the two women shared confidences about the loves of their respective lives, Madison's husband Steve and Dancer's lover Troy. Michael was mentioned occasionally, too, in an oblique way; there was some sort of a triangle between the Commander, Steve Belmont—whom Dancer still hadn't met—and his wife, but Madison never offered any information, and Dancer never asked. By the same token, even in moments of confidence, she dared not speak of Makellen.

Then came the momentous day when, following an afternoon of chasing each other around the skies, Highland took her directly to the club after landing. By this time, Dancer was proficient in the Weasel and had at least ten hours' flying time in every aircraft in the installation's inventory—including the T-12s and T-14s, instrumented in Karranganthian—with the notable exception of the Dart. Ceremoniously signing off the most recent flight in her logbook, Highland declared her ready for active duty. "After," he added with that familiar sparkle in his eyes, "you pass an operational check with Michael. And if you think that Mad and I are hardasses, you ain't seen nothin' yet."

Her reply was one of the eardrum-shattering whoops for which she was becoming infamous and a joyous dance with Blaise that thoroughly amused the few onlookers.

It wasn't until the next morning, when she went looking for Michael, that she realized the significance of the nearly empty bar on an afternoon when it should have been moderately packed. Not only was Michael nowhere to be found, but Madison and Seven were mysteriously missing, too. In fact, Dancer could scarcely find anyone to ask where they all might be.

"On a mission," was Highland's tight-lipped reply.

The compound was deserted except for the noncombatants and the children. Most of the meds were gone, and Dancer wasn't surprised to discover that the psychs also doubled as pursuit, escort, and transport pilots.

Those left behind were unnaturally subdued, even the kids, though they had no more notion of what was going on than she did. Dancer divided her time between them and patrols with Highland, and waited. Ten times a day, she asked the communications computer if Michael had returned, and ten times a day received a polite "Not yet, Dancer. I shall let you know the moment he does."

And, near evening of the third day, it did. Michael was on his way to his quarters, the silky, not-quite-mechanical voice informed her noncommittally. So that was where Dancer headed.

Chapter 24

"Michael, wait! I've been looking for you for days."

Stopping in the hallway, turning only his head, the Commander stated quietly, "You have found me."

He stood waiting as she approached, his shoulders slumped, weight on one foot, hand resting on the wall. Something told Dancer that her timing was incredibly bad, but it was too late to turn back now. "Are you all right?"

Michael moved slightly into the light, and she gasped. His uniform was covered with blood, splotched, spattered, soaked; in places, it still glistened wetly. The hand against the wall clutched sodden gloves; a stained cape was thrown negligently over the arm. As he turned to face her, she saw blood caked in his hair, smeared in his eyebrows and across the bridge of his nose where the fingers inside those gloves had pressed. Only his boots showed signs of a sketchy attempt at cleaning, wiped, from the looks of it, on the hem of the cape.

Black bootheels, the hem of a cape, flashed into Dancer's mind. Black bootheels, black cape, blood everywhere, and the hollow echo of the words *This one's still alive.*

"Dear God," she moaned, shaking her head and sagging against the opposite wall.

Michael sighed. "I can't handle that now, Dancer. I crave company, but if you haven't the stomach for it, I understand." His voice was hoarse with pain.

After only a slight hesitation, she fell into step beside him.

"Not to worry, child; very little of it is mine, if that is your concern. Don't touch me!" he commanded sharply as Dancer put out her hand to steady him. "I would prefer that you remain outside of this as long as possible." With that cryptic comment, he lapsed into momentary silence, before startling her by asking, "Dancer, are you afraid of me?"

"Not anymore," she said automatically. "Why?"

"Your reaction when you saw me just now."

"All the blood . . ." She waved a hand vaguely. "It brings back a nightmare I keep having."

"Perhaps a nightmare that we all keep having. It was a child this time, eight, ten years old; barely alive. Screamed herself into unconsciousness at the sight of me." A dry chuckle caught in his throat. "We hoped she could be saved; I held her in my arms the whole trip back. I had even decided to assign her to you."

"She didn't make it."

Michael shook his head. "Her screams still echo in my ears. So." With a sidelong glance at his companion, he opened the door to his quarters, indicated that she should precede him, and went directly to a cabinet under the window. Still holding cape and gloves, he poured himself a glassful of amber liquid from a decanter there and tossed it down in one swift, practiced motion. "A restorative, not an intoxicant," he explained, noting her shocked expression. "I still have reports to make before I rest."

"I'll leave you, then."

"No, stay! Please, I prefer that you stay; we can talk after I get cleaned up. Where is your shadow this evening?"

"You mean Serious? Some of the kids are camping out tonight

on the North Commons, and they feel safer with Seri on guard duty.''

"A camp-out? In the open? That certainly is your doing."

"Fear is acquired, not inherited," she answered defensively.

"I'm not criticizing, child; I'm just surprised that such an outing was approved. Why aren't you out on the North Commons with them?"

Dancer shrugged. "I helped get them settled, then Will took over. I was told you'd be back tonight, and I wanted to talk to you."

"That's right, you had something to tell me, didn't you? Good news?"

"I hope so. Highland thinks I'm finally ready for regular duty, if you concur."

"That *is* good news!" The prospect seemed to cheer him. "It has been a long haul for you, hasn't it? Jeremiah!"

"Here, sir," a disembodied voice answered from somewhere on Dancer's right.

"Jeremiah, pass the word along that I want two fighters ready for a dawn takeoff."

"Any preferences as to type, sir?"

"Something suitable for Dancer's operational check flight. I'll leave it to your discretion."

"You will, of course, want your Weasel?"

"No. It won't be ferried back in time. I'll take whatever's available. And have them armed. That's all, Jeremiah."

By now, Dancer had concluded that there was some sort of intercom link in the room; she was surprised when Michael explained that Jeremiah was the Command computer, and not its operator, as she had previously thought. With what was almost a smile, he "introduced" them.

"Jeremiah will keep you company, Dancer. He can give you any type of music you wish; on occasion, he has even been known to play games. If you want something, he will tell you where to find it. Please, make yourself comfortable—I fear I shall be a while." With that, and a shake of his head, he left her.

Strange man, she couldn't help thinking. Something was weighing on him so heavily that he obviously couldn't stand being alone—and yet, she could sense that he would have preferred not to have seen her. Or for her not to have seen him. Curiosity and an uneasy sense of duty kept her there; being comfortable was something else again.

Dancer finally lit on the windowsill, wondering if she could get the portal open far enough to enjoy the soft evening air. The atmosphere in here was stuffy, though the air-circulating system was working perfectly. An aftereffect of the months cooped up in the Van Wert, the psychs claimed. More likely an aftereffect of her encounter with the Karranganthians. The least bit of tension and she was ready to run outside, as far and as fast as she could across the lush green of the tended lawns, past the well-ordered gardens, into the cool, friendly, nonstructured wilderness outside the confines of the main compound.

As always, the image soothed her nerves back into the studied calm she was learning by example from the Commander. Dear heavens above, what could she do for him tonight? Dancer had rarely seen the river after dark, with moonlight echoing from the ripples in its surface—had Michael ever? Perhaps she could convince him to walk out later. Getting away from here might be good for him, too.

What was she doing just standing around, anyway? She ought to be fixing Michael something to eat, brewing him a pot of coffee, or that vile black ooze that passed for coffee here. But she doubted that he was hungry, and he'd been perfectly capable of pouring himself a drink. Without thinking, she picked up the glass, caught the few remaining drops on a fingertip, and raised it to her lips.

Strong, but not bad. Made her tongue tingle. It might be a restorative, but it certainly had an alcohol base.

"It has been altogether too long since the Commander has had a woman," a voice commented from behind her.

Dancer set the glass down with a bang and spun around guiltily. There was no one there.

"I beg your pardon?" she asked.

"I merely remarked," the voice patiently stated, "that it has been too long since the Commander has had a woman."

"He doesn't have this one," Dancer snapped back, "and just who the hell are you?"

"Jeremiah. It has only been a short time since we were introduced."

"Uh-huh." It was the voice Michael had told her belonged to the Command computer. Dancer couldn't help wondering if the Commander might not have an unexpectedly warped sense of humor, and "Jeremiah" might really be someone on the other end of a communications link. She was familiar, of course, with machines that interpreted speech and vocalized information, but she had never before known one to initiate a conversation.

"I was just trying to be friendly. The Commander did instruct me to make you feel at home."

"Is he all right?" she asked without thinking.

"The Commander? These missions always affect him. He needs only time to collect himself."

Her breath caught in the back of her throat at the specter of Michael as she had just seen him, blood-soaked and stumbling with weariness; his face, the face of war. She hadn't seen that much blood since . . .

These missions, Jeremiah had said. What missions? Rumors circulated in the other Services that the Auryx were ruthless, vengeful, cruel; that they could match atrocities with the Karranganthians and perhaps come out ahead. Funny how she hadn't thought of that before now. But then, none of them had ever met any of the mysterious Auryx, had ever seen what sensual, creative, loving people they were.

Massive quantities of the color red, like closed-in spaces, would make her uneasy for a long time to come, the psychs had warned. But instinct, and the recollection of the grim lines of Michael's face, told her that this was something more. Details of those rumors popped uninvited into her head, and she pushed them away irritably. Surely not Michael. Not Michael.

I . . . would prefer that you wait, he had told her, but if you'd rather not, I understand.

Damn. She'd been too happy at the prospect of flying operationally again to remember the purpose of it all. It wasn't a game, was it, Commander?

Well, She would wait. She owed him that much.

Chapter 25

When Michael at last reemerged from the other room, he was dressed only in a black robe, long-sleeved, ankle-brushing, tightly belted at the waist, obviously made of the same contour-forming fabric as his favorite uniform tunic. Dancer couldn't help staring;

it certainly accented the lines of his body. Shoulders not too broad but well-proportioned to his compact frame; she knew how nicely her head fit in the hollow under his collarbone—it was an experience she had always wanted to repeat. To feel the steady rise and fall of his comfortably muscled chest with his breathing, the whispered caress of his heartbeat under her cheek. To run her hands down over trim hips . . .

To distract her own thoughts, she tried to imagine him in some other color, a blue, perhaps, to match his eyes. Hers swept from the hint of dark hair peeking out of the V where his robe came together over his chest to the trim ankles and bare feet. She tried to imagine him in some other color, but black was Michael, and it became him.

Dancer's appraisal was making him uncomfortable, as close to embarrassed as she had ever seen him; yet she couldn't look away as he strode toward her, his usual easy grace accentuated by the casual drape of the robe.

"Forgive my attire," he finally said. "It seemed too much trouble to dress again, but if this bothers you, I shall."

Distracts was the word, she thought, reminding her of all the dreams—waking and sleeping—that she'd had about this man.

"Why do you always wear black?" she asked abruptly to discourage further speculation along those lines.

"I beg your pardon?" It certainly wasn't what he had expected her to say.

"Black," she pursued, realizing that she really was curious. "You always wear black. Why?"

"No one ever asked me that before." He brushed past her to pick up his glass and refill it from the decanter under the window. It seemed an attempt on his part to buy a few seconds to get his own mind back on safer ground. "Would you like something? There's food if you are hungry; I am not yet ready to eat. No? Well, you know where everything is; help yourself if you change your mind." He stared at his reflection in the window for a moment, then brushed at an imaginary spot on the pane before raising his glass to his lips and lowering it again without drinking. "Your question, Dancer. I haven't forgotten. It's just that I never really thought about it myself.

"As you know, we all have a single black uniform, for which you will, unfortunately, be fitted soon enough. I suppose I chose black because that was what I was wearing the day my predecessor died. On a deeper level . . ." He sighed, and took so long to continue that Dancer began to think he wasn't going to. "Mourning, I think, for all the lives that ended that day."

"Including your own."

He raised an eyebrow. "Very astute. Also, black stands out in a crowd. I have always liked to stand out. An important attribute for a leader, don't you think?"

Though she accepted the attempt at levity, she didn't miss the frown that briefly narrowed his eyes before he turned back to the window. Michael was younger than Dancer had first thought; not much older than she, in fact, and tonight he had an air of vulnerability that she had never seen before. How would she cope with the responsibilities resting on the shoulders under that taut black fabric? It was with great difficulty that she restrained herself from throwing her arms around him.

Good grief, I'd better watch it, she thought with surprise. Her feelings for him could easily become a lot stronger than the stalwart affection she saw in the eyes of "his people" whenever he walked by, much more than the appreciation of a well-made male form and the familiar longing for an undefined someone.

"We really must find you a lover, Dancer."

So, he was aware of the attraction, too; something about his tone indicated that it might just be mutual. "Are you volunteering?" she asked flippantly.

"Ah, child, would that I had the leisure or the constitution for an emotional attachment! I simply cannot afford the distraction. It's bad enough that I feel the loss of every one of my people as if a part of me has died. To invest even more in one woman . . . would certainly outweigh the dubious benefits of such a liaison."

"From what I hear, your predecessor had no such qualms."

"Jeremiah telling tales again, hmm?"

"It seems that he thought I was here to, how shall I phrase it, comfort you. And about time, according to him."

"I must remind Jeremiah that I can easily reprogram his 'opinions.' But yes, our late Commander indulged himself in a succession of mistresses. The last was a beautiful lady in every way, and he loved her literally to distraction. They both died for it."

For a tenth of a second Dancer felt his fingers on her wrist as he brushed by her; just long enough for her to realize that the contact was not accidental before he rearranged some cushions on the couch and sat.

"Please. Be comfortable." He gestured her into his treasured rocker, drew an Auryx harp from under the end table between them, and stretched his legs out on the couch, his back eased against the pillows on its arm.

As his fingers roamed idly over the strings, Dancer discovered with pleasure the comfortable hollows worn in the patchwork seat and back pads that she had put together for his rocking chair as part of her coordination therapy. Her entire progress, from that best-forgotten but forever memorable first simulator to her first actual trainer flight, was documented here. The clumsy early stitches, large and uneven, that she would have discarded had Michael not prevented it, to the precise, uniform joinings resulting from hours of frustration and practice. Twenty-three different stitches; her teacher had insisted that she learn twenty-three different ways to hold two scraps of cloth together. Dancer couldn't understand why anyone would want to go to so much trouble, but she soon learned that that was the way of the Sixth Service: precise, strictly attentive to detail, expert in what they did. Even as they were training her fingers, they were disciplining her mind.

All under the watchful eye of Michael, who seemed to be every-where and know everything intuitively. Again, she wondered how she would have coped with his responsibilities. She wondered how *he* did.

Michael sighed and crossed his arms over the instrument on his chest. "I did not ask for this job," he stated. "I did not want it, and when I learned that I was chosen, I tried to refuse. They wouldn't let me. So here I am. I will, of course, do my duty. But I hate it, Dancer. There is so much blood on these hands." He held up slender, immaculately manicured hands and looked at them with a distaste that communicated itself to her as she remembered the red-brown stains glistening on his gloves.

"You see it, too, don't you."

"What happened, Michael?" she asked with a calmness she was far from feeling. Whatever it was, if it had unsettled him, *she* certainly didn't want to hear about it.

The ghost of a smile was his only acknowledgment that, as usual, he had been following her thoughts. "Fragile-looking things, hands, but capable of so much force. Killing force. Two dozen men died directly by mine this time. The Sixth Service does not take prisoners, Dancer. Do you understand what I am saying?" He threw his head back on the pillows, squeezed his eyes shut, raked a hand through his hair, and continued on, as if afraid of her reaction. "When you are surrounded by the carnage, the dying, the dead, the stench of blood and the horrors that the enemy has inflicted—the anger, the hatred are overpowering. We kill and kill and kill until none are left alive. It isn't always clean and painless. More times than I care to count I myself have indulged in the more subtle forms of execution. I remember one occasion on which I particularly enjoyed it . . .''

The gleam in his eyes matched the chill in his voice, and both unaccountably frightened Auglaize. Awareness of that fact slowly penetrated his reverie; he took a deep, calming breath. "So, child. You see how I forget myself. You're fond of quotes; ponder this one. 'Vengeance is mine, sayeth the Auryx.' To us falls the honor of the so-called 'mopping up' missions. That is what I would shield you from. Avenging Angels, we are called. Or Dark Angels. Death Squad. Devils in Black. Yes, the black uniform. Chosen for its psychological impact; black has historically inspired fear. Heeled boots for added height. The sweeping cloak, you see, gives the impression of floating, of speed. Of majesty. It gives us the illusion of invincibility. The illusion. We are not invincible.''

"The bloodlust," she answered softly. "Throughout history, individuals and whole armies have suffered from it. I've heard it said that persons thus afflicted occasionally turn on their own when no enemy is left."

The look that he gave her from under lowered eyelids turned her lungs to ice. She had to force herself to breathe as he continued harshly, "And you do not yet *know* the worst. Four of those twenty-four were under my command. It was . . . not as you have said, but nevertheless . . . Have you ever killed anyone, Dancer, face to face, watching the life drain out of him like so many grains of sand through your fingers?''

Dancer nodded, unable to speak past the sudden constriction of her throat that was the memory of Troy. In a span of perhaps three seconds, she relived the last five minutes of his life. She cradled his shaven and bloody head on her shoulder, frantic for a way to ease his suffering. His voice, a hoarse croak no longer recognizable as his once hearty baritone, pleaded with her. "Auglaize, please. I can't stand any more. You are the only one strong enough to do it. For God's sake, Auglaize, if you love me!" Horror at the thought, and pain. Pain. Nothing to what he had endured, was enduring, would endure. A jerk, a twist of her manacle chains around his neck—and Dancer learned that men do not die easily. But he did die. She held his broken body until they came and dragged him from her.

"Of course you have; forgive me." Michael's voice was gentler, but just as relentless. "He was one of your command, too, wasn't he, and a friend. You understand, then, that there are some things a commander must do.''

"I am beginning to," she said levelly.

"Four of my people," he repeated. "My friends; we're a small Service, and close-knit. The determination had been made that they could not survive, and the drugs to make their passing easier could not be spared. Nor the time of the meds, who were concentrating on those who could be helped. So, you see, it was up to me. There is a method, painless to the victim, instantaneous . . .''

He sighed. "Mercer, Pike, Noble; quickly, efficiently. But the woman—that was the worst. Madison.''

"Not Merylys," she whispered, using the given name that few in the Service knew—the name that was embroidered on the patchwork under her hand because Dancer had liked the pattern the Auryx characters formed. Merylys Belmont, Madison. Her teacher and her friend. That shattering sense of loss—Auglaize was getting quite used to it by now. The hard knot in the throat would dissolve itself into tears eventually, after the shock wore off.

Michael nodded. "There was an explosion; you would not have known her. I almost didn't know her. But she was conscious, and she understood what I had to do. In the end, I did it.''

"My God, Michael." Merylys dead, and he had killed her.

"It is the way of our people. My duty as Commander.''

Expelling her breath in a harsh laugh, Dancer shook her head. "Your duty! Here we are, surrounded by an installation whose prime function is to preserve life, and you sit here calmly telling me it was your duty to kill—''

"They would not have made it back," he interrupted forcefully.

"Who made that decision, Michael?''

He met her eyes steadily, and she was the one who had to look away.

"Come now, Dancer; by your own admission, you did the same thing yourself.''

"The situation was a little different, my friend.''

"The situation was the same," he stated flatly. "You ended Morgan Troy's suffering the only way you knew how. And don't think my actions won't haunt me the way yours haunt you! I shall see the trust in their eyes in the dark of night, hear their voices . . .''

He was right; it was the same. Though wed to Steve Belmont, Merylys had died loving Michael, and he had loved her, perhaps even as Auglaize had loved Troy. " 'Will all great Neptune's ocean wash this blood clean from my hand?' '' she quoted dispassionately.

"Don't condemn me, Dancer. Not you. Don't add to my burden of guilt by suggesting that she . . . that any of my four might have survived. I did what I had to do, and if there is a merciful God watching over us, one day I'll be able to accept it myself."

"The psychs—"

"I am the Commander, child! I don't have the option of cleanly forgetting. Anything. *Anything*." The last was a whisper that tore at her heart. "What I have done, what I have been, what I have become, I must live with.

"The girl I brought back here today—I wanted her so much to survive. My vindication, perhaps. The vain hope of salvaging something from another Karranganthian slaughterhouse. Our medical transports are as fast as most fighters, but they were not fast enough this time."

"Did she truly have a chance, Michael, or was it just that you couldn't bear to let go of another life?" Dancer asked gently.

His expression was odd as he regarded her. "Everyone else knows enough to stay out of my way after a mission such as this. I'm glad you didn't."

"If euthanasia is the way of your people, why was I allowed to live?"

"Because you were alive when you should have been dead! Because when I first looked into your eyes, I knew that your mind was intact. Because, just once, I wanted to cheat the Karranganthians of a victory."

"It was you, then. I thought . . . someone else."

"It matters not who made the decision. None of us would have done otherwise. But yes, you are one of my successes, and right now, I am more than grateful for the reminder."

She was looking at him, through him, trying to remember. "The other voice. It could have been you. I don't even know if it was real any more."

"If what was real, child?"

After the briefest of hesitations, Dancer began to describe the nightmares that wouldn't stop, the indistinct murmurs and images of black and red, the utterance, "This one's still alive." There, the dream usually ended. Tonight, though, she saw again the vivid blue eyes staring down into her own, heard the husky, not-quite-familiar voice whispering, "Don't leave me now, child," and felt once more the incongruous aura of safety amid the terror. Of peace. The same safety, the same peace, Dancer suddenly realized, that she generally equated with the Commander's presence.

"It was you," she stated positively. "It was real."

"It was real, child. As real as this moment. As real as . . ." He caught himself, shook his head, gave her a distracted half-smile.

"What happened, Michael?" she probed gently. It wasn't that she really wanted to know. On the contrary, she definitely did not. What she did want, though, was to ease his mind somehow, as he had so often eased hers. The mere lending of a sympathetic ear seemed scant payback for his friendship.

Michael looked at her, shook his head again.

"There was a child," Dancer pursued. "The situation was similar to mine?"

"No, Dancer, no."

"Talk to me, Michael."

He held out for one moment more, as if torn between his desire to protect her and his need to rid himself of certain images from the waking nightmare that had been the past few days. Need won out. On a long exhalation of breath, Michael haltingly began to speak, to her, and to Jeremiah for the record.

Though his voice strove for the accustomed impassivity, he just missed it somehow. As for her—she felt herself blanch, with almost detached interest watched the room spin around her as he purged his mind in graphic detail, clung to his hand as if it were a lifeline and noted with surprise that he was clinging to hers just as desperately.

"How was it for you, Flight Leader, watching your command die?" he asked her when his report was finished, his voice not quite steady even yet. "Did you feel each of their torments as if it were your own?"

It was Dancer's turn to sigh. "I am luckier than you; the psychs haven't left me with much recollection of that. I think, in a way, Auglaize DeWellesthar did. But the part of me that was Flight Leader held herself aloof because they were looking to her for guidance, and the only way she could give it was to keep a clear head."

"Yes. Never let them know that the commander has doubts. And the killing of your friend?"

"That was rough. Troy and I were about as close as two people can be, given the circumstances of our chosen profession. The whole group of us were thrown in together after we were captured. They knew what he wanted me to do, at the end; they knew as well as I what he had been through and what he had ahead of him. Yet they were shocked when I . . . eased him out of life. It was the first sign of weakness I had ever shown them."

"Weakness? I don't understand."

"That's the difference in our philosophies. All of us knew what was going to happen. All of us were terrified of it. But we saw it as our duty to hang on and fight it through."

"And you say that *my* Service is a hard one."

"Michael, I survived. As you have said, I should have died, but I didn't. Why do you think that is?"

He shook his head and rose. "I feel as if I am just beginning to know you."

"Well," she drawled, her sense of humor reappearing unexpectedly, "that usually happens when two people spend the night together." At his startled look, she gestured toward the window. "Aren't those the dawn stars?"

"Indeed. You should have been in bed long ago, child."

"And you, my friend."

"I was afraid . . . your friendship means a lot to me, Dancer. I fear I do not always live up to my image."

"You keep telling me I can say anything to you. That works two ways, you know." Dancer stood up, stretched, gave his shoulder a quick squeeze, and started toward the door while she still had the self-control to leave him.

"Dancer." His voice stopped her in her tracks. "I have not always been completely honest with you. I can arrange for you to go back to your old Service, back to combat flying, even back to your old unit if that's what you want."

"I know," she replied, eyes still on the door. "Highland told me weeks ago."

"Yet you never asked?" The briefest of hesitations. "So. Now that you know exactly what kind of a Service we are—what we are required to do—do you still want to join us?"

"Of course."

His hands turned her to face him. "Think well, child. Are you completely certain?"

"Absolutely. But, Michael, it is not for your Service that I would lay down my life." Dancer left the rest of it unspoken. It was to him, the man, that she pledged her loyalty.

It took him a moment, but Michael understood. The lines of weariness dropped from his face, and his blue eyes were alive again. In fact, he almost laughed out loud before he caught himself. "You'll be officially sworn in immediately after passing your check flight—perhaps you would like to return to your quarters for a few hours' rest before we take off?"

"Will you sleep if I leave?"

"I think not quite yet."

"Neither will I."

"Well, then. You go get into your flying clothes, and let me get into mine. Meet you for breakfast, and then we shall watch the sun come up."

4: O'Brian's Stake

Chapter 26

As the sun came up over O'Brian's Stake, Dancer rose from the windowsill and stretched stiff muscles, her body drenched with sweat and her face wet with tears. But she knew. Knew who Auglaize DeWellesthar had been, and who Dancer was.

Who *she* was.

Shivering in the cool morning air, she pulled the black flight jacket closer around her shoulders. Funny, she didn't remember getting it out of the closet. Then—of course. Michael's, she thought, snuggling into it. The body warmth was hers, but the scent was his . . . nothing in particular, just Michael. "Thank you," she said aloud.

"I should have closed the window, but I didn't want to disturb you." He hauled himself to a sitting position on the bed as Dancer turned toward his voice, giving her a sheepish half-smile. "I seem to have fallen asleep. Sorry."

"Have you been here all night?"

"Most of it. I wanted to be close by if you needed me."

"You could have stopped me from remembering."

"To what purpose? You're different from the rest of us, Dancer— you needed to know. It has been coming on for some time; your double seems to have been the catalyst. Are you all right?"

Better than she had been since the day that routine patrol had ended in tragedy, she reflected. All she had to say was, "Yes." Michael would know the rest.

"No deep, dark, buried secrets about Flight Leader De-Wellesthar?" he asked with a smile.

"No. She sure did want to go home, didn't she? I had forgotten how alone she felt after . . . ." Dancer hesitated. "Michael—Makellen Darke. He did exist."

"You never doubted it."

"Is he dead?"

He met her searching gaze unflinchingly. "Child, accept this: They never approved of your relationship, and They finally found a way to keep you apart."

"It was you who pushed him out of my mind."

"It was I," he confirmed. "It was necessary."

"Why?"

"Child, I did what I had to do, as ordered by my superiors. Please believe me, I did not obey lightly, or without strenuous protest. Also please believe, it is as Darke would have wished it. I can tell you no more."

"And the Karranganthian," she whispered. "How could I have forgotten the Karranganthian?"

"That, child, was by your own request."

Dancer nodded, suddenly too weary to speak. She'd sort it all out later. Right now, she just wanted to sleep.

The next thing she knew, she was in Michael's arms, being lifted, carried over to the bed, and tucked in, jacket and all. He stood looking down at her for a long moment, then dropped a light kiss on the bridge of her nose and turned on his heel.

"Mike?" she called sleepily after him.

"Yes, Red?"

"There's more than enough room for you here, you know."

"Perhaps later, child. Just now, I have things to do."

With a smile, Dancer snuggled down, pulling the blankets—and the jacket—closer around her face.

Through the open door came the creak of Michael's rocker and the bittersweet strains of an Auryx harp.

Chapter 27

He should have awakened Dancer an hour ago. Still, as he stood beside the bed with a steaming cup of cinnamon cocoa—one of his second's few indulgences—Michael was reluctant to do so even now. Asleep, without the weariness of years of war haunting her features, she looked even more the child she would soon be impersonating. Or the child whose mutilated body he had held in his arms twelve years ago, whose eyes had looked into his with so much trust. Even knowing it was he who had erased that time from her mind, erased the memory of the man she had loved and refused to let go of—even knowing that he had violated her in this manner, the trust was still there. God, to be worthy of it!

Oh, he'd left her with a shadowy recollection of her time in the Van Wert, of boredom and loneliness and hours of learning Auryx language and culture to pass the time, a recollection reinforced when it came her turn to play "Guardian" to one of Van Wert's long-term patients. Of her convalescence and struggle for acceptance in her new Service, her sense of isolation and her homesickness, her triumph and delight at overcoming the stigma of "outsider," he had left her memories nearly intact. The extent of his own friendship and support during those days, he had merely blunted. It was only Darke he had actually taken away from her. Only Darke—leaving behind a void in her that no other man had been able to fill. And the one who wanted so desperately to try—well, Michael still held that knowledge back from her.

She smiled in her sleep, and his free hand was only inches from caressing her cheek before he stopped himself. How quickly years of hard-won self-control could flee! It might have been a mistake to move her up here. Then again, if it was an error in judgment, he had made worse. "Time to get up, Dancer," he finally murmured.

"Mmrph," was her sleepy reply as she rolled toward the sound of his voice. Then, "Uh!" when she opened her eyes, registered white light and acute pain, and squeezed them shut again. "Would you mind . . ."

She needn't have bothered to ask; Michael had already deposited the mug on the nightstand and was drawing the drapes.

"Thanks." Dancer cautiously raised her eyelids again, obviously finding the twilightlike dimness more to her liking. "This waking up to bright sun is going to take some getting used to."

It was Michael's turn to grunt. Snapping on a lamp, he took her lower jaw firmly in his cupped hand and forced her to look at him, then shook his head. "As I feared. Reaction to the dye. You're not going anywhere with the whites of your eyes the same color as your uniform."

"So, what's wrong with being color-coordinated?" she shot back defensively. "It's my fault that that stuff was designed for your damned Auryx blue irises? You'd think by now our research people would have come up with something compatible with my Dancer brown ones. For you, a little amber tint, and there you go. Green eyes. For me, it's the full chemical treatment."

"To which you seem to be sensitive."

"Michael, my friend, I always have been. I was just never stupid enough to let you notice before. Look, Preble gave me some drops; they're around here somewhere. I got time for a shower?"

That was his Dancer—no sweet, innocent child when she was awake. Michael sighed his exasperation, located the tiny bottle of eyedrops in the pocket of her robe, and administered them. "Drink your cocoa. Yes, you have time for a shower and for some lunch, which I have already prepared. I have also laid out your clothes for you."

"Someday you're going to make somebody a great valet," she quipped, holding up the mug. His hand closed over hers to steady it as he took a sip.

"If I ever go looking for a job, I'll count on you for a reference." The reply was automatic, almost distracted, and she noticed.

"What is it about this mess that bothers you so, Michael?"

"Your ego never ceases to amaze me. What makes you think your petty problems are my only concern?" If he could have put his reservations into words, he wouldn't have voiced them to her, anyway. "I just have a bad feeling, child. I don't want to lose you."

Did he read her reaction in her face, or did he actually feel it in his mind? Even after all these years, Michael himself wasn't sure. But he knew what she was thinking as clearly as if she had voiced it: he had, in the past, calmly sent her into places from which the percentages had been very high against her emerging intact, his last words to her a half-joking "I don't want to lose you, child." Why, then, this time, did the familiar, almost ritualistic phrase make her shiver? What, exactly, was the Commander afraid of?

What *was* the Commander afraid of?

Perhaps part of that question would have been answered had she seen, through his eyes, her reaction as her glance fell on the red jumpsuit hanging on the closet door, the spit-shined flying boots sitting on the floor under it. Dancer's smile was of pure, anticipatory pleasure. As if she were, at long last, going home.

"Very well, DeWellesthar," Michael stated dryly. "Let's get to it."

Chapter 28

The hot water stung. When Dancer looked down, she was surprised to see an angry red welt creasing her thigh. In all the excitement, she had forgotten that the point of Tonia's survival knife had restyled her khakis—and, incidentally, her leg. Ouch. Luckily, Preble's ointment was an anesthetic as well as an antiseptic. If she could remember where she'd tossed the stuff.

On closer inspection while she patted it dry with a towel, the scratch didn't look so bad after all. Sure, there was some redness and swelling, and the towel felt like sandpaper, but what did she expect? In a day or so, except for a long, thin scar, she'd never even know the skin had been broken.

Still, the tight-fitting tailored jumpsuit would irritate. Better to leave putting that on until the last possible moment. She started to reach for the tube on the back of the sink, but Michael's voice chose that moment to urge haste and she grabbed his robe off the hook behind the door instead.

"I know how it looks," she replied to his raised eyebrow. "But it was handy, okay?"

"The word is *cliché*." His fingers moved on the keyboard before him and Jeremiah digested his orders with a soft hum as Michael rose and led her to the small kitchen. With a quick look of longing at the curtained recess containing his bunk, she took the indicated chair at the dining table.

"How are you feeling?" he asked, setting a plate of stew in front of her and turning to remove what smelled suspiciously like fresh rolls from the oven.

"Hungry, thank you. Anything new I should know about?"

"Nothing pressing." He seemed almost shy with her, probably waiting for the fireworks about his tampering with her memory.

She would have been furious with him, had she not known what a powerful stimulus it took to force the Commander into actions so entirely against his moral code. Besides, if he hadn't wanted her to remember now, she wouldn't. Dancer had that much faith in his power over her.

"You're thinking about him, aren't you?" Michael asked quietly. "Darke. Even after all these years, I recognize the look. There is a certain softness around your eyes . . ."

"Is there?" she mused, toying with the idea of admitting that it had been her Commander of whom she had been thinking. No. He wouldn't appreciate that. Besides, now the gentle curve of her lips *was* for Kellen. "You know, it just occurred to me, I think I have been waiting for him all this time. I made him a promise, that he would be the first man I made love to after the Van Wert. Maybe subconsciously I have been keeping that promise."

"There really hasn't been anyone else for you since Troy?"

"I said it, didn't I?" Dancer snapped back, unaccountably angered that Michael, of all people, would doubt her word. Besides, what business was it of his? But the ironic half smile that met her display of temper dissolved it instantly. "All right, so there were a few near misses. Our own sweet Seven, for one, if you must know. But none of them ever really got under my skin for some reason. Although one . . . could have."

"Ah." The way he avoided her eyes let her know that he understood, but deliberately chose to ignore the implications. Then, his half smile blossomed into a mischievous grin. "And the fair-haired crewchief of your double?"

She grinned back at him. "You saw the sparks, huh?"

"I could hardly miss them. Although I understand you always did fall in love very easily."

"How would you know?"

"Hearsay," he teased. "I've been listening in on your conversations with Antonia, remember? If it's any consolation, I venture to guess that Callicoon spent a restless night on your behalf. Perhaps it's time you buried your dead, hmm?"

"You're telling me I should sleep with Paulding Callicoon?"

"If that's what it takes. You could do worse."

"Do you have any idea how many times you've said that to me over the years? Besides, you know what Calli is."

"I have a fairly good idea. But as long as you're aware of the dangers going in, I see no reason you can't enjoy yourself."

"You never cease to amaze me, Michael."

"I assure you, I devoutly share your wish it could be I instead of he. However, since that is not possible, coping with the jealousy of a living man whom you will probably never see again is much easier than coping with that of a memory who will be cherished by you always. Now, finish your lunch. Time grows short."

Dancer shook her head in astonishment at his cavalier delivery of this startling pronouncement, and ate her stew.

Colonel Daven enjoyed lunch at his desk, alone, as was his wont. The framed likeness of Kalelle, his favored wife, was the only company he needed, and that precluded the necessity for idle conversation. Daven preferred to enjoy the excellent Fourth Service food in silence. For dessert, it was his habit to partake of a chapter or two of one of the volumes in his predecessor's considerable library. There was much to learn here, much that would be of value in later endeavors.

When the knock sounded on his office door, Daven swallowed his irritation and called out, "Enter." By now, all knew of his midday habits—some, to their considerable discomfort—and none would dare interrupt unless the matter was vital.

Still, Summit was hesitant about actually setting foot over the threshold. Instead, he opened the door only far enough to stick his head in until he could gauge his commander's temper.

Daven sighed to himself. This ogre act really was becoming tiresome, but he had an image to maintain, and his further career depended on his ability to maintain that image. The further career he had in mind for himself was retirement from active service, and a nice, quiet hideaway where he and Kalelle could live out the rest of their lives in peace. Strange wish for someone with his past record, but there it was.

So, instead of inviting his operations officer in for a cup of excellent coffee and a civil discussion of literature, Daven found himself snapping, "What is it, Summit?"

"Sir, the punishment of DeWellesthar's maintenance team has been carried out, as you ordered. The effect upon the others was as desired—there will be no more carelessness such as that loose winglock."

Lovely news to aid digestion, Daven thought ironically. Still, it had been necessary. If fear was the best way to control, then a commander must control by fear. "Excellent."

"The same awaits her crewchief when he returns."

"No," Daven stated. "His punishment is to know that what happened to his people was his fault. That will do best for a man with his conscience. Somewhere along the way, that one has become imbued with the lamentable Fourth Service trait of loyalty to one's peers."

"But, sir—"

"Think, man! The media has been having a field day with this little incident. The girl and he are both mysterious heroes. A crewchief is in a very visible position during the exhibition flight. What kind of questions do you think would be asked if he were not in evidence during today's?"

"You're right, as always."

"We'll kill him as soon as we leave orbit," he said dismissively. "After we kill the girl."

Chapter 29

Strange, after all those years, how natural it felt to be slipping into a Fourth Service uniform again. As she had with all former impersonations, Dancer donned a new personality with the costume. This time, however, with a few attitude adjustments, the new personality was her own old one. Oddly enough, that too seemed natural.

She even found herself humming an old, half-forgotten, Fourth Service drinking song as she laced her flying boots. Like the other uniform items, these were stiffer and less comfortable than their Sixth Service counterparts, but her toes felt as if they had come home. In a couple of hours those same feet would be screaming for release, Dancer knew, but that knowledge didn't dampen her enjoyment now.

Her last, almost unconscious act before exiting her room was to pull the Academy ring off her finger and set it on the wooden base of the Gypsy model. Though Dancer parted with this talisman only under duress, Auglaize DeWellesthar had habitually left it behind when preparing to fly. And, of course, Tonia didn't have one to wear.

Michael was issuing last-minute instructions, via Jeremiah, to today's plainclothes crowd-control crew when she came out; uncharacteristically, he hesitated when he saw her. Dancer waited until he had finished, then tossed him a flip, "Well, how do I look?"

Not that she needed to hear him murmur "Incredible" to reassure her. She had a mirror. She knew that Auglaize DeWellesthar was a striking woman. What she had forgotten was that Michael had never met her. At least, not conscious and all in one piece. This was the first time he had ever seen Dancer in Fourth Service uniform.

It wasn't just a set of clothes, she realized, looking into the mirror of his eyes—it was an entire set of mind. She held herself differently, more stiffly, and moved with a confidence that crossed the border to the side of arrogance. She was Flight Leader DeWellesthar—Squadron Leader, if she had been a bit older—and she bore the responsibilities of command with a hard-edged pride. Not consciously ambitious, but, like Michael, aware that a job needed doing, and that she was the person to do it.

She was also a woman and, despite the close-cropped coiffure, managed to project that, too. Although Antonia's reasons and background were different, the overall effect was the same, and Dancer thought it was her striking likeness to the girl that left Michael speechless.

"I never realized . . ." he began, then cleared his throat and rose. "Come along, child. We have kept them waiting long enough."

With that and nothing more, he took her arm and escorted her downstairs.

* * *

My God, look at her! Michael thought as he stared at the stranger in the minutely tailored Fourth Service jumpsuit walking beside him. In truth, though he had read records and seen tapes of her, Michael's first meeting with Flight Leader Auglaize DeWellesthar was a shock. Shock? Lord, she took his breath away! This was a side of his Dancer that he had never seen. Cockier, with a hard edge that even his mind couldn't define; an edge succinctly her own that she would have to blunt if she were to be accepted as the other.

With her customary self-confidence augmented, she seemed to exude . . . authority, that was it. The wide, tinted green eyes lacked the warmth of their former brown, though that might have been simply because both she and Michael were unused to the color. Still, the depths of those eyes—and by extension, Dancer's mind—seemed to be barred from him.

Was this the minx with whom, only yesterday, he had been joking about ordering her to become his mistress? The uncomplaining subordinate content to fly his wing, sit at his right hand, quietly advise, argue, then finally follow his commands even when she disagreed with them? Try as he might, he just couldn't see his easygoing Dancer in the Confederacy officer at his side, this cropped-haired woman with an overall demeanor of easy aloofness, relaxed rigidity—not the contradiction in terms that seemed. Her erect posture and touch-me-not air were not assumed; rather, they seemed long suppressed and at last allowed to break free. Had she remained with the Fourth Service, she surely would have been a general by now; God knew she had the talent. And she certainly had the bearing.

Michael felt curiously bereft, as if his worst fears had been realized. She was leaving him. No, she already had left him. She was back among her own people, where she belonged. His mistake had been in ever thinking otherwise.

"Michael, what is it? What's wrong?"

How could he tell her? How could he admit that his fear of losing her was so great it almost immobilized him? But how could he deny her the dream of two lifetimes?

The feeling of physical danger was so strong he could almost reach out and pluck it from the air in front of them; maybe that was what triggered the overwhelming sense of loss. If only he could be with her, to protect, to share the danger . . .

Michael set his jaw and pulled himself away from feelings and speculation. His first priority was to keep her alive, and he couldn't do that unless his mind was swept clear of emotion.

Dancer . . . !

Keep her alive. If he couldn't do that, it wouldn't make any difference in which Service's uniform she was more comfortable.

Chapter 30

Antonia and Dancer would enter the conference room separately, and alone, for maximum effect. The dramatics were necessary. If they were able to keep the people who knew Dancer well guessing even for a moment—people who were trained to observe and pounce on anomalies—maybe she had a chance of pulling this masquerade off. It was one thing to impersonate someone unknown personally to your audience; that she had accomplished many times, and well. But to try to step into someone else's life, on her own territory, after only one day of study, was asking a lot of even Dancer's superior acting skills, and she knew it. Still, the physical resemblance alone would get her by for quite a while, and almost everything else could be explained away by a pointed reference to Tonia's accident. Dancer understood Michael's misgivings, but did not share them. The slightest doubt on her part would have meant automatic failure.

Subtly, her demeanor changed as she and Michael watched Tonia stride down the corridor toward where they waited for her outside one of the more commodious briefing rooms. Dancer's mantle of self-confidence slipped toward bravado; her air of command muted to arrogance as she assumed the younger girl's persona. Even her face altered, the hardness of fourteen years at war slipping away to reveal that sweet eagerness of youth she had only last night—but oh, so long ago—mourned the loss of in herself. Only behind the eyes was Dancer still evident, and that strength was masked by her adoption of Tonia's rapid, insecure eye movements.

Michael gave her the ghost of a smile, a quick nod as he slipped through the door of the conference room to become part of a large and critical audience.

"Looking good," was Tonia's greeting, after she reached over to tweak a lock of hair onto her double's forehead.

Dancer's impatient hand would have immediately pushed it back out of the way had she not consciously stopped herself. She had worn her short hair brushed to the side, but Tonia preferred an eyebrow-tickling fringe. "I'll remember," she said aloud. "Ready?"

"Good gravy, you even sound like me! Unbelievable. But are you sure you can handle the flying? I mean," she added hastily at Dancer's raised eyebrow, "it's not exactly the kind of stuff you're used to."

"I think I can compensate for the downgraded performance of the Gypsy," Dancer assured her with a straight face.

"We're ready for you, DeWellesthar." Michael's voice called from the other side of the closed door, and Dancer nodded.

"You're on, kid. Just walk across the room and stand beside Michael."

Antonia wiped her palms down her hips. "I can't believe I'm so nervous!"

"So'm I, and I know everybody. Go ahead. Just be yourself. Then stand back and watch *me* be yourself."

Tonia shrugged, squared her shoulders, and marched into the conference room as if she owned it, meeting critical stares with an assumed nonchalance that made Dancer smile as she watched through a finger-wide space between door and jamb. Reaching Michael, Antonia walked all the way around him, surveying him from head to toe from all angles, then gave onlookers a shrug of the eyebrows and a raised thumb. The girl really knew how to play to an audience.

Well, so did Dancer. She stood poised for the count of three, then hit the door with the heel of her hand and copied Antonia's entrance gesture for gesture—not a difficult task, since Tonia's mannerisms so closely resembled her own—except for the last. Dancer directed her appreciative wink and the thumbs-up over Michael's shoulder at Antonia.

Tonia's eyes sparkled as she nodded, and even Michael's taut features threatened to relax into a smile.

"He's not bad at all," was Tonia's judicious opinion. "A little on the small side, but I wouldn't throw him back."

"*On* his back, maybe," Dancer returned with a lewd gesture. "You know what they say about the small ones."

With the snort that was the closest he ever came to a laugh, Michael retreated to the sidelines, the slight upturn of the corner of his mouth signaling that he still knew which was Dancer and that she'd answer for her *lèse-majesté* later.

There was some whispering back and forth as Antonia and Dancer continued their light banter, audible disagreement as to which of them was which. Knowing Dancer so well, her colleagues immediately pounced on the mannerisms they recognized—which happened to be the ones she and Tonia shared. It seemed that the pair also shared the same warped sense of humor. They certainly shared the same feel for flying, they discovered; ignoring the now open dissension in front of them, their conversation quickly and naturally turned to that subject.

This enjoyable private discussion was interrupted by Michael. "You have proven your point, ladies. Kindly take your seats so that we can continue."

Everyone not directly involved left the room, and at Tonia's inquiring look the Commander indicated an empty chair next to Eire. Dancer, as usual, slid into place at Michael's right hand. More murmurs, quickly stilled this time as she tossed her head in the habitual gesture a long-haired person develops to fling stray locks back out of the way. To her surprise, Antonia immediately copied it, and they both laughed.

Michael just sat back and allowed his second to conduct the briefing, though there wasn't much to report. He'd set into motion all the inquiries he could think of, and the replies had either been less than helpful or had not yet arrived.

For instance, the revised show schedule. Peacekeeping forces on the five other planets that had received unannounced visits from the Team this season reported surprise, delight, enjoyment of an outstanding show, and renewed support for the Confederacy forces as the only results of the Team's Warlord in orbit around their worlds. Certainly nothing out of the ordinary, and wasn't it about time the Confederacy gave some thought to its troops out in the boondocks?

At that, Dancer snorted. Good God, you'd think that with all their vast resources, the Sixth Service would have gotten some inkling all was not as it should be with the Fourth Service Interplanetary Precision Aerial Demonstration Team long before this. Or had they just grown lazy with the signing of the latest peace treaty?

The Commander's small quirk of the lip, as telling to her as a full-blown grin, let her know he understood and shared her frustration.

"Sorry, Dancer," was Will's response. "That's the best I've been able to come up with. Nothing yet from Fourth Service Headquarters about who changed the itinerary or why. We're just too far out for instantaneous communications.''

"Efficient as always, Willtell," Dancer replied. "My impatience was not directed at you. Preble, what do you have from the medical standpoint?"

"First of all, Auglaize here"—the med wizard nodded at Antonia—"has been most cooperative. We know what compounds have been introduced into her system, and can guess at the effects of each from observation. We're working on countermeasures now, but it's slow going without knowing exactly how the components were combined. As to how Team Five was being systematically drugged without her knowledge—we can only hypothesize that, from the amounts and the blends we've found, it's been administered over a long period of time, probably in food or drink. So, be careful what you consume. Your resistance to most mood-altering drugs is phenomenal, but it's not a hundred percent reliable.''

"So noted. But I've gotta eat, Preb. You think they'd let me on board with a goodie bag from our own cafeteria? What've you got on Callicoon?''

"Callicoon?" Antonia interrupted. "Excuse me, but what is a Callicoon?''

"Paulding Callicoon," Dancer told her. "Your 'Troy's' real name.''

"How did you . . . ?" she began, then shook her head. "He told you last night?"

"Something like that.''

Dancer watched the girl's reaction as the meds reported their total frustration in trying to examine her crewchief. Tonia seemed startled; unaware either that the attempt had been made or that he had caused so much trouble.

"I understand Dancer had no such difficulties," Clermont commented archly.

"Dancer wouldn't," Preble agreed, "but then, we do differ in approach. Aside from the obvious, Dancer, what did you find out?"

She shrugged. "Not much. However, I am ninety-nine point nine percent certain that he is Karranganthian.''

She could have drowned in the silence that ensued. Tonia's eyes widened and she seemed frozen in her seat.

"Last night you told me he was human," Morrow, one of Preble's assistants, finally said accusingly.

"You forget that the Karranganthians *are* human," Michael inserted coldly. "As human as we are."

The pointed reference to shared racial roots between the mortal enemies had the desired effect.

"But our linguistics computers can identify all of the Karranganthian dialects," Gallia pursued.

"Can they?" Dancer challenged. "How do we know? Had you considered that perhaps his odd pronunciation may be the result of a speech defect, either congenital or inflicted?"

"Possible," Morrow conceded. "But what makes you so certain?"

"Part of his tongue has been removed."

A gasp from Tonia, then another as Eire quietly informed her that that particular punishment, and the method of carrying it out, was reserved by the Karranganthians for disciplining their own. "My God! How can people do things like that to each other?"

Dancer shook her head. The kid had a lot to learn, but now was not the time to enlighten her. "I'm more concerned with how and why a Karranganthian . . ." she hesitated slightly, ". . . defector comes to be in the Team maintenance cadre. Seems like, for his own protection, the Service would have hidden him away somewhere."

"But the war is over," Tonia objected. "And he truly loves his work."

"Hmm. You trust him implicitly"—a nod from Tonia confirmed the assertion—"and I must admit that I'm drawn to him myself. He may be, like Williams and Guernsey, a true defector. He may be a plant. I think the latter is the stronger possibility, but I don't know."

"Then how do you know *you* can trust him?" Gallia asked.

Dancer's reply was directed at the Commander. "Instinct." A tiny, assenting gesture from Michael settled that question. After all, for years he had urged her to trust her instincts, and they hadn't let her down yet. "Now, what kind of communications do you have for me?"

Antonia cleared her throat. "Not much, I'm afraid. Except for a tight beam reserved for official communications, the Starlifter is transmission-shielded. You can neither send nor receive without permission. There used to be amateur equipment available; PR-type stuff, you know? Some of our pilots used to talk to amateur operators on the planets we were visiting. But nobody's done that for a long time." She paused, staring off over everybody's heads. "Seems like Colonel Daven put a stop to it for some reason or other, though the equipment is still set up, in a closet off the rec room. Just down the hall from my quarters."

Michael and Dancer exchanged glances. "Well, if I have something to pass along, I either figure out how to do it through channels, or I get off the Warlord."

The Commander shook his head, but said nothing.

"I was thinking," Tonia continued, "that since you have your own private frequency, Glaize, I could broadcast instructions to you during the show."

"No!" Michael smiled gently to ameliorate the abruptness of his exclamation. "Dancer is quite prepared on that score, I assure you. It would not do for you to break her concentration at any point."

Dancer didn't remind Michael that, unlike their Darts, the Gypsy would not kill its pilot for a moment's inattention. Unless, of course, she was flying fingertip formation and was startled into colliding with the guy next to her. Antonia's single head jerk showed that she understood.

Dancer smiled in sympathy. "Believe me, I know how you feel about watching someone else do your job, but I can handle it. You have my word; I'll do you proud."

"You'd better," was Tonia's semi-joking reply.

"Count on it. All right, then. Anyone have anything else to add? No? Okay, let's get to it."

Amid the general chair-scraping, Eire immediately attached herself to Antonia. Dancer paused to watch the two of them walk out together. Children, really, though both were physically and chronologically adults and would have resented the appellation. They were so much alike, laughing, animated, as Antonia amused the younger girl with a "war story," punctuated with all the contortions and hand gestures necessary to properly relate flying anecdotes.

Given time, they could become great friends, she realized with pleasure. Perhaps Antonia could convince Eire to return to flight training where she belonged, where she would have been if she hadn't chosen to follow Michael and Dancer here. Maybe Tonia could get her the hell out of the Sixth Service while it was still possible to do so. Dancer couldn't help remembering her own initiation into Sixth, the hatred she had felt, the delight in bloodletting that shamed her still. Could she be blamed for wanting more for sweet-natured Eire?

Eire looked up at that moment to see her watching them and sobered instantly. "Dancer? We always thought that Auglaize DeWester was just a story you made up to amuse us when we were children."

"She was," Dancer answered shortly.

Eire hesitated a moment, then flung herself across the room into her arms. Dancer returned the impulsive hug, raising her eyes to meet what she thought would be Tonia's contempt. Instead, the face that was the mirror image of her own held a mixture of bitterness and hurt.

"Did you ever even give me a moment's thought?" Antonia asked in a small voice.

How could Dancer tell her about the sleep she had lost wondering how the child was, what she was—about the tears she'd shed for the little girl she would never see again? Wordlessly, she held out one arm, and was surprised when the invitation was accepted.

"All right, ladies," Michael said heartily, "break it up. We all have work to do. Flight Leader, a moment of your time, if you please. I need a word with you."

Tonia and Dancer both stepped forward, their smothered chuckles breaking the serious mood. Michael's index finger unerringly leveled itself at one chest. "You, Dancer, come with me. You, Miss," he said to Eire, "should be down in Communications, logging dispatches. Take Antonia with you so that I'll know where to find her when she's needed. While you're at it, put her to work."

"Yes, Commander," was Eire's demurely respectful response, but her blue eyes were sparkling with mischief, and she made a face at Michael's back.

"I saw that," he said without turning around. Dancer didn't have to look, either, to see Antonia's head-shaking expression—theirs wasn't quite the sort of discipline she was used to.

"Is he your father?" Tonia finally asked in a loud whisper, evidently concluding that this was the logical explanation for the Commander's bantering tone and Eire's blatant insubordination.

Michael chuckled shortly as he herded Dancer around the corner into his "downstairs" office space. Though she missed Eire's reply, she was sure that it included the words, "all us Auryx look alike."

"Dancer." The Commander motioned her to his side, all traces of humor gone. "I have some information on your friend."

She nodded, following him to the computer terminal. After a quick turn of the head to see who might be near enough to overhear, he flicked his fingers over the keys, then laid his hand on the thumbprint lock. Whatever he had discovered was highly classified.

"As you know," he began quietly, his breath tickling her ear, "his Fourth Service personnel records begin rather abruptly four years ago, and tell us absolutely nothing. There is documentation neither of his being granted emigrant nor defector status, using normal channels. So, I did a little digging." His left pinky stabbed the number 8 on the numeral pad, and the screen began filling with data.

Dancer pursed her lips in a small, involuntary whistle. Michael had done a *lot* of digging. Before her were codes denoting intelligence subfiles buried so deeply that perhaps six people in the entire Confederacy had legal access to them. Michael was not one of the six.

Paulding Callicoon—his real name, and not quite the one on his Fourth Service records—had been the top-ranking Karranganthian ace until he was caught disabling the remotely activated explosive charges in his cockpit prior to a deep-penetration recce mission. True enough; she vaguely recalled the name and reputation from old Fourth Service briefings. A brilliant tactician, albeit a ruthless adversary. Now that she thought about it, she also remembered hearing he had disappeared without a trace, and even Sixth Service sources could neither confirm nor deny the persistent rumor that he had been executed for treason.

His supposed defection thwarted, Dancer read now, he was saved from execution only by his combat record and its attendant propaganda value. He was branded in the painful, peculiar Karranganthian fashion as a warning to others, reindoctrinated, and returned to combat. Undeterred nevertheless, he had apparently bided his time, figured out how to disable the booby traps in flight, and come over to the Confederacy. Claimed he was a soldier, not a butcher. The regular Services had kept it quiet, picked his brain, and studied his aircraft before tucking him quietly away. All very routine.

So the story went. It could actually have happened that way—Fourth Service's intelligence people had certainly swallowed less plausible plot lines. But then, Fourth Service's intelligence people, thorough as they attempted to be, were not blessed with Auryx paranoia.

"Reaction?" Michael asked as she straightened.

"Too pat. If they hadn't wanted him to defect, the Karranganthians never would have trusted him with another solo mission even after, quote, reindoctrination."

"My thoughts exactly. Callicoon and I had a long talk this morning. He cooperated as fully as he was able, but could give me nothing except confirmation of what I've already discovered. I venture to guess that a combination of drugs, hypnosis, and blackmail has been used on him; that would account for his conduct with Preble's people. One thing I do know: he most emphatically does not want to return to the Warlord. Nor does he want you to."

"So. We know who landed Tonia's plane. What I need to find

out is, was it also he who sabotaged it in the first place, and if so, why?''

"That's what you need to find out," Michael confirmed. "First, though, you'd better know one other small fact not in this report. From our own records, I have confirmed that Paulding Callicoon led the attack on Lioth. Do you trust him still?''

Dancer deliberately closed her mind to the red Auryx characters staring back at her from the CRT; she banged her thumb down on the space bar to obliterate them from her sight as well. "With my life." As they both knew would be the case.

"Then be very, very careful, child.''

"Sleep with him if I will, but keep a knife under my pillow, hmm?''

The ghost of a smile lightened Michael's strained features. "Something like that. If he is ordered to betray you, he'll likely not be able to resist.''

"I'll be careful, Mike," Dancer assured him. "But can I be forgiven for hoping that whatever it is doesn't hit the fan before the airshow this afternoon?''

"You're that eager to return to your own people?''

"I'm that eager to get in a little recreational flying again. The Team *are* Fourth Service's best, you know.''

"And you are only Sixth Service's second best. Still, you ought to be able to hold your own. All right, DeWellesthar; pick up your crewchief and be on your way. Your public awaits!''

Companionably, the two walked together downstairs to the building's public sector. Aware of his sidelong glances, Dancer finally stopped, hand on her hip—one of Antonia's unconscious habits—to meet his amused smile. "The swagger," she explained pompously, "is built into the boots.''

His reply was an uncharacteristic slap to her posterior which propelled her through the open door to the lobby. Luckily, the press was being restrained on the other side of the glass entry, and their own people knew better than to comment on Dancer's stumbling over thresholds.

Uniformed and ready, Calli waited off to one side, fear in his eyes as he looked from Dancer to Michael and back again. The caged animal look made her edgy, reminding her of Michael's veiled warning: He was at Lioth.

"You don't have to go back, Calli," she told him for perhaps the twelfth time. "Stay with Tonia; I'll report that your injuries were worse than first suspected, that you couldn't be moved.''

His violent hand motion halted her. "No!" he signed emphatically. "Now it is *you* who needs me."

Once again she asked him what he meant, and once again he shook his head in frustration, unable to tell her.

Michael turned away in rigid silence.

Chapter 31

What did Tonia know, what had she seen—what was locked away in her mind, locked away so completely that even Michael couldn't catch a glimpse of it? And who held the key? He was fairly certain by this time that Callicoon had engineered the crash to get the girl away from something on the Warlord. But was it just Tonia, or was the whole Team involved?

Michael hated question marks, hated vague feelings, cursed the diluted genes that gave him such a tantalizing taste of the vast mental powers his Auryx forebears had experienced. To be able to break down the walls between himself and the truth, to put a name to the unnamed fears . . .

To never again be forced to send Dancer unarmed into certain danger.

Not totally unarmed, his rational side argued. A product of the best training two cultures had to offer, abundantly endowed with both wit and gut instinct, unhampered by vague forebodings and not admitting even the slightest chance of failure, perhaps she was the best equipped of them all to take on whatever abided aboard the Warlord.

Even so, aware of the turbulence that remained in her mind and unhappy about her necessary reliance on Callicoon, he gave her one final chance to back out as she stepped aside to adjust her cap before leaving the building. "Dancer, there are still other ways to do this."

"I'm all right, Michael," she assured him. "Take care of Tonia."

He stared into her face for a moment, his blue eyes calculatedly neutral. A faint pink halo remained around her green-dyed irises, but Preble's drops had cleared up most of the irritation for the moment. She just looked like she had spent a restless night. No one would even question.

He was looking deeper than that, though. One word from him, one small gesture, and even now the mission would be scrubbed, as well she knew. Tonia would have to be sent, unsuspecting, back into the lion's den with an open receiver implanted somewhere in her body. And Dancer would be sitting here monitoring until the Warlord's electronic dampening systems made even that much impossible, unable to do anything if the girl got into trouble.

But it had been years since Dancer had flown a Gypsy. On the edge of both her worlds, with an enemy as her backup, would she be able to get *herself* out of trouble?

"I can handle it, Michael." Her lips shaped the words, but what he read was the plea in her heart: *Let me fly with the Team, Michael, just once*. Just once. With the old dream within grasp, he knew that it was impossible for her to keep from stretching out her hand. Well, she certainly didn't need to know about his qualms.

So, against his better judgment, the Commander nodded abruptly, then inclined his head toward the door. At least returning Team Five this close to show time would limit contact with those who knew Antonia well. Even such a small advantage could mean the difference between success and failure.

Dancer thanked him by insolently turning her back on him and striding out, escorted by Greene, Seven, and, of course, Callicoon. But the Commander's voice was a whisper in her ear receiver as she boarded the shuttle for the commercial airport out of which the Team would be flying: "Watch your six, child."

The Auryx version of the traditional pilot's catchphrase—meaning, "Keep an eye on what's happening at your back"—also translated to "Good luck."

Team officials and the press observed that Auglaize DeWellesthar emerged from the shuttle smiling.

Summit's head appeared in his commander's open doorway yet again. "They've reached the Fourth Service base, sir. After the paperwork and the flight physical are out of the way, shall I bring the girl back here?"

"No," Daven said thoughtfully. "Let the media have its darling. Let DeWellesthar fly. Just keep a very, very close eye on her. I want photographs and life histories of anybody who so much as talks to her today. Understand?''

"Particularly any short, dark-haired persons who talk to her?"

Daven smiled, a predatory smile that conveyed all the warmth of a polar ice cap. "Perhaps our Auryx doctor is just a stray who quite coincidentally happened to find himself a safe haven here. Do you believe in coincidence, Summit?''

"Not where the Auryx are concerned, sir.''

"Exactly. Let's see what we've got here. Perhaps we can work in a little recreation of our own on this mission. Perhaps this is one of those lucky contingencies for which we have been preparing.''

"Yes, sir.'' Summit left grinning, no doubt with visions of commendations and bounties dancing in his head.

Those thoughts had crossed Daven's mind, too. For now, though, the task was to distract the yokels down below with an aerial circus so that his people could make their contacts. This business with Callicoon and DeWellesthar was turning out to be a bonus. Maybe, for their inadvertent part in whatever was to come, he would let them live.

Dancer knew the drill for filling out Fourth Service incident reports very well; heaven knew she had processed more than her share back in her active-duty days. She was anticipating the required interview with the mysterious Colonel Daven, the new Team commander, and resigned to the pile of paperwork in which she would be required to relate, in minute detail, all events prior and subsequent to the forced landing.

In fact, she and Callicoon were met at the shuttle by the Team's chief of security, a glowering man only slightly shorter than Calli, who asked Dancer a few general questions, then packed her off for her preflight physical. Except for some shouting from the maintenance area, where Calli had been taken, that was all. She would be flying her own bird—freshly cleaned and polished, of course—and thus was the whole matter dismissed.

A "Class C" incident shrugged off as a minor inconvenience? Outwardly, Team Five took it all in her stride. Inwardly, Dancer was puzzled. The Fourth Service Auglaize DeWellesthar had known and loved certainly hadn't condoned this that's-the-way-it-goes attitude. It was as if the investigation had already been conducted, blame assigned, and punishment meted out, and the pilot was an insignificant detail.

Her examination by the Team physician was cursory, held in the office of the Fourth Service Commander. Evidently the packet

Preble had put together attesting to her fitness was convincing, because Doc Butler checked to see if she was breathing, and that was about it. After being admonished to get a haircut, she was sent on her way. Didn't even have to unzip her flightsuit.

From there, it was a trip up to the Warlord to brief. This seemed a little odd, since all pilots, maintenance troops, and aircraft were already on the base; Dancer had assumed that they would merely use the Fourth Service facilities out of which they would be flying. That was, after all, standard Team operating procedure.

"Colonel Daven likes to give us a pep talk before every flight," she was reminded.

Oh, really? Strange that Colonel Daven's pep talk couldn't be delivered anywhere but in the Team briefing room aboard the Starlifter. Stranger still that no one thought it odd of her to ask.

Come to think about it, the overall mood of the group was wrong. They were subdued almost to the point of somberness, with none of the usual banter, rivalry, and mild horseplay that were usually in evidence to break preflight tension. Professionalism was one thing, and no one knew better than a sometime Dart pilot the necessity for intense preparatory concentration, but this was uncanny. If the thought weren't too preposterous to consider, she would have sworn that her colleagues were mechanical dolls—or heavily drugged.

It was the oddest briefing Dancer had ever attended in either of her two lifetimes. The barest minimum of attention was paid to atmospheric conditions, the entire demonstration was passed over with, "Usual routine; no changes," and then the room darkened. From hidden sources, ripples of illumination danced over the walls and their faces. It was most soothing, the swirls of color and starbursts like a symphony for the eyes. In fact, she could almost hear music. Or voices. Soft, caressing voices that remained just outside her grasp.

Dancer surreptitiously glanced around at the rapt faces of the other Team pilots and the two alternates chosen for today's standby. Some were nodding, some moved their lips to a tune only they heard, some sported the bemused expression of a plebe cadet in love. Her own features, she discovered, had of their own accord relaxed into an attitude of amused tolerance. A comparatively subtle brainwashing technique, the analytical part of her brain informed her. Great God in heaven, when had the Team begun to resort to this type of nonsense to ensure perfect demonstrations?

The answer to that was obvious to one who knew from experience the pride the Fourth Service placed in performance: they hadn't.

The symphony of lights and its subliminal melody receded and finally died away, leaving the room in total darkness, but only for a moment. Three candles were solemnly lit on the podium, and a rustle like a collective sigh went around the room as full shot glasses were distributed. Dancer took hers with the same appreciation demonstrated by those around her, passing it quickly by her nose. A brandy of some sort, she guessed. *Alcohol* as a routine part of a Fourth Service preflight briefing?

Why the hell not? It made as much sense as the rest of what was going on. Michael would certainly be interested in hearing about all this. There had to be some way she could get a message to him.

Lead Solo rose and intoned a preflight toast, the liquid contained behind the crystal looking ominously like blood in the uncertain light. "To our fallen comrades," was his hushed proclamation. "May they never be forgotten."

A chill ran down Dancer's spine at the words, which had been inscribed behind every bar in every recreation club on every forward Fourth Service base, the first and last toast of every evening and a constant reminder of their wartime mission. But certainly not appropriate here. A quick glance around at the glittering, intense eyes of her fellows as they repeated, "To our fallen comrades," assured her that these people were prepared to go out and kill.

She stiff-armed the drink with the rest of them, but suspicion kept her from swallowing. On impulse, she fumbled in her leg pocket for Preble's eyedrops, twisting off the cap and dumping the contents into the sweat-absorbent lining of the show suit. On the pretense of a cough, she spat as much of the drink as she could into the bottle, then swallowed the rest. Whatever it was had already begun to be absorbed into her system through the lining of her mouth, anyway, so a little more wouldn't hurt. She would figure out how to get the sample to Michael when the time was right.

The lights came up, and the mechanical dolls around her came to life with a change of mood that was astounding. It was as if they had all been released from thrall—here were the jokes, the banter, the friendly admonitions, the rivalries that were normal to the place and time. Dancer insinuated herself with an ease that would have amazed the pretender to her name. After all, faces changed but the language remained the same, though she did have to be careful of the idiom. Colonel Daven, she noted almost parenthetically, had never put in an appearance.

The shuttle ride back down to O'Brian's Stake was quite different from the one up to the Warlord. Everyone was animated—teasing challenges were exchanged, uniforms straightened, preshow jitters aired and calmed and, as the shuttle touched the ground, PR smiles fixed firmly in place. The show began for them as soon as that shuttle door opened. They lined up in order of introduction and awaited their signal to emerge.

Chapter 32

The narrator was already well into his spiel. Thousands of pairs of eyes had turned skyward to follow the progress of the shuttle as it plummeted earthward; thousands of throats were primed to burst into cheers as each Team member was introduced and ran, waving, to an assembly point center stage. Behind them, as they stood at what appeared to be rigid attention, waited their aircraft and their ground crews, also dressed for show and also at attention. Dancer was relieved to see Calli's bulk in the shadow of Number Five.

All, pilots and maintenance cadres alike, held their poses for a full five minutes after the last alternate had taken his place in line as the narrator intoned the requirements for membership on the Team. Dancer was gratified but not surprised to know that she, herself, exceeded all of them. Antonia had claimed the minimum number of combat hours, which meant that she must have excelled in "natural talent and abilities." As Dancer's thoughts followed their own course, the narrator went on to outline the selection process and remind the crowd again of the Team mission. It was an impressive sight: fifteen dedicated pilots, fifteen combat aircraft physically unmodified except for the distinctive high-visibility color, markings, and insignia package; an image to be recorded for thousands of personal scrapbooks and for later media broadcast, so that those who didn't make it to today's show would be motivated to come to tomorrow's.

Fifteen hands snapped crisply to fifteen brows in simultaneous salute as the Confederacy anthem was played by a local school band. Dancer remembered the thrill she had felt as a child at the sight, how fervently she had wished to be on this side of the cordon. Well, here she was, on Antonia's credentials. Mother Fate did have a sense of humor.

As the last notes echoed in the still air, fifteen bodies did an about-face without a ripple in the line and marched back to their airplanes. Then came a precision, by-the-numbers preflight check of the external aircraft, each hand lifting at the same moment, each voice in chorus with the standard responses. It was really just a cursory inspection, since the craft had already been thoroughly examined by the maintenance people—just for show and to further impress the spectators. They would have been disappointed to know that the pilots all took their timing cues from the notes of the band, which was now rendering the Fourth Service song.

Though Calli's nod assured Dancer that all was in order, she habitually took her preflight seriously, closely eyeballing wing-locks, checking for any forgotten "remove before flight" flags, sniffing for faint but distinctive odors of unseen fluid leaks, making sure that all external stores—for the first part of the show, smoke canisters dummied up to symbolize the full array of weapons options available to the Gypsy—were securely bolted in place.

After that came close-order cockpit drill. Calli strapped his pilot in as crewchiefs all down the line did the same, helped her into her helmet, and hooked up and tested her life-support apparatus. After that, control surfaces waved to the crowd as if motivated by a single hand as the pilots brought their flight computers on-line. Again, a bit of illusion: they would hand-fly the actual show, but their computers would warn them with admonitory lights, tones, and caustic comments—if there were time—should they stray overmuch from preprogrammed positions. The skill came in avoiding these tell-tales, and in responding immediately and correctly should they not. Low-altitude midair collisions in the Gypsy were not survivable.

The cockpit chores out of the public view were described by the narrator, whose voice droned softly in fifteen earphones. Again, if the pilots needed the prompt, this background voice would give them cues and relay the attitude of the crowd over the next couple of hours. Normal air-to-air and air-to-ground communications could be carried on over the top of it. Unfortunately, these were recorded and monitored; there would be no chitchatting with Michael on these business-only frequencies, though Dancer knew that Antonia would be nervously eavesdropping back at Eire's communications post. She was worried that the counterfeit Team Five would besmirch her reputation, no doubt. Oh, well; were the positions reversed, Dancer would be biting her fingernails, too.

Finally, canopies winked closed sequentially down the line, sealing with a sigh that seemed to say *Welcome home!* It felt good. Dancer of the Sixth receded into memory as the past twelve years took on the quality of a long dream from which she had now finally awakened. She *was* Auglaize DeWellesthar.

It was time to power up the engines. As her practiced fingers automatically set the throttles for a quick run-up, Auglaize's ears strained for any audible clues to possible malfunction and her body gauged the slight vibration of the airframe. Everything "felt" right. When the voice of Control chimed in her headphones, she could reply with the formula, "Team Five checked and ready, sir!" that would be broadcast to the crowd. Calli gave her thumbs-up, snapped her a rigid salute, and strode off toward the sidelines.

Then, with an impressive roar staged for the benefit of the spectators—with their new engines, Gypsies under normal operations just sort of hummed along—fifteen aircraft wheeled about, the thirteen show aircraft taxiing into takeoff position and the two alternates removing themselves to the sidelines.

Number One, Team Lead and primary solo pilot, or "Ace," was first into the air. His extra-long takeoff roll served to conceal the true performance of the aircraft while letting the audience get a good look at it and providing a sharp contrast to his "maximum performance climb," where he quite literally stood the Gypsy on her tail and blasted straight up. Almost out of sight from the ground, he did an inside loop, dropping back down to streak over the heads of the rest of his Teammates, so low that if he had put his gear down he would have snagged a canopy. This was their cue to simultaneously hurl three four-ship echelons into the air in formation on him. Cleverly placed canisters of quick-dissipating chemical smoke were activated, giving the illusion of a solid link between each member of the three echelons. Then thirteen Gypsies jockeyed into position to become thirteen aircraft beads on a smoke string, wingtips so close that, but for the white contrast between, they looked from the ground to be touching. In this Beads on a String formation, pilots executed a series of simultaneous—then sequential, then alternating—loops, rolls, spirals, and flips.

Auglaize's time in the paper simulator yesterday—had it been only yesterday? She felt as if she had been flying like this at least half her life!—had really paid off. Working with a confident precision that amazed even herself, she throttled forward slightly, to the left and to the rear of Number Four, to the right and ahead of

Number Six, to assume her position in a large circle. The basic formation dated back to the beginning of air warfare and had gone by several names: Lufbery Circle, the Wagon Wheel—or just Wheel—or, in Dancer's cadet days, Ring Around the Rosy. The Team had, of course, added several refinements all its own.

There was a lot more space between the aircraft this time; when twelve were firmly in position, Thirteen wove in and out of the circle between them. After two such circuits, he maneuvered Ace out of his position, the even numbers throttled back, and the odd numbers leapfrogged over them in a giant circle dance over the heads of the spectators. By the time this maneuver was reversed, returning all to their original positions, Auglaize was grateful for the moisture-absorbing lining of her show coverall—but she was having the time of her life.

It was Ace's turn to run the basket weave through the circle. As he passed each Team aircraft, however, it spiraled up and off in a different direction. Ace then took the only course open to him, straight up. While all eyes were trying to follow him, the rest of the aircraft screamed in from twelve compass points, seemingly hell-bent on converging in the same spot at the same time. At the last, breathtaking moment, they pulled up into a starburst, Ace coming in low from nowhere to shoot up through the center. Auglaize let out a whoop of pure exhilaration.

After what seemed to be the finale, they broke up into smaller groups for an intricate aerial square-dance seemingly called by the narrator. This gave each a chance to showcase his or her particular skills, while Ace and Thirteen, Lead and Second Solos, continued to dazzle the audience with their expertise. For the first time in years, Auglaize got to cartwheel a Gypsy, a barely possible, highly impressive maneuver given just the right touch. This was Antonia's particular trick, and Dancer could almost see her holding her breath and mumbling instructions that would have been unnecessary even if coaching had been allowed. "All right! Good on you, Dancer!" Auglaize heard in her ear as she rejoined her element. Antonia hadn't been able to resist broadcasting that one comment. Auglaize gave her the slightest waggle in acknowledgment, then grinned. Michael would have something to say to both of them later—but what difference did a small break in radio silence make when one had the only receiver for the transmitted frequency? Chalk up another unrepented transgression.

Finally, the aerobatic portion of the show was over. Pilots landed one by one to thunderous applause, allowing their aircraft to take their bows. As soon as Auglaize's canopy seal was cracked, Calli handed her a cold drink that tasted like fruit punch with a slight metallic tang and was rich in the electrolytes lost through perspiration. She held the can in one hand while the other rested in sight of all outside observers. On either side, Four and Six relaxed in identical attitudes, and the self-same actions were being performed up and down the line. Assured that each pilot's ten fingers were occupied well clear of the controls, ground crews stripped off the smoke canisters with combat efficiency, replacing them with practice weapons, cameras, and sensors for the operational part of the demonstration. These troops strove not to impress their audience with precise, simultaneous motions, but with a contest to see which crew could work the fastest. As usual, Ace's hand was the first to disappear from view, signaling that his externals were mounted and ready and he was reprogramming the computer for combat.

Auglaize half listened in amusement to the cheers and exhortations of the audience, spurred on by the narrator, as she waited a further six seconds for Calli's signal to withdraw her own hand. Whether they came in second, third, or fourth, she neither knew nor cared. Her mind was already in combat mode. Her fingers flew with practiced ease over the cockpit drill, then she alighted with her fellow pilots for yet another close-order check. Again, Calli strapped her in; and again all canopies closed and sealed in unison.

The upcoming attack on the mock city constructed on the other side of the field was designed as an actual combat operation in miniature, with distances and altitudes vastly compressed for demonstration purposes, and the thirteen Gypsy fighters playing the parts of several different types of aircraft. Given enough noise, fireworks, and fancy flying, few in the crowd would complain if authenticity was compromised. First up would be the four ECM birds—electronic countermeasures planes tasked with suppressing any ground resistance. They would also relay back any changes to the route as briefed. Dancer was in the element of six CAP or Combat Air Patrol craft, which would neutralize opposing aircraft—a job for which she, the real Auglaize DeWellesthar, had close to a hundred and fifty missions' Fourth Service combat experience. After them, and high above, would follow the single craft whose job it was to photograph and direct.

All these aircraft were support for the remaining two, the primary and alternate strike aircraft. Had this been an actual mission, primary would have been the only one to reach the target; the alternate was there in case, for some reason, primary was unable to complete his task, or on the off chance that he missed. In this simulated attack, all Team members would have a chance at the target, and all carried the same externals instead of more or less as their individual chores required. Under normal operational conditions, many would also have been picking up a special-systems officer at this point, but that little detail did not work well into the choreography of the show. In Auglaize's time, it had been a sore point with most SSOs—and probably still was.

Auglaize had to admit that it gave her a bit of a thrill, swooping down and unloading on target, seeing the pyrotechnics indicating another direct hit, and hearing, via the narrator, the appreciative roars of the crowd. One would have thought that by now the spectators would be tiring, but in fact they were still enthralled with the performance, building to a fever pitch of enthusiasm for the finale, and her favorite part: the close-in aerial free-for-all, odds against evens, Ace wild—playing both sides, or neither.

One by one, aircraft swooped down almost to the deck as their pilots punched off their externals in the field beside the runway. Regaining an altitude safe enough to maneuver but still low enough to be easily seen, they formed into six two-ships. Auglaize took her assigned position as cover for Three, then they wheeled off with the rest of "the friendlies" to turn and engage the evens in an unrehearsed, unchoreographed battle for air supremacy.

In the days of knights and jousting tournaments, the event had been called the melee. As far as Auglaize knew, the Team was the only aerobatic organization in history to incorporate the idea into an airshow; though unlike in the ancient tourneys, no actual weapons were used. What it boiled down to, in effect, was a fast-paced free-for-all, again compressing the vast distances of a typical air-to-air engagement into an area easily observable by the audience. In most actual battles, the closest Auglaize ever came to seeing the enemy—or the rest of her own flight, for that matter—was as colored shapes on her combat array. This close in, though, she always thought the tussle took on the characteristics of what Rhombyan described as a "good, old-fashioned dogfight."

There was a training refinement in the computers that allowed them to track a theoretical shot and alert the opposing computer of an ensuing hit. The pilot was informed with a distinctive chime; corresponding controls were cut off to simulate damage sustained. In the event of a kill, the plane's tail number would be illuminated. Again, the only time the computers interfered with the pilot of the aircraft was when there was immediate danger to either the pilot or someone else. The Team hadn't lost an airplane in air-to-air yet, which, all things considered, was a minor miracle.

Odds against evens, and where was Ace playing? Which side

would he choose, or would he just sit back and pick off the survivors? Auglaize stuck with Three until he went down, then joined on Nine until she, too, was dispatched. Then Five was hit, the computer informing Auglaize that she had lost control of the left side of her Gypsy. It could have been fatal; she didn't realize it then, but to Antonia, it would have been fatal. Auglaize just didn't have sense enough to give up. Combat experience—in the Fourth Service and the more radical Sixth—had taken over her reflexes shortly after takeoff, and before her mind registered the handicap, she had already compensated for it. All unconsciously. Dancer didn't even know she had done anything unusual until her computer tapes were reviewed at debriefing; her only awareness at the time was of an overwhelming instinct to survive. Which meant eliminating all competition. Even when it was just herself against Two and Eight, and Ace dropped down out of the clouds to take their side.

Then it was just Ace and Auglaize. He had full control and full weapons-charge.

And then there was just her. Awakening to an empty sky and Michael's voice saying, "Out*stand*ing performance, Dancer!"

Auglaize grinned to herself at the pride in his tone, then let out another whoop as she sideslipped the computer-crippled Gypsy toward home.

As Calli helped unstrap her from the seat she felt as though she had grown to, the cheers of the spectators—and her Teammates—hit her like a solid wall.

"Congratulations, Dancer. Looks like you're the hero of the house," was Michael's amused comment. Good grief, what had she done to deserve all this? Hurriedly she brushed the chemical cleaner through her hair—the special linings of the coveralls made it certain that the crowd would never see a Team pilot sweat, and this ten-second dry wash ensured a perfectly groomed coiffure. Image was all.

Auglaize tossed her head, laughing triumphantly as she threw her leg over the side of the plane and dropped to the ground.

To be reminded immediately, jarringly, agonizingly of a recent, untended knife wound in her thigh. She would have fallen but for Calli's unobtrusively supporting arm; as it was, there was a collective gasp which the narrator smoothed over with a comment about her needing a moment to regain her equilibrium.

True enough. Stiffening her spine and gritting her back teeth together, Auglaize went forth confidently to meet the public.

Still on duty, her Teammates and she didn't have the time to wander through the other static displays or catch more than a glimpse of the other flying demonstrations. The rest of their afternoon was spent giving interviews and being photographed, signing programs, mingling with the crowd, showing off the Gypsies, answering innumerable questions, and diplomatically fending off propositions. The audience was mostly comprised of civilians, of course, though Dancer saw what seemed to be an inordinate number of Fourth Service security people in full working regalia. The Auryx contingent was much less obtrusive: very few khakis, and the occasional Auryx face in the crowd recognizable as such only to her or other members of her Service. The smattering of midnight-blue duty dress interspersed amongst the spectators startled her until she recalled that the 21 pilots and 339 support troops of the Team were merely freight. The Warlord Starlifter itself belonged to the Fifth, or Space, Service.

Auglaize was sitting on the canopy rail, having just lifted the umpteenth child into and out of the pilot's seat—with the computers off-line, none of the classified displays were visible—when she spotted a relatively short, dark-haired man in a khaki uniform standing shyly on the fringe of her audience. Trust Michael to find a way to talk with her when she had neglected to do so for him.

Her hand automatically reached to smooth the fabric over the inconspicuous bulge in her pocket where the tiny bottle was hidden, then she half rose with Antonia's typical imperiousness to beckon him forward. "Want to see inside?"

He ducked his head. Embarrassment, it would seem to the others, but Dancer knew he was hiding a smile.

"You're one of the Confederacy police types, aren't you? Of course; who else would wear such a drab uniform? What's your name?"

"Mike," was all that was audible.

Dancer stifled a smile of her own. "Come on up here, Mike. I won't bite you. Are those wings of some sort on your shirt? Unbelievable, a shy pilot. Speaking of a contradiction in terms."

Michael good-naturedly let himself be jostled forward, then looked up to give her the full force of those eyes.

"Need some help?" she offered.

"I think not." Ignoring the stairs rolled up for the use of the public, he had grabbed a hand and foot hold and swung himself over her into the pilot's seat before she could react.

"You've got style, Mike; I'll grant you that."

"Thank you. So have you. That was some act today," he said neutrally. Then, as Dancer's head bent closer to his, ostensibly in explanation, his tone changed again. "Are you all right? We saw you stumble."

"Antonia's gift. Hurts like hell, but I'll survive."

He nodded his comprehension, then pointed to the computer power switch. "Find out anything yet?"

"God, Michael. Subliminals. Drugs. Hypnotism." A tug on the booted foot dangling down the side of the Gypsy reminded her that time was limited; her hand dropped out of sight to the leg resting on the instrument console and removed the bottle from her pocket. "This is from Brief," was all she had time to say. "The pilots were like zombies until they drank it."

Michael palmed the vial and transferred it to his own pocket as he stood up. "Thank you," he said with a dazzling smile. "See you later, maybe."

Auglaize shrugged off the ensuing jokes about fraternizing with the natives and helped still another child over the side of her airplane.

Colonel Daven's video coverage of the Team's performance would have been the envy of all planetary broadcast networks. Coverage was so complete, in fact, that it took a bank of monitors and two assistants to keep track of everything. There were six angles of the show itself for him to choose from, as well as tracking on each aircraft, surveillance on the ground crews, and close-ups of individual audience members, quite aside from the O'Brian's live media coverage of the event. Always one to exploit the resources at his disposal, Daven had ordered into use all of the Warlord's vast array of sensing equipment. Somewhere down there in the estimated press of 200,000 bodies was the key to fame and fortune, and he aimed to find it.

The Team's routine he had seen enough times by now to find boring, but still he watched. Watched the redhead's plane for any signs of hesitation, anything—he wasn't quite sure—anything that was out of the ordinary for her. Even his practiced eye could find no faults, though. In fact, her performance seemed even smoother, less mechanical than usual. That nagged at him.

Senses alerted—to what, he didn't know yet, but these feelings hadn't let him down once in a long career—he paid close attention to the free-for-all that closed the show. What he saw astounded him. DeWellesthar had always done respectably well here, but today, she showed remarkable skill. "Remarkable" was the word. That kind of flying could only be the product of hours upon hours of training, practice—and actual combat.

"Looks like our media darling got incredibly lucky today," Summit remarked over his commander's shoulder. "General consensus is that the accident certainly didn't hurt her style any."

"What do you say?" Daven asked, curious as to just how observant his ops officer was.

"If I didn't know better, I'd swear someone slipped in a ringer."

"Indeed. If I thought for even an instant that that were possible . . . but where the Auryx are involved, everything is possible. Rerun the close-ups of the introduction for me, and take a very careful look."

The requested video appeared almost instantly on a corner monitor. No, that was DeWellesthar's face, all right, down to the last freckle. Her eyes looked a little odd—tired—but it was DeWellesthar's face. And her cocky walk, her trim, lithe body, her . . . damn! Now was not the time for such thoughts! Daven turned away almost angrily.

"I need to think," he said abruptly. "I'll be in my office. Call me if you see anything interesting."

"Yes, sir . . . Colonel, wait! Look at this. I think we've got something."

The scene was of DeWellesthar sitting on the side of her airplane, as she had been doing for quite some time, talking animatedly to another awestruck townie in the pilot's seat. Daven was about to dismiss the scene when a closer look at the townie arrested him. Slight, raven-haired, wearing Confederacy khakis . . . "Give me a close-up on him," he barked instead.

A handsome face set in a quizzical half-smile filled the screen directly in front of Daven. The lips were moving. "Can we hear what they're saying?"

"Uh . . . no, sir, too much background noise."

"No matter. That one wouldn't give anything away, anyhow. He would expect to be watched."

Summit nodded. "An Auryx. I knew it when I saw him."

"Not just 'an Auryx,' " Daven told him, the certainty growing within him even as he said the words. "I do believe we have before us *the* Auryx. Summit, take a good long look at Michael, Commander of the Sixth Service."

"But, sir. How do you know? Even our intelligence people don't have a photograph of Michael."

Daven shook his head, suppressing his own excitement. One of his greatest assets over the years had been the legacy of his own trace of Auryx blood—not enough to endanger him or his family, but enough to allow him to recognize an Auryx on sight. Just enough to allow him to state with absolute certainty, "As sure as we're sitting here, that's Michael. Look at those eyes. Feel the power behind them."

The face on the screen tightened almost imperceptibly as the Auryx turned fathomless blue-black eyes directly into a camera that he had no way of knowing was there. Daven felt both the chill that rippled down his own spine and his assistant's shiver simultaneously. "And Michael, I think, is aware of us. But he doesn't know for sure. And he won't. At least, not in time."

"But what has DeWellesthar got to do with . . . wait a minute. Colonel, wasn't there some story going around years ago about a red-haired Auryx?"

"Yes. But unless the Auryx have added shape-changing to their repertoire, that is our Team Five. Even the Auryx couldn't effect such a perfect counterfeit overnight."

"I wonder. Earlier, one of our O'Brian contacts reported receiving an odd radio transmission."

"So?"

"On one of our unique frequencies?"

"When? What?"

"He didn't remember the exact words; something about congratulating a dancer. The transmission wasn't very clear."

"When?" Daven repeated with more patience than he felt.

"Come to think of it . . . it would have been just about the time DeWellesthar was landing after the show. Would somebody have been congratulating her, do you think?"

"Does DeWellesthar have a nickname?"

" 'Dancer,' maybe? I've never heard her—or anyone else here—called that, but I'll check right now."

"Do." Dancer. Dancer. Dancer. Why was that name so familiar?

"Uh, Colonel Daven? Only thing that comes up under the word 'Dancer' is 'Dancer Flight,' Fourth Service slang for 'D-Flight,' and—"

Dancer Flight! It wasn't Summit's matter-of-fact voice he heard, it was an ear-piercing shriek. Dancer Flight! Lioth, about a dozen years ago. There had been a redhead among the captives from Lioth.

Of course! How could he have forgotten the damned redhead who'd almost cost him his career—and his life?

Could it be? No. She was long since dead; he had made sure of that.

"I want to see Callicoon as soon as he's back aboard," Daven ordered thoughtfully.

Chapter 33

Finally, the last of the civilian visitors had been shepherded off O'Brian's small Fourth Service base, and the Team pilots adjourned to a quiet corner of the ready room for a spirited debrief as they watched the "official" show videos. Auglaize found herself on the spot, trying to translate into words the reflexes with which she had so brilliantly won the day.

"God, I can't believe it actually worked!" she told them. "I read an article somewhere about how this Gypsy pilot managed to compensate for all kinds of battle damage and get himself home in one piece, and I've wanted to try it ever since. I've been practicing cockpit drills on the ground, but this is the first time I've actually had the nerve to *do* any of it. I figured, what did I have to lose—and it worked!"

"You lucked out, kid." Woods echoed the general consensus. "Don't let it go to your head."

At that, the few O'Brian's Stake Fourth Service pilots who had been sitting apart, listening, were called over to join the group. For a long while, they all lounged around sipping soft drinks and swapping war stories. Luckily, the session broke up before the discussion of what was now called the Lioth Massacre got into full swing. Two of Auglaize's Teammates had been sent there with the relief troops, and she didn't especially want to hear what they had to say.

Oddly enough, the Team pilots were not allowed to accept their newfound Fourth Service friends' blanket invitation to a dinner in their honor in the base officers' mess. Always before, that had been part of the job description for Team pilots. Thou shalt graciously allow thyselves to be entertained by thy hosts, thus furthering the friendly image of thy Team. Looked like for some reason the rules had been changed again. However, after dining aboard the Starlifter, they might return for a few drinks in the stand-up bar. Providing, of course, they drank only the light beer allotted to alert pilots.

Auglaize's feelings weren't hurt in the least. She had had about all she could take for one day; after a hearty, excellently prepared meal in the Team's private dining area, her plans for the evening included some light reconnoitering and some heavy relaxation. Judging from the increasingly less animated demeanors of her Teammates, most of them felt the same way. Some of them had even returned to that zombielike state which had characterized her first preshow shuttle ride to the transport. With newfound perspective, Auglaize wondered if her original suspicions about the lethargy being drug-induced might not have been only unfounded paranoia on her part. She now exhibited all of the same symptoms herself, traceable directly to exhaustion. In fact, she was so tired that she didn't even feel the vague claustrophobic discomfort of being "trapped" on the Warlord, discomfort that had become almost routine for her when faced with spending time aboard any spacegoing vehicle over which she herself did not have complete control.

Except that Dancer of the Sixth had routinely endured "days" twice as long, three times as wearing, and with the added attraction of live ammunition coming at her from the aircraft she battled. That no one thought it the least bit out of character when Auglaize excused herself to go to her quarters didn't matter. That *she* didn't find it so should have been telling.

A handful of the others elected to return to O'Brian's Stake, but the majority, like Auglaize, sought their bunks. She would rest for a while now, she rationalized, then do that scouting around in the middle of the night, when everyone else was asleep. The first thing she would check out would be all of those new off-limits areas . . .

Michael was lying down when the knock came at his door; a quiet word from him, and the portal swung open to admit Willemtell. The Commander couldn't help smiling at the serious young man who, as a gangling, smitten adolescent, had taken his Service name from the hero of the yarns Dancer had spun to amuse the children.

"Sorry to disturb you, Commander," he began.

"I wasn't asleep," Michael replied, swinging his legs over the side of his bunk and sitting up. "Merely waiting. What have you to report?"

"We just received an answer to our inquiry from Fourth Service headquarters. They have no idea who decided to change the FSI-PADT's itinerary, or when, or how. Everyone seemed to think that somebody higher up was responsible, and that was that. No problem; their reports indicate the changes are working out well. 'After all'—this is a direct quote—'what's the big deal? It's not like there's a war on.' "

Michael snorted. "I've heard that before."

"I've also been checking out the other new planets on the Team's schedule. There are several rather significant similarities. All are relatively small, fringe populations, in more or less a straight line—well, of course, it makes sense they would be. All have only a small Confederacy presence, limited off-planet contact, as little government as they can get away with, no planetary-guard military forces."

"The buffers."

"Exactly. The only types of human colonies that certain of our nonhuman Confederacy partners will tolerate anywhere near their territories. If the Karranganthians—"

"Pure speculation, mind you, since the Karranganthians are a conquered people," Michael interjected with a straight face, his mind already leaping ahead to Will's conclusions.

"Oh, of course. But if they wanted to smash the Confederacy to splinters . . ."

"And when haven't they?"

"All they'd have to do is plant some subversives, bide their time, take over a few nongovernments . . ."

"Trivial stuff for them . . ."

"And they'd have ready-made bases conveniently located to launch simultaneous strikes against both us and our intolerant allies," Will finished. "Remembering, of course, that the creed of the Confederacy is to allow each member species to fight its own internal battles—as they classified the last war—*unless another member species is attacked.*"

"And we know that the Karranganthians already have allies among the nonhuman species."

"Exactly. It would take years for the plan to mature, but they've got all kinds of time."

"Time," Michael stated, "for us to reduce our military even more. Time for us all to be lulled even further into thinking that the last war has been fought."

"Time for the Karranganthians to garner sympathy among *our* former allies. Can you believe that, even now, they are appealing for 'humanitarian aid,' and getting it? More and more rational, intelligent people are refusing to believe the Karranganthian atrocities ever took place?''

"Tell that to Dancer," the Commander said shortly. "You know how fantastic this entire future-war scenario sounds, don't you?''

"Yes. But I believe it is happening.''

"So do I. But no one else will. Not as long as there's still the shadow of a chance that the Fourth Service might be up to something itself with the Confederacy's full blessing. We need irrefutable proof before we can legally take any action to stop it.''

"Mike . . .''

Will hesitated, and Michael raised a quizzical eyebrow. That was another thing the lad had picked up from his red-haired idol—this habit of addressing his Commander by a diminutive when his brain was skipping far ahead of his tongue. None of the older-generation Auryx would even consider such a thing, under any circumstances. The Commander found himself liking it. "Wiliard," he responded, calling the boy by the real name that he had probably forgotten himself. "What?''

A slight blush and the flicker of a smile were all of Will's reaction. "It's . . . about Dancer.''

"What about Dancer?''

"I've had this tremendous crush on her ever since the first time I saw her," he said hurriedly. "My fourteenth birthday, remember? When my parents sent me that crossbow thing, and Dancer showed us how to use it? I always knew that she was Auglaize DeWester. It's been like a secret just between the two of us all these years. Anyway.'' The blush deepened considerably. "I have this feeling about her right now that's just about driving me crazy.''

Michael's eyes sharpened. "What kind of feeling?''

"That she's in terrible danger. Nothing definite, you understand. Just a feeling. No, a certainty.''

The Commander sighed inwardly. He had long suspected Will to be one of the few remaining Auryx who shared the curse. He'd have to have him tested and trained, of course; there was no getting away from that now. Should have done so long ago while he was still a teenager, but Michael had hoped to spare the boy some of the proprietary control, the emotional blackmail by the Council that he had suffered himself. As for Will's admission . . . "I share that feeling, lad. There is an alert team standing by. At this point, it's all I can do.'' That, and hope that "all he could do'' would be enough.

Chapter 34

Dancer shouldn't have been surprised at the luxurious accommodations accorded Team pilots, but, having spent considerable time aboard active-service Warlords in the course of her career, she knew that the normal crew's quarters weren't exactly spacious. In fact, they were more like plastic-walled boxes barely large enough for double-decker bunks, a chair, and a fold-down desk bolted to one wall.

On the other hand, Antonia had a pleasant, good-sized cabin to herself. A comfortable bunk, nice pictures on the walls, lots of clutter. The closet—itself almost the size of some of the transport accommodations Dancer had known—contained, besides more civilian clothes than the O'Brian's Stake Sixth Service contingent's entire costuming section, two more of the tailored show suits, three regular-issue Fourth Service flightsuits, and two—*two!*—obviously frequently worn sets of full-dress ceremonial regalia, as well as numerous examples of every other uniform combination known to the Fourth Service. Auglaize found the emerald-and-gold-patterned caftan that Antonia had described as her favorite—it so closely resembled the treasured hand-embroidered Auryx robe Merylys had made for Dancer long ago that she couldn't help being startled—and hung her jumpsuit a little apart from the girl's. That item of apparel should have been sent out to be laundered, but there was no way it would have been returned in time for the next day's show. From a hook in the back of the closet she removed the ballet slippers that were Tonia's accustomed footwear, with a small smile at the irony of the kid as an aspiring dancer.

A housekeeper, Antonia certainly wasn't. Or perhaps it was that her lifestyle just contrasted so greatly with Dancer's rather Spartan one. Weariness helped her resist the urge to tidy up, though having so many . . . things . . . just tossed around made her uncomfortable. A jacket adorned the arm of one upholstered chair, a flight cap and tie the back of another. The dresser and bookshelves were littered with all sorts of memorabilia and books, a good dozen well-worn volumes of which Dancer recognized as her own. A battered stuffed bear occupied the place of honor in the middle of Tonia's pillow, and Dancer smiled when she saw it—it was still wearing the remnants of Antonia's red dress.

The kid had it good, Auglaize thought as she sank down onto the bunk—which, she noticed, was big enough for two. A guitar case lay open across its foot, and she lifted the instrument out lovingly. No surprise; it had also been Flight Leader De-Wellesthar's. It had cost her more than a term's savings in her cadet days, this handmade, cherished friend. She gave it an experimental strum and automatically reached up to tighten a tuning peg. How had Tonia ended up with all the things that had meant the most to Auglaize? Were their tastes really all that similar, or was it just part of the role?

Dancer's leg was throbbing by this time; she'd be lucky if she could walk at all tomorrow, let alone fly. Since cursing herself for previous neglect was a waste of breath now, she simply eased the leg up onto the mattress. Mind over matter. She had blocked worse pain than this, and for longer periods of time. "Good work, DeWellesthar," she couldn't help chiding herself aloud, relocating to a chair the flightsuit carelessly tossed across the pillow.

Antonia had mentioned a contraband bottle of whiskey in the bottom drawer of the nightstand, and Auglaize suddenly felt the need for a good stiff drink. It was while trying to make room for the full glass that her eyes fell on the framed photograph tipped over into the clutter on top of the nightstand. Two casually dressed, laughing adults and a happy little girl in what looked like her Sunday best. At first glance, a charming family portrait. Then a lump formed in Auglaize's throat as she slipped it out of the frame to read the precise schoolgirl script on the back: *Glaize, Troy and me at the Fair*, with a date thirteen years old. At the bottom was the postscript, *We had fun*. Not such a little girl, after all. Tonia had been, what, eleven? Twelve?

Dancer moved the bear and leaned back thoughtfully into the pillows with her drink and her guitar, picking out an Auryx ballad with her left hand. It sounded strange, haunting, as she hummed the harmony; too strange. Abruptly, she realized what she was playing and switched to a mournful Fourth Service ballad that suited her mood almost as well. Even with her eyes closed, she could see the images on that picture and read Tonia's three-word epitaph: *We had fun.* Indeed. Auglaize remembered that last leave: Antonia had been in a choral competition or some such, hence the dress. She had won, too. That's right; Auglaize and Troy had been so proud of the kid they'd just about "bust their buttons," in Grama D.'s parlance. That had been just before Tonia cut her waist-length hair to look more like her heroine. Dancer shook her head. Again, irony. The spice of life. She drank to it, draining her glass, then refilled it to the brim.

"You'd better be careful with that stuff," remarked a disapproving voice from the doorway.

"I didn't hear you knock," was her pointed reply to the man who stood there. Terrence Woods, Team Leader and good friend. Very good friend, if he could get into Tonia's room through a locked door.

"Since when do I have to knock?"

Dancer shrugged, liking his dark plainness, the overlong, crooked nose and large, uneven teeth that gave character to the high-cheekboned angularity of his face. Perhaps the smoke-gray eyes were set a shade too close together, but there was an intelligence lurking behind their studied blankness. "Have a seat, Woody. I know there's another glass hiding around here somewhere."

The chair he accepted, though with a frown that brought his black eyebrows crashing together over the narrow bridge of his nose. "You know the penalty for drinking the night before a show."

Dancer didn't, but arranged her face in Tonia's pixie grin and shrugged. "I won't get caught."

"You just *got* caught, DeWellesthar."

"Woody, the day you turn me in is the day *I* turn in my wings." Shifting her weight slightly, she stifled a gasp at the pain in her leg.

His expression immediately changed to one of affectionate concern. "You all right, Glaize? That was a weird song you were playing when I came in. Gave me the shivers. It's not like you to be moody."

"Huh," she snorted. "Coming this close to being the star attraction in a smoking hole can make a person real moody real fast, you know? I'm also tired, Terry. Very, very tired."

He nodded. "I'm not surprised, after what you've been through. We debated letting you fly this afternoon, despite the flight surgeon's assurance that you were fit. Daven said you fly, so you flew. You were good, though—even better than usual."

"Thank you," both selves answered. Dancer couldn't help being pleased at being told she was better than Antonia. "I'm after your job."

"Keep it up, and I might start worrying. You seemed to have picked up a . . . I don't know, a finesse. That knock on the head obviously didn't hurt you any."

It was a very good thing that this masquerade would end soon. In the not-too-distant future, these discrepancies would begin to add up—Dancer could see the speculation in his eyes already.

"I should leave you to get some sleep, but we're all curious. What really happened, Auglaize?"

"Damned if I know. I pranged my bird. I don't know."

"It was a hell of a recovery. We thought you'd bought it for sure."

"So did I." No lie there. She shivered again as if reliving a terrible moment and hoped that he wouldn't press for details.

He didn't take the hint. "Come on, Glaize, this is your old buddy Terry here, not Daven's inquisition. You can tell me. What really happened? Practicing some of those 'compensations' you mentioned at debrief today?"

"Are you crazy? In the middle of a tight-formation practice? What the hell do you think I am, a total idiot?" And what do you really want to know? she wondered. Would everything she said be duly reported to someone, or was their conversation even now being monitored? Dancer looked him straight in the eye and told him truthfully that Auglaize DeWellesthar had no memory of the incident. "All I know is, one minute I'm flying along, minding my own business, and the next, I'm flat on my back getting the third degree from some guy in a black suit with the creepiest eyes . . ." She shuddered, repressing with difficulty the feeling of warmth that always accompanied thoughts of Michael.

Woods's hand on her shoulder was reassuring, but the expression in the back of his eyes was unfathomable. A shade had fallen when she mentioned the black clothing, and Dancer suddenly recalled Tonia's reaction to her first sight of Michael. What the hell was wrong with her, anyway? Something very strange was going on, and here she was, sitting on her ass getting comfortably relaxed on Tonia's bootlegged whiskey when she should be out trying to discover what that something was. It didn't even occur to her that the high resistance to drugs she'd so long taken for granted might not be quite so high as she'd thought.

Woods lifted the glass out of her hand and rose. "You get some sleep. That's an order."

"Terry, wait. Just out of curiosity—what's the official story on this? I honestly don't remember."

"That crack on the head would explain the amnesia, I suppose.

They say that your plane had a loose winglock, though how something like that could have gone unnoticed through inspection is anybody's guess. At any rate, the negligence was unforgivable. Your on-board maintenance crew has already been punished.''

"You make it sound like they were summarily executed."

"They were."

Dancer stared up at him in genuine shock. He wasn't kidding. It wasn't so much what he said that made her blood run cold as the way he said it—imperturbably, indifferently, as if executions were trivial, commonplace occurrences in a Service that she knew for a fact imposed the death penalty only in extreme circumstances.

Then came another thought even more shocking. "My God," she whispered. "Callic—Troy. My crewchief. What happens to him?"

"I guess that depends on what kind of mood Colonel Daven is in, doesn't it?" He shrugged. "Most of us would think him a small loss, though Daven's making an example of the others was more than enough for even the strongest stomachs. But what's this 'Callic' stuff? Never heard you call him anything but Troy before."

"Callicoon. It's his name," her voice answered, her mind still trying to digest the fact that the new Team commander made examples of his troops by executing them. Luckily, the banter came easily. "And there are a lot of things you haven't heard me call him, old buddy. Unless you've got my bed bugged."

"Uh-uh. You snore."

"I do not! And anyway, how would you know?"

He flashed a grin that was three-quarters leer. "Your Terry Bear's been there, remember?"

"It's been a long time since I've seen my Terry bare," Dancer cooed back, automatically replying to the implication of his last statement.

"And it'll be a hell of a lot longer time before you do again. I've lost all desire to be your pet anything."

So Tonia treated all of her men the way she treated Callicoon, hmm? Sweet child. Was that part of her caricature of Auglaize, or was it a refinement all her own? Dancer couldn't help but wonder how the kid had managed to keep this one's friendship. "Did I ever tell you I was sorry things didn't work out for us?"

"Dear Auglaize, could it be that you are possibly thinking about somebody other than yourself for a change? You really must be tired. Get some sleep. I'll see what I can find out about your . . . crewchief for you."

"I do appreciate you, Terry Bear."

He hesitated as if there were something more he wanted to say, then shrugged, bent to press his lips firmly but quickly to hers, and found his own way to the door.

Auglaize let her fingers wander over the guitar strings again, a lot more careful of where they fell, and started assembling the pieces of the jigsaw puzzle she had been handed.

Chapter 35

Callicoon had failed. Well, maybe he'd half succeeded. Auglaize was safe—at least the one he had known as Auglaize—but the DeWellesthar who was now called Dancer was in greater danger than she could ever know. Not only had he put her there, but as much as he wanted to, he couldn't even warn her.

Not wouldn't, couldn't. "Induced selective aphasia" was the term used for this short-circuiting of the pathways between certain thoughts and speech inside Callicoon's head. The words arranged themselves in orderly progression in the front of his brain; he could see them there as clearly as if they were written on the air before his eyes. But he was physically unable to transfer them into communicable sound. It wasn't just his impediment preventing him; he also couldn't sign or write the characters for the words that would save Dancer's life. His . . . commander . . . had seen to that as part of his mental conditioning.

Callicoon had been confident that he'd cleanly escaped his past masters. His years with the Confederacy, first as an "intelligence consultant," then as an instructor at the Fourth Service's secret tactics school, had been fulfilling, even enjoyable. Furthermore, at war's end the Confederacy had promised him a home anywhere he wanted to live and a comfortable income for the remainder of his life. This sudden assignment to the Team—as a maintenance crew-chief, no less!—had come as a surprise, but it had sounded like it might be fun.

Until he met—and recognized—his new commander. That was when it became clear to him that he wasn't free. Never had been, never would be. They had let him go, all right, but only until they found further use for him. His family, after all, was still living under their control—added insurance in case the drugs and conditioning weren't enough to bind him to them. Not that they needed him for anything except show once they all returned home. And not that he had any hope now of returning home . . .

Auglaize . . . what was her real name? Antonia? She might survive this, anyway. Falling in love with her had been foolish on his part; besides the fact that it had given them another weapon against him, the kid wasn't yet mature enough to know the meaning of the word "love." Still, he was a lonely man and she had flattered his ego. Aside from which, face it—she was very good in bed.

What had he been thinking of, trying to escape with her? That wasn't so hard to figure, O'Brian's Stake being the last stop on the Team's new itinerary. After that, Daven wouldn't have any real use for the Warlord's crew, though Callicoon was certain the colonel had something in mind for the Warlord itself. He'd hoped he could keep the girl out of Daven's hands long enough for the drugs to wear off—he, himself, had already worked through the conditioning to a certain extent—to warn someone that all was not as it should be with the Fourth Service Interplanetary Precision Aerial Demonstration Team.

Dancer's coming back in Antonia's place had been a good idea, except that her razor-sharp perceptions were already being dulled. Quite aside from that, somehow Daven knew who she really was.

Callicoon held himself stiffly after his last encounter with the supposed Team commander. It had been unpleasant, to say the least. He had managed not to betray Dancer; if there was one thing you learned rising through the ranks in the Karranganthian military, it was how to take a beating. Even in the face of the evidence he had been provided, he had bluffed for her sake. It had earned him cracked ribs and bruises, but nothing worse. He was more valuable to them alive, at least until after tomorrow's show.

Then, damn her, she had inadvertently betrayed herself, strumming that distinctively Auryx ballad on her thrice-cursed guitar. Why hadn't she taken for granted that her room would be monitored, and been more careful?

He couldn't even warn her. Worst of all, Daven had decreed that Callicoon be the instrument of her downfall. Her death. He wouldn't carry out their orders. He did not want to carry out their orders. Somehow, he'd find a way . . . but, from bitter experience, he knew better. He *had* to carry out their orders. Tomorrow.

Tomorrow. He had neither eaten nor drunk anything since his return to the Warlord, nothing except some snacks and soft drinks surreptitiously purchased from a local vendor at the airshow this afternoon. Maybe by tomorrow he'd be able to break free of the chemical effects, anyway. That just might be enough.

As for tonight, Callicoon aimed to make that as pleasant for the both of them as he was physically able. He knew that to be very pleasant, indeed.

"Sir, you're just letting Callicoon go to her?"

Daven smiled at the dismay in his second-in-command's voice. "Why not?"

"Good grief, one look at him, and she's going to know something's wrong!"

"Summit, think. Dancer of the Sixth would not be here if she didn't already know something is 'wrong.' What good is it going to do her? She can't communicate with anyone on the planet, and she can't leave the Warlord without our knowing about it. Callicoon certainly can't tell her anything."

"But what if she starts getting nosy?"

"I fully expect her to. However it is my impression that our slow-witted friend there has other ideas. He'll do us the favor of keeping her in her room tonight, and I must say I envy him the task."

"And if he doesn't? Keep her in her room, I mean?"

"Then we get to have a little fun with her. This redhead holds up amazingly well under torture."

Chapter 36

The locked door opened a second time as Auglaize lay, three-quarters asleep, in the bunk in Antonia's darkened cabin. Either these locks were totally worthless or Tonia was very free with her keys, Dancer thought wearily, feeling for the small but deadly knife that was never far from reach.

The intruder paused, accustoming his eyes to the gloom of the built-in nightlights that kept the room from total blackness. It was with wary relief that she recognized Callicoon's shadowy bulk. His appearance wasn't totally unexpected, but after her conversation with Woods, Dancer had been anxious about Calli's well-being.

Without a word, she watched him shrugging out of his uniform jumpsuit—no concealed weapons there—and then moved back against the wall to make room for him beside her. How far she would let this go, she wasn't sure yet, but it promised to be an interesting night.

"Do you mind?" he signed. His movements in the dark abbreviated to a kind of shorthand, but her mind filled in the blanks for a smooth translation. "Open secret that I sneak in here often; always the night before a show."

"Don't want to arouse suspicion tonight, hmm?"

"Not suspicion," he articulated carefully.

Dancer ducked the fingers reaching for her hair, but she couldn't avoid the heat of his body. Eyes squeezed shut at the involuntary contraction in her lower abdomen, she fought giving in. She couldn't, she *wouldn't* play this game now! her mind told her treacherous body, but even her mind was only half listening.

"No," Dancer told him firmly, pushing the big, sensitive hands away from flesh that ached for their touch.

Teeth flashing in a smile, he pressed her palms flat against his chest where she could feel his rapid heartbeat.

"No," she repeated regretfully, sliding a hand up over the slight bristle on his chin. "I am not Antonia."

"I am not Troy." He formed the words with exquisite care. "We both know who—and what—the other is. So, why not?"

"Because even with my eyes wide open I don't need this kind of trouble, friend." As much as she wanted it. Dancer started to push him away, but didn't have to; he flinched from the pressure of her hand on his ribs, and his gasp wasn't motivated by passion.

In one motion, Dancer flung back the covers and snapped on the reading lamp over the bed. "My God," she breathed, taking in his bruised side and swollen face in a single sweeping appraisal. "Are you all right?"

He nodded, the corners of his eyes crinkling in a rueful smile that didn't reach his mouth. "Well enough," he signed. "I was lucky. They still have use for me; I got off with a warning."

Two of his fingers were taped stiffly together; her own flexed in unconscious sympathy. "What's going on here?"

Again, that tortured look as his throat worked in frustration. "I cannot tell you. As much as I want to, I cannot. Anyway, there is nothing you can do tonight. Please, Dancer!"

With a sigh, she dimmed the light and lay back down beside him, a hairsbreadth of air between them. "All right. If you must stay, at least let me get some sleep. Yes?" She hoped he was a sound enough sleeper himself not to notice when she climbed over him in a couple of hours. She had a feeling that if he knew about the nocturnal prowling she had planned, he would try to discourage it.

He grasped her hand to get her attention. "Your Michael told you everything, didn't he?" he signed. "I asked him not to; I said it did not matter. Evidently he thought it did."

"He told me who you are," she signed back.

"I see. Did we ever meet, do you think? I thought I recognized something in your style today. Fearless, and the tiniest bit unorthodox. It would have been a terrible blow to your pride to have lost this afternoon's contest."

"You're probably right about that. Doesn't it seem strange to you that a few years back we were hell-bent on killing each other?"

Callicoon's forehead furrowed. "Interestingly enough, we saw *you* as the monsters. We were told that we were fighting to protect our homeland. Can you imagine that a supposedly intelligent man could be so gullible?"

Though his gestures dripped bitterness she was certain was genuine, Dancer couldn't resist a cold smile. "I don't know; how gullible do you imagine me to be?"

"Dancer. Dancer!" His hissing whisper underscored the urgency of his words as his fingers signed. "No matter what Michael told you, I had nothing to do with what happened on the ground, not on Lioth, not anywhere else. You *must* believe that. We didn't even know, most of us. When I found out . . ." A jerk of his head and a click of his teeth finished the sentence.

No matter what Michael had told her. How much more about Calli had he known and kept to himself? And was the man now trying to tell her that he had defected because of the Lioth Massacre? "It's frightening, isn't it, how easily truths can become twisted?"

"Believe mine."

"I am here in spite of Michael's warning, am I not?"

He raised his hand in the peculiarly Karranganthian gesture that approximated a shrug, the kind denoting good-humored concession. "You 'speak' well. Better than your double. If it is no state secret, where did you learn?"

"Both Standard sign and small sign are required courses at the Academy. You?"

"Same. Only, our Academy puts somewhat less emphasis on Standard. At the time, however, I never thought I'd be solely dependent on it to communicate!"

"Indeed. So you're a 'Grad', too, huh? It seems that you and I have a lot in common, Paulding Callicoon."

"Perhaps one day, when we have more time and fewer mistrusts, we can discuss it over a drink." He chuckled warmly. "Savor it— who would ever have thought to find a Karranganthian and an Auryx in bed together?"

Williams and Guernsey and their Auryx wives, Dancer thought whimsically while signing a noncommittal, "Indeed."

"I do like you, Dancer."

His choice of modifiers gave the verb a much stronger meaning that she quite deliberately ignored as she returned the sentiment, adding, "But I am not Antonia."

"I think we adequately covered this subject before, but I will assure you once again that I am very well aware of who you are not."

"What is it with you, Callicoon? Is it because I am so like her, or do you just welcome challenges?"

"Because you are like, and because you are unlike. Because you are Dancer, and because you are Auglaize. And because any man, who is a man, would want to make love to you. Have I stated it in words simple enough for you to understand?" How had she ever underestimated this man's intellect? He was articulate, witty, warm, and a genius at concealing his genius. From years of security briefings, Auglaize remembered that what Paulding Callicoon didn't know about a Karranganthian T-12 would never be discovered, and that he had had some say in the design of the improved '14. On top of that, he was very, very attractive. God help her, she could visualize with delight a lifetime of evenings spent with him. "It must gall you to be treated the way you are here, not to be able to fly . . ."

"It's not so bad. I am respected for my knowledge and skill at maintaining the Gypsy," he replied, inserting a sidelong glance to make sure that she caught the irony, since in all the years of the war, no state-of-the-art Gypsy had ever fallen into Karranganthian hands. "And she—what did you call her, Antonia?—occasionally lets me get in some stick time. It's a game to me to be deliberately clumsy. We converse, though not so much, because she does not have your fluency with sign and becomes frustrated when she cannot understand me. She often asks for my advice, and sometimes even takes it."

Dancer rolled onto her side and propped herself up on one elbow to study him, partially because she was getting a stiff neck from trying to watch him with just her head turned, and partially because she wanted to see his shadowed emerald eyes in what little light there was. "I *am* looking forward to that long talk, Callicoon."

"But not now, hmm? Come, lie down, then, my little Auryx. Be at peace. This Karranganthian won't force you to do anything against your will . . . How is your hurt?" He smoothed the fabric of Tonia's nightshirt down over her hip with an incredibly sensuous motion of his thumb.

Auglaize wasn't worried about anything happening against her will—her will and his had never been that divergent. "You won't give up, will you?"

"It feels swollen. You must not fly tomorrow."

"I'm fine." The stresses of today's show had badly irritated the laceration, and Dancer knew for certain now that it had become infected, but the excitement and concentration of today's show had pushed the pain from her mind. She had no doubt that she could do the same tomorrow.

"You are not fine, and you must not fly tomorrow!" he stated with peculiar emphasis. As if he were trying to warn her about something. "For tonight, I can make it better." It was his turn to push back the blanket; the guttural grunt as he eased up her night-shirt was comment enough.

Dancer's protest was shushed sharply as Callicoon took a small tube from his jumpsuit pocket and squeezed its contents into his palm to warm. "Trust me, love; I would not willingly cause you any more pain."

She gasped when he touched her and tried to writhe away from the sting; he used his superior strength, coupled with an unexpected gentleness, to keep her still. Gradually, she relaxed under his knowledgeable ministrations, setting herself adrift on the tips of his fingers as he expanded his attentions to other parts of her body. It had been a long time, Dancer thought in drowsy contentment—long enough to have forgotten this sense of serenity and well-being, long enough to have convinced herself that she didn't need it any more.

Maybe Michael was right. (The Commander is always right, a voice intoned in her brain.) Maybe Callicoon was just the thing for her tonight. With this rationalization, she managed to keep logic at bay until Calli had caressed off the nightshirt, dropped it into a heap on top of his jumpsuit, and led her gasping to the point where she knew the world would end if she couldn't have all of him.

A whispered nagging in the back of Dancer's head brought her abruptly back to the time and place. Her eyes widened in shock at what her own hands were doing—shock not that she had let herself lose control to this extent but, unreasonably, that she would try to regain it now. The voice that had whispered a second before had become silent again; her unspoken "why?" remained unanswered.

"Despite what Antonia believes, this is not like me," Dancer found herself murmuring. Then, with another fleeting thought of Michael, she shook her head at Callicoon's questioning glance and surrendered herself once and for all.

When the voice whispered at Dancer again from her pillow, she dismissed it as the dying gasp of rationality. She and Calli were alone here, and though indeed he was using his mouth to communicate, it wasn't with words. A man skilled in love didn't need words to tell a woman he found her infinitely desirable, any more than that woman needed words to answer.

The pillow was pushed to the floor and forgotten, Dancer's head resting now on a smooth-skinned golden arm, now on the sheet-covered mattress as the two continued to explore each other. This could go on all night, she thought voluptuously. She hoped it would go on all night.

There was the oddest sensation in the back of her throat, a vibrationlike tickling that persistently intruded on her overall sense of well-being. Dancer tried clearing her throat; Calli paused in his contemplation of her breasts long enough to kiss the pulse points in her neck, and the tickling went away.

Then, quite clearly, came a hollow, distorted voice from over her shoulder. "Under the circumstances, I think the second approach would be the best."

But there was nothing behind Dancer except the bulkhead. Again, her ear receiver vibrated; again, that strange itching tickle across the back of her throat. Turning slightly, she caught a second voice, garbled, sounding like it was encased in sheet metal under ten feet of water. ". . . a roger," it was saying. "Plan two. What about the pilot?"

It was as if a light snapped on in Dancer's head. "Oh, my God!" Half of her mind listened while the other half analyzed. If not Auryx-originated, she should not be able to pick up this conversation. Each of their ear receivers was tuned to a separate splinter frequency of a spectrum accessible only to Auryx technology. Transmit-only on the part of the communications computer; receive-only on her part. Except that they had already ascertained that the shielding of the Warlord made it impossible for Michael's messages to get through to her.

The transmission upon which she was eavesdropping was, at least on one end, originating aboard the ship—probably from the amateur equipment in the rec room a couple of doors down. The other end was probably on O'Brian's Stake. From the lack of clarity, she gathered that someone had stumbled onto a frequency approximating hers, not close enough for her to have monitored continuously, but which pure dumb luck let her pick up now.

And if *she* could hear *them*, had they been listening to messages directed at her all afternoon?

Right on cue, the first voice was saying, "Dancer of Sixth is my problem. You do your job half as well, and your reward will be great."

They knew! She had to get the hell out of there! Without even thinking, she braced her back against the bulkhead, drew her knees up, and kicked Callicoon in the stomach.

"Damn you!" Dancer cried, her feet hitting the floor a split second after he did. "You filthy Karranganthian maggot! Damned straight they still had a use for you! Keep me dumb and happy until they could collect me at their leisure. Good God, I knew what you are, and I still trusted you! I ought to kill you where you lie."

Trembling with rage and the shock of betrayal, she stood looking down at him long enough to catch her breath before turning to snatch from the chair the first article of clothing that came to hand. Struggling into Tonia's rumpled flightsuit, Dancer tried to shut out Callicoon's barely articulate pleas for an explanation, tried to deny that the sick bewilderment she had seen in his face was real.

He was the enemy. Dancer could ill afford to forget it again!

Though she heard movement behind her as she groped under the chair for the other ballet slipper, she refused to look at him. If he was to attack, she would feel it coming. And she would kill him. Even filled with anger-induced hatred, she knew she couldn't do it unless he posed an immediate threat.

A moment later, Dancer regretted her weakness. As she swung the door open, he slammed it shut again and barricaded it with his body, fending off her physical resistance simply by hooking his ankle around hers and holding her, off-balance, against him until she couldn't breathe. With the last of her strength, she pounded her fists on his chest. Not Calli! she wanted to scream. Not this beautiful, charismatic man whom she had known so short a time but had already come to love.

He could have very easily crushed her ribs, but he didn't. In fact, as she relaxed, so did his grip, the hands becoming the hands of a lover once more as he bent to lay his cheek on the top of her head.

"What have I done?" he asked in a slow whisper when she had calmed down enough to pose no further danger to him.

Tersely, Dancer explained the situation, watching as his expression changed from hurt to horror. She knew then that he was being used, perhaps knowingly, but certainly not willingly. God alone could guess what he had been threatened with to ensure his cooperation in keeping her in her quarters this night. Or, judging from his condition and what she had already surmised about his attempts to protect Antonia, what *she* had been threatened with.

His hand flashed in front of her eyes. "We must get you out of here!" he signed imperatively. Zipping up the jumpsuit that he had managed to pull on but hadn't had time to fasten, he thrust his head out the door, checked the corridor up and down, and hauled her out after him.

Dancer started off in the direction she knew the hangar deck to be in, but he grabbed her hand and dragged her around the opposite way. "Trust me," he signed when she would have protested. *Trust me.* How many times had she seen that repeated in the past day and a half?

With no choice but to pound along after him, she was reminded of her injured leg about fifty feet down the corridor. After a hundred feet, a stabbing pain shot through it every time the sole of her ballet slipper hit the deck. Dancer pushed on, trying to ignore it, until finally she stumbled and would have fallen had Calli not still been grasping her hand. Without discernible pause he jerked her to him, tucked her under his arm, and carried her the rest of the way like a rag doll.

It was neither a dignified nor a comfortable way to travel, but Dancer wasn't complaining. She wouldn't have made it on her own.

Once on the hangar deck, he tossed her bodily into the front seat of an alert Gypsy, fueled and waiting just outside its launch tube as was Warlord SOP even in peacetime, indicating that she should try the radio while he jockeyed the fighter onto the catapult and readied it for launch.

"Calli, wait!" Auglaize tried to detain him, not caring for precious seconds lost, because what she had to say seemed more important.

He disentangled her fingers from his sleeve impatiently. "All quarters are monitored," he signed. "They are already on their way."

"I'm sorry for what I said back there, for what I thought—"

"Later, Dancer, when we are safe." But he pulled himself back up and leaned into the cockpit for a hasty kiss. Auglaize knew she was forgiven, and that mattered much more to her than it should have, considering the circumstances.

Shaking her head to try to clear it, she powered up the computers and crossed her fingers. If whoever she had overheard was still transmitting, there was a chance of getting a message to Michael. And if she started transmitting now, the computer would, on command, repeat the message continuously. As soon as the Gypsy was clear of the ship and its transmission shielding, her call for help would get through, even if Calli and she were otherwise occupied. Otherwise occupied—a euphemism for dead?

Callicoon even now would be at the console, punching in the launch sequence. In a few seconds, he would climb into the rear cockpit and secure the canopy. A few seconds. They might just make it.

Dancer took a deep breath, stringing together in her mind the appropriate coded phrases. Though she hadn't completed her mission, she was certain that there had to be a connection between the arms cache and the Warlord, and that whatever was happening would happen tomorrow, probably using the airshow as a diversion. And that whoever was behind all of this now knew of the Sixth Service's involvement. Between Michael, herself, and Jeremiah, they could figure out the rest in time to forestall it. Please God, it was just a simple smuggling operation. But even as she thought it, she knew better.

"This is D-Dancer, D-Dancer." She coolly intoned the identifier for life-threatening situations, repeated twice the prearranged phrase from an Auryx nonsense rhyme which described the situation. That should be enough. Calli was at the side of the airplane as she started to reach for the switch marked Repeat. Then all hell broke loose.

Calli's bellow of warning came as Dancer was pulled from the Gypsy and thrown to the unyielding floor below. She was aware first of a tearing sensation, then of the oozing, sticky wetness inside the leg of her jumpsuit that signaled the reopening and deepening of Antonia's "scratch." Dancer gave it only glancing attention. Her immediate concern was evasion of the three Fourth Service security men who were bent on Calli's and her destruction.

Or, at least, Calli's destruction. She was half-stunned and having such difficulty regaining her feet that they obviously considered her no serious threat. A negligent shove was all that was required to keep her on the floor while Callicoon fought for both of their lives, and the knife she always carried lay on the floor half under Antonia's bunk. Under other circumstances, Dancer would have enjoyed watching Calli's animal grace as he tried to keep the attackers well away from her while edging both of them back toward the launch-ready Gypsy. It seemed to be a game to him; he was smiling even as a booted heel slammed down and ground into his bare foot, even as a double-fisted blow to the jaw snapped his head back.

Then he went down.

The hangar deck revolved around her in shades of yellow and black as she fought her own weakness to go to him. "Can't see from here? Let me help you." A rough hand on her collar hauled her erect long enough to drag her to where Calli lay.

These three all wore sidearms; why didn't they simply stun her and Calli into submission, as was standard Fourth Service security procedure? Obviously, because these sadists in Fourth Service garb weren't Fourth Service. Dancer sagged to the floor again as the one who had been supporting her picked up a wrench and returned his attention to Calli.

Callicoon was still fighting them, but more and more feebly, and there was despair in his eyes when they met Dancer's. He had been injured far more in that earlier "warning" than he had let on. Sickeningly, she realized that she had hurt him badly, too. If she only had that knife!

Still, it was Dancer's name, not Antonia's, that he gasped out as he lost consciousness.

At least, Dancer thought, that would be the end of it. They would be taken into custody, locked up somewhere, and she could try to keep him alive until help came.

That was what she thought, but still the three men rained blows on him. Rising to a crouch, she hurled herself into their midst, whether trying to pull them off or just shield Calli from further harm, even she didn't know. "For God's sake, enough!" she cried. "He's dead. Leave him be!"

Fury made her quick, desperation made her strong, but even without a leg she could barely stand on she would have been no match for these three barehanded. Still, she had the satisfaction of hearing the scream that was the product of a well-placed kick of her own, seeing blood other than Calli's as it became apparent that she wasn't striking out so indiscriminately as it first appeared, feeling muscles go slack between her hands as she wrenched an arm back to pop a shoulder joint, smelling the sweat of fear as they realized that she was not only highly motivated to kill them but suddenly capable of doing so—and tasting defeat not at the hands of her three adversaries but through her own weakness. She tried to support all her weight on that damaged leg once too often, and it buckled.

When she attempted to rise, her leg was kicked out from under her. Head swimming, Dancer realized that a fourth man had come from behind the Gypsy where he had been observing. She had a feeling it was the elusive Colonel Daven, and that she was in for it now.

As if to confirm those fears, the newcomer chuckled. "That leg seems to be giving you some trouble. You ought to have the flight surgeon take a look at it."

He moved back slightly and Dancer once again started to rise—until a pair of black boot-toes planted themselves in her line of sight, right between her hands.

Black boots . . . not now, she willed silently, squeezing her eyes shut against the recurring vision. When she dared look again, the boots were still there. Dancer eased into a sitting position so that she could tip her head back far enough to take in the rest of the picture. A small part of her instantly wished she hadn't.

Boots, black leather, calf-hugging, handmade, the tops of which disappeared under black trousers. High-collared, finely tailored tunic of a soft, form-fitting fabric, also black. The hair, she knew without looking, would be thick and glossy and of the hue that some called ebony. The eyes were a startling, hypnotic blue, cold and glittering, and Dancer flinched when she met them with her own.

Michael! her mind screamed.

Chapter 37

Michael's head snapped back; his irises dilated to bottomless black pools, and Antonia felt her blood freeze. They had been just sitting there on Dancer's bed, chatting amicably about this and that—Michael had been giving her a very personal history lesson about both her cousin and the man Tonia had been calling Troy, who unbelievably turned out to be a Karranganthian fighter ace by the name of Paulding Callicoon. Now the Commander was the very picture of the vicious bloodthirsty Auryx of Colonel Daven's security briefings. Granite-hard face, ice-cold eyes. He had even, for a moment, ceased to breathe, and his entire body was rigid.

Tonia was afraid to ask why. Then a terrible light glowed in his face as he ground out an order, seemingly to the air: "Strike teams ready *now! Dancer's in trouble.*"

What kind of trouble? How did he know? What . . .

The next thing she knew, a bundle of black cloth was flung at her along with the admonishment, "Put this on if you're coming with us."

Well, of course she was going with them. They'd already discussed that; she knew her way around the Warlord, and would be invaluable to them. Reacting to the tone rather than the sense of Michael's command, she shook out a suit of night black, from the cut and size obviously Dancer's. *Death Squad.* The words echoed in her mind, and Daven's briefing video danced before her eyes. "No!"

"I don't have time to argue," Michael said from the doorway, half out of his own clothes. Had the man no modesty? "Dancer is in danger, do you understand? We need to get to her as quickly as possible. She may already be dead.''

Dead? Auglaize? Auglaize had been dead for twelve years. A hysterical giggle worked its way past Antonia's lips.

The Commander seemed to fly across the room to grab her shoulders and shake her hard. ''*Now,* DeWellesthar!''

''I have my own uniform,'' she managed to get out.

''Child. We've been over this. If there is resistance, it is better that you be instantly identifiable as one of us.''

If there was resistance—she would be fighting her own shipmates. As a member of the Death Squad, for God's sake. How could her shipmates hurt Auglaize?

''Dress, or I will dress you,'' Michael was threatening. At the stricken look on her face, he changed tack. ''Child. We need you. Dancer needs you.''

That did it. Antonia struggled into unfamiliar garments that were a lot heavier and denser than they looked.

Michael caught her questioning look. ''Body armor. Fairly good protection against energy weapons, some from projectiles. We need all the advantages we can get.''

Protection against energy weapons, such as those carried by the Fourth Service security patrols? Her own people were going to be shooting at her? No. It was an adventure, after all. It was only a dream . . .

Dancer had to admit it; anyone who had never known an Auryx would swear that this man was one. The effect was incredibly, frighteningly real, except for the eyes. The color was perhaps under some circumstances correct, but anyone who had ever looked into the fathomless depths of true Auryx eyes that seemed to probe the mind, the very soul, would know this man for an impostor. But because of the eyes, in spite of the darkened hair and disguise, Dancer recognized him instantly. The Karranganthian. ''Harla Davenger,'' she breathed. How could this be?

He smiled slightly and inclined his head in acknowledgment. ''So, Dancer. It is Dancer, isn't it? I never even suspected that you were not the same Auglaize DeWellesthar who left here yesterday until your friends radioed their congratulations. Strange that after all our years of research to discover the Auryx communication bands, we should accidentally stumble onto one of them at this opportune time, isn't it? I am surprised, though, that you remember me.''

Remember him? He was the author of all her nightmares. Flight

Leader DeWellesthar and her people had spent altogether too much time pinned like insects under those razor-sharp eyes. Snake eyes, some of her culture had called them. Not she—she had always considered snakes benevolent enough creatures, which struck only when provoked. No, if in any of God's creations there lived a monster who killed for the sheer joy of it, who fed off the terror, humiliation, and anguish of its victims, that creature would look like Harla Davenger.

Dancer had believed him dead, killed in a manner he deserved in the Auryx cleanup of his installation. She had been *assured* that he was dead.

"I know, I was surprised that you were still alive, too," he continued conversationally, as if enjoying the most-sought-after of reunions. On his part, that might well be true. Dancer kept her face carefully neutral.

"Still not a talker, are you? We never did get much out of you." He shrugged. "No matter. I seem to have been given a second chance. Nothing to say to that, either? Ah, but what can you say? The pleasure is all mine."

Dancer heard the faintest of sounds off to her left, nothing more than the tap of a fingernail on the floor, yet she knew it was Callicoon's way of signaling her that he was still alive. If she wanted to keep him that way, she had to distract these clowns and come up with some plan to get them both out of there.

Once again, she started to rise, and watched in fascination as her reflection in the polished toe of Davenger's boot caught her squarely under the chin, just hard enough to push her off balance and sit her down again. On the festering, swollen, blood-stiffened mess that was her left thigh. Her involuntary groan was one of frustration as much as pain—and, though it pleased Davenger, it also covered a similar, barely audible noise from Calli.

"Sit back and relax, Dancer; we haven't finished chatting yet. I'm sure you have all kinds of questions, hmm?" The boot again, poised over her hand, gently tapping her fingers. It took all of Dancer's willpower to keep them from flexing, to keep from snatching her hand out of his way. The effort diverted her mind from imagining the crunching waves of pain she would experience if he shifted all his weight onto that foot. "For example, oh, what am I doing in command of a Fourth Service aerobatic team?" Each syllable precisely spoken and punctuated by a toe-tap on a fingernail.

Dancer had to admit that she was curious about that and a lot of other things. And she had to admit that she didn't think she could live through having her knuckles crushed again, and she desperately needed something to prod her drugged and paralyzed mind back into action.

Dancer Flight! she wanted to scream. He had her again, and she didn't care how or why. The Karranganthian had her, and she was more afraid than she had ever been before in her life. This time, she knew what was ahead. This time, she couldn't possibly survive.

Dancer Flight! Troy. Meig. Putnam. Ross. Crawford, and the rest. Even now, names and faces came back to haunt her. Once again, she felt the emotions of the commander too young to cope with watching friends die while powerless to prevent it. And once again the certainty assailed her that a more experienced officer would have been able to do something to spare them. Something. How could she have thought that their pitiful acts of defiance had made any difference?

Dancer Flight—it was anger that had sustained them then, the same anger that was surging through her now. As if the intervening years had never been.

Somehow, Dancer hauled herself to her feet, drew herself erect, and stared into those ice-hard eyes. This time, it was Davenger who looked away.

Dancer had never lived, and therefore could not die. Auglaize DeWellesthar was long dead, and could not die again. What, then, was there to fear? "So tell me, Davenger, is this all just for me?"

Surprise flickered across his face. "I would like to be able to say that it was; believe me, if I had known before just who and where you were, I would have gone to any lengths to get you back. You and yours cost me much. The soldiers among us were moved to admiration at your continued resistance. The others, however—those who counted—were cheated out of the promised spectacle. They got their fill of blood, but where was all that lovely groveling and begging for mercy they lusted for? No military secrets blurted out unasked in return for the quick death, and you—there are those who enjoy hacking up corpses, but not I. Worst of all was the effect on morale of watching the supposedly cowardly enemy displaying more fortitude than most of them would have had under similar circumstances. My superiors were . . . most displeased."

So maybe that defiance hadn't been so futile after all. You have just given me a greater gift than you will ever know, she thought.

"This," Davenger continued with a sweeping hand gesture, "is a very neat setup, masterminded by yours truly, for transferring arms and supplies to and from our people in some of the more strategic locations, such as O'Brian's Stake. Planting seeds, so to speak. When the time is right, they and their allies amongst the indigenous populations will replace undesirable governments with their own.''

"Pretty subtle—for a Karranganthian." She didn't need to ask how those "allies amongst the indigenous populations" were recruited—after a couple of generations, even the colonies had their dissidents, often youngsters unhappy with policies they considered old-fashioned. By the time they realized the monster they had given birth to, it would be too late: the Karranganthians would have their stepping-stones across this section of the galaxy. "Could take years. Think your superiors will be able to wait that long?"

"I think so. They don't exactly have the resources yet for any type of major confrontation. Although twenty-five of the latest Gypsy modifications aboard this vessel—not to mention the vessel itself—are an excellent start. As far as your people will know, all will have been lost without a trace in an unfortunate accident in deep space. By the way, I use the term 'your people' loosely. By the time we're finished here, the Auryx truly will be extinct.''

"Auryx? Excuse me?"

"Come now. There was something familiar about that cocky, redheaded DeWellesthar, though I couldn't put my finger on it. It has been rather a long time, and the name didn't mean anything to me; we don't bother to record the identities of our captives. As you well know, we quite frankly don't care, and should the records fall into the wrong hands, they can only give aid and comfort to the enemy.

"But I digress. This DeWellesthar haunted me. Where had I seen her before? It was your own Commander who gave me the answer, when he was patting you on the back for your fine performance this afternoon. 'Dancer.' Of course. How could I forget Dancer Flight? I consulted your excellent Fourth Service computer records, and started adding a long column of figures. She couldn't have survived, and yet if she had . . . the Auryx have been known to accomplish some amazing things.''

"There you go, using that word again. Look, I'm just a poor Confederacy flunky who happens to resemble one of your pilots who crashed on a planet under our protection. The circumstances of the crash were suspicious, so . . .''

"Yes, I ought to thank DeWellesthar and her traitorous maintenance chief for that. If it hadn't been for his idiocy in trying to save her from us, we wouldn't have stumbled into Sixth Service's secret nest.''

"Callicoon?"

"We planted him some time ago. Marked as a traitor to us, he was readily accepted by your people. The weak fool made the mistake of becoming sentimental over a spoiled child who treated him like a lap dog. Don't regret the manner of his death. He deserved much worse."

"Forgive me. I had become fond of him." Dancer's gaze was drawn to the pool of blood that was spreading just within her peripheral vision. Calli's blood. She turned away abruptly. "Can we continue this conversation elsewhere?"

"My dear Dancer, don't tell me you find the sight of blood disturbing?"

What she found disturbing was watching Callicoon's life seep out as she stood there chitchatting. If she couldn't help him directly, at least she could draw Davenger and company away so that he might help himself. The confirmation that he was a Karranganthian spy did nothing to dampen her affection—or her trust. She still believed him to be a true defector. And if Michael could receive even a part of her message, there was a chance for both of them. It wouldn't be the first time the Commander had been cast in the role of savior.

Now the obscene imitation Auryx was examining her right hand, turning it back and forth between his, then raising it to his lips to touch the forked vein on the inside of her wrist. "I'd heard that the Auryx have accomplished miraculous reconstructions, but I had no idea the results were so exact. Tell me, is this actual flesh and blood, or are you just an exquisitely formed robot with a human brain?"

"I expect you'll find out for yourself soon enough." She began to edge toward the door. Surprisingly, she was allowed to. More surprisingly, Davenger came with her after bidding his wounded underlings to seek medical aid. She became bolder, striding out of the hangar deck in spite of the discomfort it caused, turning down the corridor that would eventually lead to her quarters.

"Once, you would not even speak to me, let alone share a joke. You have changed. I wonder how much?"

"I'm sure you'll find that out soon enough, too."

"Tell me, Dancer, are you afraid of me?"

"You'd damned well better believe I am."

Chapter 38

The calm, straightforward statement threw her captor off balance, and Dancer smiled to herself. Every second she could stall was another second for the cavalry to arrive. She did not doubt that it would arrive—Michael hadn't let her down yet.

Davenger recovered quickly. "Yes, you have changed. Not that I remember anything about you but your 'death.' It will be interesting to see how you react this time."

"Interesting to you, perhaps. I would rather forgo that dubious honor."

"I like you, Dancer." His penetrating gaze swept her from head to heel and back again, and she could easily anticipate his next line. "Very much. Perhaps we could strike a bargain—for your life and my pleasure."

"Spare me the melodramatics, Davenger." Then Dancer told him, in fluent colloquial Karranganthian, that before becoming his bed partner she'd fornicate with the slimiest of parasites and take more pleasure from it than she ever would from him. This, one of the crudest insults in a culture that proliferated crude insults, earned her a clip just behind the ear that felt like it spun her head around twice on her neck.

Somehow, she came up smiling. "Now, that's the Harla Davenger I know and loathe." His hand rose again, and her head turned slightly. "Plant one on this side, why don't you. Even me out."

The hand connected with her cheek, all right, but in the gentlest of caresses. "Your life and *my* pleasure, Dancer. A night for a day. It may take weeks for me to tire of you."

"So, my people are going to think I stayed here of my own free will?" she snorted. "Davenger, they *know*. Your whole operation here is blown."

It was his turn to laugh. "At last you abandon the masquerade.

234

No one is coming for you, Dancer. You are mine. Do you actually think your pathetic little radio transmission got through?''

"You know how it is," was the breezy reply. "If you're going to be out after curfew, call home. Since I figured this party would probably run longer than expected . . ." Dancer smiled and shrugged. "Old habits are hard to break. But you seem to forget that they do have DeWellesthar.''

"She can't tell them anything. She knew little enough to begin with, and remembers none of it. You surely realize how easy that was to manage.''

"After all the publicity today, if I'm not in tomorrow's show, they're going to wonder why. And when I don't report back, Michael will come after me.''

"Oh, I think not, Dancer. By the end of tomorrow's show, your Michael will have much more to worry about than your pretty neck. On the off chance that he'll be alive to worry about anything.''

"Don't tell me you've come all this way just to assassinate the nominal head of an insignificant occupation force.''

"Come now, Dancer. Michael is hardly insignificant. We have agents everywhere, don't you know that by now? Some, like your friend there, are obvious. Some—ignorant inhabitants of a backwater planet who don't take kindly to being policed from without.

"O'Brian's Stake is ours, Dancer; and after the second show, our mission will be completed. I've also prepared for the contingency that we might, somehow, run into a nest of Auryx in our travels. With a spectacular finale of fireworks tomorrow afternoon, we will eliminate your entire Auryx secret service—and its Commander, Michael, will be in my hands.''

Into Dancer's mind came the first thought she had had upon viewing a low-flying Team plane: she had thanked whatever deity existed that it hadn't been armed. She knew firsthand the damage one Gypsy could do; it took no imagination to visualize the impact of thirteen Gypsies dumping full ordnance on a certain building on the outskirts of town. There would be no piece bigger than her clenched fist left within a radius of ten miles.

With no advance warning, would Seven be able to put up any kind of defense? Not hardly. And the two recce birds, though always in the air, were unarmed by peacetime law. "Suck fish, Davenger. How do you plan to substitute your pilots, what with the big PR entrance and all the autographed programs we handed out yesterday?''

"Quite unnecessary. I know how to utilize existing raw material. And if you're still thinking that you will be missed—one redhead looks pretty much like another at a distance. Because of all the public exposure at the last show, the natives here will be able to testify that it was, indeed, Team pilots who attacked and destroyed their occupation force. They'll probably be touted as heroes.''

One redhead might look like another to him, but not to Michael. Nor to Antonia, for that matter, who would have already been alerted by Calli's absence. Which, in turn, might make them suspicious enough to notice that the show dummies had been replaced by live ordnance. Dancer didn't like the word "might."

"It's not going to work, Davenger," she said hurriedly. "If you think you'll be using Fourth Service pilots for this strike, you're going to be sadly disappointed. Fourth Service is under the delusion that the war is over.''

"Come, now." He unobtrusively herded her down an intersecting corridor, deeper into the heart of the Warlord. Armed guards in Fourth Service garb fell into step behind them, in an area marked with warning signs declaring it off-limits to unauthorized personnel. Under the circumstances, Dancer could have been forgiven her lack of curiosity as to why.

"You know how easy minds are to bend," Davenger continued. "Of course, we don't have the vaunted innate Auryx facility to do so; we have to resort to artificial means. Drugs to induce the proper emotional states, and a little unabashed propaganda. We have a lively little video cleverly titled 'The Demons in Black' which graphically illustrates Auryx atrocities. It's become quite a favorite here; what a shame you won't be able to view it.''

"Know your enemy, hmm?" It was all too fantastic to be true, yet she had seen enough films of that type—she had even helped make one or two—to know what they could do even without chemical enhancement. "I trust you have ground support. The local Fourth Service element doesn't boast much, but it—"

"Won't have time to get anything off the ground to save your people. All they'll accomplish is to eliminate the attackers on their way out. My crowd-control people will, of course, neutralize your crowd-control people. The weapons are being distributed from their hiding place even as we speak.''

That much, at least, was under Sixth Service observation. But was it enough? She took a deep breath—and laughed.

"Please," Davenger said not at all pleasantly. "Share the joke, Dancer. What could you possibly find humorous in the thought of total destruction of your fortress?''

"Hardly a fortress," she gasped, wiping her eyes. "A converted high-rise. If you think you're finally getting rid of the Auryx, you've got another think coming. We're everywhere, too. It's true, Michael is *our* leader, but do you actually believe he commands this entire so-called secret service you seem so obsessed with? Good lord, Davenger, Mike's no more the Commander than I am.''

"We'll see," he said, his humor restored. But was there a shadow of doubt behind the bluster? ''If what you say is true, I can't help but wonder how much *you* might be able to tell us. Why don't you reconsider my offer? I have some imaginative ideas that might appeal to you.''

She replied flippantly that he would very likely find adequate sexual fulfillment with a number of inanimate objects while watching her torture.

"Indeed," he said thoughtfully. "Or perhaps with one or two of your fellow pilots. It's amazing what some people will do out of fear for their lives.''

"Some people." Perhaps it was a way to keep breathing a little longer, but she didn't delude herself. Chances were that she'd endure a couple of hours of his perversions only to be slowly strangled at the height of his passion. It wouldn't be a much easier death than the one she was facing now. Still, she might be able to buy some time so that she could somehow warn Michael. Or stop the second show. Then Dancer knew, looking into Davenger's eyes, that she had no chance. He'd been playing the game, too, with no more intention of letting her live to see the sunrise than she had of begging for the privilege.

Moving slowly, casually, she glanced around, gauging distances, her weakness, the speed of those with her—looking for some small miracle that she could make happen. If there was one, she didn't see it.

"I think we have you this time, Dancer.''

"You thought that before, too." Her voice was steady enough even as the knowledge penetrated that the game was over. Michael was not coming. She had to play this one out on her own, and Davenger held the winning hand. It would be as he said; her friends would all die as her friends had died before, and she was as powerless to stop them as she had been twelve years ago.

And Michael. Dear God, he knew the location of every Auryx outpost—every Auryx—left in the worlds. He was strong, but when Davenger's interrogator started with him, would he be strong enough? She thought of advanced Auryx technology, Van Wert's secrets falling into the hands of the Karranganthians, and Williams and Guernsey, God help them. She thought of the children. Above all else, Michael would not betray the children. For this alone, he would be made to suffer until the medieval concepts of hell would seem like blessed relief in comparison. A skilled interrogator could keep him alive—and in agony—indefinitely.

Perhaps Michael would not let them take him alive. If he did . . . well. Her predeceasing him meant that at least this time, she wouldn't have to live with the consequences of failure on her conscience.

Then, another thought struck her, not cheering, but enough to give her the courage to get through. Dancer's death itself would carry the warning that would save her Service, a world, perhaps even the Confederacy. Sometime during the small hours of the morning as she drew her last agonized breath, Michael would stop whatever he was doing, his mind turned inward on itself, and know that another of his number had perished. She had seen it happen time and time again. Unless the empathy was very strong, he would not instantly have the identity of the deceased, but in Dancer's case this hardly mattered. She was the only one of his people in immediate danger.

Michael would feel her loss, and the pieces of the puzzle would fall into place like marbles rolling downhill. All hell would break loose on O'Brian's Stake as he struck out efficiently, legally—savagely. She turned her head so that no one would see the small gleam of triumph in her face.

Davenger bent his thumb fractionally, and Dancer had a guard clutching either arm. She welcomed their support. Her leg had turned to jellied fire and wouldn't hold her weight much longer; the world around her had begun to slosh back and forth like water in a nudged bowl.

She was half marched, half dragged into an elevator and through another maze of corridors. Davenger stopped once to run his hands over her face; she suffered his touch with exasperated impatience. "The corpse with the beautiful, beautiful skin," he murmured. "It won't matter this time. Whatever's left of you will be disposed of with the rest of the day's refuse. A pity." His probing fingertips traced the outline of her skull, then stopped at the tops of her jaws. "There it is."

A door opened in front of her, and she was shoved, stumbling, over the threshold into a cell-like room. It was claustrophobic, that room: walls, floor, ceiling all the same nauseating off-white, bare of furnishings except for a few chairs, for spectators who got a thrill from blood spatters, and the wrist cuffs that hung from the center of the ceiling. There she would dangle, just inches off the ground, until her arms felt like they were being torn from their sockets. One wall would be opened to reveal a spectators' gallery, and other prisoners would be lined up along the side to wait their turns. If there were others. She couldn't help but give silent thanks that they thought Calli dead. The executioner—no, this time Dancer had something they wanted; she would rate an interrogator—would bring his own tools.

Davenger had discovered the receiver implanted behind her ear. The first thing they would do would be to cut it out for analysis, and probably remove the ear, too. She would, of course, survive that, since they would know enough not to cut too deeply. Then what? The fingers, joint by joint? She shuddered. At least it would be over in a few hours. A few very, very long hours.

As the uniform was torn from her body and the cold steel clamped around her wrists, a thousand emotions passed through her brain to coalesce into a single, resigned thought:

"Here we go again . . ."

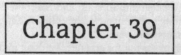

Chapter 39

One more chance. That was all he had left, just one more chance. For Dancer, for Antonia, for himself. One more chance . . .

Callicoon started inching himself toward the Gypsy the minute Dancer pulled everybody's attention away from him. After all, he was dead. He wasn't going anywhere. Surprise, Davenger! Another thing you learned working your way up through the Karranganthian military system: how to make them think they'd broken you up a lot worse than they had.

Although the way he hurt, he knew that it was just a matter of time. He was a walking—crawling—bruise. Most of the bleeding was internal, so at least he didn't have to look at much more than that pool from the compound fracture of his leg that had so upset Dancer. He'd already controlled that. The broken ribs, he could pretty much ignore—except for the one that had punctured the lung.

It would have been all right if he hadn't had to breathe, and to keep breathing—at least long enough to get a message to Michael, letting him know that Dancer was now in Davenger's hands.

In all actuality, Callicoon probably was dead; he was just too stubborn to admit it.

The Gypsy. Damned tall airplane. Funny he'd never noticed how tall. Of course, he'd never looked at it from quite this angle before, flat on his stomach beside the right main landing gear. Flat. One shattered leg, one separated shoulder. God only knew what else was broken in between. Everything, from the feel of it. Topped by a skull that seemed to shower sparks whenever he moved his head. No way. No way was he going to be able to get into that airplane. Even if he did—assuming a miracle—the stresses of launch would crush out any inkling of consciousness left in him. Give up. Die here. Quit hurting.

Ah, Dancer. Too bad; what a woman she was! What his Antonia could be when she grew up. Of course, he'd never live to see it. Nor would Dancer. Callicoon had no doubts whatsoever concerning Davenger's plans for the redheaded Auryx. Even now, perhaps . . .

The thought pushed him forward another foot, the sleek side of the fighter looming over him now like a cliff. A cliff he had to climb with his fingernails. No way.

Memories, things taken for granted. Vaulting into a cockpit with the grace and agility of a wild cat. One of those beauties that leaped snarling through the air for the sheer joy of movement. Movement. Pain bordering on agony. Where was this rumored shock that was supposed to keep the severely injured from hurting? He could use a little of that right now.

Another foot. Standing—almost. Was there enough strength in the good arm to pull him up far enough to get the weight off his less damaged leg so that he could brace it in a foothold long enough to pull himself up again with the good arm? Just thinking about it exhausted him.

But he did it. Got himself into the seat. Strapped in sufficiently to survive launch, if he was lucky. Canopy down and sealed. Rest for thirty seconds, then . . . come on, engine. Start. Start. Computer, launch sequence. God. Dancer. Go!

The silence unnerved Antonia, the silence and the cool, calm, unconcerned faces of the black-caped troops boarding the shuttle. What were a dozen—thirteen, counting her, but she counted herself worthless—against the hundreds aboard the Starlifter? Even granting them the element of surprise?

According to Michael, contingency plans for extricating Auglaize from the Warlord had been worked out with her before she left the confines of Sixth Service headquarters. Simplicity was the key; they'd merely pretend to be an innocent Fourth Service shuttle returning a Team pilot who'd partied a little too much and "missed the bus" home. Michael had even gone so far as to single out a likely subject from the half-dozen who returned to O'Brian's Stake to socialize after dinner. A lithe, ebony-haired Auryx beauty named Fulton had taken it from there; she was, even now, entertaining Marko Rhyan in the VIP suite of a local hostelry. Presumably, Rhyan would awaken around noon with a pounding headache, thinking he'd had one hell of a good time—and knowing Fulton, Michael had commented, the Team pilot undoubtedly *would* have had one hell of a good time. Once on board the Warlord, the Auryx would have to play it by ear. Tonia took that to mean that they would fight their way through the entire ship if they had to in order to get to Auglaize.

Meanwhile, the Sixth Service body now filling Marko's flying boots actually fooled even Antonia at first glance. Will had submitted to having his hair and eyebrows dyed light brown on the off chance that this subterfuge would be needed; even now, as he sat in the first passenger seat behind the man garbed as a Fourth Service shuttle pilot, he was popping in the lenses that would camouflage the characteristic Auryx blue of his eyes under Marko's tawny brown. He'd put his foot down at having his irises dyed; for the short time the color change would be needed, contact lenses would suffice. They were easier and less uncomfortable to put in—and easier and less uncomfortable to get rid of.

The two members of the shuttle crew, husky Seven and the brown-haired woman named Perry, looked about as Fourth Service as one could get in their red uniforms. Maybe Perry was a bit on the short side, but since Fourth had no height requirement for shuttle crew, she'd be accepted without question.

As far as Antonia could see, the shuttle itself, though normally stabled in a hidden Auryx complex just outside of town, was standard Fourth Service issue. At that observation, Michael had just smiled.

"But the Warlord has all sorts of sensors," she thought aloud as the vehicle climbed through the first layer of clouds. "Surely they'll be suspicious of a dozen people returning one Team pilot."

Seven half turned in his seat. "There's no security measure that can't be circumvented. The Warlord will see only three bodies on this shuttle.''

"But how—"

Michael stopped her with a gesture. "Even our allies are not fully apprised of our technology," he said so quietly she had to strain to hear him. A small, graceful, black-gloved hand brushed the fastening of the cape at his throat, and his eyes touched hers impassively.

So, was the fabric he'd described as "fairly good protection from energy weapons" also impervious to sensor scans? Or was there some sort of jammer aboard? Or both? She'd put her money on both. The question was in her face, but the Commander didn't answer it.

Silence again as the shuttle drew nearer to the Warlord. Several members of the Black force even seemed to doze.

Tonia shook her head. What about Michael's certainty that Auglaize was in some kind of deadly danger? He looked like he didn't have a care in the world. She didn't believe it. These people all had ice water running through their veins!

As Michael again turned that glacier gaze on her, she tried to stop her hands from shaking so that he wouldn't see. Well, he saw, all right. His pointed look was followed by a barely perceptible softening of the muscles around his jaw—then, incredibly, a slow wink.

What the . . .

"Commander, there's a Gypsy fighter being launched from the Warlord," Seven murmured. "I'm preparing for evasive action."

Michael's attention snapped back to the forward viewer. "Dancer?"

That was Antonia's first thought, too, but given the craft's erratic flight path, she found herself hoping not.

"Message coming through."

Michael's hand raised for silence as Dancer's voice repeated a nonsense rhyme, followed by an odd tapping. Antonia felt that she should have been able to identify the rhythms, but knowledge eluded her. She was just too plain scared. "Auglaize?" she asked in a whisper. Why had she ceased voice transmissions?

"No," Michael answered shortly. "A recording. Hush."

Perry was busy even then talking with Warlord Control. "What was that?" she asked them in apparent surprise. "Do you people need some help up there?"

"Negative, Shuttle. We're handling it. An alert catapult misfired during routine maintenance."

"We seem to be intercepting a distress call," Perry continued.

Hesitation. "The Gypsy is unmanned. We read a computer malfunction. Say again your mission, Shuttle?"

"Warlord Control, we are returning one of your pilots. He was, uh . . ." Perry's voice dropped insinuatingly—these Auryx all seemed to be frustrated actors!—"partying a little too strenuously, if you get my drift."

"Understood," came back on a chuckle. "Pilot's name?"

"Marko Rhyan."

A few seconds' delay as Warlord Control obviously ascertained that Team Pilot Rhyan had, indeed, gone planetside, and was not peacefully asleep in his own bed.

"Dancer's been taken," Michael whispered into the lull.

"How do you know?" was Tonia's reaction.

"Callicoon," Seven answered briefly. "Modified dot code."

"Shuttle, this is Warlord Control. Bring 'im home."

"Roger," Perry responded.

"Commander!" Seven said almost simultaneously, drawing their attention to the shuttle's electronic "rearview mirror."

As the Warlord's landing-bay doors opened in front of them, the fighter crashed on the planet below.

God, was all Tonia had time to think. Did they say Callicoon?

Unreal. Absolutely unreal. The shuttle glided onto the indicated landing pad as if nothing unusual had happened in the whole of recorded history; the three Auryx in Fourth Service red calmly prepared to disembark as soon as the bay was repressurized and atmosphere restored around them.

"Escort's on the way," a new voice on the radio told them. "I'll be right down to help you turn 'er around for launch."

"Thanks." With her best smile, Perry directed a wave at the glassed-in monitoring booth just in front of and above them. "Seems to be just one up there," she reported to Michael.

"That's about right for this time of night," Tonia confirmed. "Probably sent him down from Main Control when they saw us coming. They're not even suspicious!"

"They're suspicious," Michael returned. "Stay on your toes."

With a silent flutter of black, Antonia and nine Auryx moved deep into the shadows in the rear of the shuttle. There, out of sight of the main hatchway, they watched on a hidden monitor as Seven and Perry helped a stumbling Will disembark. Instantly, a large Fourth Service security team, weapons drawn, materialized as if from thin air around the trio. Antonia again silently nominated the three Auryx for the highest acting awards.

"What the . . . !" Seven yelped in feigned surprise. "For God's sake, you don't need twenty men with guns to put one intoxicated pilot to bed, do you?"

Will's mumblings were less distinct and more profane as he slipped to the floor; the four hands that had been supporting him were now resting on their owners' heads at a pointed request accompanied by the whine of a weapon charging.

Seven didn't even turn his head as half a dozen of the "escort" disappeared inside the shuttle. They were too late: only a moment before, Antonia had followed in a daze as the good guys wearing black silently slithered out of a concealed hatch in the shuttle floor. From under cover of the vehicle, Michael made a quick reconnaissance, then issued a rapid series of orders in an abbreviated sign that Antonia couldn't even begin to follow.

"Stay put," was his terse instruction to her. As if she had any intention whatsoever of moving!

After all the tension, it seemed ridiculously easy. She had the impression of a brief scuffle, one muffled scream, and some heartfelt cursing. From her vantage point, all she *saw* was a herd of booted feet. For some dumb reason, Warlord security had not deemed it necessary to surround the shuttle. The Auryx took advantage of the fact to show them how it should have been done, sneaking around behind the red-shirted security force while Seven, Perry, and Will provided a vocal distraction. Without a shot being fired, a dozen and a half well-trained Warlord security people were disarmed and marched into the shuttle to join the six of their number already trapped inside.

"Don't forget the keys," Perry called out jokingly; Seven replied that controls and communications were already locked to prevent prisoner interference.

Then Michael was hauling Antonia to her feet and urging her to take them into the bowels of the ship, the new Off Limits section, the place where . . . had she actually seen an execution carried out there, or was it just a drug-induced hallucination?

At any rate, like her cousin's, Tonia's curiosity had always been piqued by Off Limits signs that appeared for no reason, so she was able to lead her assault team straight to it. No one challenged them. In fact, no one was visible in the corridors at all. It was odd, frightening, like the lull before a storm, when even the birds don't sing.

Michael seemed to know instinctively just which closed door to shoot the lock off, which small room for them to rush into, weapons drawn.

The four surprised men in that room scarcely had time to blink before the black-clad swarm was upon them. Intent upon something else as the door burst open, they were quickly subdued. Again, Tonia brought up the rear, unable at first to see what caused the collective gasp among the Auryx rescue party. Unable to see, at first, her cousin.

Across the small room, held fast between Seven and Will, stood a man in black whom part of her mind immediately identified as Colonel Daven. What was he doing in Auryx uniform, anyhow? And what was that he was babbling, about not even having touched her? Touched whom? Then, Antonia found her horrified eyes riveted on the focal point of the room. Glaize. Hanging limp, steel bracelets clamped around her wrists, fingers entwined in the chains between those bracelets and the high ceiling. Blood ran freely down one mangled leg and fell with an audible *drip, drip, drip* the few inches to the floor below her feet. And her eyes—flat, empty, staring fixedly at the opposite wall.

"My God," Tonia breathed. "Is she still alive?"

The Commander's gaze flickered from this specter across to Daven. "Release him," was Michael's low-voiced command.

The two Auryx obeyed instantly, and Michael flashed into action. He had kicked the legs out from under Daven before Antonia—or any of the rest of them—realized he'd moved from her side; kicked Daven's legs out from under him, wrenched an arm behind his back, and pulled him upright before smashing his face into the wall a couple of times.

Daven's scream was almost simultaneous with the crack of his arm breaking; the sounds propelled the stunned Auryx into action. This one had to be brought back alive! But Tonia was certain that if it wasn't for the need to appease Confederacy law, they all would have just stood there and watched Michael kill the man who had done—that—to Auglaize. As it was, it took six of them to separate their enraged Commander from his captive, six of them and soothing murmurs in a language Antonia didn't understand to snap Michael back to himself.

With that same dreamlike sense of unreality, Tonia watched as Gallia and Fayette lowered Auglaize gently into Michael's arms, watched him tenderly enfold her inert body in his cape, watched his hand caress the staring eyes shut.

"Dear God," Antonia repeated, pleading for reassurance. "Is she still alive?"

The eyes Michael raised to hers were as empty as those his fingers had just closed.

"No," she murmured, denying that any of this—any of it!—was happening. *"No!"* Vaguely, she heard an annoying whining behind her. The words didn't matter; it wasn't an Auryx, it was indecent, and it irritated her. "Shut up," she snapped. "Just *shut up!*"

The whine separated into intelligible words denying responsibility for Auglaize's condition and protesting his, Daven's, treatment. Antonia whirled without thinking and, with a booted foot forcefully placed, silenced him.

Gradually she became aware that in the stunned quiet that ensued, everyone was looking at her.

God. She had actually kicked a man—there! She had actually kicked her colonel! What had gotten into her? She'd never lost her temper like that before. Embarrassed, she raised her eyes to Michael's, sure of the censure she'd see.

Instead, to her immense surprise and added confusion, she met approval, even a tiny sparkle of humor.

"You'll do," was the Commander's assessment.

Antonia didn't believe it. With all that had happened in the last fifteen minutes—with Glaize lying on the floor, wrapped in Michael's cape—what she felt, after that small praise from the Commander, was the same mixture of pride, jubilation, and dismay she'd experienced the first time she'd soloed one of Mydge Ashland's airplanes. That hadn't seemed quite real, either.

Chapter 40

Black. Black and red. Boots. Uniforms. Blood. Two men, one good, one evil. Good, and evil. Evil and good. Both clad in black. Black bootheels, the hem of a cape. Dancer's face, looking into Dancer's face. Dancer's voice. "Dear God, is she still alive?" Another voice, a man's. Words that meant . . . nothing. A swirl of black, an explosion of red—then oblivion.

5: O'Brian's Stake, Quarters of the Commander, Sixth Service

Chapter 41

Jeremiah, please record and edit the following account to be entered into the Official Report of Michael, Sixth Service Commander, to the Auryx Ruling Council. NOTE: Additional commentary provided by Seven, one of several who accompanied me in this action. Pick it up where we left off. Ready?

Of course I had an assault team primed and ready before Dancer had even set foot on the Warlord. I also knew that she was on her own until we could get to her, and that worried me. Why? She asked me that at least a dozen times—"Michael, what is it about this one that bothers you so?"—and I never gave her a satisfactory answer. I was afraid of losing her back to her own Service. It was as simple as that. Even suspecting Karranganthian involvement, I was certain that she could handle any outside threat. None of us had any idea of the magnitude of the danger she actually faced.

Immediately upon receipt of the drink sample Dancer smuggled out to us, I put our entire medical section to work analyzing it. It turned out to be the key to the neutralizing agent which we had been seeking. Interestingly enough, the alcohol that this was administered in wasn't just a convenient carrier as first thought; it turned out to be an integral component of the compound. No wonder the severe strictures limiting drinking among Team pilots! After another delay to manufacture the chemical antidote in our labs, we then administered it to Antonia DeWellesthar. She was thereafter able to "remember" many odd happenings aboard the Team Warlord.

It had seemed strange to them that a new Team commander—and a nonflying one, at that—would have been assigned at the third stop on a very successful tour, and that he should also bring with him four dozen replacements for the Warlord crew, most notably the security contingent. When it was noted that the former, very popular, Team commander had left without a word to anyone, rumors started buzzing. But not for long.

Before anyone outside of the Starlifter could question, the Team had embarked on a new schedule that the Fourth Service hierarchy had evidently been persuaded would better serve their mission. NOTE: Request for investigation of this matter has already been forwarded through proper channels.

At this time, a new cook was also introduced, classified security films depicting the "atrocities committed by our supposed allies, the Auryx people," became a triweekly routine, and predemonstration briefings began to include a light show "to promote proper concentration" and the toast "To our fallen comrades." We know now, of course, that Davenger was drugging all food and drink and subtly brainwashing the entire cadre to keep them subdued while he smuggled arms and insurgents and, incidentally, sought out the remnants of our Service. If he found us, this ongoing conditioning would ensure unquestioning participation by Team pilots in our destruction. The Fifth Service captain and crew, though by tradition segregated from their "cargo" anyway and having no idea that anything untoward was happening, were handled in a like manner to guarantee their noninterference.

From what we could piece together later, we were discovering this information at about the same time Dancer was. Antonia volunteered to lead us into the Warlord when she realized exactly what was happening; since she knew her way around the transport better than we did, I consented. At first she balked at wearing Dancer's black uniform, a lingering effect of Davenger's conditioning which I felt had to be dispelled before she would be completely trustworthy.

There remained the problem of getting aboard. We agreed that initial contact should be made by a single Fourth Service shuttle, which would carry a dozen of our people. Logic dictated that launching our Dart interceptors and trying to blast our way in would have accomplished nothing but to give away our strength and guarantee Dancer's death and the deaths of many other innocent people. That she was still alive at this point, I knew—it is one of the curses of a Sixth Service Commander to have such an empathy for his people that each death strikes him as a physical blow.

For Dancer, I hoped we wouldn't be too late. A vain hope, as it turned out.

We approached the transport on the pretext of returning a Team pilot suffering the effects of too much celebration. Contact had just been made with the night crew when a lone Gypsy fighter hurtled toward us out of the Number Four stern catapult. It wavered unsteadily on launch, as if the craft or pilot were grievously hurt.

Our first thought was that we were under attack. Shuttles operating on and around such buffer planets as O'Brian's Stake, even those used by our Service, are, by law, unarmed. We could only watch helplessly and attempt evasive action.

Then Seven detected a continuous message coming from the Gypsy in modified dot code. It was Paulding Callicoon, who had returned with Dancer to the Warlord, repeating Dancer's transmission and enlarging upon it in the only way he could be sure we would understand him. Her few well-chosen words let us know she had been found out and was in danger; Callicoon added that she had been captured and was almost certainly under torture at that moment. I could but pray that she would sense we were on our way, and hang on just a little longer.

The Gypsy wavered again and then regained control, streaking groundward as Callicoon attempted to duplicate his earlier spectacular recovery and landing. Our rearward eye, as we glided through the open hangar door, told us that he did not entirely succeed.

The door closed behind us, the atmosphere was renewed, and Seven, Perry, and Will disembarked. As expected, they were met by two dozen Karranganthian infiltrators using Fourth Service weapons—suspicious of a shuttle visit at this hour of the night, but not suspicious enough to take more than the most rudimentary of precautions. With Davenger preoccupied with Dancer, his second-in-command was in charge; thanks to the Karranganthian policy of discouraging independent thought among subordinate officers, Summit was unsure how to cope with two unusual situations simultaneously. As Sixth Service interference was totally unexpected at this point, Callicoon's flight and radio transmissions were deemed the greater threat.

We sustained only one casualty, and that minor, as Logan tripped and fell at the door of the shuttle, breaking his arm.

So far, so good. The trick now was to find Dancer. Antonia was able to lead us into the restricted area of the ship, unopposed—the few guards on night duty had already been dispatched to O'Brian's Stake to recover Callicoon. Our people were at the crash site, waiting for them.

Davenger had converted one of the smaller cargo compartments into a torture cell where, Antonia told us, many horrors had been perpetrated, in the name of "discipline," by the order of a dark-haired man in a black suit. I understood now both her unreasonable fear of me and my unreasonable fear for Dancer's safety. Or, perhaps, not-so-unreasonable fear, considering how both women had come to us originally.

At any rate, it was in this torture cell that we found Davenger—and Dancer.

Damn, I thought we got there in time, this time! There wasn't a mark on her except for the reopened wound on her thigh and the darkening bruises of resistance. They hadn't yet touched her. They hadn't yet touched her, and still her eyes had the cold, flat stare of death.

Ten minutes! If I had reached her just ten minutes sooner, she would be sitting here with us, joking and drinking spiced chocolate instead of . . . !

Yes, Seven, I know. Self-recrimination serves no purpose.

At least her body still lives, and I will reach her mind again. Let the "experts" assert her brain dead and clamor for euthanasia; I *know* that she is reachable! She shall not die by my hand unless at her own request—I made her that promise years ago. And by *our* law, no one else can touch her.

I am that certain, Seven. When they took her down and laid her in my arms, she looked into my eyes, and she knew me. She knew me!

NOTE by Seven: the Commander has been momentarily called away, but will pick up this report here later.

Antonia hesitated outside the door of the Commander's quarters, unsure of her welcome. Faintly, from within, she heard the strains of some sort of stringed instrument accompanying a man's voice in a tune that made her heart rise into her throat even though she couldn't understand the words. Michael must have one of the local broadcast stations turned on for background noise, she decided. Before she left, she'd have to get the name of that song so that she could buy a recording.

"Who wishes to see the Commander?" a voice inquired pleasantly from nowhere. Tonia jumped, looking behind her, before she remembered that Michael's computer talked.

"It's Antonia DeWellesthar." Odd how easily her own name slipped out after all this time of using Auglaize's. Michael's influence, surely. Lying to him was like cursing in church.

The door immediately slid open; the music stopped just as Antonia stepped across the threshold. As she looked around the room, she was surprised to see Michael not at his workstation, but rising from a rocking chair beside a cupboard of some sort, coming toward her with a smile of welcome on his face and a harplike instrument in his hands.

"Come in, child," the Commander was saying. "This is a surprise."

"Was that you singing?" At his nod of assent, she continued, "I was, uh, down in the Medical Section checking on Troy . . . Callicoon . . . and was wondering about my cousin. Dr. Pebble, is it?"

"Preble," Michael corrected. "Just Preble. How is Callicoon?"

"Hanging on. Preble says he's really dead but the word hasn't gotten to his brain yet, and that it's probably just a matter of time. Mentioned something about transporting him to a hospital somewhere anyhow."

"AES Six," Michael supplied. Chances were slim that even Van Wert could put Callicoon back together again, but the mere fact that the man was still breathing signaled that he was worth the effort.

"Whatever. I talked to him even though he's unconscious. At the very least, I owed him an apology. And a thank you, for what he tried to do for me, for what he tried to do for Auglaize. Preble told me you had her brought up here."

"I thought it best." He led Tonia across the room. Upon closer examination, what she'd taken for a cupboard turned out to be a bed of some sort, on which lay—

Antonia gasped at the bluish white face of her cousin, stark against the black of the bed covers. Without thinking, she brushed the marble cheek with her fingertips, then drew her hand back hastily. Auglaize was ice cold, despite the sheet and blanket covering her. In fact, Tonia could see no sign of breathing, and when she hesitantly touched Glaize's neck she felt no pulse.

"She's dead," the girl murmured, sinking into the conveniently placed rocker. That beautiful song that Michael had been singing—Michael? Singing?—must have been some sort of dirge.

"No," said the Commander in his soft voice. "Not dead. Just . . ." he gestured vaguely, "away. What we need to do is find some way to bring her back to us."

Antonia eyed him incredulously. She couldn't believe the Commander standing here calmly denying the obvious. Mr. Ice Water, himself? Mr. I-Can-Take-Anything, refusing to admit to the plain fact that Glaize was dead? "Michael," she began, shaking her head. "She's not breathing. She has no pulse. That means she's—"

"Hush, child," he interrupted with a cryptic half smile. "I am perfectly aware of appearances. Your cousin has—how can I put this so you'll understand?—retreated into herself, into her own mind, and is blocking out everything outside that place where she is hiding."

"I don't understand. Are you saying Glaize is in a coma?"

"Not exactly. There is no physical cause for Dancer's condition; she has willed it upon herself. Her mind has slowed her pulse and respiration rates so much that they seem to be nonexistent."

"Wait a minute. She's put herself into a trance of some sort?"

"Biostasis, your friend Preble terms it. Or suspended animation, if you will. It saved her life once before; we believe it is an unconscious reaction to being trapped and in immediate danger of torture and death aboard the Warlord. The problem is, I can't get through to her to let her know she's safe now. I've tried. I've tried, but . . ." He sighed and shrugged.

For the first time, Antonia really looked at him. "You're exhausted," she stated flatly. He looked like death warmed over.

"Thank you, I'm fine."

Well, that certainly was a matter of opinion, but Tonia wasn't about to argue with him. Instead, she asked, "How can you be sure Glaize isn't dead?"

"Jeremiah," Michael said in answer, "Dancer's condition, if you please."

"Unchanged, Commander," the machine replied smoothly. "Pulse and respiration barely perceptible, but present. Still no evidence of brain activity, though."

Michael's hand brushed the side of Auglaize's neck, lifting her hair and turning her head slightly so that Antonia could see the tiny silver patch at the base of her skull. Smaller than the nail on Michael's little finger—Lord, he had tiny hands for a man! Just a hairsbreadth broader across the palm than her own!—the sensor shone reassuringly. If the computer said Glaize was still alive, then Glaize was still alive.

"You said this bio-whatever, this suspended animation, saved her life once before. How did you get her out of it then?"

Michael's eyes stared, unfocused, across the room toward the window. "With great difficulty," was his characteristically brief reply.

Undaunted, Tonia pursued. "Well, how long did that take?"

"Something on the order of three months."

"Three—What happened to her, Commander? Why did she do this to herself?"

"Initially? She was . . . tortured," he admitted reluctantly. "To death, or so they thought."

This was all too much to cope with at once. "Oh, no," Tonia protested. "Auglaize was killed in the Lioth Massacre."

"She was captured in the Lioth Massacre. She and seventeen others, Morgan Troy among them."

Tonia's stomach turned over, and she was glad for the support of the chair at her back. Glaize had mentioned something about perishing in a Karranganthian torture cell, but Antonia had concluded she was just being overdramatic. Trying to scare her. But it was true? Tonia had seen firsthand how the Karranganthians worked . . . She kept talking to keep herself from thinking. "No wonder she wouldn't tell me how Troy died. But how did this . . . mind thing save her life?"

"You've seen for yourself. All body functions have been slowed to the lowest levels possible. What wasn't necessary to sustain her existence was simply shut down. The Karranganthians didn't destroy anything vital, and blood loss was minimized when—"

"I'm sorry I asked," Tonia interrupted. The last thing she wanted were all the gory details. This was *Glaize* he was discussing so dispassionately. "I don't believe this. Can she hear us? Does she know we're here?"

"She doesn't even know that *she's* here. If she did, she'd wake up."

"Just like that? You said it took three months, before."

"I'll be perfectly honest with you, child. The meds nor psychs neither one expect her to awaken this time. As far as they're concerned, she's gone."

Tonia shook her head. "How do you know she's not?"

"I know," he said simply.

"Like you knew she was in trouble to begin with?"

"Yes."

"That's good enough for me. What can I do?" There it was again, that brief sparkle of approval in his eyes—Glaize was right, he did have beautiful eyes.

"Your responsibilities lie aboard the Warlord. Dancer is my responsibility. Unfortunately, she's not the only one."

"That's why you brought her up here, so you could keep tabs on her yourself. Is that your shirt she's wearing?"

If Tonia hadn't known better, she would have sworn that the Commander blushed. "I thought it would make her feel more . . . secure," he explained. "What was she like when you knew her, Antonia?"

Tonia smiled at the recollection, in spite of herself. "So alive! No, larger than life. Not in size; she weighed less then, I think, then she does now. I remember looking at her wrists, so thin I could see the bones. So delicate looking, for the strength in them. Fact, you could say that about Glaize, too. And it seemed like she was always laughing, even when she was talking about something serious. Like the time she and Troy were joking about this friend who died. I said, if he were her friend, why wasn't she sad that he was dead? She said—I remember this like it was yesterday—that as much as she missed the guy and was sorry that he wasn't there for her anymore, she wasn't sorry for him, because he'd 'gone out in a blaze of glory, just like he wanted to.' For a long time, whenever I'd start feeling sorry about Glaize being dead, I'd think, well, she went out in a blaze of glory, just like she wanted to. Except she didn't, did she?"

"In her own way. She earned those medals, child, and a few they don't give."

A few they don't give. Whatever he meant by that, Tonia felt it, too. Auglaize was going to be all right, though; Michael said so. Michael knew. How Michael knew was beyond her, but she'd seen for herself: if that man said something was so, it was so. Then, looking at the contrast of red hair with that milk-white profile—like blood on snow—she wasn't quite so sure. Her eyes filling with tears, Antonia turned blindly away.

Straight into Michael's arms.

Chapter 42

It was a man's voice, dimly heard at first as though her ears were stuffed with cotton, then suddenly sharp and clear as she came awake. Another voice answered in a language she didn't quite understand.

A weight across her eyes prevented her from opening them; her throat was so dry that when she tried to speak, all that came out was a croak. The voices ceased instantly as someone rushed to her side. A cool hand brushed the hair off her forehead, then its mate curved its palm over her cheek.

The owner of that hand murmured something; each syllable was clear and distinct, but she had no idea what any of them meant. "In Standard, please, Makellen," she managed.

A few seconds of silence, so heavy it was almost suffocating. "I asked how you were feeling, child."

A groan intimated what Auglaize thought of the question.

"Perhaps this will help." An arm went behind her shoulders to lift her up as he held a cup to her lips. Cinnamon cocoa. Lukewarm, and not much left, but she sipped appreciatively. "I seem to have developed a taste for this," he said apologetically. "Seven will fix you a cup of your own if you like."

"Yes, thank you." Auglaize started to raise a hand to her face—surprised, because she shouldn't be able to move—and he intercepted it.

"You've hurt your eyes. You'll have to leave them covered for a while longer."

It was then that she realized she could feel her whole body, with the exception of a leg she knew was there only because it lay touching its mate. She shouldn't be able to move or feel. She should be in the Van Wert. Wasn't that what happened next? Or had she already skipped ahead to the part where she was out of the Van Wert? If that was the case, then Makellen wasn't dead after all, because he was right here beside her.

"Mak, you've come back! I thought you were—"

"Hush, child. The drugs are confusing you, ours and theirs. You'll be fine in a few days."

"How can that be? The Karranganthians had me." Her forehead puckered in a frown. If the Karranganthians had had her, common sense asserted, she would be dead. Except that she had been rescued, and . . . then it struck her that this must be a dream. Of course. A follow-on to the dream of terror, black boots, and blood. She had dreamed such dreams before, of a black-haired man with brilliant blue eyes and a touch that made her spine tingle. Her hand reached to explore his face, his fine, smooth hair, and she giggled when his lips brushed her palm. Yes, many times had the dreams been this real.

"Ah, here's Seven with your cocoa."

He arranged the pillows so that she could sit up and another man placed a steaming mug in her hands. "I don't remember a Seven," Auglaize said fretfully. "I think I meet him later, don't I?"

It didn't really matter. Things seldom made sense in dreams. Soon, she'd be waking up to Troy's teasing, and the two of them would marvel at a dream so vivid she could actually taste the rich, creamy chocolate with just a hint of cinnamon that was her other vice. A dream so vivid that she actually burned her throat on the drink. A dream so vivid—wait a minute. Did they drug your cocoa in a dream?

The Commander rose, turned away from the bunk, and pretended to stretch out the muscles in the back he presented to his friend.

"Dancer?" Seven asked hesitantly.

"She's asleep, Sev," Michael answered in a strained voice.

"Asleep?"

"Asleep. As in, the opposite of awake." With a shaky hand, he set the empty mug on the table and closed his eyes.

"You mean, *asleep* asleep," Seven pursued, "as opposed to . . ."

"That's exactly what I mean."

"She didn't know us. She thought she was dreaming."

"Perhaps she was. We'll ask her about it when she wakes up, shall we?"

"She's going to be all right?"

"Yes, Seven, she's going to be all right."

Seven let out a whoop. "Yes!"

"She's really going to be all right," Michael repeated. The tremulous smile he finally allowed his face to relax into was followed by a whoop of his own. Good thing the kid was a sound sleeper, he reflected whimsically. All this yelling and back-thumping he and Seven were indulging in would certainly have woken her up, otherwise.

Chapter 43

Voices in the background again, Michael's and her own. But it couldn't have been her own, because she wasn't talking. Auglaize remembered a tall redhead with her face, dressed in black and leaning over her . . . "What the hell?" she croaked.

"Do you know who you are?"

She cleared her throat irritably. "After twelve years, don't tell me *you* don't know who I am, Commander. What is all this nonsense?"

"Good to have you with us again, Dancer." Michael's tone was amused. Relieved? She reached up to remove the folded cloth impeding her vision, but her hands were firmly pushed away.

"Let me." The weight lifted, and Dancer tried to open her eyes, but they seemed to be glued shut. "For once in your life, you are going to follow Preble's instructions. If you had done so to begin with, it would have saved everyone a lot of trouble." As he talked, he sponged her eyes with something wet, mediciney, but very pleasant smelling, then patted them dry and slipped a pair of darkened lenses onto her nose. "There you go."

It took her a minute to focus. "What am I doing in your bed—in your shirt, in the name of Third Earth? How long have I been here?"

"Sleeping, it was more convenient for me, and a couple of days. In that order."

"A couple of . . . wait a minute." Shaking her head, Dancer pushed partway to a sitting position and squinted against the sunlight.

Michael moved from the edge of the bunk to his rocker, which had been pulled close beside. He wanted to touch her, she could tell, but wasn't quite sure whether he ought to. That in itself made her nervous. What had been going on around here? She reached

259

for his hand, knowing that he wouldn't tell her anything until he was ready to and wondering what he was waiting for.

"I can't feel my leg, Michael."

"Preble put in a nerve block. We thought it best under the circumstances that you not be distracted by pain. I can remove it if you like."

"Thanks, I'll wait on that." If Preble had thought it necessary to insert one of his tiny electronic pins, that leg must be in pretty rough shape. Dancer tried to remember what she could have done to herself, but drew a blank. Michael's influence? She stared at him with aching eyes over the protective glasses.

His reply was a smile. "What's the last thing you remember, child?"

His favorite opening gambit when he didn't want to give anything away. "The last thing? A crazy dream I had about Ma . . . never mind."

"By any chance did this 'Ma . . . never mind' offer you cinnamon cocoa?"

Dancer's raised eyebrow asked the question and his lighthearted shrug answered it. It hadn't been a dream. She had been awake, remembering nothing of her present life except a name that had once meant security. Michael must have been half out of his mind with worry.

"Actually, I was relieved. But I'll tell you the whole story later. What do you remember before that?"

"Before that—looking up into my own face." After thinking about it for a minute, she sighed in relief. "Antonia's, of course. I'm not going crazy. It was her voice I heard just now." She looked around, half expecting to see the girl making herself at home in Michael's quarters.

"Yes, I was talking to her a moment ago. She called from the Warlord to inquire about your condition. You'll have to get back to her when you feel up to it. She's been very concerned about you. We all have."

He was watching her closely—too closely, as if he expected her to shatter in front of his eyes. Dancer felt her forehead pucker. What had been going on? Antonia . . . the Warlord . . . flying the show. The Warlord again, Callicoon coming to her quarters—of course. "Davenger," she thought aloud.

"Davenger," the Commander confirmed, relaxing his guard slightly at her matter-of-fact tone.

"For a while there I thought I was a goner. I take it our message got through."

"Yes and no. I . . . heard you calling for me."

Dancer met his eyes steadily for a moment, then nodded her understanding. She no longer questioned Michael's talent, just accepted it as a fact of life. One for which, right now, she was very, very grateful. "I don't remember your coming aboard. What happened?"

His shrug was not a very satisfactory answer.

"You're not going to help me a bit, are you? All right, then. Calli came to my room, we made nice-nice, I heard . . . they were transmitting on my receiver frequency, did you know that? Or close enough. I heard them aboard the Warlord. They, on the other hand, appear to have been listening to your transmissions to me all afternoon. That's how they discovered I wasn't Tonia."

The Commander's voice sharpened. "Do they know? I mean, was it intentional, or . . ."

"Accidental." Good Lord, what a threat to Sixth's security that chance discovery could have been! She hadn't really been in a position to give it much thought before. "They stumbled onto it, but Davenger knows it was one of ours."

"I doubt that he's told anyone yet, and I'll make certain that he'll never be able to pass the word along," Michael stated positively. "Still, I'd best get our comm wizards on it."

"Good. Good. I get a headache just thinking about it. And don't tell me not to think!" she added automatically.

"I wouldn't dream of it." The Commander smiled.

"Hmm. Where was I? Oh, yes. I thought Calli'd set me up, but he tried to help me escape. We made it to the alert Gypsy—two more minutes, and we would have been out of there. Two lousy minutes! Then Davenger's flunkies kicked the crap out of Calli, left him for dead, and took me down to . . ." She broke off at the memory of that off-white room in the bowels of the Warlord. "Ah. Now, I understand."

Understood why she didn't remember something as exciting as a Sixth Service rescue. Understood why Michael had shown relief when she'd awakened before, even though she hadn't recognized him. Understood his treating her as if she were a fragile piece of porcelain now. Well, she wasn't a fragile piece of porcelain! "I blanked out again, didn't I?" she said in disgust. "God, what a coward I am!"

"Coward?" Michael echoed. "Hardly that, child. Listen." With a gentle smile, he instructed Jeremiah to replay for her information the unedited version of his dictated report, recording for inclusion her comments as they went along. A detailed summation would come later, when she was strong enough to handle the brusque interrogation that would accompany it.

"Callicoon?" she asked abruptly when Jeremiah signaled the end of the file.

Michael shook his head. "He was dying before the crash. Preble has done all he can, but holds out little hope."

"Before what crash?" was Dancer's automatic response. Then, the words "he was dying" sank in. In her mind she saw it all again, three savages brutally beating Calli into unconsciousness and beyond, herself powerless to stop them. "I want to see him," she whispered through teeth so tightly clenched it was that which brought the tears to her eyes, nothing else. She had known Calli couldn't survive. And she had learned a long time ago that simply wanting something badly enough did not automatically make it happen.

"Child—it would serve no purpose. Besides, he is aboard the Warlord now. There is talk of transporting him to AES Six, but the outcome remains doubtful."

As usual, the Commander was right. Seeing Calli, broken and battered, would serve no useful purpose. Still—"Antonia should be told what sort of man she was keeping for a pet."

"I took the liberty of informing her," Michael said levelly. "Her affection for him is as real as yours. As is her grief."

Dancer's voice hardened. "What of Davenger?"

"Alive. Our Antonia got in the last lick—or should I say kick?—with a very well-placed boot to the groin. But we are unfortunately constrained by law, now." His eyes turned to flint. "Though I cannot be in the same room as that Karranganthian hellkite without wanting to jerk his testicles out through his nostrils."

"If you ever decide to do it, can I watch?" she asked flippantly.

"Unfortunately, unless by some happy chance he gives us a reason otherwise, we are ordered to transport him and his surviving crew members—intact—back to trial before the Confederacy Worlds Court's War Crimes Tribunal."

"War Crimes Tribunal. Now, there's a mockery of the legal system if I ever heard one. Still, this is what we've been hoping for. If the Confederacy can keep him alive long enough to reach trial."

"Indeed. Ah, Dancer," he said slowly, leaning back in his chair and rubbing the bridge of his nose. "I truly feared I had lost you this time."

Dancer remembered blue eyes staring down into hers, remembered sensing safety there. It seemed that Michael had saved her life yet again. She looked at him for a second, then moved shyly toward him. The Commander met her halfway in a rib-cracking embrace, letting her feel exactly how frightened for her he had been. It was Dancer's turn to administer a reassuring caress and press a kiss on the bridge of *his* nose.

"I'm surprised at Antonia, though!" she exclaimed when Michael at last extricated himself from her embrace. "Hauling off and giving Davenger a good swift kick. The kid's got guts."

"Yes," Michael said dryly, "uncanny how much alike the two of you are, isn't it?"

Good food, a comfortable bed—even for prisoners. These Auryx had it soft! And though Davenger could sense that they would just as soon kill him as look at him, so far no one but the medical personnel had laid a hand on him. Painkillers—they'd even given him painkillers! It was a crying shame what the advent of peace had done to a formerly worthy foe. No wonder any self-respecting free society would want to rid itself of the Milquetoast yoke of Confederacy law!

Still, even with their lax peacetime vigilance, they had destroyed his plans of a quiet retirement in the pine-covered hills of Karran. My apologies, Kalelle, he thought whimsically. I shan't be home from work in time for dinner tonight.

He would, however, get home. It was only chance that had delivered him unto the Auryx on the last stop—the last stop!—of a hitherto successful mission. Chance, and that damned redhead. Correction, those double-damned redheads! Who ever would have thought that there could be two such spawn of Satan? He should have dumped the younger one down the garbage chute when he had the opportunity. And the older one, the now-Auryx! She had more lives than a sorceress's cat! He'd overheard the doctor telling someone not five minutes ago that she had come out of whatever vegetative state her terror of him had sent her into. Well, next time, no games. He'd kill the bitch outright. A shame, but gad! After they heard his side of the story, even the vaunted Confederacy Worlds Court would rule it justifiable homicide!

Of course, he had no intention of letting himself be taken to trial. Soft and lax these Auryx had truly grown; he would slip away from them. Just as soon as he could walk, he'd be out of here. Or, failing that—there was no way the Confederacy troops could hold him if he didn't want to be held. After all, he had bloodlessly—all right, almost bloodlessly—commandeered one of their fully manned Starlifters, and Fourth Service's famous Team to boot, right under their noses!

I'll lie in your arms soon, Kalelle, he vowed. First, though, he would have his revenge on the redhead.

Chapter 44

Preble had poked and prodded to his heart's content, removing both nerve blocks and nutrient and medication patches. Sandusky the psych had come and gone, apologizing for pronouncing her dead before giving her a chance to live and pleading affection-bred fear as the reason for his mistake. Seven had stopped by long enough to reassure himself that, indeed, she was herself, then had carried the welcome news of her recovery to the rest of the installation. Antonia had checked in briefly, promising a long chat when things were back to normal again aboard the Warlord and she wasn't so busy. Michael had fed Dancer, bathed her, reclothed her in her favorite red jumpsuit, and gotten her settled into her own bed before grudgingly letting his duties reclaim him. Now she was finally alone except for the ever-vigilant Jeremiah and, though somewhat weak, she was restless.

She did try to lie down for a while, per Michael's orders, but though her body relaxed, Dancer couldn't seem to turn off her brain. Davenger had brought back such feelings of horror, fear, and loathing—coupled with violent, irreplaceable loss—that her mind was still reeling under the impact. A call to Preble would bring instantaneous relief in the guise of a candy-coated chemical introduced into her still-sensitive system, but the numbing effects of sleep were notoriously limited. The problem would still be there when she awoke. Less immediate, perhaps, but still there. The psychs, with their compelling eyes and hypnotic voices, offered a solution of sorts, too; but this time, she had to work it through for herself.

Projected against the insides of her closed eyelids were the faces of friends and a lover long dead, and a would-be lover on the brink of death. It was Calli's image she reached out for, his ready smile and sharp, inquiring eyes.

Paulding Callicoon, the counterfeit traitor who had, in the end, saved her life. Another body to bury; another loss to mourn. How much like Troy had he really been, and how much had been the projection of wistful thinking based on a roughly similar physique and a quality of personality so indefinable as to be totally disregarded in any rational analyses?

Suddenly, Dancer wanted to see them again so badly that the pain was sharper, more real than the one in her leg. She grabbed Preble's drops to clear her vision as she hobbled over to Jeremiah's main station to do something she had seldom done before: flip through those pages of the personal file that she had labeled "Dancer Flight."

All Sixth Service members had these necessary encroachments on Jeremiah's precious memory space, used to store images of mementos they couldn't actually carry with them. Accessible only to the individuals initiating them—and to the Commander, of course—the personal files were requisite links to the pasts that each otherwise had to deny.

Dancer's held mainly people; also the aircraft photos that decorated her quarters, and some of the more attractive places she had been, but mostly people, gleaned from official photos and other sources—including blatant theft from her brother Alex's computer while she and Michael had been traveling incognito with him. Perhaps not exactly theft; as a gift to her, Michael had copied those images with which she had entrusted her brother for safekeeping when she had been moved to a forward base. Her family, her friends—many still living, though all were dead to her. There was a reason she didn't look at them often.

She did not look at them now, but thumbed through to the middle of the file, the part she had deliberately closed off and marked "No Trespassing" to herself. A flick of the wrist, and there it was: the group photo of Dancer Flight, informally posed to become part of the decor of the Club. Funny how alien this clean-cut, severely uniformed crew looked now to eyes used to the casual, dark-haired, blue-eyed, slightly built Auryx. Twenty-three smiling faces and their slender, merry-eyed flight leader, with just a minute tightness across the cheekbones suggesting the pressure of her responsibilities. Twenty-three smiling faces, of whom two had survived the slaughter of their Lioth base—only to die in desperate, forgotten battles defending the godforsaken skies of outposts no one in their right minds would have wanted to invade.

No debates as to the futility of war, please; the party was getting maudlin enough. A drum of her fingers on the keyboard replaced the group photo with the head and shoulders of Morgan Troy, whose features, even in the stiff official photograph, still settled into a quizzical half-smile. Part of that was the result of an old scar across his right cheek, invisible except where it pulled up the corner of his mouth. Mostly, though, his habitual expression mirrored the way he had looked at his world. A born leader, except that he lacked the ruthlessness necessary to the commander of a fighting force. No, nature had fashioned Troy as a lover, not a fighter, Dancer thought with a half-smile of her own, remembering the wide, all-seeing green eyes heavy-lidded with passion, the neat sandy hair tousled and the smiling lips swollen after a night spent with only enough sleep to enable them to turn to each other yet again. It was a hell of a way to prepare for a mission, but they always managed to arrive at the morning's briefing with adrenaline flowing and all senses alert. Anybody else she would have grounded.

"This image seems to interest you, Dancer. Would you like me to enhance?"

Jeremiah's voice shattered her reverie, bringing her back to O'Brian's Stake with a jarring thud. She shook her head, forgetting that the machine couldn't see her, then supplemented the gesture with an emphatic "No!" Dancer preferred her memories two-dimensional. Computer-enhanced holographs always seemed to her like having a head in a box. An empty head, without the spark of life that was Troy.

Ah, well, better to remember a head in a box than a corpse in her arms. Or a slumbering god awakening under her touch.

Dancer chuckled suddenly. Michael was right: it was time she found herself a lover. She was missing too much, trying to live up to the example of her Commander.

Equilibrium restored, she had Jeremiah display the rest of the file at a leisurely rate. They were all there: her parents, Uncle Ash as much at home in his Fourth Service uniform as Mother in her apron or Dad in his overalls, her prim and pretty sisters, brothers Alex, Adam, and Alan, orphaned cousin Amadeus, raised with them and like a brother, three screens of family reunion with all the rest of the cousins, twelve-year-old Antonia—looking very much like twelve-year-old Auglaize—proudly showing off a swimming trophy to a hometown newspaper photographer. Antonia at fifteen, again in the news for being at the top of her class. Antonia as a baby, at one, at two, at three, yearly intervals up to the mate to the framed photo of Tonia, Troy, and Dancer at the fair. And she had asked if Dancer had ever thought of her. She should see this rogue's gallery sometime. Perhaps Dancer would let her, before the Warlord left orbit.

All there, her friends, Fourth Service, Auryx, well-met-along-the-way. Madison, whose untimely death had so conveniently provided a body to occupy Auglaize's grave in the little churchyard a mile and a half from her family's farm. Highland, who had survived years of combat to return to flight testing. Van Wert, rebuilder of broken bodies. Even Michael, in the cerulean-blue robes and clipped beard of an Auryx ambassador.

All there. All—save one. And no record of that one existed. Or did it? With little hope of success, Dancer tried the obvious, invoking her enhanced status as Michael's second when Jeremiah protested her security clearance. She herself scanned directories of records of personnel, actions, and casualties, closed personal files, active personal files, personnel on other stations, personnel with other organizations. No listing for Darke, Makellen, or any variation thereof. Not even a decoy file. That would have been too easy.

"Okay, Jeremiah, that'll be all for now." She sighed, shutting off his voice-recognition function. She wasn't finished, not by a damned sight, but she dared take no chances that Jeremiah's Michael-programmed intelligence would figure out what she was about to attempt. The Commander would not be forgiving even of his second if he caught her breaking into the Star files.

Dancer was one of the privileged few who even knew about these most secret of Sixth Service records, the who-had-been-who listings of real names, personal histories, and details of recruitment. Information to which she had never wanted to be privy—horror stories like her own of massacre and mutilation. Information to which no one but the Commander and the Council had access, and they, only with difficulty; there would have been no reason to purge files to keep them from imaginative but unauthorized prying. If Makellen Darke didn't show up in the Star files, then, despite Michael's hinted assurances, he truly had never existed.

It was an obsession, this longing to see his face again; it was a challenge, matching wits with the Sixth Service's best. Besides, Dancer had nothing better to do.

One deep breath, steady, think. She would only get one chance. Another deep breath. No hesitation, now. Remember the positions of Michael's fingers as he typed in the access codes last time you had reason to consult the Star files, and hope the codes weren't periodically changed. Michael's fingers—the thumbprint lock. Plastic spray-on bandage from the first-aid box, a bit of sponge, a dirty glass from the kitchen, and a little luck—the method had worked before. It worked again, but she still had a voice lock to circumvent. Without even thinking, she hit the button marked with the Auryx character for communications. "Michael," she said briefly. Then, "Three o'clock and all's well," with her hand hovering over the voice-recognition switch.

A chuckle. "Confirmed," whispered his voice in her ear—and Jeremiah's security system.

The screen cleared, then a coded directory appeared. Hardly daring to believe she'd gotten this far, she hummed the first half-dozen bars of the Auryx ballad only she and Michael knew to be his favorite. Immediately, the random characters marched into line as easily decipherable listings. Though her eyes faltered over "DeWellesthar, Auglaize," and she was tempted, there were still things she didn't want to know.

Then she spotted it, the name just above hers. Dancer's trembling fingers picked out "Darke, Makellen, D*D." D-Star-D. Dead by Decree, declared killed in action to the Real World so that he could take on a new identity in the shadow service of Sixth. Darke, the startlingly lifelike blue eyes staring into her own in that contemplative gaze she found so compelling and yet had so seldom seen. It was his smiles she remembered, and that expression of quiet contentment which they punctuated.

And his laugh. "Ah, what I would give to hear that laugh again!"

Instantly, the serious image dissolved into one of uncontrollable mirth, the sound of his voice filling this sixth-floor suite just outside the capital city of O'Brian's Stake. Dancer started, then realized that it was only Jeremiah, dredging through his memory in answer to her request. The voice recognition was still in the on position.

She chuckled as Mak tried to compose his features, running a nervous hand through longish raven hair in a habitual gesture that had always left her craving the feel of the shining, silken strands between her own fingers. Her palm was on the screen before she remembered that this was a three-dimensional projection, not four. Dancer had wanted to see him again. She had to content herself with that.

"Enough, Seven!" the laugh-roughened voice commanded. "This record-updating is supposed to be serious business."

Words in the background that Dancer couldn't make out caused his eyes to crinkle and his shoulders to shake again, but he regained control quickly. "I have better things to do with my time than spending all day here talking to a computer."

Another background murmur, and another grin. "You've got that right. *My* redhead, and no one forget it."

Lord, he was talking about her. Of course. The last update would be first in the records. This one must have been done just before he . . .

"I'm ready now, and I'd appreciate it if you'd cut out all that clowning before."

Reassurances were duly given by a technician who had no intention of complying with the request, and the dark head lifted, eyes level, facial muscles set in a deadly serious mask.

"I am Darke, of the Sixth Service," he stated, and that was all she cared to hear.

"Freeze," she barked, and the living, breathing man was once more a captive instant of history. The professional in her demanded that she find out the rest of what she wanted to know, that each second she delayed multiplied the chances of discovery, yet Dancer couldn't help lingering to study the face she had thought to have known so well.

Strange, she didn't recall that stubborn set of the chin, and there certainly was none of the remembered softness evident in these lips, parted slightly in speech. The hair still touched the vivid blue collar, but the endearing look of boyishness was gone. And behind the eyes the color of that uniform, a blank wall.

Still, this face was even handsomer than the one she had carried in the back of her mind for so long, perhaps for the same reason Troy and her Fourth Service friends now seemed so alien: her perceptions had altered drastically in the years since she had known them. Too, here was a side of Makellen she had never seen—Darke of the Sixth Service, emanating confidence and authority. The voice was different than she remembered, somewhat lower in pitch, rougher, but still melodic and soothing to the ear.

Dancer drew closer to the two-dimensional face, her own reflection staring back at her from the blankness behind those terrifying eyes.

"My God, Dancer, what have you done?" exploded in her ear as Michael's hand closed over her arm, jerking her to her feet to face him.

Though she involuntarily flinched, Dancer still managed to meet his eyes. There was anger there, a scathing fury that she had seen many times and hoped never to have turned on her. There was something else there, too, something that she'd never thought to expect from the Commander—fear.

"What happened to him, Michael?" she asked calmly.

In the space of a breath the full force of that fury swept over her; for a held breath she knew he wanted to kill her. Because he loved her. Then, something seemed to snap inside him, and he thrust her back into the chair.

"Shall I show you what happened to your precious Kellen Darke, Dancer? Then look, damn you! Look!" He forced her head around, and when she recoiled from what she saw, forced it around again. "Take a good, long look, DeWellesthar. Look at the face. Look at it!"

But there was no face. Just a three-dimensional pool of blood, and two blue eyes staring out of it.

"Enough. Enough." Michael banged the control panel with his fist, then turned and stalked out.

Dancer limped into the bathroom and threw up.

He had been so hard on her. Too hard. Still, what she had done had been unforgivable.

No, not unforgivable. Dangerous. He could still lose her, best not to forget that. Best never to forget that. Hadn't he lost everyone else he'd ever loved?

He'd go back to her, apologize, of course. And, of course, she'd forgive him. After all, she had been in the wrong.

Damn Darke! Michael should never have allowed Dancer to remember him. Even unknowingly, she'd carried him in her heart all these years.

Well. He would go back and apologize. Later, when he wasn't so angry, so shaken. So . . . jealous.

Chapter 45

The nightmare came back as soon as Dancer dropped off to sleep. Now that she knew it to be memory, it no longer had the power to affect her—or shouldn't have had. Until it transmuted itself into something even more horrifying than she had ever before imagined.

It began, as usual, with the familiar patterns of black and red, eventually resolving themselves into blood and bootheels, the hem of a cape tickling her face. Then, the voice—to whom it belonged she had never been able to discover—should have made its incredulous query, and it should have ended. Dancer waited resignedly for this to happen, but it didn't. Instead, her eyes traveled up the boots, up the black-clad legs and body to the face—her face, coldly impersonal as it had to be on these occasions, and crowned by a braided coronet of hair a darker red than that spattered on her uniform. I am attractive in black, she thought; funny that she had never before noticed how very much it suited her coloring.

With startling sharpness, her perspective shifted, and Dancer was looking down at the body whose oozing life made the floor slippery under foot; her compressed lips parted to utter the words, "Is he still alive?" It was not Auglaize DeWellesthar lying there, as she feared, but a man—a slender, nicely proportioned, once-handsome Auryx who now had no face under the gore- and grime-caked black hair, just a blob of reddish pulp and bone splinters between two staring blue eyes. She backed away, shrieking, but those eyes followed her, patient yet pleading, full of an anguish it seared her soul to see.

She turned to run but fingers caught in her cape, dragging her back, dragging her down onto the floor, fingers reaching, grasping, holding with a strength too great for a dead man. Dancer fought, screaming until her throat closed off, screaming soundlessly around her own knuckles jammed against her teeth.

"Dear God, Kellen, I didn't know. I didn't know! Forgive me, please forgive me, I didn't know," she sobbed over and over. Finally, exhausted, she gave up the struggle; the arms that held her down were too strong, and it didn't matter anyhow. "Forgive me, Michael," she whimpered into cupped palms dripping with her own tears.

"Hush, child, hush. It's all right now. It's all right." The voice was pitched to be soothing, the hands on her back were meant to be caressing, and it was only a dream.

"Michael?"

"I'm here, child. Open your eyes and look at me."

"Don't worry, it was only a dream," she murmured.

"I know. It's all over. Here, look at me. All right now?"

A nod. "I think so. It was so horrible, Michael. He was . . . oh, God."

"Wipe your face and tell me about it."

Sniffling, Dancer closed her eyes and shook her head. "I can't. I just . . . can't."

Reality was only now beginning to penetrate. It was Michael who had held her, Michael's arms against which she had struggled. Relief that he was no longer angry made her tremble. "I hit you, didn't I?"

"I'll have a few bruises in the morning, yes. And my hearing will never be the same. I wonder that someone isn't up here investigating."

"They probably just think we're doing something kinky."

He didn't crack a smile. "Child, those were the screams of a lost soul in torment. If you ever frighten me like that again . . ." His voice broke and he swallowed the rest of the sentence.

Wonderingly, Dancer looked up into his face and glimpsed, briefly, the other Auryx face that she had loved. Her fingers traced the curve of his cheekbone, the planes of his jaw, smoothed the bridge of his nose and the lines around his eyes.

He took her hand, kissed the palm, and cradled it against his cheek as understanding dawned. "So that's it. God forgive me, I should not have shown you that picture."

"I'll never forget it, Mike. Never."

"I think perhaps you will, if you'll let me help you. Hush, I know, you don't want to forget, hmm? Would that *I* could!"

"You were there?"

He nodded, easing himself back onto a pillow propped against the headboard and crossing his legs in front of him. "I was there."

"He was dear to you, too, wasn't he?"

Michael's eyes stared from under his curved lashes for perhaps ten heartbeats before he shook himself free of his thoughts. "That's not as I would have phrased it, but yes. We were close."

"What happened?"

"It was an iron bar," he stated flatly with no preamble. "Darke walked right into it. Diagonally, between the eyes." His finger sketched a line from just below his right cheekbone to above his left eyebrow. "Then, he was hit again, once, maybe twice more. Seven was close enough to catch him as he fell, but not close enough to save him. Kellen never knew what hit him; he felt nothing except perhaps a moment's surprise."

"Did you . . . ?" The words she needed to ask, if he had been the one to end Makellen's life, stuck in her throat.

"I did what I was required to do."

"I have always been afraid that it was . . . that somehow *I* was responsible for what happened to him."

"No, child. Kellen was just in the wrong place at the wrong time. If Seven had been first through that door, it would have been he instead of his dearest friend. Sometimes, I think he would have preferred it that way."

Dancer shook her head in an attempt to assimilate all she had heard. "I can't believe that after all these years, it should hurt so much. Why did you keep this from me?"

"Because, after all these years, it still hurts so much," he answered simply. "Dancer, do you think it has been easy for me, this reopening of old wounds that were still, even now, only half healed? Looking at Antonia, and seeing only the child with whom the child that I was was so much in love? The woman, with whom the man in me is still . . ." His fists clenched and his eyes turned toward the night-black sky outside the window.

How had she not guessed before? "Then it was you who tried so hard to separate us."

"God, no, Dancer! That would have made it so much simpler; with him gone, I could have just stepped in. No. The same elusive 'They' who had forbidden him you also forbade me, and for the same reason. I was not born Commander."

"He would have been . . . ?"

Michael nodded again. "A position Darke wanted no more than I. I watched you heal, did you know that? So many times I sat watching you sleep, wanting to make myself known to you, to hold you, understanding that if I so much as put a finger to your hair, They would have had you out of my reach permanently almost before I could draw my hand back. I hated you for it, at the same time wanting you so much." He shrugged.

"Finally, I came to terms with it. They had been right to keep us apart; I had to establish myself, with no distractions. I needed to develop that single-minded devotion to duty that has enabled me to do whatever I must all these years. For the good of the Service."

"Ah, yes, the altar on which we are required to sacrifice our all," Dancer stated sarcastically.

"The good of the Service," he repeated, as if he hadn't heard her. Perhaps he hadn't. "I was so cruel to you when you most needed a friend. When I most needed you. You understand now? And all those times I had to send you to what I feared was your certain death, when what I really wanted to do was keep you by my side where I could protect you."

"All these years, I have stayed by your side to protect *you*."

He allowed himself a tiny, ironic smile. "You did well, Dancer. Times without number you saved my sanity. Through the blood and the killing, the horrors that made me question my own right to live, you were there. Occasionally, your friendship was all that kept me from . . . You know, you're probably the only person in the known worlds who isn't in awe of me. Even so, it hasn't been easy, being so close to you and not being able to . . . touch you."

"That I know well."

"Try not to hate me too much, child."

Dancer felt him looking down at her and tilted her head back so that she could see his face. "Hate you? Don't be ridiculous." Her dear, dear Michael, with that wise, sad smile. Even now, he didn't want to hear that she loved him, that she had always loved him, that her adored Makellen had long since been replaced in her dreams—and in her heart—by this devil in black. She smiled at the thought, acutely aware of the warm hip pressed against her own and the strength of the thighs hiding under the light fabric of his black robe. She saw it all clearly now. It hadn't been Kellen she had waited for all these years, it was the Commander. "Is this where you tell me for the seventy-five thousand three hundred and fifty-sixth time that 'we have to find me a lover'?"

Michael chuckled. Mak, Dancer couldn't help thinking, would have laughed, a great, warm, sexy, infectious sound that had bubbled out of him as naturally as water bubbled from a spring. Had she ever heard Michael laugh?

"I'm forgiven, then?" he asked.

"For doing what you were forced to do? When have I ever presumed to judge you?"

"More than once, I fear." His hand cupped her cheek, pressed her head into his shoulder; then, abruptly, he rose. "What I have told you tonight, I should have kept to myself. Even now, it can be no different with us."

"I am losing you, too, then?"

"No, child. Not while I live."

"Yet it can be no different with us."

"I am what I have become. Sleep now, Dancer." His voice became brusque, back to normal. "I need you back on your feet as soon as possible."

She said nothing as he walked toward the door.

His hand on the knob, he paused. "Dancer . . ." he began, his voice oddly hesitant. "I wasn't going to ask, but I have to. How . . . what do you feel for me?"

After all these years of reading her thoughts, he shouldn't have needed to ask. But then, Michael never had put much trust in his own emotions. As he waited in silent misery, she pondered which to answer: her friend or her Commander. In the end it was the same, either way. "I wish the war were over," she finally said, hoping he would understand.

"So do I," he replied cryptically. "So do I."

He had to get out of the room, away from her, *now*. Now, or he'd do something they would both regret.

"Michael!" she cried reflexively as he crossed the threshold and started to pull the door closed behind him.

He stopped dead in his tracks, her voice tearing at his heart like a thousand barbed hooks tearing at his flesh. "Child?" he said gently, his back to her, his eyes on the lights of the living room, and safety.

"I'm afraid to be alone. I'm afraid that . . . as soon as I close my eyes, it'll come back."

Michael's spine stiffened at the anguish in her voice. She was saying something else, something about fearing the dark. He was glad of the dark, glad that it masked from her his struggle to regain the iron self-control he had cultivated over the past twelve years. The self-control that had cost him so much of himself.

Please don't go, Michael. She was begging him, not with words, but with her heart. He never had been able to resist that appeal.

With a deep, almost unconscious sigh—like a man bowing to the inevitable—he turned on his heel, three strides taking him back to her side. "Tell me all about it, child," he said softly, settling his aching back once again into the pillow she'd propped against the headboard. "Perhaps we shall be able to banish it together."

Haltingly at first, she told him everything. Everything. He managed to listen to the recitation, harden his feelings against her as she spoke of her love for Darke. Not enough, though, to keep the sharp-edged guilt from ripping through him as she groped for words to describe her nightmare of the destroyed face that anger and jealousy had driven him to force her to see. He used the fire of this guilt to quench the other fire deep inside him, the one he must continue to deny. In its place came the ice-cool caring calm, tender friendship peering out through the mask of Commander that he had forced himself to wear these many years.

The calm that allowed him to keep his heartbeat slow and steady when it wanted to race; the control that enabled him to listen to her admissions of feelings for him that caused him, simultaneously, overwhelming joy and unfathomable despair, without allowing her an inkling of the turmoil within him.

The calm that, finally, imparted itself to her, allowing her to snuggle down into the refuge of his arms, at peace.

He could have left her to sleep then. He should have, he knew it, but . . . what was the purpose of it all? "For the good of the Service" just wasn't good enough anymore. Not when she had come so close to dying. Why couldn't he, just for one night, just for one hour of one night, let himself be a man, not Commander— just long enough to tell her what she meant to him?

For twelve years, he had been forced to deny his love for her; for twelve long years, his mind had pounded his body into submission. Unbidden, the memory of Madison in his arms that last time rushed over him like a geyser, scalding, suffocating. Madison— Merylys, his Merylys—dead by his hand. If Dancer hadn't been there for him to go back to . . .

Not again, he'd told himself. He would not love again. He would not lose again. Not Auglaize. Not his bright, beautiful, shimmering Auglaize.

He pulled back far enough to look down into her face. Her eyes sparkled in the silvery light of the moon through the window; eyes mildly curious, completely unafraid, and with an underlying depth of affection that took his breath away. He was used to the adoration of his people. This kind of love was something else again.

Without thinking, he dropped his mouth to hers. She broke away from that first exploratory kiss with a gasp and a whispered "Dear God, Michael!" that was both a prayer and a plea. As she came back for more, he met her halfway.

His mind still held out, detached, amused even. Play if you will, child; I won't let it go any farther.

The mind continued to hold out—until the tip of her tongue touched his lower lip, tickling, teasing, and he parted his teeth to respond in kind. Then his body took over. At long last, he was going to make love to her as he had dreamed of doing since the first time she had smiled at him.

She was perfectly content to let him. Dancer. Beautiful courtesan. His beautiful courtesan.

They played, chuckling together at silly little jokes; they danced to the varied rhythms of the senses, sometimes he leading, sometimes she; they sparred, they teased, they kissed and touched and finally clung together with the increasing urgency of their mutual need. Michael quickly learned to divert the self-control that had denied her to him for years into prolonging his enjoyment of her for lifetimes. Their enjoyment of each other. In between passed long, contented moments with her breathing synchronous with his breathing, her heartbeat echoing his heartbeat until it was hard to tell where one left off and the other began.

They were good together, he found himself thinking with surprised satisfaction. Then—so, this is what those words meant, "good together," this intricate game of give-and-take, this physical complementing of bodies, this intense delight in taking pleasure by giving it. This incredible, emotional sharing, meeting a need he had never recognized in himself. He was filled with love, and a feeling of power—power greater than he had ever experienced from being merely the Commander of a Service with responsibility for the preservation of an entire race. Then, thought was once again suspended in the novel, overpowering oblivion of emotion and senses.

Somewhere toward morning, Michael finally fell asleep memorizing the feel of her body curled trustingly against him. It had been a glorious night, but it was over.

Because he was still the Commander, and the commanded. Because They could still send her so far out of his reach that he'd never be able to touch her again.

It was full daylight outside the window when Dancer awoke, stiff and sore in places she'd forgotten could get that way. Incongruously, her leg itched. It took a minute for her to remember where she was, and another full minute for the realization to penetrate that the warmth in her bed was not entirely her own. There was definitely a pair of male arms around her, a cozy, firm, living pillow cradling her head. But who? Whose bed was she in, and where? she wondered drowsily. What she'd been doing, her body had already reminded her.

Callicoon? Her mind catalogued length and breadth and texture. No. Michael. She knew by the scent of the skin under her cheek, the way they fit together, the sense of rightness. With a tender smile, she eased back slightly and, supporting herself on an elbow, watched Michael sleep.

Short of the occasional illness or injury when he had no choice in the matter, Michael rarely let anyone see him asleep. He was always first up and last down, even when someone else had the watch, even when exhaustion showed in every line of his body and fatigue was etched so deeply into his face that he looked like walking death. Many times Dancer had awakened with his eyes on her, but the reverse was a rare treat.

A ray of sunlight cut through the cloud cover outside to chase the shadows from his face. His eyelids tightened and, with a small sound deep in his throat, he turned toward her out of the brightness.

Dancer treasured the moment, recalling the narrow bunks they had shared on outward-bound freighters, traveling as man and wife—she the bodyguard and he the target ripe for assassination. Her hair had been black then more often than its natural but all-too-recognizable red. Shining, silken ebony waves, fanning out over the pillow and both of them. Michael's hand caressingly brushing it out of their faces, blue eyes shining as he settled them more comfortably in accommodations barely adequate for one. The innocent pleasure they had taken in each other's proximity then, and occasionally since.

She wanted to touch that deceptively youthful face, push the heavy black hair back from the smooth forehead, trace those long eyelashes with a fingertip. The lightest touch, though, the slightest sound, and he would awaken and leave. For this instant, at least, he was hers.

He stirred; she felt the light breath of his sigh as tension returned to his face and the blue eyes opened to stare quizzically into hers.

"Good morning, my Dark Angel." Dancer whispered the greeting from those former occasions and, without thinking, he replied in kind.

"Good morning, my wife." A quick furrow appeared between his eyebrows as his mind reluctantly returned to the here and now. "Would that you truly were my wife."

"Perhaps in a manner of speaking I am, hmm?"

"I thought I had been dreaming."

"Not this time, love."

A smile of pure joy washed over his face then, colored by a hot blush as he recalled how they had spent the better part of the night. He turned away from her in embarrassment.

"It's truly for me, isn't it?" he asked, his voice muffled by the pillow. "What I see in your eyes, feel in your body, is for *me*. Not for the surrogate of a beloved ghost, not for the godlike Commander, but for Michael the man."

"Why are you so surprised? You know that's the way I've always seen you. I love you, Michael-the-man," Dancer said, just to see that smile again. He didn't disappoint her. Of their own volition, her fingertips moved over his face, memorizing features already indelibly imprinted on her mind.

He imprisoned her hand in one of his and pressed a kiss into the palm, then leaned over to recapture her lips with his. She melted into him.

"Michael," she whispered into his mouth, fighting back the tears welling up behind her eyes and threatening to spill over.

"I know, child. I know." His smile was tender as he first sensibly wiped her cheeks with the edge of the sheet, then traced a tear-track from the corner of her eye with the tip of his tongue. When finally his mouth found hers again, Dancer wasn't about to let it go . . .

And the bedroom door crashed open, accompanied by Seven's anxious voice. "Michael, are you in here?"

Chapter 46

The joy froze in the Commander's face as he slowly pulled away from Dancer; the eyes he turned on his friend were as cold as the vacuum and as hard as diamond sheathed in steel.

"Sorry, Michael," Seven stammered. "We couldn't reach you; Davenger—"

Michael cut him off with a look. "Not even you," he said quietly.

Seven paled, nodded, and backed out, closing the door carefully behind him.

"I'm so sorry," Dancer murmured.

"Hush, child," he interrupted, once again the affectionate lover. "It's my fault. I thought that just once, just for a few hours, they could get along without me. The first time you fell asleep in my arms last night, I left word with Jeremiah that I wasn't to be disturbed for anything short of a full-scale invasion."

"You did that?"

"Unfortunately, I put a time limit on the injunction. Still, I slept better than I have in a long, long time."

"Neither of us got all that much sleep," Dancer corrected with a smile that mirrored his own.

"I require but little. Although I wouldn't have minded an hour or so more."

"But the real world awaits, hmm?"

"The real world," he repeated, his gaze intensifying as he searched her face. "No matter what happens, remember this: *you* are the real world to me, Auglaise DeWellesthar. I will always love you."

"And I you, my Dark Angel." His skin slid soft under her fingers as he eased himself out of bed, out of reach, into his clothes.

Dancer watched, still warm and fuzzy-brained as her newfound lover transformed himself back into the Commander. He sat on the edge of the bed to pull on the calf-hugging boots he still preferred to all other footwear, smiling when she wrapped her arms around his waist and pressed her face into his hip.

"You rest awhile longer," was his gentle command before his eyes caught hers again and held them for all too brief a moment. "Always, Dancer. Remember." His lips bridged the space between her eyebrows, then he was gone.

Her orders for the day, Dancer discovered when next she awoke, were simply to rest and do nothing. That wasn't hard; physical and emotional strains were catching up with her, and all she wanted to do was sleep. Preble came in to ascertain that yes, indeed, her thigh was healing nicely, and yes, indeed, her eyes were still sensitive to the light. His advice was to stay off her feet for a few more days, and avoid the sun.

Someone brought meals in at the appropriate times; she was too sleepy to know who it was, or to care. The only thing she did realize was that Michael didn't come in to check on her. Nor did she hear his voice in her ear receiver. He must have gotten reports from the meds and not wanted to disturb her. And there was all that work he had been neglecting; he'd have a mountain of catching up to do.

The second day, Dancer was ready to tackle her own backlog of paperwork. However, the Command computer had orders from a higher authority not to cooperate if she tried to use him for anything but games, music, or company. "The Commander says you have been exercising my information retrieval systems altogether too much lately," Jeremiah told her.

So she wandered around the kitchen for a while, then tried to read the new science-fiction novel that Eire, knowing her passion for books, had thoughtfully provided. A week ago, Dancer had been griping that she never had enough time to read for pleasure—today it was a chore, and she gave up after the third chapter. The suite which she had not long ago considered spacious now seemed no better than a six-by-eight-pace cell. And when she opened the door to leave, she found an apologetic Logan—his left arm in a sling—standing guard outside it.

Granted, Dancer agreed that too much exercise might damage her infection-weakened leg and, rapidly as it was healing, it still hurt like hell to put her full weight on it.

She also had to admit that until the psychs were assured that her mind was stable and not likely to turn itself off again in a critical situation, Michael was justified in forbidding her to resume her high-pressure duties, which would inevitably bring her into contact with their Karranganthian prisoners. She would have made the same decision under the circumstances. As she saw it, there were two things she needed to do before she could certify herself emotionally fit: confront Davenger, and spend some time alone in a certain small white room aboard the Warlord.

So, all right, her "house arrest" was warranted! Dancer would have thought, though, as chronically shorthanded as they always were—even more so now, with a contingent on loan to get things straightened out aboard the Warlord—there would have been some area into which she could be temporarily reassigned. Even Antonia was busy, too busy to talk. Dancer voiced her complaint to Jeremiah, who was as sympathetic as a machine could be.

"The Commander's instructions were explicit, Dancer. However, he did leave a gift for me to pass along to you if you became too bored. Are you bored, Dancer?"

A gift? She hadn't been totally out of Michael's mind, then. "I certainly am, Jeremiah."

"I'm to tell you first that it is in your personal file, so you can find it on your own whenever you like. But you are not to share it with anyone else, is that understood?"

What could Michael have inserted into her electronic scrapbook that would constitute such a breach of security? Apprehensive now as well as curious, Dancer slid into the chair and agreed to Jeremiah's terms.

Even not knowing what to expect, she was totally unprepared for what she then saw—or heard. Makellen Darke was smiling at her from Jeremiah's monitor, and his laughter warmed the room around her. Her own voice—actually hers this time, not Tonia's—demanded to know what the joke was; then the thrum of an Auryx harp accompanied the Standard translation of a bawdy song he had obviously just sung to her in his own tongue. There was a dreamlike familiarity about the scene which haunted her until, in a rush, she realized that she was viewing one of the monitoring tapes from her time in the Van Wert. A quick check showed about a dozen of these vignettes, carefully edited to focus on her companion instead of, as they originally had, on her.

Michael had given her back Makellen Darke, and a missing chunk of her own life. She couldn't reach him to thank him, but Jeremiah promised to pass the word along.

The Commander sighed as the unobtrusive blue light blinking on the side of his terminal console caught his attention. Someone else wanting to talk to him. Another problem, no doubt; no one ever bothered him with solutions. What now? Seven with more insurrections aboard the Warlord? Clermont, going head to head with the O'Brian police division about who had jurisdiction over the Karranganthian sympathizers on-planet? Liaison difficulties between the Sixth Service troubleshooters he'd sent to the other five planets on the revised Team schedule and the standard-forces Confederacy peacekeepers there?

He briefly debated ignoring the light and returning to the three crises he was already juggling, but didn't. The Commander never ignored a communication . . . unless, a small part of his mind nagged, it came from a certain redhead currently residing in his quarters. He'd been guiltily dodging contact with her since Seven had interrupted them in bed, when, two days ago? Had it really been that long?

"Yes, Jeremiah," he finally acknowledged.

"Commander, Antonia DeWellesthar wishes to speak with you from the Warlord."

Antonia? Now what? His finger reflexively tapped a switch. "Yes, Antonia," he said.

"Commander, I know you're busy, and I really hate to bother you, but . . ."

"What is it, child?"

"I've just made a decision that's probably going to ruin my life, that's all. Would you . . . I mean, the other day when we talked, you said you'd do whatever you could to back me if I made the right choice, and I'm on my way to talk to the interim Team commander now, and . . ."

The interim Team commander, memory supplied, was a man by the name of Terrence Woods, who had flown the Lead Solo slot in the last show. Incidentally, Dancer had informed him, a former conquest of Tonia's who only carried a small grudge at the way the girl had treated him. Under the circumstances, and given his need to prove himself able to handle his new command, a chance to exact revenge might be difficult for him to resist. "Would it be easier if I were to accompany you?"

"Yes," she answered in a small voice. "I mean, I know you're busy. Forget I asked."

"I have business aboard the Warlord in any case." That was only half true; Will and Seven had been handling details at that end quite satisfactorily, but it wouldn't hurt for the Commander to put in an appearance to look over the situation for himself. "Shall we meet in, say, half an hour?"

"That would be terrific. Thanks."

"Your quarters?"

A hesitation as she mulled over his implicit offer to accompany her to the office of the Team commander. "No," was her firm reply. "I have to do this myself. But if you were waiting outside that office door when I came out, I wouldn't pretend I didn't know you, that's for sure."

Michael smiled inwardly. Antonia really did sound like her cousin at times. She showed a lot of promise, if handled right. And he sincerely hoped he was handling her right. "I think I can manage that. Good luck, child."

"Thanks, Michael. I have a feeling I'm going to need it."

Maybe. Or maybe her luck would come in the form of a black-clad Confederacy enforcer who believed the girl deserved a second chance. She'd worked hard the past few days helping to pull the Team back together in light of the aftereffects of shock, drugs, and Davenger's conditioning. Surely her past transgressions counted little in view of that.

And, if the Fourth Service didn't see it his way, he had a little leverage he could use. Michael always had a little leverage.

Chapter 47

Once again, of all the people Dancer talked to the next day, Michael was not among them. If he had come in at all, she had missed him; she couldn't help wondering if he was avoiding her for some reason.

Though she was still confined to quarters, at least it was no longer solitary confinement. Sandusky dropped in even before Preble paid his wake-up call. Perhaps it was Dusky's own guilt that made him so easy to convince she was not only rested enough for callers but would be climbing the walls before the morning was out if he didn't authorize visitors. At any rate, he passed the word along that Dancer was available for consultation—on a limited basis.

The first thing she did was to have Greene drop by and return her cropped hair to its natural color. Unfortunately, they could do nothing with the length but joke about gluing the clipped locks back on. Ah, well, it would grow back—although she might just harass Michael for a while about keeping it cut short. When she'd mentioned it in passing the other night, he'd positively snarled at her until he realized she was teasing.

The other night. A languorous warm glow suffused her body as the circumstances of that teasing pushed their way into her mind. Ah, Michael. Almost dying was a small price for such a night in his arms. Not one she could afford to pay very often, though!

With a chuckle, Dancer pushed such thoughts to the back of her mind to make room for the deluge of typical day-to-day problems that were the answer to her complaints of boredom. Things that would have driven her crazy any other time she tackled with relish now: police reports, duty rosters, supply screwups, an unlamented shortage of soap in the public restrooms—these were what kept her from remembering that she had not yet been rigorously debriefed on her latest misadventures, a task usually handled by the Commander himself.

Finally, late in the afternoon, she called a halt—or rather, Jeremiah did by refusing to let anyone else through the door. A snack break seemed in order; Dancer had just stepped into the kitchen when a most unexpected and unwanted visitor stepped out of the bedroom.

She spun around to face him at—what? The *ssshush* of feet on the carpet? A ragged breath? A "sixth" sense of the intent behind the handgun he trained on her? She could see the tremor in the hand that aimed the weapon, a tremor in sync with the one that shook her at his sudden appearance.

Adrenaline surged into her system, a scalding rush of impotent rage and naked hatred that blurred the room in front of her. God, she wanted him dead! She wanted him cold and white and lifeless as a snow-swept tundra; she wanted to hurl herself at him, rend his flesh with her bare hands until he screamed as Meig had screamed, as Troy had screamed! Instead, she clamped down hard on the emotions—as Michael would have said, anger was counterproductive in this instance. It would only give the intruder the upper hand.

Where are you when I need you, Commander? her mind called out, the thought of Michael, as always, providing the steadying influence she needed. Now, if she could just quell the nausea that spun like a gyro through her insides . . .

"So, Harla, what brings you to my humble abode?" she managed to ask calmly, even pleasantly. "I don't recall issuing you an invitation."

Davenger walked into the living room with something less than his usual swagger. The limp that he tried to disguise and the way he held his right arm across his chest indicated that he was hurting; his face was purplish with old bruises, his nose was taped, and one eye was still swollen almost shut. Compliments of Michael, Dancer recalled, landing Davenger in the med section instead of the holding cells. Whence he had escaped. While Michael and she were sleeping in each other's arms, no doubt, precipitating Seven's rude interruption. And, she had a sneaking suspicion, the guard posted at her door. The guard who had been somewhat relaxed today because there had been so many people in and out. Why hadn't they warned her?

"You're going to get me out of here, then I am going to kill you," Davenger said reasonably.

"Oh, really?" His bravado amused rather than frightened Dancer. A quick and clean death seemed a mild threat considering the havoc he had already wrought on her and hers, and he was hardly in any condition to accomplish even that. "I don't know how you managed to escape Med, hide out for three days, then break in here, but I assure you, you're not going anywhere but back to the holding area, with or without me. I was just fixing myself something to eat. Why don't you sit down and join me? You look like you could use a good meal." With that, she gathered her courage and turned her back on him—a deliberate insult—to open the refrigerator.

"Or maybe I'll just kill you here and now," he pursued.

"And they say *I* have a one-track mind. So, kill me. What will that gain you? Bread. Here we go. One thing you can say about Michael—he knows how to stock a pantry. Look at you; the way your hand is shaking, you'd miss me and put a hole in the wall. Besides which, Michael himself is probably standing outside that door right now, waiting for my all-clear to barge in here and wrap your arms around your neck. Right, Jeremiah?"

"Security is standing by," the voice of the computer acknowledged.

Davenger started, looking over his shoulder, and she relieved him of his stolen weapon. "In the third place," she continued, pushing him into a chair and tossing a hastily made sandwich at him, "where do you think you're going to go once you're out of the building? You aren't the type to be happy stuck on O'Brian's Stake for the rest of your life—short though that may be, since Michael has seen fit to make your crime public—and it's next to impossible to get off-planet without authorization. I would have difficulty doing it myself. So eat your lunch. Then Jeremiah will open the door and you will be escorted back to a place of relative safety."

The Karranganthian stared at his former captive, torn between anger, hunger, and bewilderment. "After all I have done to you, you're concerned about my safety? I don't believe that any more than I believe there's a security force at the door. What's in this, anyway?"

She leaned over to bite a corner off his sandwich, though swallowing it became a silent battle of the will between her mind and her rebellious stomach. "Some concoction of Michael's between a couple of slices of whole grain bread from the bakery down the street. Go ahead; it's quite tasty. Certainly not poisoned; I wouldn't waste good food. Jeremiah?"

The suite's door whooshed open and four Sixth Service security people charged in, led by a glowering Seven; they stopped short behind Davenger at her gesture. "Let him finish eating. By the way, Harla, in case you have any doubts about my intentions: I shall very likely be part of the team that escorts you to your trial; I will most definitely testify against you as the only living witness of that little party you held for your Lioth captives; and I shall certainly be part of the escort if, by some miscarriage of justice, you are sentenced to rehabilitation instead of humane execution. I assure you, you would meet with a very *in*humane accident en route. However," she added ironically, pointedly stripping him with her eyes, "you aren't unattractive. Perhaps we could strike a bargain for your life and my pleasure, hmm?"

Davenger rose stiffly, all fury and injured pride. "We'll meet again, on my terms," he said, imperiously beckoning the guards to take him away. The remains of the lunch she'd thrown in front of him were still clutched in his good hand.

"Think about my offer, Harla," she shot back. "I have some very imaginative plans for you that you might enjoy."

The door closed on his snarl, and Dancer turned on Seven. "Good of you to warn me he was on the loose!" she snapped, wrapping her arms tightly around her body to stop its shaking as reaction set in.

"Dancer," he said simply, reaching for her. She shrugged off his hands, turned her back on him, stiffened her spine, and then about-faced to pin him with a dagger glare.

"Don't 'Dancer' me. You didn't just look over your shoulder in your own supposedly secure quarters to find that vermin standing behind you!"

"I know. I know. What can I say? We thought our precautions were enough. I'm sorry. Michael didn't want you worried."

"Yeah, you all thought I would flip out at the mere mention of his name, didn't you? Spare me your misdirected efforts at protection! You ought to know me better than that by now. Speaking of Michael, where is he? Why didn't he run to my rescue himself if he's so concerned?"

Seven shifted uncomfortably. "He was outside that door almost before Jeremiah alerted us to your danger. When Jeremiah passed along your conversation, and we saw that you had the situation under control, the Commander left it in our hands. It's best that he stay as far away from Davenger as possible right now."

It sounded plausible, but Seven was talking past her instead of to her, so she knew he was still hiding something. "All right, I'll let you off the hook." She sighed. "This time. The Commander, however, is another story. Davenger is not here now."

"You know Michael," Seven said evasively. "Has to be in three places at once. Now that he's proven a Karranganthian plot, everyone and his brother is clamoring for his guidance."

"All the more reason for him to consult with his second-in-command, wouldn't you say?"

"Listen, Dancer, I owe you an apology for barging in on you and the Commander the other day. I should have known when he wasn't in his own bed and the door was closed that . . . oh, damn!"

She looked at him levelly for a moment, then it struck her: whatever he knew about Michael, he could no more reveal to her than she could reveal Michael's personal confidences to Seven. Confidences that included wall-banging, furniture-throwing, crockery-smashing rages, confidences that included her holding the Commander's head as his anguished tears scalded her skin . . .

"All right, Sev," she finally said, allowing him to change the subject. "Apology accepted. You realize, of course, that that was the first time Michael and I had ever . . . been together."

"Ah—no. We'd all thought . . . hmm."

"I know what you all thought," she returned ruefully. "Only in my dreams, I'm afraid."

"Wish I'd known that. I definitely would have tried to take advantage of the situation. Oh, good grief!" Seven's voice took on an exasperated edge. "Speaking of dreams, Red, I came up here in the first place to make a delivery. Wait a minute."

Ducking out into the hallway, he retrieved an opaque plastic garment carrier, which he hung on a fold-out arm next to Michael's bunk. "Your presence is required tonight at a dinner in your honor aboard the Team Warlord," he stated formally. "The uniform for the evening is ceremonial dress. I know Sixth doesn't have one," he added hastily as her eyes narrowed. "That's why Michael requested me to bring you this."

"Right. Why wasn't I informed earlier so that I would have had a little more time to get ready?"

"So you would have had more time to think of a way to weasel out of it, you mean."

"Your point. Why didn't Michael deliver this invitation himself? I trust he's attending?"

"He's, uh, busy tying up a few loose ends here and there, and may not be able to get away until later. If you want an escort, I'm always available."

Dancer's automatic smile was remote. If Michael wasn't avoiding her, then he was giving a real good imitation of it.

"That's all right, Dancer; I wouldn't choose me over Michael, either," Seven said softly after a moment. "I never could understand why Madison did."

"Wait a minute. You were Merylys's Steve? Of course! I knew he was Michael's best friend; why have I never made the connection before? Because Michael didn't want me to?"

Seven shrugged, and his completely candid brown eyes met hers. "It's possible. We have a very long history of both loving the same woman," was his light reply. "I suppose it's only fair; I got Merylys, and he got you. Though in the end, we both lost 'Lys, too."

"I'm still not sure who's got whom, as you put it." On impulse, she reached over and grabbed his hand. "Keep your eye on the Commander for me, will you? He has a tendency to push himself too hard."

He murmured something in Auryx so softly that she caught only the last two syllables, and she wasn't completely certain of them. Then, his voice rose to match his eyes, carefully neutral. "This affair has put some unusual pressures on him, that is true. It's a delicate situation."

"Seven . . ." She halted, not sure why she was going to say it. "I made a mess of things, didn't I?"

"Not yet, child. Not yet." With an enigmatic smile, he left her to her thoughts.

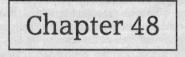

Chapter 48

Actually, truth be known, it was a relief to be back in custody again. Davenger wasn't feeling quite himself yet, and had missed that soft bed and good food. All right, he'd missed the painkillers, too. His ridiculous showing with the redhead convinced him of his physical weakness; much as he hated to admit it, she was right. He wouldn't have gotten very far on his own with the shape his body was in now. Certainly wouldn't have been able to contrive a way off-planet.

No, the best thing for him to do was to let the Confederacy lackeys take care of that for him while he kicked back and regained his strength. Transportation would almost certainly be aboard the Warlord and, though security would be much tighter on him this time, he'd find a way to turn the situation to his advantage. He'd taken over the entire vessel once; he knew its strengths and its weaknesses. In fact, in many ways, its strengths *were* its weaknesses. Surely he'd be able to manage a simple escape and evasion before he was turned over to Confederacy intelligence forces. He would have to, because once he was in the hands of those professionals, his chances to get home alive dwindled with astonishing rapidity.

Not that the Confederacy posed a threat. No, it was his own superiors who couldn't afford to let him live to reach trial. Most of his people had no idea what took place on conquered planets; nor, from Davenger's observations, would it be healthy for them to find out. Whether the fear that one man's public testimony could, in effect, topple the Karranganthian government was founded or not, his government had no intention of testing the theory.

No matter; it wouldn't come to that. He'd be back with Kalelle before the idiots aboard the Warlord even knew he was missing.

As for not ending the life of that redheaded nightmare Dancer when he'd had the chance—she was wrong. If he had fired at her, he would not have missed. Something had stayed his finger on the trigger, something more than the desire to see her smile again. She was tough, she was cocky, she led a charmed life, and, much as he hated to admit it, he was actually growing to like her. If Dancer indeed was part of the team to escort him to trial, that simple escape and evasion would take on much more of a challenge.

He would, eventually, exact his revenge on her, of that he was certain—even if it took another twelve years. And the time and place would be of his choosing. For now, rest, food, and healing were his priorities.

Let her sleep soundly, thinking him out of her life. He knew better.

Preoccupied, Dancer opened the garment bag Seven had left her and began dressing herself in the not-unexpected Fourth Service combination it contained. First came the light, sleeveless, collarless, white underblouse which, as close as she had ever been able to figure out, existed solely to protect the torso from the chafing of the rest of the uniform. Next came the socks, because after she drew on the slenderizing high-waisted red pants she wouldn't be able to bend over comfortably, and the legs were too tight to push up even if she could. Luckily, the shoes were of the slip-on variety. She took a deep breath before fastening the hooks of the wide, belly-flattening waistband under her ribs, knowing that it would be the last comfortable breath of the night, repeating the familiar curse against the designer of the outfit.

Fourth Service ceremonial dress existed solely for looks; once the twenty-three tiny hidden buttons down the shoulder and right side of the jacket had been fastened and the crossbelt arranged, the body was imprisoned in an exhausting posture of rigid erectness until someone helped to unfasten them again. The uniform was designed that way, cleverly manufactured to convey the illusion of ease and comfort while making it impossible for the spine to bend or the shoulders to slouch. Sitting was achievable only if one knew the trick; on occasion, the ensemble had been used at the Academy as a training aid for those cadets who had trouble mastering the basic cadet attitude. Wearing it to a Dining-In was sheer torture if the food was worth eating, because one couldn't. Couldn't even drink enough to make it bearable, because that would tarnish the image that Service hierarchy had invented this nightmare to perpetuate. Dancer hated the thing; every Fourth Service officer she had ever known did. She couldn't figure Michael for requesting— no, commanding—her to put it on now.

Before her still hung the stiff, heavily decorated ceremonial jacket of a Fourth Service flight leader. Dancer ran a reluctant hand down the fabric that looked so soft and inviting to the touch but held the body so rigidly constrained. Inside the stiff red stand-up collar, she automatically fastened the even stiffer white liner that would chafe, even cut the neck if the head wasn't held just so. She measured with her eye the white border to see that it was precise, then repeated the process in each tightly buttoned cuff. Stepping back to brush an imaginary speck of dust off the sleeve, even she had to admit that it looked damned good. On the hanger, or some other poor slob's body.

The nametag said DeWellesthar—the uniform had probably come out of Antonia's closet. But the wings over the left breast touted the star-in-circle of actual flight-level command and the lightning bolt denoting combat proficiency, neither claimed by her double even with faked records. Dancer's wings—there was the minute nick in the third point of the star—kept out of her belongings so long ago by Michael and nonchalantly tossed to her across a crowded bar in celebration of her return to active flying in the Sixth.

And it was her career detailed by the campaign and award ribbons ranked neatly below the wings. Her Academy ribbon, red with the three diagonal gold slashes of the outstanding graduate. Marksmanship ribbons, proclaiming proficiency with a number of weapons. Unit citations, awards for leadership, bravery, and getting them before they got her, topped by the highest honor meted out by Fourth Service—edged discreetly in black to denote a posthumous award. There'd be a correspondingly ornate medal pinned on the black-and-gold embroidered diagonal of the crossbelt. Station ribbons, one for each base she had served, Lioth's also edged in black to show where Flight Leader DeWellesthar had met her demise.

There should have been a KIA, gloss black with red slashes, signifying Fourth Service killed in action. Hers had had the gold holder for "conspicuous gallantry." Dancer laughed out loud. What gallantry? They had been fighting for their lives. It was easy to be brave when you knew you were going to die anyway.

But then, the KIA hadn't been designed for the recipient, but as a panacea for the grieving next-of-kin. Something to show off proudly, if tearfully; a ribbon pinned to the pocket of a body for burial. If they had a body. More often than not, her comrades had ended in scattered atoms in the skies they defended, or in smoking holes in the earth below.

Instead of her KIA, Dancer found the MIA, red slashes on a white background. The ribbon for Missing In Action, whose recipients occasionally came back to wear them. So, Michael or whoever had gone to all the trouble of researching the ingredients for the fruit salad on her tunic had made a mistake. Dancer would enjoy pointing that out to him later.

In either case, the gold border meant it went on the top row, between the commendation and final station. She switched them without conscious thought.

Impressive. Damned impressive. That row of black would certainly catch the eye of anyone looking her way, the incongruity of the white causing him to look more than twice.

The words of an ancient hymn popped into Dancer's mind: "I once was lost but now I'm found . . ." That was when it dawned on her: no mistake had been made. Michael had intentionally substituted the white ribbon for the black, which would have instantly proclaimed Sixth Service to those rare individuals who would understand.

"I once was lost but now I'm found/Was blind but now I see," was the entire quote. And what she now saw struck her like a blow to the solar plexus.

Michael was sending her back.

Chapter 49

At the Dining-In tonight, in front of Antonia, God, and everyone, Michael was going to officially return Auglaize DeWellesthar to the Fourth Service. No wonder Seven hadn't been able to meet Dancer's eyes when she had asked him about the Commander. Seven had known his plans. Everyone probably knew. Everyone but her. What a day. First Davenger, then this!

She snatched the jacket off the hanger, wadded its stiffness into a ball, and hurled it with all her strength across the room. Damn Michael! How could he do this to her? *Why* would he do this to her?

"Jeremiah!" she blazed, jerking at the fastenings of her pants so that she could move freely.

"What's wrong, Dancer?" was his immediate query.

"I need to talk to Michael. Now."

"I'm sorry, Dancer. The Commander is unavailable at the moment."

"You tell the Commander . . ." Tell him what? That Dancer wasn't pleased with being named his second one day and thrown out of the Service the next? He should be able to figure that one out for himself.

It was better to settle this face to face, anyhow. Michael had to return to his quarters to dress for his part in tonight's human sacrifice; she would just sit here and wait for him and have it out when he did. And if he sent someone to drag her out before he came back, she'd create a scene on the Warlord that would make the past war look like a minor skirmish.

If he wanted to send her away, that was his prerogative, but he'd have to do it by the laws of his—their—Service. He'd have to bring her up on charges. The fight would be public, and, on her part, it would be vicious. But at least she would know what her transgression had been, to merit such harsh punishment.

Hot and cold running damn! A few nights ago, Michael had confessed a long-standing love. Now he was sending her away.

The two thoughts connected, and her knees gave way under her. Dancer grabbed the back of the couch for support. It seemed preposterous, yet . . . was he sending her away because they had made love? Because his hard-won control over emotions and body had finally failed him, and he would never again be able to face her because she knew? Or because it might happen again?

Jeremiah reminded him of the hour for the third time in fifteen minutes, and Michael snapped back that he was damned well aware of how long it would take him to shower, dress, and transport himself to the Warlord. The truth be known, he'd just as soon not put in an appearance at all. This sort of affair wouldn't have appealed to him even if he weren't handing over his second-in-command, cherished friend—and lover—to a Service that wouldn't know how to fully utilize her unique talents even when it discovered the extent of them. Of course, the choice to return to Fourth was hers. But he'd known, ever since that communique requesting that the offer be put to "Auglaize DeWellesthar's double, who flew so brilliantly in the recent demonstration flight"—he'd known what Dancer's decision would be. Hadn't she always wanted to go home? He remembered those early days when she had confided a homesickness so acute he had hurt for her. Granted, it had been years since she'd mentioned it, but he'd seen the eagerness in her eyes when the lifelong dream of flying with the Team became a reality. He knew she'd been studying the computer files of her family and former friends. He could feel . . . something indefinable whenever Dancer looked at Antonia when she thought no one else was watching. Not jealousy, exactly, but some sort of longing.

Well, it was almost the perfect solution. The perfect solution would have been for her to have been accorded a "detached duty" status from Sixth, but both Services involved had made it abundantly clear that this was not an option. Michael had been decidedly unhappy when that same communique had ordered him to place Davenger and his crew into Fourth Service custody for transport to "an unspecified destination" to await trial. A round-the-clock Sixth Service armed guard would have been his choice. Face it, the Warlord was still in a state of civil war with the Fourth Service cadre blaming the Fifth Service captain for the near success of Davenger's plot, and vice versa. In some cases, his people had even had to break up brawls between the two factions when the arguments became too enthusiastic.

That was the first thing Dancer would straighten out; an order to be read at this function tonight would make it abundantly clear who the new Team commander would be.

They still didn't know what name to call her by other than Dancer; Antonia hadn't been able to tell them. Michael had given Tonia two options: either forgetting she'd ever seen her cousin again, or— much more difficult—remembering everything that had transpired on O'Brian's Stake, but never being able to tell anyone about selected portions. Antonia, predictably, had opted for the latter. He would need another hour or so with her before the Warlord left orbit to make sure whatever blocks Dancer chose to leave in Tonia's mind remained so, but that would be almost enjoyable, since it was the last he would ever see of either of them.

At any rate, the mere fact of Dancer's Sixth Service tenure, along with reports of her flying, were recommendations enough to those who ruled the Fourth. Good decision on their part, but God! How was he going to get along without her?

Enough of that. Just do what you have to do, and think about it later. For three days, ever since Fourth had contacted him directly with its proposal, he'd been telling himself that. Easier said than done. At the oddest moments, he'd find himself remembering how she had felt in his arms, her drowsy morning smile. The stormcloud show of temper when frustrations became too much for her to bear uncomplainingly. Her smile, her touch, her light breath on the back of his neck as she peered over his shoulder at a computer screen. Her laugh in his ear receiver as they shared a long-distance private joke.

It had been so wonderful to contemplate going home to her every night, though the time either of them spent in their quarters was severely limited; past wonderful to actually walk into his suite and find her there waiting for him. And when he'd heard that Davenger was in there with her, threatening her life—he'd been ready to break the door down and kill for her . . .

"Michael?" With a guilty start, the Commander realized that Seven had been standing there in front of him for some time. "Sorry," he said ruefully. "How's she doing?"

"Oh, just fine, considering she's been trying to figure out exactly what she did to make you so mad at her you haven't been near her for three days."

"I have been near her."

"Right. Sneaking in to look at her when she's asleep doesn't count."

"Fine. I'm a coward. I can't face her. I admit it. Is that what you wanted to hear?"

"I don't need to hear it. I already knew it. Look, you're going to have to talk to her sometime. What's wrong with now?"

"Seven. What have I to say to her? Nothing that matters. When the Warlord leaves O'Brian's Stake, she'll be on it."

"What makes you so damned sure, Commander?" Seven returned.

"She wants to go home, Sev. And to command the Team—how can she refuse?"

"I don't know; have you even considered telling her that you want her to refuse?"

"How can I do that without her thinking I'm ordering her to stay with us?"

"Come on, Michael; you know better than that. Don't let her leave just because she hasn't any better reason to stay. And don't give me that look; I'm not afraid of you, and you know exactly what I'm saying."

Yes, Michael knew exactly what he was saying. But . . . did Seven have any idea what it would do to him if the Commander were to remind the love of his life that she *was* the love of his life, and she still chose to leave? It was not a risk he could take. Besides, such touching emotional declarations still couldn't change what was. What had to be.

Another reminder of the time. Well, at least Dancer would long since have been on her way to the Warlord. He could return to his quarters and dress in leisure. Dress . . .

The germ of an idea was growing in his mind. No, he couldn't. Still . . . no. His door opened soundlessly before him—yes, he was alone—and he found himself rummaging through the wardrobe at the foot of his bunk to find a small, locked storage area. He had one more ace to play, and his superiors on the Auryx Ruling Council be damned! He was going to play it.

Chapter 50

One of the benefits of sharing Michael's quarters was that Dancer also got to share his balcony. That was where her feet, of their own volition, had taken her in her agitation. With an effort she'd finally gotten herself in hand, breathing deeply of the rain-washed air and staring, unseeing, at the gardens of the courtyard below.

Dancer knew for certain now what she had been suspecting. Michael had purposely avoided her these past three days, coming upstairs only when she was asleep, being too busy to talk whenever she tried to communicate with him. She missed his voice in her ear, the small jokes, the wry comments, even the occasional reprimands. She hated the knowledge that from now on, she'd be living without it.

The hell of it was that this was all her fault, though even with 20/20 hindsight she couldn't see what she could have done to prevent either his emotional admissions or the logical progression leading to their physical consummation.

No, that was wrong. What she could have done was curb her curiosity, restrain herself from the electronic breaking and entering which had apparently precipitated the rest. She could have stopped him before that first kiss. Or the second. She could have done any number of things, if she just hadn't been so headstrong. So weak.

Dancer was sure that was the way he felt—weak and ashamed, as if he had let down his precious Service. Possibly as if he had let her down, too. He had hated her once. Did he hate her now, so much that he couldn't even tell her face to face? Or was there some other reason he felt he must stay away from her?

Damn! She had been so stupid! If she had just let well enough alone, if she had just kept her mouth shut, if she had just . . .

She brought herself up short. No use berating herself with what she should—or shouldn't—have done. What she had to decide now was what to do next.

The best alternative probably was to get as far away from him as possible, to let him regain his equilibrium and whatever else she had taken away from him. It was obviously what he wanted. Her mind flinched away from the thought, and she ruthlessly forced herself to examine it. She would be welcome almost anywhere; she would be back to her first love—flying. Sure. Sure, then the exhilaration of having her head in the clouds would make up for the boredom of daily peacetime patrols and training exercises. If she could find a sector that was still a little unsettled, maybe she could even get in a few air-to-air duels. Keep her wits sharp. Forget Sixth and everyone in it.

Yeah, right. Not in this lifetime.

But the psychs could help her dull the pain. Two sessions with Sandusky, and she'd be saying, "Michael who?" It would be a way out, and she knew that the psychiatric people were just waiting for a chance to dissect her subconscious. Well, Dancer had news for them: they would mess with her mind again the day they all met for a snowball fight in hell!

Besides, due to the nature of his responsibilities, that avenue was not open to Michael. He would have to sort out his own feelings, work through his own duality, come to terms with himself—by himself. For her to do any less would be contemptible.

Ah, Michael. Even now, Dancer longed for the pressure of his arms around her. "Damn it all, I do love you," she whispered, surrendering to the unbidden, bittersweet memory of their lovemaking.

That he felt the same for her, she no longer had any doubt. All right, then. The best thing she could do for him now—for both of them—would be to get away from here. As far and as fast as possible.

Go back to flying. Accept with good grace, without argument or demands for explanations, the transfer back to Fourth that he had already arranged.

With a sigh, she set down the drink she had been toying with and leaned back in her chair. She had never before realized how much she liked it here. Funny to think she would miss this ball of rock. Emptying her mind of all thoughts, she relaxed to watch the reflection of the sunset stain the mountains.

The snow-capped peaks were a blood-soaked red when Dancer felt, rather than heard, Michael come out behind her. Neither spoke for a long while, nor looked at one another, nor moved. "It has been a long, long while since I have taken the time to watch a sunset," Michael finally said, pulling up a chair beside hers.

"Mmm. I haven't had much else to do lately."

"How are you, child?" he asked softly.

"I might ask you the same question, Commander," she replied, still not looking in his direction.

"The sky is such a beautiful deep blue just before it falls dark."

"The color of your eyes," she added without thinking.

"So I have been told."

Silence again, except for the soft breathing of the wind and the muted night sounds drifting up from the city.

"I thought you might like to know," he began, then seemed to shake himself. "I thought you might like to know that Antonia has been grounded."

"Grounded? Why? Is she all right?"

"Very much so. She confessed that she was using your name and your records. She is off the Team, pending investigation."

"Did she?" At that, Dancer was surprised. Gratified, too. Thou shalt not take my name in vain . . . "Any idea what will happen to her?"

"She'll spend some time as second-string, then they'll reinstate her."

"What did you have to do with it?"

"Nothing. Well, not with her decision, at any rate. After I heard about it, though, I did put in a good word for her with the Board."

"Thank you. She has the ability. Antonia just needs to find Antonia."

"I know. She has made the right start."

"Troy would have been proud of her, I think," Dancer added reflectively, her thoughts on a time and place far away.

"She will be pleased to hear that, Dancer. As well you know, she idolized Troy."

"And Morgan adored her. He always wished he could have acknowledged paternity." The words came out before she recalled that Michael didn't know the truth of Antonia's parentage. It was something she had seldom admitted to herself over the years. It was easier that way.

Well, Michael knew now, as his sharp intake of breath confirmed. "No," he stated, denying his own conclusion. "No, you were little more than a child yourself when she was born."

"Second year at the Academy."

"Dancer . . . ?"

Dancer fixed her eyes on the moon, just struggling its way out from behind a bank of clouds, and took a deep breath. Might as well get it all out in the open. What did it matter now, anyhow? "Tonia was lucky. Under other circumstances, I would have been given the choice of her or my career. As it was, I was allowed to remain, as long as I could keep up with my class. Isolated, you understand, to save embarrassment all around; even my medical records show a highly contagious recurring viral infection. When it was all over, Tonia went home with a childless aunt, and I rejoined Academy society."

Silence again, as he tried to assimilate the information, then a quiet, "Now I remember; you were raped by a classmate."

"Makellen told you everything, hmm? You two really were close. Or were you one of my monitors? No matter. Yes, that was true, but I've always preferred to think that Troy was Antonia's father."

"He knew, of course."

"How could he not? She had his eyes, his chin, his smile, before she so blithely had them changed. His hair was lighter, but hers is close enough to the DeWellesthar red not to excite comment. Troy knew, Ash knew, my parents knew, and now you know."

"And Antonia?"

"I'd hoped that she would be told one day, but they must have figured it didn't matter, with Troy and me both dead. I must say you've accepted the whole thing very easily."

He expelled a long breath and drummed his fingers on the arm of the chair. "Guess again. I thought I knew you. I thought I knew everything there was to know about you."

"We all have one or two secrets, don't we, Michael."

"One or two." With a sigh, he let it go at that, returning the conversation to the track he desired it to take. "You know, Antonia's looking forward to seeing you tonight. Perhaps there is something you want to say to her, too."

Dancer stiffened, thinking about the Fourth Service dress coat lying in a heap on the floor of Michael's living room, and what it had told her about the purpose of tonight's Dining-In. Of course Antonia had confessed her masquerade. Tonight, Auglaize DeWellesthar was being returned to the world of the living. No matter that she was being dragged there kicking and screaming.

Michael moved restlessly. "If . . ." He paused, deliberating. "If it were within my power to grant your greatest wish, what would that be?"

You, she thought instantly, but didn't say it. Even knowing her serious, he would have passed it off as a joke. Instead, she smiled wryly into the gathering darkness and shook her head. "Once, what

I wanted most in the worlds was to fly with the Team. Circumstances have already granted that.''

"Was it all you had anticipated?"

"Definitely."

"Would you do it again, if you had the chance?"

"In a minute! Your question earlier, if you could give me anything I want, what would I ask for. There is something that you could manage, if you would talk to the Team Powers-That-Be."

"Yes?" She could feel his eyes upon her, curious, waiting, but she couldn't meet them yet.

"One hour alone with a Team Gypsy in restricted airspace."

"Is that all? Done!"

The two sat in silence for a time, watching lights winking on one by one in the city below, then Michael shifted in his seat again. "Dancer, we are expected on the Warlord momentarily. They wish to do you honor."

Again, the crumpled dress coat flashed through her mind, the white MIA ribbon glowing like a beacon. *I once was lost, but now I'm found* . . . It was difficult to repress a shudder. "An honor I would refuse if I could."

"Perhaps it would be more enjoyable for you if I told you what they had in mind. A few days ago, they asked my permission for you to join the Team."

Dancer's heart skipped two beats as she continued to stare straight ahead. Here it was. "Did they. And your reply?"

"That the decision, of course, is yours."

"Then I choose not," she said, much more calmly than she felt. "Make that two Gypsies, Michael. I've always wanted to challenge you on my own turf."

"As you will," he replied mechanically. Then, "Did you say no?"

"I said no."

"Did I mention that they want you to join the Team as Lead Solo and commander?"

"Do they? How flattering," was her dismissive reply.

"Think well, Dancer. Things can be no different with us. I'll not have you give up a dream that you can grasp for one that can never be a reality."

Was this the same man who, not so very long ago, had assured her that, no matter what, she *was* his reality? "You always mean what you say, don't you, Mike?"

"You know I do."

"So do I. I made my choice the day I swore that oath to you and to the Sixth. Nothing has changed. What is in my genes, I cannot help. In my heart, I am Auryx.''

"Are you certain?"

"Absolutely."

"Thank God," he whispered, enfolding her hand in both of his. "I have been suffering the tortures of the damned, trying to accustom myself to your absence, so certain was I that you would choose to go."

"You mean, you're not sending me back?" Dancer whooped. "I thought you were *sending* me back!"

As she turned on him incredulously, words froze in her throat at the jolt of a world stopped turning. Surely her eyes were playing tricks on her. She blinked rapidly, shook her head in denial even as the increased pressure on her fingers told her it was true.

The sleeve of Michael's dress coat, so buttery smooth against her arm in the moonlight, shimmered with the brilliant deep blue of a nightening sky.

The blue once and forever registered to Makellen Darke.

About the Author

Aviation researcher/historian Michelle Shirey Crean was born and raised in Olean, a small town in southwestern New York state. After marrying a USAF officer and shuttling back and forth across the country for several years, she has settled in Benton Harbor, a small town in southwestern lower Michigan, with her now-civilian resident computer expert and her eight-legged doorbell (two large, obnoxious hounds). *Dancer of the Sixth* is her first novel.

DEL REY DISCOVERY

Experience the wonder of discovery with
Del Rey's newest authors!

. . . Because something new is always
worth the risk!

TURN THE PAGE FOR AN EXCERPT FROM
THE NEXT *DEL REY DISCOVERY*:

The Drylands
by Mary Rosenblum

The ride was a bad one. Nita Montoya sat stiff and straight in the seat of the decrepit Winnebago as it groaned around another bend in the road. Twilight was falling, and the air reeked of cheap perfume. A bottle must be leaking somewhere in the jumble of black-market items that filled the rear of the RV. Beside her, clutching the wheel, the man reeked of lust. Rachel squirmed on Nita's lap, fussing, her face screwed up, fists waving.

"Easy, love." She bounced her daughter gently on one knee, watching the dark, bearded driver from the corner of her eye. Andy, he had said his name was. He was a trader, doing the little town markets, selling black-market clothes, electronics, pharmacy-labeled medicines and cosmetics. He had offered her a ride this afternoon and she had accepted, because she was tired, and there was a long way yet to go. He had felt all right then.

"You sure you want to chase after this old man of yours?" His grin turned into a grimace as the old RV tried once more to lumber off the narrow, broken road. "Anyone who'd walk away from a sweet thing like you ain't worth it. I make a pretty good living, doin' the markets. These Dryland hicks can't trade for squat. You wouldn't believe what I can twist 'em out of."

Asshole. "I think I'll get out pretty soon." Nita hugged the fussing Rachel to her chest. "She's going to cry like this for a long time."

"No problem." His smile revealed his yellowed, uneven teeth. "I don't mind kids."

He was lying. A darkness had been building inside him for the last hour—a gathering storm charged with lust and threaded with the red lightning of violence.

She felt it. Since she could remember, Nita had felt it all: Mama's pain, Ignacio's anger at the dusty world, and Alberto's terrible res-

307

ignation. Joy, lust, fear, anger. The world around her shrieked with the noise of humanity. It had driven her into herself as a child, the more frightening because the adults in her life hadn't understood. It wasn't until much later that she had learned why, that she was unique. A freak. A mutation, David had said, trying to be kind. *That's how the species evolves.*

Unique was another word for alone.

The Winnebago was slowing. The dark storm inside this man was about to break. Nita sucked in a quick breath, stifled by the stuffy air, struggling with the urge to fling the door open, leap out with her daughter, and run, run, forever, get away . . .

She could die without her pack and her water jugs. Rachel could die. Rachel was screaming now, back arched, feet kicking. "Easy, love. Rachel, it's all right." Feeble words—they didn't touch the fierce brilliance of her daughter's distress. But they covered the motion as she tucked her struggling daughter into the sling she wore across her chest and slid her hand into her pocket. The switchblade clicked open. He was thinking about fucking her, hurting her, his erection a hot ache in his pants. This close to him, she felt it, too, couldn't help but feel it. The RV was edging off the road. Nita swallowed and leaned toward him, her throat dry with his storm. "We're getting out now."

He started to laugh, then flinched as the blade pricked through his shirt. The RV swerved and the muscles in his arms bulged, corded tight with fury. Rachel shrieked. Teeth clenched against the black and crimson deluge of his rage, Nita tried to keep her hand from shaking. I will kill him, she told herself. If he moves. The decision made, her hand steadied. He made a small sound in his throat as she edged the blade deeper, his anger collapsing.

"Stop now, and turn off the engine. Keep your hands on the wheel."

He did, and sat very still as she reached behind herself to open the door. He was afraid now, afraid that she would stick the knife into him anyway, hurt him. He could understand hurting, Nita thought, and disgust clenched her belly. She groped behind the seat, awkward with the weight of Rachel in the sling, and swung her pack one-handed out the door. It thudded onto the dusty asphalt. Carefully, she backed out the door. "If you come near me, I will kill you," she said between her teeth.

"You fucking bitch." His lips trembled. "I'll get you, you little tramp."

She slammed the door and stepped back, clutching Rachel to her. If he wanted to, he could shoot her. He must have a gun in there and who would know, out here? Who would care? He could run her down with the RV. There were only fields beside the road; neat lines of sugar beets, with nowhere to hide. Stupid! She should have tied him up, locked him in somehow—but his dark violence had battered at her, drowned rational thought in a primitive urge to get away. Nita shoved the now-useless knife into her pocket, slung her pack onto her shoulder, and ran. Behind her, she heard the Winnebago's engine growl and then catch. Rachel hiccuped and cried as Nita pounded through the drifted dust at the verge of the road.

A house! Preoccupied with escape and emotion, she hadn't noticed it. Old and weathered, sprouting the black wings of solar arrays, it would belong to the beet farmer. It might save her, if this guy was afraid of witnesses. Yes! The Winnebago roared past her on the far side of the road, raising a cloud of dust that stung her eyes and coated her throat. Panting, *safe*, she staggered to a stop.

"Are you all right?" A figure limped out of the deepening dusk, an old man with wispy white hair. "That was Andy Belden's rig, wasn't it? The trader?" He stopped in front of her, weathered and stooped, his worry clouding the darkness. "He's a slimy bastard— gonna get himself hung one of these days. Or shot. Did he . . . hurt you?"

"No. No, he didn't." Nita tried to laugh, but it wanted to turn into a sob. "I just decided to walk."

"It's too dark for walkin'. You come on inside now. My name's Seth." His smile crinkled his face into a thousand folds. "I got an extra bed for you and the baby, and I'd love the company."

His worry was soft against her mind, like gentle winter sun. "Thank you," Nita said, and let her knees begin to tremble. "I would be very pleased to stay."

The house was pleasant inside. There was a kitchen-dining room with a table and cupboards. A shirt hung on the back of a chair and a worn Bible lay on the tabletop, beside a small clutter of odds and ends. He ushered her into a small adjoining living room. It was crowded with upholstered chairs, a table, a china cupboard, and a sideboard of dark wood. Curtains hung at the window, striped with darker fabric at the edges where the sun hadn't bleached out the blue-flowered print.

"You sit," Seth told her. "Stew's almost done. I'll bring you a glass of water."

Nita sat down gratefully in one of the oversized chairs. Rachel was hungry, groping at her. She looked around the small room as she lifted her shirt and tucked her daughter's small warmth against her. It was neat and very clean, but it had an unused feel to it, as if Seth didn't come in here very often. The glass shelves in the corner cupboard were filled with small china animals: dogs, horses, ducks, even a white goat with curly horns and a golden bell around its neck. A memorial, she thought. They had belonged to the woman who must have lived here once. Her picture stood on a shelf. It had to be her—there was a respectful space around it that made it the focus of this clean, unused room. Nita studied her as Rachel nursed. She had a wide smile, but there was a subtle sadness to her eyes. In the picture she was young, with only a few gray hairs in her dark curls.

"Here we are." Seth appeared in the doorway, a tray in his hands. A blue ceramic pitcher stood on the tray, flanked by two matched glasses. "I thought we'd do it formal." He set the tray down on the table. "How's the young one?"

"She's fine." Nita watched him pour a silver stream of water into the glass, her throat tightening. You were always thirsty out here in the Drylands. You put it away in the back of your mind, ignored it, until someone offered you a glass of water. And then, suddenly, you were dying of thirst. She picked up the glass, forcing herself to drink slowly. It tasted so sweet, water. No, not really sweet—honey was sweet. Maybe it was *life* that she tasted. That's what water was. "Thank you," Nita said. "For the water, and for letting us stay."

"Like I said. I get lonely. Leah was always proud of this room." He gave the picture a quick smile, as if she were listening to him. "I don't use it much, and that would make her sad. She'd be pleased to see me use the pitcher, too. I gave that to her for our twentieth wedding anniversary. Got it in Portland."

"It's lovely," Nita said. His grief was new and sharp, but the love beneath it had a timeless feel to it. Nita felt the last of her tension draining away, leaving her tired. Secure.

Seth was watching her over the rim of his glass, legs crossed, eyes sharp and dry as the land outside. "You on your way somewhere?" He leaned forward to tickle Rachel's belly. "She's kind o' young for wandering around, ain't she?"

Curiosity gleamed through his words. He wanted her story. News was the coin of the Oregon Drylands—personal or general— payment for water and hospitality. Nita stifled a sigh. "We're on our way to The Dalles." She settled the sleepy Rachel more comfortably on her lap. "David—my husband—heard of a job there," she said reluctantly.

"The Dalles, huh? What kind of job?" Seth leaned forward to refill their glasses.

"Working for the Corps. Pipeline work."

"Yeah?" His sparse white eyebrows rose. "I heard there's trouble up that way. Trouble about the Pipe. Hope he got his job. Where you from, anyway?"

"The Willamette Valley, west of Salem." Nita stirred uneasily. She knew the questions that were coming—knew them too well. She didn't want to hear them from this man's lips, but Rachel had fallen asleep, and her sleeping weight pinned Nita to the chair.

"All the way from the Valley? That's some hike." Seth whistled. "How come you got stuck on your own? Seems like this David of yours'd be worried sick if he knew. There's not a whole lot o' law outside the big towns like The Dalles and La Grand. Lot can happen out here."

He was referring to Andy and his stinking RV. Nita's lips tightened. "I haven't heard from David." She said the words because they had to be said out loud, had to be faced every morning with the silent, rising sun. "I couldn't go when he got the word about the job. Rachel was too little, and it was honey-flow season. We were bee-hunters," she said. "We'd have missed the harvest, if we'd both left. So I stayed until it was over."

He was supposed to have sent word when he got settled. He had planned to come back for her, if he could. For four months, she had waited. Nita stroked Rachel's sleeping face, listening to the murmur of her daughter's dreams. "We hunted bees way up in the coast range," she said, and heard the defensiveness in her tone. "Messages get lost all the time."

He heard it, too, and his sympathy was like the soft hum of bees on the still air. "Yeah, messages do get lost." He picked up the tray and got stiffly to his feet. He didn't tell her that people get lost, too. He didn't have to.

"I'll go dish up the stew," he said, and put out a hand as she started to rise. "You stay put. When I got the table ready, you can put her down on the bed."

Nita blinked back tears as he shuffled out of the room. A lot of dusty miles lay between their tent in the mountains and The Dalles. Andy and his stormy violence wasn't the worst she could meet out here. It was easy to die in this dry land. But it wasn't his death that haunted her dreams. Nita stroked a wisp of hair back from Rachel's face. *She looks like you,* David had said, and he had been afraid. He had always been afraid of her, deep down inside. Ever since he had understood what she was—that she would always know what he felt. *It's all right,* he had told her. *I don't mind.* And part of him didn't. Part of him was happy when she translated the bees' soft song for him, told him how the hive was content or nervous or happy. Part of him liked it that she knew when he needed a touch, or a little private space.

And part of him was afraid.

He wouldn't look into that shadow, wouldn't face it. But it had always been there. After Rachel's birth, it had grown darker. He had been full of a nervous restlessness, like the bees before they swarmed.

She looks like you. He had said it so many times. It was easy to die in this dry land. It was easy to walk away, too. You could disappear down the road, vanish into a horizon of dust and sun and never look back. The Drylands ate yesterday. They buried it in dust, dried it up, and blew it away.

"Think you can put the little one down?" Seth stuck his head through the door.

"I think so." Nita scooped Rachel gently into her arms and carried her into the tiny back bedroom. Seth didn't seem to have noticed her tears. Nita laid her sleeping daughter on the bed and wiped her face on her sleeve. "You're not like me," she murmured. "You're normal." *Normal.* The word hurt her. "You can't hear him. He doesn't have to be afraid of you."

Rachel whimpered softly in her sleep—she would look like Nita, yes, and like David, too. "I love you," Nita whispered. She tucked the spread around her daughter and tiptoed out of the room.

Seth had cleared off the table and spread a flowered tablecloth across it. He had set out thick white china and a cut-glass bud vase full of golden grass stems. "You get sloppy living alone," he said as he ladled bean-and-vegetable stew into a bowl. "I'm glad I got an excuse to set a proper table."

She took the filled bowl with a smile, but something was wrong. There was a stiff uncomfortableness to him that hadn't been there a few minutes ago.

"This is great," she said as she tasted the stew. "You're a wonderful cook."

"Thanks. It's garlic does it. You can't never get too much garlic in a dish." He put the pot back on the small electric ring on the counter and sat down. "You know, if you want to hang around until tomorrow afternoon, I can give you a ride on into Tygh Valley. You could likely find someone heading north on One-ninety-seven who could get you closer to The Dalles."

He was lying to her. Why? Nita's earlier sense of safety began

312

to leak away. "We're close to One-ninety-seven, then." Nita made her voice light. "I wasn't sure."

"Yeah, you're close." Seth put his spoon down, eyes fixed on his stew, as if a fish had suddenly jumped in the middle of his bowl. "We got a good weekly market there. Folk come in from all around. Few weeks back we had some excitement." He poked fork tines into a thick cube of squash. "Some guy come through doing magic tricks. Cards and stuff, but more than that." He looked up suddenly, frowning. "He made stuff . . . appear. Frogs and butterflies and such. Out of the air, like. It was a gadget, he said. Little black box." He reached for his water glass, took a long swallow. "Good thing for him. Couple of us kind of got him aside, eased him on out of town. He got the message real quick, and beat it."

"What kind of message?"

"That folk around here don't have no sense of humor when it comes to that kind of thing. You know, a lot of weird stuff happens in the Dry." He held his glass up, stared into its crystal depths. "Kids get born strange. Some folks say it's the water, or the dust." He shrugged. "The Reverend, he says it's the devil. Rev says we've killed the land with our wickedness and now its ghost is raising up, looking for vengeance. It's taking over our children, right in the womb, turning 'em evil. You got to stop it 'fore it gets out of hand."

There was something hot and hard running through the softness that she had felt before—a shining thread, like a thin stream of molten metal. It frightened her, that hot thinness. It was aimed at Rachel. He had overheard her in the bedroom. Nita put down her spoon. "You're wrong," she said, and her voice caught in her throat.

For a moment, he looked her in the face, his eyes dry and pitiless as the sky. The hot-metal feel of him burned her so that she clutched the tabletop to keep herself from leaping to her feet. She felt the weight of the knife in her pocket, but it didn't reassure her. Not this time.

Seth looked down suddenly, and the hot glare faded. "I don't know," he said, and his voice was unsteady. "Leah and I, we had three kids. They all died. She said it was the will of the Lord, Leah did. That it was God's way. Maybe, but a little bit of her died with each of 'em." He looked at her, looked away. "I believe in the Rev," he said slowly. "He's a pure man. I believe God speaks through him. When he holds out his hand, the dust storm ceases. But . . . I don't know. The Robinson boy was a good kid—but when he touched someone, they . . . glowed. Like colors in the air—all around. He said you could see sickness that way. Leah tried to stop

313

'em when they started to throw stones. He got away—the Robinson boy. The Rev said she was a weak vessel, that God would punish her. She died a month later.'' He picked up his fork again and ate the cube of squash. "It was my fault," he said, and guilt beat in him like a second pulse. "I should've taken her home."

"I'm sorry," Nita whispered. The stew tasted like dust, but she ate it, a spoonful at a time, afraid to reject the food, afraid, period.

They had stoned a child. Because he was . . . different.

She helped Seth with the dishes, hiding her fear. He told her that he got up early to soak the beets before it got hot. The scary part of him was watching her, waiting for her to go to bed first. Nita smiled for him and shut the bedroom door tightly behind her. There was no lock, but she jammed the back of a chair beneath the doorknob. *Don't tell people what you can hear.* David had told her that years ago, when he had first understood. *"Different" scares people,* he had said. *Scared people can hurt you.*

Oh yes. David had known about being scared. Rachel's diaper was wet, and Nita changed it, wrapping the wet one in the plastic bag from her pack. No time to let it dry now. She sat down on the edge of the bed with the switchblade in her hand. Listening.

Part of Seth grieved for that boy, and for his own dead children. But another part of him was forged from that hot, molten ugliness. She heard his footsteps in the hall, soft and careful. Nita held onto her knife, fear a stone in her chest. The doorknob turned gently. The chair creaked a little and skidded an inch or two across the wood floor. Silence. Nita held her breath, hearing only the rush of blood in her ears. She watched the single window, waiting for a face to appear, for the glass to smash in.

Silence.

Perhaps . . . just perhaps, the grieving part of him had coaxed his body to sleep. She didn't dare hope, but . . . perhaps.

Silence.

After a long time, when the house had creaked and groaned itself to sleep, she gathered up her daughter, her pack, and her water jugs. Heart pounding, she climbed though the window. No Seth. The moon was up high enough that she could see to walk along the cracked asphalt of the county road. She fished the map from her pocket and spread its creased folds out on the moonlit asphalt. Yes. If she took this road, it would bring her to 197 well north of Tygh Valley. Nita refolded the map, slid her arms through the pack straps, and tucked Rachel into her sling. An owl screeched thinly as she started walking, and fear lurked in the darkness behind her, nipping at her heels.

314